Critical acclaim for David Baldacci's novels

'As ever, Baldacci keeps things moving at express-train speed'
Daily Express

'Yet another winner . . . The excitement builds . . . The plot's many planted bombs explode unpredictably'
New York Times

'As expertly plotted as all Baldacci's work'
Sunday Times

'It's big, bold and almost impossible to put down . . . I called this novel a masterclass on the bestseller because of its fast-moving narrative, the originality of its hero and its irresistible plot'
Washington Post

'Baldacci cuts everyone's grass – Grisham's, Ludlum's, even Patricia Cornwell's – and more than gets away with it'
People

The Will Robie thrillers by David Baldacci

The Innocent

Master assassin Will Robie is the US government's most indispensable asset. But when he refuses to pull the trigger, he's putting more than his own life at risk . . .

The Hit

Will Robie may have met his match when he's ordered to kill rogue agent Jessica Reel. With the trap set he quickly finds that there is more to her betrayal than meets the eye.

The Target

A deadly assassin from North Korea is ordered to destroy the enemy at all costs. With the stakes so high, Will Robie and Jessica Reel face their most lethal mission yet.

The Guilty

Returning home after twenty years brings back painful memories for government assassin Will Robie. His father has been arrested for murder, but could he really be guilty?

End Game

Will Robie returns to the US following an explosive mission in London to discover his boss has vanished. Calling on an old friend, the investigation begins to track him down.

The Innocent

David Baldacci is one of the world's bestselling and favourite thriller writers. With over 130 million copies in print, his books are published in over 80 territories and 45 languages, and have been adapted for both feature-film and television. He has established links to government sources, giving his books added authenticity. David is also the co-founder, along with his wife, of the Wish You Well Foundation®, a non-profit organization dedicated to supporting literacy efforts across the US. Still a resident of his native Virginia, he invites you to visit him at DavidBaldacci.com and his foundation at WishYouWellFoundation.org.

Trust him to take you to the action.

Also by David Baldacci

The Camel Club Series

(An eccentric group of social outcasts who seek to unearth corruption at the heart of the US government)

The Camel Club • The Collectors
Stone Cold • Divine Justice • Hell's Corner

King and Maxwell series

(Two disgraced Secret Service agents turn their skills to private investigation)

Split Second • Hour Game • Simple Genius
First Family • The Sixth Man • King and Maxwell

Shaw series

(A mysterious operative hunting down the world's most notorious criminals)

The Whole Truth • Deliver Us From Evil

John Puller series

(A gifted investigator with an unstoppable drive to find out the truth)

Zero Day • The Forgotten
The Escape • No Man's Land

Will Robie series featuring Jessica Reel
*(A highly trained CIA assassin
and his deadly fellow agent)*
The Innocent • The Hit • The Target
The Guilty • End Game

Amos Decker series
*(A damaged but brilliant special agent
who possesses an extraordinary set of skills)*
Memory Man • The Last Mile • The Fix • The Fallen

Vega Jane series
(The bestselling young-adult adventure series)
The Finisher • The Keeper • The Width of the World

Other novels
Absolute Power • Total Control • The Winner
The Simple Truth • Saving Faith • Wish You Well
Last Man Standing • The Christmas Train
True Blue • One Summer

Short Stories
No Time Left • Bullseye

DAVID BALDACCI

The Innocent

PAN BOOKS

First published 2012 by Grand Central Publishing, USA

First published in the UK 2012 by Macmillan

This edition published in the UK 2018 by Pan Books
an imprint of Pan Macmillan
20 New Wharf Road, London N1 9RR
Associated companies throughout the world
www.panmacmillan.com

ISBN 978-1-5098-5967-2

5 7 9 8 6

A CIP catalogue record for this book is available from the British Library.

Printed and bound by CPI Group (UK) Ltd, Croydon, CR0 4YY

To Mitch Hoffman, my editor and,
more importantly, my friend

CONFIDENTIAL

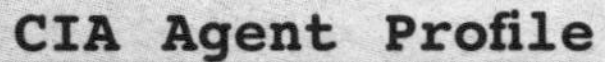

CIA Agent Profile

Name: Will Robie

Date of Birth: Classified. Early forties but doesn't look it. On the outside. On the inside, he's about 110.

Place of Birth: Cantrell, Mississippi, USA

Marital Status: Single. Never married. Too much baggage.

Physical Characteristics: 6 foot, 1 inch. 180 pounds. Athletic build, physically ripped. Dark hair, kept short.

Distinguishing Marks: Previously broken nose. Old wounds and scars over his torso and limbs. Right arm surgically repaired; scar tissue removed, tendons and ligaments all tidied up. Tattoos on one arm and also on back. One tattoo displays a large tooth from a great white because he's a predator like the shark. The other is a red slash of lightning on fire because that's how fast he strikes and what you feel like after he does. The tattoos effectively cover up old scars that have never healed properly.

Relatives: Daniel Robie (father); Tyler Robie (half-brother). Mother (current status unknown).

CONFIDENTIAL

Service Career: Began his career in the Special Forces. Robie is a dangerous and incorruptible CIA assassin. Possibly trained as part of SEAL, Delta Force, or United States Army Rangers. Details permanently classified. Reports to 'Blue Man'.

Notable Abilities: Immense endurance levels and off-the-chart tolerance to pain. Expert military-grade weapons and vehicle training. Deadly in close-quarters combat. Relies more on quickness and endurance than sheer strength. Will kill you before you even realize it with a gun, his finger, or a household appliance.

Favorite Film: *Reservoir Dogs*. He likes it because it's not nearly as violent as his line of work, so it allows him to relax.

Favorite Song: Queen's 'Another One Bites the Dust', of course.

Dislikes: Faulty scope/ammo, soulless bad guys, clueless bureaucrats, anyone pointing a weapon at him.

Likes: Jessica Reel, Blue Man, Dan and Tyler Robie, Julie Getty, Shane Connors, Nicole Vance, and last but not least, John Carr AKA Oliver Stone. Full stop.

1

Will Robie had closely observed every one of the passengers on the short flight from Dublin to Edinburgh and confidently deduced that sixteen were returning Scots and fifty-three were tourists.

Robie was neither a Scot nor a tourist.

The flight took forty-seven minutes to cross first the Irish Sea and then a large swath of Scotland. The cab ride in from the airport took fifteen more minutes of his life. He was not staying at the Balmoral Hotel or the Scotsman or any of the other illustrious accommodations in the ancient city. He had one room on the third floor of a dirty-faced building that was a nine-minute uphill walk to the city center. He got his key and paid in cash for one night. He carried his small bag up to the room and sat on the bed. It squeaked under his weight and sank nearly three inches.

Squeaking and sinking were what one got for so low a price.

Robie was an inch over six feet and a rock-solid one hundred and eighty pounds. He possessed a compact musculature that relied more on quickness and endurance than sheer strength. His nose had been broken once, due to a mistake he had made. He had never had it reset because he'd never wanted to forget the mistake. One of his back teeth was false. That had come with the broken nose. His hair was naturally dark and he had a lot of it, but Robie preferred to keep it about a half inch longer than a Marine buzz cut. His facial features were sharply defined, but he made them mostly forgettable by almost never making eye contact with anyone.

He had tats on one arm and also on his back. One tattoo was of a large tooth from a great white. The other was a red slash that looked like lightning on fire. They effectively covered up old scars that had never healed properly. And each held some significance for him. The damaged skin had proven a challenge for the tattoo artist working on Robie, but the end result had been satisfactory.

Robie was thirty-nine years old and would turn forty the following day. He had not come to Scotland to celebrate this personal milestone. He had come here to work. Of the three hundred and sixty-five days in a year, he was working or traveling to do his job on about half of them.

Robie surveyed the room. It was small, adequate, unadorned, strategically located. He did not require much. His possessions were few, and his wants fewer still.

He rose and went to the window, pressed his face to

the cool glass. The sky was gloomy. It was often that way in Scotland. A full day of sun in Edinburgh was routinely greeted with both gratitude and astonishment by its citizens.

Far to his left stood Holyrood Palace, the queen's official residence in Scotland. He could not see it from here. Far to his right was Edinburgh Castle. He could not see that battered old edifice either but knew exactly where it was.

He checked his watch. A full eight hours to go.

Hours later his internal clock woke him. He left his room and walked up toward Princes Street. He passed the majestic Balmoral Hotel that anchored the city center.

He ordered a light meal and had tap water to drink, ignoring the large selection of stouts offered on the board over the bar. As he ate he spent some time gazing at a street performer juggling butcher knives atop a unicycle while regaling the crowd with funny stories delivered with an embellished Scottish brogue. Then there was the fellow outfitted as the invisible man taking pictures with passers-by for two pounds each.

After his meal, he walked toward Edinburgh Castle. He could see it in the distance as he ambled along. It was big, imposing, and had never once been taken by force, only stealth.

He climbed to the top of the castle, peering over the gloom of the Scottish capital. He ran his hand along cannon that would never fire another shot. He turned to his left and took in the full breadth of the sea that had made Edinburgh such an important port centuries ago as vessels came and went, disgorging freight and picking up fresh cargo. He stretched tight limbs, felt a creak and then a pop in his left shoulder.

Forty.

Tomorrow.

But first he had to make it to tomorrow.

He checked his watch.

Three hours to go.

He left the castle and headed down a side street.

He waited out a sudden chilly rain shower under a café awning and drank a cup of coffee.

Later he passed a sign for the ghost tour of Underground Edinburgh, adults only, and only conducted after full darkness had set in. It was almost time. Robie had memorized every step, every turn, every move he would have to make.

To live.

As he did every time, he had to hope it would be enough.

Will Robie did not want to die in Edinburgh.

A bit later he passed a man who nodded at him. It was just a slight dip of the head, nothing more. Then the man was gone and Robie turned down the doorway the man had vacated. He shut and locked it behind him and moved forward, quickening his pace. His shoes were rubber-soled. They made no sound on the stone floor. Six hundred feet in he saw the door on the right side. He took it. An old monk's cloak was hung on a peg. He donned it and put the hood up. There were other things there for him. All necessary.

Gloves.

Night-vision goggles.

A recorder.

A Glock pistol with suppressor can attached.

And a knife.

He waited, checking his watch every five minutes. His watch was synched to the very second with someone else's.

He opened another door and passed through it. He moved downward, reached a grate in the floor, lifted it, and skittered down a set of iron handrails set into the stone. He hit the floor silently, moved left, counted off his paces. Above him was Edinburgh. At least the "new" part.

He was in Underground Edinburgh now, home to several ghost and walking tours. There were the vaults under South Bridge and parts of old Edinburgh such as Mary King's Close, among others. He glided down the dark brick-and-stone passages, his powered goggles letting him see everything in crisp definition. Electric lamps on the walls were set at fairly regular intervals. But it was still very dark down here.

He could almost hear the voices of the dead around him. It was part of local lore that when the plague came in the 1600s it struck impoverished areas of the city—such as Mary King's Close—especially hard. And in response the city walled up folks here forever to prevent the spread of the disease. Robie didn't know if that was true or not. But it wouldn't surprise him if it were. That's what civilization sometimes did to threats, real or perceived. They walled them off. Us against them. Survival of the fittest. You die so I can live.

He checked his watch.

Ten minutes to go.

He moved slower, adjusting his pace so he would arrive seconds before he was supposed to. Just in case.

He heard them before he saw them.

There were five, not counting the guide. The man and the peripherals.

They would be armed. They would be ready. The peripherals would think this was the perfect place for an ambush.

They would be right.

It was stupid for the man to come down here.

It was.

The carrot had to be especially big.

It was.

It was as big as it was total bullshit. Still, he had come because he knew no better. Which made Robie wonder how dangerous the man really was. But that was not his call.

He had four minutes to go.

2

Robie rounded one final bend. He heard the guide talking, giving the memorized spiel and delivering it in a mysterious, ghostlike voice. Melodrama sells, thought Robie. And in fact the uniqueness of the voice was vital to the plan tonight.

There was a right-angle turn coming up. The tour was heading for it.

So was Robie, just from the opposite way.

The timing was so tight that there was no margin of error.

Robie counted the paces. He knew the guide was doing the same. They had even practiced the length of their strides, to get them perfectly choreographed. Seven seconds later the guide, who was the same height and build as Robie, and wearing a cloak identical to his, came around the bend a mere five paces ahead of his party. He held a flashlight. That was the one thing Robie could not duplicate. Both of his hands had to be free, for obvious reasons. The guide turned left and disappeared into a cleft cut into the rock that led into another room with another exit.

As soon as he saw this, Robie pivoted, putting his back to the group of men who would round the corner a few moments later. One hand slipped down to the recorder on his belt under the cloak and turned it on. The guide's dramatic voice boomed out, continuing the tale that he had momentarily halted to take the turn.

Robie did not like having his back to anyone, but there was no other way for the plan to work. The men had lights. They would see that he was not the guide. That he was not doing the talking. That he was wearing goggles. The voice droned on. He started to walk forward.

He slowed. They caught up to him. Their lights swept across his back. He heard their collective breaths. Their smells. Sweat, cologne, the garlic they'd had in their meals. Their last meals.

Or mine, depending on how it goes.

It was time. He turned.

A deep knife strike took out the point man. He dropped to the floor, trying to hold in his severed organs. Robie shot the second man in the face. The sound of the suppressed round was like a hard slap. It echoed off the rock walls and mingled with the screams of the dying men.

The others were reacting now. But they were not truly professionals. They preyed on the weak and the poorly skilled. Robie was neither. There were three of them left, but only two would be any trouble.

Robie hurled the knife and its point ended up in the third man's chest. He dropped with a heart split nearly in half. The man behind him fired, but Robie had already moved, using the third man as a shield. The bullet hit the rock wall. Part of it stayed in the wall. Part of it ricocheted off and found purchase in the opposite wall. The man fired a second and third time, but he missed his target because his adrenaline had spiked, blown his fine motor skills and caused his aim to fail. He next executed a desperation spray and pray, emptying his mag. Bullets bounced off hard rock. One slug hit the point man in the head on a ricochet. It didn't kill him because he'd already bled out, and the dead could not die a second time. The fifth man had thrown himself to the hard floor, hands over his head.

Robie had seen all of this. He dropped to the floor and fired one shot into the forehead of man number four. Those were the names he had given them. Numbers. Faceless. Easier to kill that way.

Man number five was now the only one left.

Five was the sole reason Will Robie had flown to Edinburgh today. The others were just collateral, their deaths meaningless in the grand scheme.

Number five rose and then backed up as Robie got to his feet. Five had no weapon. He had seen no need to carry one. Weapons were beneath him. He was no doubt rethinking that decision.

He begged. He pleaded. He would pay. An unlimited amount. Then when the pistol was pointed at him he turned to threats. What an important man he was. How powerful his friends were. What he would do to Robie. How much pain Robie would suffer. He and his whole family.

Robie did not listen to any of it. He had heard it all before.

He fired twice.

Right and left side of the brain. Always fatal. As it was tonight.

Number five kissed the stone floor, and with his last breath hurled an expletive at Robie that neither of them heard.

Robie turned and walked through the same cleft as the tour guide.

Scotland had not killed him.

He was thankful for this.

Robie slept soundly after killing five men.

He awoke at six and ate breakfast at a café around the corner from where he was staying.

Later he walked to Waverley Station next to the Balmoral Hotel, and boarded a train to London. He arrived at King's Cross Station over four hours later and took a cab to Heathrow. The British Airways 777 lifted off later that afternoon. With a weak headwind the plane touched down seven hours later at Dulles Airport. It had been cloudy and chilly in Scotland. It was hot and dry in Virginia. The sun had long ago begun to drift low into the west. Clouds had built up during the heat of the day, but there would be no storm because there was no moisture. All Mother Nature could do was look threatening.

A car was waiting for him outside the airport terminal. There was no name on the placard.

Black SUV.

Government plates.

He got in, clicked the seat belt shut, and lifted up a copy of the *Washington Post* that sat on the seat. He gave the driver no instruction. He knew where to go.

Traffic on the Dulles Toll Road was surprisingly light.

Robie's phone vibrated. He looked at the screen.

One word: *Congratulations*.

He put the phone back in his jacket pocket.

"Congratulations" was the wrong word, he believed. "Thanks" would be the wrong word too. He was not sure what the right one would be for killing five people.

Perhaps there was none. Perhaps silence would suffice.

He arrived at a building off Chain Bridge Road in northern Virginia. There would be no debriefing. No record of anything was better. If an investigation ensued, no one could discover a record that didn't exist.

But if things went wrong Robie would have no official cover.

He walked to an office, not officially his, but one that he sometimes used. Even though it was late there were people working. They did not talk to Robie. They didn't even look at him. He knew they had no idea what he did, but they also knew not to interact with him.

He sat at a desk, hit some keys on the computer, sent a few emails, and stared out a window that wasn't really a window. It was merely a box of simulated sunlight, because an actual window was just a hole that others could get through.

An hour later a chubby man in a wrinkled suit with pasty skin walked in. They didn't greet each other. Chubby placed a flash drive on the desk in front of Robie. Then he pivoted and left. Robie stared down at the silver object. The next assignment was already prepared. They had been coming at an increasing clip these last few years.

He pocketed the flash drive and left. This time he drove himself, in an Audi that was parked in a space in the adjacent garage. When he slid into the seat he felt comfortable. The Audi was his, had been for four years. He drove it through the security checkpoint. The guard did not look at him either.

The invisible man in Edinburgh. Robie knew how it felt.

Once he hit the public road he shifted gears and accelerated.

His phone vibrated once more. He checked the screen.

Happy Birthday.

It didn't make him smile. It didn't make him do anything other than drop the phone on the opposite seat and punch the gas.

There would be no cake and no candles.

As he drove, Robie thought of the underground tunnel in Edinburgh. Four of the dead men were bodyguards. They were hard, desperate men who had allegedly murdered at least fifty people over the last five years, some of them children. The fifth man with two holes in his head was Carlos Rivera. A trafficker of heroin and youngsters for prostitution, he was immensely rich and had been visiting Scotland on holiday. Robie knew, though, that Rivera actually had ostensibly been in Edinburgh to attend a high-level meeting with another criminal czar from Russia in an effort to merge their business interests. Even criminals liked to globalize.

Robie had been ordered to kill Rivera, but not because of his human and drug trafficking businesses. Rivera had to die because the United States had learned that he was planning a coup in Mexico with the aid of several high-ranking generals in the Mexican army. The resulting government would have been no friend of America, so this could not be allowed to happen. The meeting with the Russian crime czar had been the setup, the carrot. There was no czar and no meeting. The offending Mexican generals were also dead, killed by men like Robie.

When Robie arrived home he walked for two hours

through the darkened streets. He ventured down by the river and watched the headlights on the Virginia side cut through the night. A police patrol boat slid past on the calm surface of the Potomac.

He stared up at the drab, moonless sky; a cake without candles.

Happy Birthday to me.

3

It was three a.m.

Will Robie had been awake for two hours. The mission set forth on the flash drive he'd been given would cause him to travel well past Edinburgh. The target was yet another well-protected man with more money than morals. Robie had been working on the task for nearly a month. The details were numerous, the margin of error was even less than with Rivera. The preparation was arduous and had taken its toll on Robie. He could not sleep. He was also not eating very much.

But he was trying to relax now. He was sitting in the small kitchen of his apartment. It was located in an affluent area with many magnificent dwellings. Robie's building was not one of them. It was old, utilitarian in design, with noisy pipes, odd smells, and tacky carpet. Its occupants were diverse and hardworking, most just starting out in life. They left early every morning to take their place at law firms, accounting practices, and investment concerns spread over the city.

Some had chosen the public-sector route and took

the subway or bus, biked, or even walked to the large government buildings housing the likes of the FBI, the IRS, and the Federal Reserve.

Robie did not know any of them, though he saw all of them from time to time. He had been briefed on all of them. They all kept to themselves, immersed in their careers, their ambitions. Robie kept to himself too. He prepared for the next job. He sweated the details because it was the only way he could survive.

He rose and stared out the window, down to the street where only one car passed by. Robie had traveled the world for a dozen years now. And everywhere he went someone died. He could no longer remember the names of all the people whose lives he had ended. They didn't matter to him when he was killing them and they didn't matter to him now.

The man who had previously held Robie's position had operated during a particularly busy time for Robie's clandestine agency. Shane Connors had terminated nearly thirty percent more targets than Robie had in the same amount of time. Connors had been a good, sound mentor to the man who would replace him. After his "retirement" Connors had been assigned to a desk job. Robie had had little contact with him over the last five years. But there were few men Robie respected more. And thinking about Connors made Robie dwell for a bit on his own retirement. A number of years off, it would eventually happen.

If I survive.

Robie's line of work was a young man's game. Even at forty Robie knew he couldn't do it another dozen years. His skills would erode too much. One of his targets would be better than he was.

He would die.

And then his thoughts came back to Shane Connors sitting behind his desk.

Robie supposed that was death too, simply by another name.

He walked to the front door, placed his eye against the peephole. Though he didn't personally know any of his neighbors, that did not mean he wasn't curious about them. He was, in fact, *very* curious. It wasn't hard to explain why.

Their lives were *normal.*

Robie's was not.

Seeing them going about their everyday lives was his only way to stay connected to reality.

He had even thought about starting to socialize with some of them. Not only would it provide good cover for him—attempting to blend in—but also it would help prepare him for the day when he would no longer do what he did now. When he might have a normal life of sorts.

Then his thoughts turned, as they inevitably did, back to the upcoming mission.

One more trip.

One more kill.

It would be difficult, but then they all were.

He could very easily die.
But that was also always the case.
It was a strange way to spend one's life, he knew.
But it was *his* way.

4

The Costa del Sol had lived up to its name today.

Robie wore a straw-colored narrow-brim hat, a white T-shirt, a blue jacket, faded jeans, and sandals. There was three days' worth of stubble on his tanned face. He was on holiday, or at least looked to be.

Robie boarded the large, bulky ferry to cross the Strait of Gibraltar. He looked back to the mountains rising along the rugged and imposing Spanish coastline. The juxtaposition of the high rock to the blue Med was captivating. He admired it for a few seconds and then turned away, forgetting the image just as quickly. He had other things occupying his mind.

The high-speed ferry headed to Morocco. It pitched and swayed like a metronome as it left Tarifa Harbor on its way to Tangier. Once it gathered speed and hit the open waters, the ride smoothed out. The belly of the ferry was filled with cars, buses, and tractor-trailers. The rest was crammed with passengers eating, playing video games in an arcade, and purchasing duty-free cigarettes and perfume by the carload.

Robie sat in his seat and admired the view, or at

least pretended to. The strait was only nine miles wide and the ride would take only about forty minutes. Not a lot of time to contemplate anything. He spent it alternately gazing out at the waters of the Med and studying the other passengers. They were mostly tourists, eager to say they had been to Africa, although Robie knew that Morocco was very different from what most people probably would think when they imagined Africa.

He walked off the ferry in Tangier. Buses, taxis, and tour guides awaited the masses. Robie bypassed them all and left the port on foot. He entered the main street of the town and was instantly besieged by peddlers, beggars, and shopkeepers. Children pulled on his jacket, asking for money. He directed his gaze down and kept walking.

He passed through the congested spice market. At one corner he nearly stepped on an elderly woman who looked to have fallen asleep while holding on to a few loaves of bread for sale. This had probably been her entire life, thought Robie. This corner, and a few loaves of bread for sale. Her clothes were dirty, her skin the same. She was soft and plump but malnourished, as was often the case. He bent down and put some coins in her hand. Her gnarled fingers closed around them.

She thanked him in her language. He said "you're welcome" in his. They both somehow understood the exchange.

He walked on, increasing his pace, taking any steps he encountered two and three at a time. He passed by snake charmers who placed exotically colored and defanged reptiles around the necks of sunburned tourists. They wouldn't take the snakes off unless five euros were placed in their hands.

A nice racket if one could get it, thought Robie.

His destination was a room over a restaurant promising authentic local food. It was a tourist trap, he knew. The food was generic, the beer warm, and the service indifferent. The bus guides led unsuspecting folks there and then hurried elsewhere to eat a far better meal.

He headed up the stairs, unlocked the door to the room with the key he had previously been given, and locked the door behind him. He looked around. Bed, chair, window. All he needed.

He put his hat on the bed, looked out the window, and eyed his watch. It was eleven a.m. local time.

The flash drive had long since been destroyed. The plan was in place and the movements practiced at a mock facility back in the States that was the exact duplicate of his target. Now he simply had to wait, the hardest part of all.

He sat on the bed, massaged his neck, working out kinks from the long trip by plane and boat. This time the target was no idiot like Rivera. He was a cautious man with professional assets who wouldn't spray bullets around. This one would be harder, or at least it should be.

Robie had brought nothing with him from Spain because he had to pass through customs to get on the ferry. A weapon found in a bag by Spanish police would have been something more than problematic. But everything he needed would be in Tangier.

He took off his jacket, lay back on the bed, and let the heat from the outside make him drowsy. He closed his eyes, knowing he would open them again in four hours. The sounds from the street receded as he fell asleep. When he woke, nearly four hours had passed and it was the hottest part of the day. He wiped sweat from his face and went back to the window, looked out. He watched big tour buses navigate streets never built for anything so large or cumbersome. The sidewalks were full of people, both locals and visitors.

He waited another hour and then left his room. On the street he turned east and double-timed it. In a few seconds he was lost in the hustle and bustle of the old city. He would collect what he needed and move on. All these items would be for the mission. He had traveled to thirty-seven countries and had never purchased a single souvenir.

Seven hours later it was quite dark. Robie approached the large, stark facility from the west. Over his back was slung a hardened case and a knapsack with water, a pee jar, and provisions. He did not plan on leaving here for the next three days. He looked around, taking in the smells of a third-world country. The air was also heavy with the threat of rain. That would not bother him. This task was an inside job.

He checked his watch and heard it approach. He

ducked down behind a cluster of barrels. The truck passed by him and stopped. He approached it from the rear. Three strides later he was under it, holding on to metal jutting out from its underside. The truck drove on and then stopped once more. There was a long, wrenching sound of metal on metal. It started up again with a jolt that nearly caused Robie to lose his grip.

Fifty feet later the truck stopped once more. The doors opened, feet touched the floor. Doors clunked shut. Footsteps headed off. The wrenching sound came again. Then hardened locks were clicked into place. There was quiet, except for the footfalls of the perimeter patrol that would be there 24/7 for at least the next three days.

Robie timed it so he was out from under the truck and racing away just as the wrenching sounds stopped. The facility technically had been cleared and put in lockdown. This was the only opportunity Robie had to get in. Mission accomplished, at least this part.

He took the steps three at a time, the hard-sided case hitting him in the back.

Next came the race against the clock.

He reached the top, grabbed the girder, and did a monkey crawl, hand over hand, to the targeted spot. He swung to the left and then the right and then made his leap.

He landed nearly silently on metal and skittered to a spot eighty feet distant, in one of the darkest corners of the space.

He did so with five seconds to spare.

The lights clicked off and the alarms came on. The interior space was instantly crisscrossed with beams of energy that were invisible to the naked eye. But if anything with a pulse touched them sirens would go off. All intruders found would be executed. It was just that sort of place.

Robie turned over on his back, his face to the ceiling.

Three days, or seventy-two hours, to go.

It seemed his entire existence was one uninterrupted countdown.

5

It was time.

The prayer rugs came out. Knees dropped to the ground and all heads turned east and then lowered to rest near the knees. Mouths opened and the familiar chants flowed.

Mecca was twenty-five hundred nautical miles away, about five hours by plane.

For the folks on the rugs it was a lot closer.

Prayers said, religious duties fulfilled, the rugs were rolled back up and stowed away. Allah was also put away, in the backs of his followers' minds.

It was too early to eat. But it was not too early to drink.

There were places in Tangier that accommodated this, Muslim teetotalers or not.

The two dozen men went to one such place. They did not walk along the streets. They traveled in a four-Hummer motorcade. The Hummers were armored to American military standards and would defeat all bullets and most missile strikes. Like the buses, these vehicles seemed far too large for the narrow streets. The main man rode in the third Hummer, where his front and rear were covered.

The man's name was Khalid bin Talal. He was a Saudi prince. A cousin to the king. With that sole connection he was accorded respect in almost all corners of the Muslim and Christian worlds.

He did not come to Tangier very often. Tonight he was here to do business. He was scheduled to leave during the early morning hours in his private jet that cost well over one hundred million dollars. A staggering sum to virtually anyone, it was less than one percent of his net worth. The Saudis were close allies of the West in general and the Americans specifically, at least in public. A stable flow of petroleum made for good friendships. The world moved around at speed, and men from a desert country where few things would grow could afford aircraft costing nine figures.

However, this Saudi prince was not such a friend. Talal hated the West. He hated the Americans most of all. That was a dangerous position to openly take against the world's remaining superpower.

Talal was suspected of the kidnapping, torture, and murder of four U.S. servicemen, abducted from a club in London. Nothing could be proven, though, and the prince had suffered no consequences. He was also suspected of bankrolling three terrorist attacks in two different countries, resulting in the deaths of over one hundred people, a dozen of them Americans. Again, nothing could be proven and there were no repercussions.

But those actions eventually had put Talal on a list. And the payment for being on that list was about to come due with the full blessing of the Saudi leadership. He simply had become too bothersome and ambitious to let survive.

The people he had come here to meet did not much like the West or the Americans either. They and Talal had a lot in common. They envisioned a world that did not have the stars and stripes leading the way. The gathering was to discuss how to make such a world happen. This caucus was a closely guarded secret.

Their mistake was letting the closely guarded secret no longer remain a secret.

The club was entered through a metal door with a number pad. Talal's lead guard hit the ten-digit code that was changed daily. The six-inch-thick hydraulic-powered door clanged shut behind them. There were blast walls set up at strategic points. The interior perimeter was ringed by armed guards. This was serious security for the few people who could afford it.

The prince and his group sat at a large round table in a roped-off area that was hidden behind drapes and set atop an elevated teakwood platform. The prince's eyes continually moved, sizing up the environment around him. He had survived two assassination attempts, one by a cousin of his and another by the

French. The cousin was dead and so was France's best contract killer.

Talal trusted no one. He knew the Americans wouldn't be far behind now that their French ally had failed. His guards were vetted and loyal and a close-knit group that allowed no outsiders in. There were no whites, blacks, or Hispanics anywhere near his inner circle. He was armed. He was a good shot. He kept his mirrored sunglasses on even indoors. No one could tell where he was looking. The lenses were also specially designed. Their magnification levels allowed him to see things his naked eye could not. But he did not have eyes in the back of his head.

The uniformed waiter approached not with drinks but merely with napkins. The prince brought his own glasses and liquor. Being poisoned was not on his agenda. He poured his Bombay Sapphire and added the tonic. He sipped, his gaze swiveling, his mind partly focused on the upcoming meeting. He was prepared for every contingency.

Except an enlarged prostate.

It was an annoyance that even his wealth could not overcome. He could not have someone else piss for him.

His men made sure the bathroom was empty of enemies and free of explosives, and inaccessible except for the one door. An aide wiped down the sink, commode, and stall with an anti-bacterial spray. Billionaire royalty do not frequent urinals.

Talal went to the cleansed stall, closed the door behind him, and latched it, using a handkerchief to do so. He had discarded his robes before coming here. He wore a custom-made suit that cost ten thousand British pounds. He had fifty such suits and couldn't remember where they all were, since they were spread over his many properties around the world. He had never flown commercial even as a young man. He had teams of servants at each of his homes. When he stayed at hotels they were the finest, and he rented out entire floors so he would not have to endure seeing a common person when he went to his room. He was whisked everywhere either by motorcade or helicopter. People of his wealth did not sit in traffic. His life of rarefied luxury was unimaginable. And that was fine by him, because in his mind, he was unlike other human beings.

I am better. Far better.

Yet he still had to unzip his fly to do his personal business, just like every other man, rich or poor. He studied the wall in front of him, the graffiti and filthy language written there. He finally looked away in disgust. It was the Western influence that had brought such things, of that he was convinced. In that world, women could drive cars, vote, work outside the house, and dress like whores. It was ruining the world. Even his country now said that women could vote and do other things that only men should be able to do. The king was insane and, worse, a puppet of the West.

He hit the flush lever with the sole of his shoe,

zipped his pants, and unlatched the stall door. While he washed his hands, he stared at his image in the mirror. A fifty-year-old man looked back at him: gray in the beard and quite large in the belly. He was worth well north of twelve billion dollars, making him the sixty-first richest person in the world according to *Forbes* magazine. He had taken his oil money and leveraged it into many profitable operations using his business savvy and international connections. He was sandwiched on the list between a Russian oligarch who used gangster tactics after the fall of the Soviet Union to snap up state assets for virtually nothing and a twenty-something tech king whose company had never made a dime in profit.

He left the bathroom and walked back to the table with his guards organized in a hard-diamond pattern around him. He had copied this tactic from the American Secret Service. His personal physician traveled with him, just like the U.S. president. Why not emulate the strongest? was his thinking.

And in his mind, he was just as important as the American president. In fact, he would have liked to replace him as the de facto leader of the free world. Although the world would not be nearly as free with him in charge, starting with the women.

Drinks finished, they moved on to their evening meal at a restaurant that had been completely rented out so that the prince could dine in peace without the fear of strangers interrupting. After that he changed back into his robes and returned to his jet, housed in a secure hangar back at a private jet park outside the city. The Hummers pulled past the open doors of the hangar and stopped in front of the massive jet. While most planes were painted white, this one was all black. The prince liked the color. He thought it was masculine and powerful and possessed a tangible element of danger.

Just like him.

The hangar doors closed before he got out of the Hummer.

There would be no targets for long-range rifle shots between open hangar doors.

He walked up the steps, puffing slightly as he neared the top.

The hangar doors would reopen only when the plane was ready to take off.

The meeting would be held on the plane, while it was on the ground. The meeting would last for one hour. The prince would control the meeting.

He was used to controlling situations.

That was about to end.

6

There were two guards at the bottom of the stairs leading to the jet. The rest of the security was in the plane, surrounding what would be the main target for any attack. The fuselage door was closed, locked. It was like a vault. A very expensive vault. But as with all vaults, there were weaknesses.

The prince sat at the center of the table in the main part of the cabin. The interior was entirely of his own design. The plane consisted of nearly eight thousand square feet of marble and exotic woods, oriental rugs, and exquisite paintings and sculptures by long-dead, museum-quality artists that he could admire at forty-one thousand feet and five hundred miles an hour. Talal was a man who spent his money and thereby enjoyed his wealth.

He gazed around the table. There were two visitors here. One was Russian, the other Palestinian. An unlikely partnership, but it intrigued the prince.

They had promised that for the right price they could accomplish something that virtually everyone, the prince included, would have thought impossible.

The prince cleared his throat. "You're sure you can do this?" His tone was full of incredulity.

The Russian, a big man with a full beard and a hairless head that gave him an unbalanced, bottom-heavy appearance, nodded slowly but firmly.

The prince said, "I am curious as to how this is possible, because I have been told that it is absolutely pointless even to try."

"The strongest chain is defeated by its weakest link." This came from the Palestinian. He was a small man, but with a fuller beard than the Russian. They were like a tugboat and a battleship, but it was clear that the small man was the leader of the partnership.

"And what is the weakest link?"

"One person. But that person is placed next to the one you want. We own that person."

"I cannot see how that is possible," said the prince.

"It is not just possible. It is fact."

"But even so, access to weapons?"

"The person's job will allow access to the necessary weapon."

"And how do you own such a person?"

"That detail is not important."

"It is important to me. This person must be willing to die, then. There is no other way."

The Palestinian nodded. "That condition is met."

"Why? Westerners do not do that."

"I did not say that the person is a westerner."

"A plant?"

"Decades in the making."

"Why?"

"Why do any of us do anything? We believe in certain things. And we must take steps to realize those beliefs."

The prince sat back. He looked intrigued.

The Palestinian said, "The plans are in place. But as you know, significant funds are required for something like this. Much of it in the aftermath. Our person is secure, for now. But that could change soon. There are eyes and ears everywhere. The longer we wait, the greater the chances of the mission failing before it has been given a chance to succeed."

The prince ran his fingers over the carved wood of the table as he glanced out the window. The windows were extra large, because he enjoyed the views from his high perch.

The subsonic round hit him squarely in the forehead, exploding his brain. He fell back against his leather seat and then slowly slid to the floor. Gray matter, blood, bone, and tissue covered the plane's once beautiful interior.

The Russian leapt up but had no weapon. It had been confiscated at the door. The Palestinian just sat there, paralyzed.

The guards reacted. One pointed to the shattered plane window. "Out there!"

They rushed to the door.

The two guards outside the plane had drawn their weapons and fired at the source of the fatal shot.

Shots pinged around Robie's position. He aimed and fired back. The first sentry fell with a kill shot to the head. The second collapsed a few moments after that with a bullet wedged in his heart.

From his high perch Robie pointed his rifle's muzzle at the door of the plane. He sent five shots right through the center, destroying the opening mechanism. He swiveled around and took out the cockpit window and with it the plane's controls. The big bird would be grounded for a while. It was fortunate for his mission that bulletproof material was too thick and heavy to carry on planes. That made it simply a hundred-million-dollar vault with a very large Achilles heel.

Then he was done with killing.

Now came the hardest part.

The exit.

He tightwalked down the girder until he reached a wall on the far side of the hangar. He pushed open the window, attached his cable to the support ring he had bolted into place the night before, and rappelled down the wall. His feet touched the asphalt and he ran due east away from the hangar and the dead prince. He scaled a fence, dropped to the other side. He heard shouts behind him. Some beams of light broke the darkness. Shots headed his way, all far off target. He knew that could change.

The car raced up. He threw his gear in the backseat, jumped in, and it drove off before his door was even shut. Robie did not look at the driver and the driver did not look at him. The car traveled for only a few miles, into the outskirts of Tangier, before stopping. Robie slipped out, headed down an alley, walked another five hundred feet, and entered a small courtyard. A blue Fiat was there. He slid into the driver's seat, snagged the keys from under the visor, and started it up. He gunned the engine and left the courtyard. Five minutes later he neared the center of Tangier. He drove through the city and parked the car at the port. He popped the rear hatch and pulled out a small bag packed with clothes and other essentials, including travel documents and local currency.

He boarded not the high-speed ferry back to Spain, which he had taken to get here, but instead the slow ferry from Tangier to Barcelona. It took twenty-four hours to go from Barcelona to Tangier and three hours longer in the other direction.

His employer had sprung for a three-person family berth rather than simply a seat. He went to this space, stowed his bag, locked his door, and lay on the bed. A few minutes later the ferry slipped away from the dock.

Robie could see the logic. No one would expect an assassin to escape via a boat that took over a full day to get to its destination. They would check the airports, the high-speed ferries, the highways, and the train stations. But not the lumbering old bathtub that would take twenty-seven hours to go a few hundred miles up the Med. He would actually arrive two days from now, since it was nearly midnight.

Robie had had with him a long-range surveillance cone that had allowed him to hear the conversation on the plane between the prince and the two other men. Access to weapons. Decades in the making. Significant funds for the aftermath. It would have to be followed up. But that was not his job. He had completed his task. He would make his report and others would now take over. He was certain that even the Saudi royal family would be relieved that one of their black sheep had been killed. Their official statement would condemn such an act of violence. They would demand a full investigation. They would posture and fume and whine. Tense diplomatic communications would be exchanged. But in private they would toast the ones responsible for the killing. In other words, they would toast the Americans.

It had been a clean operation. Robie had had the prince in his crosshairs from the moment he'd gotten out of his SUV. He could've taken him out then, but wanted to wait until the prince and his guards were on the plane. It would allow him more time to get away if the security detail were trapped inside the aircraft. He had lost sight of the prince for about half a minute right after he had entered the plane, but had reacquired him as he walked down the aisle and sat at the table.

Robie had aimed for the head of Talal even though

it was a tougher shot, because of something he'd seen through his scope. When the prince had leaned forward in his chair, Robie had seen the straps underneath the man's robes. He was wearing body armor. One did not wear body armor around the head.

Robie had spent three days and nights of his life perched high up, peeing into a jar and eating power bars while waiting for his target in a facility that was supposedly in lockdown and totally secure.

Now the prince was dead.

His plans would die with him.

Will Robie closed his eyes and slept as the ferry gently swayed on its slow ride over the calm waters of the Med.

7

This one was different.

It was close to home.

So close that it *was* home.

Nearly three months had passed since Tangier and the death of Khalid bin Talal. The weather was cooler, the sky a little grayer. Robie had not killed anyone during that time. It was an unusually long period for him to be inactive, but he did not mind. He took walks, he read books, he ate out, he did some traveling that did not involve the death of someone. In other words, he acted normal.

But then that flash drive had appeared and Robie had had to stop being normal and pick up his gun again. The mission had come to him two days ago. Not much time to prepare, but the mission was a priority, the flash drive told him. And when the flash spoke Robie acted.

He sat in a chair in his living room, a cup of coffee in hand. It was early in the morning and he had been up for several hours. As the next mission grew closer it had been difficult for him to sleep. It had always been that way with him—not so much nervousness as a desire for heightened preparation. When he was awake part of his brain was constantly refining the plan, finding errors and fixing them. He could not do that while he was asleep.

During his downtime he had adhered to his earlier plan of socializing more and even accepted an invitation to an informal party held by one of his neighbors at the man's apartment on the third floor. Only a dozen people had attended, some of whom also lived in the building. The neighbor had introduced Robie to several of his friends. However, Robie's attention had quickly focused on one young woman.

She was a recent renter here who made the trek to the White House as early as four a.m. on her bike. Robie knew where she worked because he had received a briefing on her. He knew she left that early for work, because he had often watched her through his peephole.

She was a lot younger than Robie, lovely, intelligent, at least from what he had observed. They had made eye contact on several occasions. Robie sensed she might be as friendless as he. He also sensed that if he started talking to her she wouldn't have minded. She had worn a short black skirt and a white blouse. Her hair was swept back into a ponytail. She had a drink in hand and every so often she would glance in Robie's direction, smile, and then look away as she continued her conversation with another person whom Robie didn't recognize.

Several times Robie had thought about approaching her. Yet he had left the party without doing so. As he was walking out he'd glanced back at her. She was laughing at a comment made by someone, and never looked his way. It was probably better that way, he'd thought. Because really, what would have been the point?

Robie rose and stared out the window.

It was fall now. The leaves in the park had started to turn. The evenings were chilly. The humidity of summer was sometimes still with them, but its intense edge had measurably eroded. The current weather was not bad for a city that was built on a swamp—and still was a swamp by many people's estimation, at least the part where the professional politicians nested.

Robie had done his recon in the abbreviated time allotted. The run-throughs, logistically harder in this situation, had still been performed.

And he still didn't like it.

But it was not his call.

The location would not involve Robie stepping on a plane or train. But the target was different as well. And not in a good way.

Sometimes he went after people intent on global menace, like Rivera or Talal. Or sometimes he simply went after a problem.

You could take your pick of labels, but in the end they all meant the same thing. His employer decided who among the living and breathing would qualify as a target. And then they turned to men like Robie to end the living and breathing part.

It made the world better, was the justification.

Like flinging the planet's most potent army against a madman in the Middle East. Military victory was ensured from the start. What could not be wholly predicted was what came after victory. Like a morphing chaos you couldn't escape.

Trapped in a trap of your own making.

The agency Robie worked for had a clear policy on operatives who were caught during a mission. There would be no acknowledgment that Robie even worked for the United States. There would be no steps taken to save him. It was the opposite of the U.S. Marines' mantra: Everyone in Robie's world was left behind.

Thus on every mission Robie had employed an exit plan known only to him, in case the operation went awry. He had never needed to employ his personal backup plan, because he had never failed a mission. Yet. Tomorrow was simply another day for something to go wrong.

Shane Connors was the one who had taught Robie this. He had told Robie that he had to use his backup plan once, in Libya, when the operation, through no fault of his, had imploded.

"You're the only one out there who really has your

back, Will," Connors had told him. That advice had stayed with Robie all these years. He would never forget it.

Robie surveyed his apartment. He'd been here four years, liked it for the most part. There were restaurants within walking distance. The area was interesting, with many unusual shops that were not part of homogeneous national chains. Robie ate out a lot. He liked to sit at tables and watch people go by. He was a student of humanity in a way. That was why he was still alive. He could read people, often after observing them for only a few seconds. It was not a natural talent. It was a skill he had built up over time, as most useful skills were.

In the basement of his building was a gym where he would go to work out, hone his muscles, ratchet up his motor skills, practice techniques that needed practicing. He was the only one who ever used the facility. For training involving weapons and other necessary tools of his trade there were other places he went. Other people he worked with.

At forty years of age it didn't come any easier.

He toggled his neck back and forth and was rewarded with a satisfying pop.

He heard a door open and close in the hall. He stepped to his peephole and watched the woman walk her bike down the hall. This was the woman from the party, the one who worked at the White House. She sometimes wore jeans on the way to work and then presumably changed into her official duds when she got there. She was always the first to leave the building in the morning, unless Robie had already departed for some reason.

A. Lambert.

That was the name on the mailbox downstairs. He knew the A stood for Anne. His background briefing on her had told him that.

His own mailbox simply said *Robie.* No first initial. He had no idea if people wondered about that or not. Probably not, though.

She was in her late twenties, tall, long blonde hair, thin. He once had seen her in shorts when she first moved in. She was somewhat knock-kneed, but her face was elegantly structured, with a mole under her right eyebrow. He had heard her during a discussion in the hall with a fellow tenant who did not support the current administration. Her replies had been sharp and informed. Robie had been impressed.

He had started referring to her in his own mind as "A."

Robie stepped back from the door when she disappeared into the elevator with her bike. He moved back to another window overlooking the street. A minute later she left the building, shouldered her knapsack, swung onto her bike, and was off. He watched her until she turned the corner and the reflector strips on her backpack and helmet disappeared from view.

Next stop: 1600 Pennsylvania Avenue.

It was four-thirty in the morning.

He turned back from the window and surveyed his living space. There was nothing in his apartment that would tell anyone searching it what he did. He had an official position that would be backed up to the fullest in case anyone questioned anything. But still, his apartment was nondescript and contained almost nothing of personal interest. He preferred that to having others invent a past for him, placing photos of people he didn't even know around his apartment and passing them off as relatives or friends. "Hobbying" a residence with tennis rackets or skis or stamp collection books or a musical instrument was standard procedure. He had turned all such offers down. There was a bed, a few chairs, some books he'd actually read, lamps, tables, a place to eat, a place to shower and use the toilet.

He reached up to the pull-up bar he kept over the doorway leading to his bedroom and did a quick twenty. It was good to feel his muscles in motion, pulling his weight up to the bar with relative ease. He could run most twenty-somethings into the ground. His strength and motor skills were still excellent. Yet he was forty now and clearly not what he once was. He could only hope to counter the inevitable erosion of skills and physicality with increased field experience.

He lay down in the bed but didn't put any covers over him. He kept the apartment cold. He needed to sleep.

The coming night would be busy.

And *different*.

8

Robie was in the basement gymnasium of his building. It was nearly nine p.m., but the place was open twenty-four/seven for the residents. All you needed was your key card. In one respect Robie's workout routine never varied: He never did the same workout twice in a row. He focused not on strength or stamina or flexibility or balance or coordination or agility. He focused on them all. Every exercise he did required at least two and sometimes all of those elements.

He hung upside down on the pull-up bar. He did stomach crunches and then worked his oblique muscles while holding a medicine ball. The U.S. Army had devised a functional fitness regime that mimicked what soldiers did in the field, the sorts of muscles and skills required on the battlefield.

Robie held to the same concept and worked on things he needed to survive *out there*. Lunges, thrusts, explosiveness from his calves up. He worked everything in synergy. Upper body and lower body at the same time that he was pushing his core past the breaking point. He was chiseled but never took his shirt off. No one would ever see him strolling along displaying his six-pack unless he needed to as part of a mission.

He did a half hour's worth of yoga until he was drenched in sweat. He was holding an Iron Cross on the pull-up bar when the door opened.

A. Lambert stared over at him.

She didn't smile or even acknowledge him. She closed the door behind her, went over to a corner, and sat down cross-legged on an exercise mat. Robie held the cross for another thirty seconds, not to impress her, because she wasn't even looking at him. He held it because he had to push his body past what it was used to. Otherwise he was just wasting his time.

He let go and dropped lightly to the floor. He snagged his towel and wiped off his face.

"I think you're the only one who uses this room."

He slid the towel down to find her now looking at him.

She was wearing jeans and a white T-shirt. The shirt and jeans were tight. No place to conceal a weapon. Robie always checked that first, male or female, young or old.

"You're here," he said.

"Not to work out," she replied.

"What then?"

"Tough day at the office. Just chilling."

He looked around the small, ill-lighted room. It smelled of old sweat and mold.

"Must be nicer places to chill than this," he said.

"I didn't expect to find anyone else here," she answered.

"Except me, maybe. From what you said, you knew I used this room."

She said, "I just said that because I saw you here tonight. I've never seen you down here before, or anyone else, for that matter."

He knew the answer but asked, "So, tough day at the office. Where do you work?"

"The White House."

"That's pretty impressive."

"Some days it doesn't feel that impressive. What about you?"

"Investments."

"Do you work at one of the big firms?"

"No, I'm on my own. Always have been."

Robie draped the towel around his shoulders. "Well, I guess I'll leave you to your chilling." However, he didn't really want to leave just yet. Perhaps she sensed this. She rose and said, "I'm Annie. Annie Lambert."

"Hello, Annie Lambert."

They shook hands. Her fingers were long, supple, and surprisingly strong.

"You have a name?" she asked.

"Robie."

"First or last?"

"Last. It's on the mailbox."

"And your first?"

"Will."

"That was harder than it should have been." She smiled.

He found himself grinning back. "I'm not the most outgoing guy you'll ever meet."

"But I saw you at the party on the third floor the other night."

"It was a little out of character for me. First time I've had a mojito in a long time."

"Me too."

"Maybe we can go out for a drink sometime." Robie had no idea why that offer had come out of his mouth.

"Okay," she said casually. "Sounds good."

"Good night," said Robie. "Have a nice chill."

He closed the door behind him and took the elevator back up to his floor.

He immediately made a phone call. He didn't really want to do it, but any contact like that had to be reported. Robie didn't think there was anything to be worried about with Annie Lambert, but the rules were clear. Annie Lambert would be investigated to a greater degree. If anything turned up Robie would be notified and appropriate action would be taken.

As he sat in his kitchen Robie wondered if he should have made the call at all. He could not look at anything normally ever again. Someone being friendly to him was a potential threat. It had to be reported. A woman "chilling" and saying hello to him had to be called in.

I live in a world that isn't remotely normal anymore. If it ever was. But it won't always be like this. And there's no agency rule against having a drink with someone.

So maybe he would. Sometime. He left his building and walked across the street. The high-rise there had a perfect view of his, which was the point. On the fourth floor was an empty apartment. Robie had a key for it. He entered the apartment and went directly to the corner of the front room. Set up there was a surveillance scope that was rated as one of the best in the world. He powered it up and turned its muzzle toward his building. He pushed and pulled on dials, making corrective adjustments until a certain part of his building came into sharp focus.

His floor, down the hall three doors. The lights were on, the shades raised three-quarters. He waited. Ten minutes. Twenty minutes. It was all the same to Robie.

Annie Lambert's front door opened and closed. She moved down the hall. He swung the scope in measured movements, following her trek. She stopped at the kitchen, opened the fridge, and took out a Diet Coke. With his scope he could read the label clearly. She closed the fridge with a swipe of her hip. She filled a glass halfway up with the soda and the other half with rum pulled from a cupboard over the stove.

She walked down the hall. Before she got to her bedroom she unzipped her jeans, slipped them off, and tossed them into a laundry basket. She set her drink down on the floor while she pulled her top over her head. Her underwear was pink. She was not the thong type; her underwear fully covered her bottom.

Robie had not seen this. He had turned his surveillance device off when she had started to unzip her pants. The scope cost nearly fifty grand. He was not going to use it for pathetic voyeurism.

Robie returned to his building and rode the elevator to the top floor.

An access door that was locked led to the roof. The lock was not a complicated one for him. Robie took a short flight of steps up to the very top of the building. He ventured to the edge and looked out over the city.

Washington, D.C., looked back at him.

It was a lovely city at night. The monuments looked particularly magnificent when mood-lighted against the darkness. In Robie's mind, D.C. was the only city in the United States to truly rival the great cities of Europe when it came to official decoration.

But it was also a city of secrets.

Robie and people like him were one of those secrets.

Robie sat down with his back to the wall of the building and gazed upward.

A. Lambert had officially become Annie Lambert. Knowing it from the briefing paper wasn't the same as hearing it in person.

And he had reported her for nothing more than probably just being friendly.

Tough day at the office. Just needed a place to chill.

Robie could relate to that. He had some tough days at the office. He could use a place to chill.

But that would never happen.

He showered and changed into fresh clothes. Then he gunned up. It was time to go to work.

9

Another foster home she did not want to be in. How many now? Five? Six? Ten? She supposed it didn't really matter.

She listened to the screams coming from the downstairs of the duplex she had called home for the last three weeks. The man and woman downstairs yelling at each other were her foster parents. Which was more than a joke, she thought. It was criminal. *They* were criminal. They had a string of foster kids through their home and made them pickpocket people and deal drugs.

She had refused the pickpocketing and the drug dealing. So tonight would be her last night here. She had already packed her backpack with her few belongings. There were two other foster kids living in the one bedroom with her. They were both younger and she was loath to leave them here.

She sat them on the bed and said, "I'm going to get you guys help. I'm going to let Social Services know what's going on here. Okay? They're going to come and get you out of this place."

"Can't you take us with you, Julie?" asked the girl tearfully.

"I wish I could, but I can't. But I'm going to get you out of here, I promise."

The boy said, "They won't believe you."

"Yes they will. I've got *proof.*"

She gave them each a hug, opened the window, climbed out, wriggled down the drainpipe to the flat roof of the attached carport, worked her way down a support pole, reached the ground, and ran off into the darkness.

She had one thought in mind.

I'm going home.

Home was a duplex even smaller than the one she had just left. She took the subway, then a bus, and then she walked. Along the way she pulled out an envelope, walked up the steps of a large brick government building, and pushed the envelope through the mail slot in the door. It was addressed to the woman who was handling the foster care placement for her and the two other kids back at the duplex. She was a nice lady, she meant well, but she was completely swamped with children no one seemed to want. In the envelope was a photo card with pictures capturing the couple in the middle of abusing their foster kids, engaging in clearly illegal activity, and sitting stoned out on the couch with crack pipes and piles of pills in full view. If that didn't do the trick, she thought, nothing would.

She reached the house an hour later. She didn't go

in the front door. She did what she always had done when getting home this late. She used a key she kept in her shoe to go in via the back door. She tried to turn on a light, but nothing happened. This did not surprise her. It merely meant that the electricity had been turned off because the utility bill had not been paid. She felt along the walls and used the moonlight coming in through the windows to see well enough to reach her bedroom on the second floor.

Her room was unchanged. It was a dump, but it was *her* dump. A guitar, sheets of music, books, clothes, magazines were piled everywhere. There was a mattress on the floor that served as her bed, but it wasn't easily visible under all the other stuff. She rationalized that her parents had not cleaned up her room because they knew she would be back.

They had problems. Many of them.

They would be regarded by most people as pathetic, drugged-out losers.

But they were her parents. They loved her.

And she loved them.

She wanted to take care of them.

At age fourteen, she was often the mom and dad, and her parents were often the kids. They were her responsibility, not the other way around. But that was okay.

They should be asleep by now, she knew. Hopefully not stoned.

Actually things were looking up. Her father was

working on a loading dock and had been gainfully employed there for a whole two months. Her mother labored as a waitress in a diner where a two-dollar tip was the exception rather than the norm. It was true that her mom and dad were recovering addicts, but they got up every day and went to work. It was just that the drug problems and the stints in jail had led the city to sometimes deem them unfit to have custody of her.

Hence the banishment to the foster care system.

But not for her. Not anymore. Now she was home.

She fingered the piece of paper in her jacket pocket. It was a note from her mom. It had been sent to her school and left at the office. Her parents had plans to move away from the area and start over afresh. And they, of course, wanted their only child to go with them. Julie hadn't been this excited in a long time.

She went to their bedroom across the hall to check on them, but it was empty. Their bed was like hers, simply a mattress on the floor. But the room wasn't messy. Her mother had tidied up. Clothes were put away, albeit in baskets. They had no dressers or armoires. She sat on the bed and removed a photo of the three of them that was hanging on the wall. She couldn't see it that well in the dark, but she knew exactly who was in it.

Her mother was tall and thin, her father shorter and even skinnier. They looked unhealthy and they were. Years of drug abuse had left permanent scars, chronic problems, lives that would be significantly shortened. Yet they had always been kind to her. Never abused her. Looked out for her when they could. Fed her, kept her warm and safe, again when they could. They never brought problems back to the house. The abuses they had committed were done away from here. She appreciated that. And every time she had gone into foster care they had worked hard to get her back.

She put the photo back on the wall and pulled out the note from her mom that had been sent to her school. She read it again. The instructions were clear. She was excited. This might be the start of something great. Just the three of them in a new life away from here. The only thing that bothered her was the contingency plan her mom had put in the note, if for some reason they didn't hook up with their daughter. There had also been cash along with the note. The money was for the contingency plan. Well, there was no reason that her parents wouldn't be able to meet up with her. She assumed that they would be leaving in the morning.

She started to the door to return to her room and pack up her belongings that she hadn't taken to the foster care home.

And then she stopped.

There were noises, which didn't completely surprise her, since her parents sometimes kept odd hours. They must just be getting home.

The next sound she heard erased all other thoughts she had.

It was a man's voice. Not her father's.

It was raised. Angry. It was asking her father what he knew. How much he had been told.

She heard her father whimpering, as though he were hurt.

Then Julie heard her mother's frantic voice. Asking the person to leave them alone.

Julie crept down the stairs, her body shaking.

She had no cell phone or else she would have called the police. There was no landline phone in the house. Her parents couldn't afford it.

When she heard the gunshot she froze and then started running down the stairs. When she reached the lower level she saw her father slumped back against the wall in the darkness. A man held a gun pointed at him. There was a dark patch on her father's chest growing bigger. His face was ashen. He fell to the floor, his arms whipsawing around and knocking over a lamp.

The man with the gun turned and saw her. He pointed the pistol at her.

"No!" her mother shrieked. "She doesn't know anything."

Though barely a hundred pounds, she hit the man in the back of the legs and he collapsed to the floor in pain, his gun spinning out of reach.

"Run, honey, run!" screamed her mother.

"Mom!" She called back. "Mom, what is—"

Her mother screamed again, "Run! Now!"

She turned and ran back up the stairs even as the

man spun around and landed a crushing blow to the top of her mother's head.

She reached her room, grabbed her backpack, sprinted to the window, and grabbed hold of a trellis of metal over which someone long ago had planted ivy. She climbed down so quickly that she lost her grip and fell the last six feet. She got up, slung her backpack across her shoulders, and ran off.

A few seconds later a second shot came from the house.

When the gunman ran outside, the teenager was already out of sight.

But he stopped, listened. The sounds of footfalls reached him. He set out west, moving deliberately.

10

The woman walked to her car. She was probably thinking a million different things as she slipped her briefcase in the backseat of her Toyota sedan, right next to the kiddie seats. Busy professional, mother, housekeeper—the list went on and on, as it did for many women.

Her black suit was a discount off-the-rack model, like most of her clothes. It was a bit grimy after a long day and her heels were nicked in several places. She was not wealthy, but the work she did was important for her country. That made up for a paycheck that was smaller than she could have earned in the private sector.

She was in her middle thirties, five feet nine, more than thirty pounds overweight from her last pregnancy and no time to do anything about it. She had a pair of kids, ages three and less than a year. She was in the process of getting a divorce. She and her soon to be ex-husband currently had joint custody of the kids. One week on and one week off. She wanted full custody, but that was difficult to manage with the work she did.

There had been a change of schedule tonight. She had one stop to make before heading home. She drove off, her mind swirling with thoughts of work issues mixed with the demands of two active children. There was no room in there for her. But that just came with motherhood, she supposed.

Robie stared up at the five-story apartment building. It looked like his place. Old, decrepit. But he lived in a nice part of the nation's capital. This was a part of D.C. that suffered from a lot of violent crime. However, this particular neighborhood was becoming safer. You could raise a family here without worrying too much about your kid dying while walking home from school because he was caught in the crossfire of drug crews battling for street supremacy.

There was no doorman here. The outer entrance was locked and one needed a pass card to get in. He had that. There were no surveillance cameras. They cost money. The folks who lived here couldn't afford that. Or a doorman.

Robie had gone from cartel bosses to Saudi princes to this. The dossier on tonight's target was particularly light. Black woman, age thirty-five. He had her picture and her address. He had not been told the specific reason why she must die tonight other than she had ties to a terrorist organization. If Robie had to label her, he would probably put her in the "problem" box his employer sometimes used to justify death. He couldn't visualize anyone living here as being a global menace. They tended to matriculate to fancier addresses or else hid out from the law in some country that did not extradite to the United States. But terrorist cell members were trained to blend in. She apparently was one of them. In any event, the reason why she had to die was above his pay grade.

He looked at his watch. The building was all condo but less than half occupied. After the financial meltdown fifty percent of the folks here had suffered foreclosure. Another ten percent had lost their jobs and been evicted. The woman lived on the fourth floor. She was a renter and could never afford the mortgage on this place, foreclosed or not. There were only two other people living on that floor, an old woman who couldn't see or hear, and a security guard who worked the night shift and was currently fifteen miles away. The apartments above and below the woman were also empty.

He toggled his neck, felt the pop. He pulled up his hoodie.

The plan was set. There was no stand-down button to push. The rocket was fueled and the launch was commencing.

He looked at his watch. His spotter had seen her go into the building alone hours ago, grocery bag in one hand, briefcase in the other. She had looked tired, the spotter had reported to Robie. That would be a good look, compared to what was coming.

It was moments like this that made Robie wonder what he would do with the rest of his life. He had no problem killing cartel trash or rich, megalomaniac desert sheikhs. But tonight Robie had a problem. He reached a gloved hand inside his pocket and felt the gun there. Usually it was reassuring for him to touch his weapon.

Tonight it was not.

She would be in bed. Her apartment was dark. At this hour she would be sleeping.

At least she would feel nothing. He would make certain his strike caused instant death. Life would go on without her. Rich or poor, important or not, life just did. He would leave by the fire escape. It emptied out to an alley, as many of these buildings did. He would be back at his house by three a.m. Just in time to go to sleep.

To forget tonight ever happened.

As if I can do that.

11

Robie swiped the card through the reader and the door clicked open. He pulled his hoodie tighter around his head. The hallways were poorly lighted. Fluorescent tubes popped and flickered. The carpet was soiled and pulled up in certain spots. The paint on the walls was peeling.

He opened the door to the stairwell and headed up. The air was filled with the smells of cooked food. Mingled together in the air, they did not make a pleasant aroma. He counted the floors. On the fourth one he exited the stairwell and closed the door behind him.

This hall looked just like the one on the first floor.

Number 404 was the one he wanted.

The blind and deaf lady lived at the end of the hall on the left. The security guard in absentia resided at 411. The lock on 404 was a deadbolt, probably engaged by his target tonight. Robie had noted that most of the other exterior condo doors had simple locks. The deadbolt meant she was security-minded. Yet it took him all of thirty seconds to defeat the lock using two slender pieces of metal in concert.

He closed the door behind him and put on his night-vision goggles. His gaze swept the small living room. There was a night-light inserted into an outlet, providing a bit of illumination. It didn't matter. Robie had been given the plans of the apartment and had memorized all relevant details.

His fingers closed around the gun in his pocket; the suppressor can was already spun on the muzzle. No wasted time.

In one corner of the room was a round particleboard table. On it were a laptop and stacks of paper. The lady had brought her work home, it seemed. There were books on a small shelf. There was no carpet, only worn area rugs.

In one corner was a collapsible playpen. On two walls were pieces of construction paper taped up. There were stick-figure kids and a stick-figure woman with messy hair. In childish script were the word "I" and the word "mom" separated by a crude drawing of a heart. There were also toys piled in one corner.

All this gave Robie pause.

I'm here to kill a young mother. The flash drive said nothing about kids.

Then in his headset came the voice.

"You should already be in the bedroom."

This was also what was different about tonight. He wore a pinhole camera that conveyed live video feedback, and an earwig through which his handler could prompt him to do his job more efficiently.

Robie moved through the room, stopping at the closed door to the bedroom.

He listened at the cheap wood for a few moments and heard what he expected: low breathing, soft snores.

He gripped the knob with his gloved hand, pushed the door open, and stepped through.

The bed was set against the window. Directly outside was the fire escape. In many respects this was far too easy, like a movie set properly lighted and waiting for the actors to execute a pivotal scene.

It was dark in here, but he could still see her lying in the twin bed. Her heavy body made a substantial hump under the covers. Much of her weight was carried in her hips and buttocks. Robie knew it would take some effort to lift her corpse onto the gurney after she'd been pronounced dead. The cops would look for clues, but there would be none. Ordinarily Robie would police his brass. But he was chambering dum-dum rounds tonight, so most likely they would stay inside her. And if so, the medical examiner would find them during the post. But what he would never have was a gun to match them to.

He lifted the Glock out from his pocket and moved forward. When you wanted to make sure that one shot would do the trick, there were any number of places where this could be accomplished.

To avoid the blowback of blood and tissue on his person that inevitably came with a contact shot, Robie had opted tonight to make the kill shot from a few feet away. He would fire once into the heart, and then for insurance he would place a second shot into the aorta, which was the width of a garden hose and ran vertically up to the heart. There were things in front of the aorta, but if one knew where to shoot and the angle was right, the shot would sever the hose ten times out of ten. The bleedout would be lightning fast. And if the bullets somehow passed through her, the mattress would probably collect them.

Quick, clean.

He moved to the front of the bed and raised the pistol. She was lying flat on her back. He lined up her heart in his gunsight. Instead of his target he momentarily saw in his mind the toys, the playpen, the drawing that said, "I heart mom." He shook his head clear. Refocused. The drawing stormed back into his mind. He shook his head again. And—

Robie jerked slightly when he saw the small hump next to her. The head with the wiry hair sticking out. It had been hidden under the covers. He did not pull the trigger.

In his ear the voice said, "Shoot."

12

Robie did not shoot. But he must have made some sound.

The wiry head moved. Then the little hump sat up. The boy rubbed his eyes, yawned, opened his eyes, and stared directly at Robie standing there, his pistol pointed at the boy's mother.

"Shoot," the voice said. "Shoot her!"

Robie did not fire.

"Mommy," said the boy in a fearful tone, never once taking his gaze off Robie.

"Shoot," said the voice. "Now."

The man sounded hysterical. Robie couldn't put a face with the voice because he had never met his handler in person. Standard agency procedure. No one could ID anyone.

"Mommy?" The little boy started to cry.

"Shoot the kid too," said the handler. "Now."

Robie could fire and be gone. Taps to the chests. One big, one small. One dum-dum fired into the child would destroy his insides. He would have no chance.

"Shoot now," said the voice.

Robie did not shoot.

The woman began to stir.

"Mommy?" Her son poked her with his fingers but kept staring at Robie. Tears slid down his thin cheeks. He started to shake.

She slowly woke. "Yes, baby?" she said in a sleepy voice. "You're safe, baby, just a nightmare. You're safe with Mommy. Nothing to be scared of."

"Mommy?"

He tugged on her gown.

"Okay, baby, okay. Mommy's awake."

She saw Robie. And froze, but only for an instant. Then she pulled her child behind her.

She screamed.

Robie put a finger to his lips.

She screamed again.

"Shoot them," the handler said frantically.

Robie said to her, "Be quiet or I shoot."

She didn't stop screaming.

He fired a round into the pillow next to her. The stuffing flew out, and the round deflected off the mattress springs and drilled into the floor underneath the bed.

She stopped screaming.

"Kill her," the handler roared in Robie's ear.

"Stay quiet," said Robie to the woman.

She sobbed, hugged her son. "Please, mister, please, don't hurt us."

"Just stay quiet," said Robie. The handler was still

screaming in his ear. If the man had been in the room Robie would have shot the asshole just to shut him up.

"Take what you want," mumbled the woman. "But please don't hurt us. Don't hurt my baby."

She turned, hugged her son. Lifted him up so they were face-to-face. He stopped crying, touched his mother's face.

Robie realized something and his gut tightened.

The handler was no longer screaming. His earwig held nothing except silence.

He should have picked up on that before.

Robie lunged forward.

The woman, thinking he was about to attack them, screamed again.

The window glass shattered.

Robie watched as the rifle round passed through the boy's head and then drove through his mother's, killing them both. It was an enviable shot made by a marksman of enviable skill. But Robie was not thinking of that.

The woman's eyes were on Robie when her life ended. She looked surprised. Mother and son fell sideways, together. She was still holding him. If anything her arms, in death, appeared to have tightened around her lifeless child.

Robie stood there, gun down. He looked out the window.

The fail-safe was out there somewhere with a fine sight line, obviously.

Then his instincts took over and Robie ducked down and rolled away from the window. On the floor he saw something else he had never expected to see tonight.

On the floor next to the bed was a baby carrier. In the carrier sound asleep was a second kid.

"Shit," Robie muttered.

He crawled forward on his belly.

His earwig came alive. "Get out of the apartment," his handler ordered him. "By the fire escape."

"Go to hell," Robie said. He ripped the pinhole and earwig off, powered them down, and stuffed them in his pocket.

He snagged the carrier, slid it toward him. He was waiting for a second shot. But he did not intend to give the shooter a viable target. And the man on the other end of the kill shot wouldn't fire without that, Robie knew. He had sometimes been the one holding the rifle out there in the darkness.

He moved clear of the window and stood, holding the baby carrier behind him. It was like lugging a large dumbbell. He had to get out of the building, but Robie obviously couldn't go out the way he'd planned. He glanced toward the door. He had to get something before he left.

He carried the child out of the bedroom and scanned the living room with a penlight. He spied the woman's purse. He set the carrier down, rifled through the purse, and took out the woman's driver's license. He snapped a picture of it with his phone. Next he photographed her ID card. Her government ID card.

What the—? That fact wasn't on the flash drive.

Finally, he spied the blue item partially hidden under a stack of papers. He grabbed it.

A U.S. passport.

He snapped photos of all the pages, showing the places to which she'd traveled. He put the license, ID card, and passport back and grabbed the carrier.

He opened the front door of the apartment and looked right and then left.

He stepped out and hit the stairwell four strides later. He raced down one flight. The layout of the building was whirring through his mind. He had memorized every apartment, every resident, every possibility. But never for such a purpose as he had now: escape from his own people.

Number 307. A mother of three, he recalled. He went for it, his feet flying down the hall, touching only lightly on the crappy carpet.

Miraculously, the little one slept on. Robie had not really looked at the child since he had picked it up. He glanced down now.

The hair was wiry, like that of his dead brother. Robie knew the child would never remember the brother. Or the mother. Life sometimes was not just unfair, it was beyond tragic.

He set the carrier down in front of 307. Robie

knocked three times. He did not look around. If someone in another apartment looked out they would only see his back. He knocked once more and glanced again at the baby that was starting to stir. He heard someone coming to the door and then Robie was gone.

The child would survive the night.

Robie was pretty certain that he wouldn't.

13

Robie went down one more flight to the second floor. He had two options.

The rear of the building was out. The long-range shooter was there. The fact that his handler had wanted him to leave by the fire escape told Robie all he needed to know. A bullet in the head would be his reward for being stupid enough to try to get out that way.

The front of the building was out for a similar reason. Well lighted, one entry—he might as well paint a bull's-eye on his head when the backup team showed up a minute from now to clean up this mess. That left the two sides of the building. His two options, but Robie had to narrow it to one. And quickly.

He was moving as he was thinking: 201 or 216. The first was on the left of the building, the second on the right. The shooter in the rear of the building could move over to the left or right and thus cover the rear and one side simultaneously.

So left or right?

Robie moved, thought.

The handler would be helping the shooter, feeding

him where he thought Robie would go. Left or right? He strained to remember the composition of the area. There was this high-rise building. The alley behind. A block of small businesses, gas station, strip mall. On the other side of that another high-rise that looked abandoned to Robie when he had done his earlier recon. The shooter had to be in there. That was the only sight line that worked. And if the building was abandoned, the shooter would have room to roam, to reset his position and turn his scope to Robie.

So which will it be? Left or right?

His original target, 404, was closer to the left side of the building. The handler might think Robie would go that way because he was closest to that side already. The handler didn't know that Robie had gone to the third floor to drop off the other kid and then proceeded down another flight. But the handler would figure Robie would have to go down. He hadn't brought anything to rappel down the side of the building.

Robie thought this through. In his mind's eye he visualized the shooter sliding his position over to his right—Robie's left—setting up his bipod, adjusting his scope, and waiting for Robie to appear.

But Robie hadn't appeared yet when speed was essential. The shooter would take this into account. Robie, he knew, was trying to outguess him. Zig when they expected zag. So to the right instead of the left. That would explain the time that had passed thus far. Not dropping off the second kid.

In Robie's mind he now slid the shooter to the left, or Robie's right, on his mental chessboard.

The time for thinking was over.

He sprinted down the hall toward the building's left side.

Number 201 was empty. Another foreclosure. Small personal miracles sometimes grew from large economic disasters. Ten seconds later he was inside. The apartments all had the same layout. He didn't need a light or his goggles to navigate. He reached the back bedroom, opened the window, and climbed out.

He gripped the windowsill, looked down, gauged the drop, and let go.

Ten feet later he hit and rolled, cushioning the fall. Still, he felt pain in his right ankle. He waited for a shot to hit him.

None did. He had guessed correctly. He ran at an angle away from the building, hid behind a Dumpster for a few moments, recalibrated his senses to the new surroundings. Then he was up and over a fence and sprinting up the street five seconds later.

They probably hadn't seen him leave the building or else he'd be dead. But they had to know by now that he'd gotten away. A response team would be searching for him. Grid by grid. Robie knew the drill. Only now he had to defeat it.

For as long as he'd been doing this Robie had known that what had happened tonight was a possibility. Not a distinct possibility, but one he had to account for. Like for all his other missions, he had a contingency exit plan in place. Now it was time to execute the plan. Shane Connors's advice to him had finally come into play.

"You're the only one out there who really has your back, Will."

He walked ten more blocks. His destination was up ahead. He checked his watch. Twenty minutes to spare if the schedule hadn't changed.

The year-old Outta Here Bus Company had taken over an old Trailways terminal near Capitol Hill. The company obviously didn't have a lot of start-up capital, and the station still appeared like it was shut down. The company's buses parked here did not look as if they could pass even a routine inspection. This trip would definitely be economy class all the way.

Robie had used a fake name to reserve a ticket on a bus leaving in twenty minutes. Its destination was New York City. He paid for the ticket in cash. Once he got to New York he would execute the second step in his contingency plan, which would entail leaving the country. He planned to put as much space between himself and his own people as he could.

He waited outside the terminal. Its location was not all that safe, especially at two in the morning. But it was far safer than the situation Robie had just left. Street criminals he could deal with. Professional killers with long-range rifles were far more formidable.

He looked at the other people awaiting the arrival of

the bus that would carry them to the Big Apple, counting thirty-five passengers, including himself. The bus would hold nearly twice that, so he would have some buffer space. It was open seating, so he would try and snag a place away from everyone. Most of the people had bags, pillows, and knapsacks. Robie had nothing except his night-vision goggles, his pinhole camera, and his Glock pistol in an inside zippered compartment of his hoodie.

He ran his gaze over the line of people again. He deduced that most were poor, working-class, or otherwise down on their luck. It was an easy assumption. Their clothes were old, tattered, their coats threadbare, their expressions tired, beaten down. Most people with even limited financial means would probably not choose to ride to New York City in the middle of the night on a dilapidated bus carrying their own pillows.

The bus pulled into the parking lot in a wide arc and came to a stop near them with a screech of rusty brakes. They all lined up. That's when Robie noticed her. He had already counted her as one of the thirty-five, but now his gaze came to rest fully on her.

She was young. Maybe twelve, maybe barely a teenager. She was short, skinny, dressed in faded jeans with holes in the knees, a long-sleeved shirt, and a dark blue ski parka without arms. She had on dirty, scuffed tennis shoes and her dark, stringy hair was pulled back into a tight ponytail. She carried a backpack in one hand and her gaze was set resolutely on the ground.

She seemed to be breathing hard, and Robie noticed that both her hands and her knees had traces of dirt on them.

Robie looked for but did not see the small rectangular shape in her jeans pockets, front or back. Every teenager had a cell phone, especially the girls. Yet unlike most teens, she might have kept it in her jacket pocket. In any event, it was none of his business.

He looked around, but saw no one who could be her parents.

He edged forward in the line. It was not out of the realm of possibility that they would find him here before the bus departed. He gripped his pistol in his pocket and kept his gaze down.

On board the bus he shuffled toward the back. He was the last on, and most people had taken seats nearer the front. He sat in the last row, near the bathroom. There was no one else in this row. He sat next to the window. From here he could remain invisible while still seeing anyone coming, through the gap in the two seats in front of him. The windows were tinted. That would foul any attempted shot from outside.

The teenage girl sat three rows up from him on the opposite side of the aisle.

Robie looked up as a man hustled onto the bus right before the driver shut the door. He showed his ticket and moved toward the back. As he neared the girl he looked the other way. This was passenger number thirty-six and the very last to board.

Robie sank lower in his seat and pulled his hoodie closer around his face. He gripped his pistol in his pocket and edged the muzzle up and forward so that it was aimed at a spot the man had to cross if he continued to head Robie's way. Robie had to assume that they somehow had found out about his contingency plan and had sent this man to finish the job.

But the fellow stopped one row beyond the teenage girl and sat in the seat directly behind her. Robie's hand relaxed slightly around his pistol but he continued to watch the man through the gap.

The girl got up and put her bag in the overhead rack. As she stood on tiptoes to accomplish this, her shirt edged up and Robie saw that her waist was tattooed.

The bus pulled off with a grinding of gears and the driver headed out onto the surface street that he would take to the interstate and then on to New York. There were few cars at this hour. The buildings were dark. The city would awake in a few hours. D.C. was not like New York in that regard. It *did* sleep. But it rose early.

Robie's gaze settled back on the man. He was Robie's size and age. He had no bag. He was dressed in black slacks, gray jacket. Robie's gaze went to the man's hands. They were gloved. Robie looked down at his own gloved hands and then gazed outside. It was not that cold. He saw the man engage the lever to slide his seat back a bit. He settled in.

But Robie's instincts told him it wouldn't be for long.

This man was not on the bus simply to travel to New York.

14

Professional killers were a unique lot.

Robie thought this as the bus motored along. The vehicle's suspension was for shit and thus the ride was too. They would have to endure two hundred miles of this, but Robie was not focused on that. He stared through the gap, watching, waiting.

When you were on a mission you looked for things that other people would never focus on. Like entry and exit points. Always have at least two of each. Gunsight angles, positions from which others can strike back at you. Sizing up opponents without seeming to do so. Trying to ferret out intent by reading body cues alone. Never let anyone notice you noticing him.

Robie was undertaking all of these tasks right now. And it was totally unconnected with his plight. He had people after him, clearly. But just as clearly the girl had someone after her. And Robie now knew that he was not the only professional killer on board this bus tonight.

He was looking at the second one.

He slipped the Glock from his pocket.

The girl was reading. Robie couldn't see what, but it was a paperback. She was intent on this, oblivious to all other things. That was not good. Young people made easy targets for predators. Young people were glued to their phone screens, thumbs ramming keys, firing off messages of importance, like Facebook status, the color of their underwear that day, girl problems, hair problems, sport stats, where the next party was. They also always had earbuds in. With the music roaring, they could hear nothing until the lion struck. Then it was too late.

Easy prey. And they didn't even know it.

Robie lined up his shot between the seat gap.

The other man leaned forward in his seat.

They had been traveling for only a few minutes. They were passing through an even more derelict part of the city.

There was no one sitting next to the girl in the window seat. There was no one across the aisle from her. The closest person to her was an old woman who had already fallen asleep. Most in the bus had settled down to sleep, though they'd barely gone a half mile as yet.

Robie knew how he would do it. Head and neck. Pull right, pull left, the same method the U.S. Marines teach. Because the target was a child, no weapon would be required. No loss of blood either. Most people died silently. There was no melodramatic dying sequence. Folks just stopped breathing, gurgled, twitched, and then went quietly. People close by were clueless. But then most people were clueless.

The man tensed.

The girl shifted her book a bit, letting the wash from the overhead light hit the page more fully.

Robie eased forward. He checked his gun. The suppressor can was spun on as tight as it would go. But in the close confines of the bus there was no such thing as a silenced gun. He would worry about explanations later. He had watched two people tonight lose their lives, one a little boy. He did not intend to make it three.

The man set his weight on the balls of his feet. He lifted his hands, positioned them in a certain way.

Pull-pull, thought Robie. Head left, neck right. Snap.

Pull-pull.

Dead girl.

But not tonight.

15

Robie could read a lot from a little. But what happened next was not something that he had anticipated at all.

The man screamed.

Robie would have too, since pepper spray stung like hell when it hit the eyes.

The girl was still gripping her paperback, keeping her current page. She had not even turned in her seat. She had just fired the spray backward over her head, nailing her attacker directly in the face.

However, the man was still moving forward, even as he screamed and clawed at his eyes with one of his hands. The other hand found purchase on the girl's neck at about the time Robie's pistol collided with the man's skull, sending him crashing down to the floor of the bus.

The girl looked around at Robie as most of the other passengers, awakened now, stared at them. Then their gazes drifted to the fallen man. One old woman wearing a thick yellow robe started screaming. The driver stopped the bus, slammed it in park, turned to look at Robie standing there, and yelled, "Hey!"

The tone and the stare indicated to Robie that the driver thought he was the source of the problem. The driver, a heavyset black man of about fifty, rose and started down the aisle.

When he saw Robie's gun, he stopped and put his hands in front of him.

The same old woman screamed and clutched at her robe.

"What the hell do you want?" exclaimed the driver to Robie.

Robie looked down at the unconscious man. "He was attacking the girl. I stopped him."

He looked at the girl for support. She said nothing.

"Would you like to tell them?" Robie prompted.

She said nothing.

"He was trying to kill you. You nailed him with pepper spray."

Robie reached over, and before she could stop him he'd ripped the canister from her hand and held it up.

"Pepper spray," he said in a confirming tone.

The other passengers' attention now turned to the girl.

She looked back at them, unfazed by their scrutiny.

"What's going on?" asked the driver.

Robie said, "The guy was attacking the girl. She pepper-sprayed him and I finished him off when he didn't back down."

"And why do you have a gun?" asked the driver.

"I've got a permit for it."

In the distance Robie heard sirens.

Was it for the two bodies back at the building?

The man on the floor groaned and started to stir. Robie put a foot on his back. "Stay down," he ordered. He looked back at the driver. "You better call the cops." He turned to the girl. "You have a problem with that?"

In response the girl rose, grabbed her backpack from the overhead bay, slipped it over her shoulders, and walked down the aisle toward the driver.

The driver put up his hands again. "You can't leave, miss."

She drew something from her jacket and held it in front of the man. From where he was standing behind the girl Robie was blocked from seeing what it was. The driver immediately retreated, looking terrified. The old woman screamed again.

Robie knelt down and used the fallen man's belt to efficiently tie his hands and ankles together behind his back, completely immobilizing him. Then he followed the girl down the aisle. As he passed the driver he said, "Call the cops."

"Who are you?" the driver called after Robie.

Robie didn't answer, because he could hardly tell the man the truth.

The girl had worked the lever to open the bus door and stepped off.

Robie caught up to her as she reached the street.

"What did you show him?" he asked.

She turned and held up the grenade.

Robie didn't blink. "It's plastic."

"Well, he didn't seem to know that."

Those were the first words she had spoken. Her voice was lower than Robie would have expected. More grown-up. They moved away from the bus.

"Who are you?" asked Robie.

She kept walking. The sirens drew closer and then started to fade away.

"Why did that guy want to kill you?"

She picked up her pace, moving ahead of him.

They reached the other side of the street. She slipped between two parked cars. Robie did the same. She hustled down the street. He picked up his pace and grabbed her arm. "Hey, I'm talking to you."

He didn't get an answer.

The explosion knocked them both off their feet.

16

Robie came to first. He had no idea how long he'd been out, but it couldn't have been very long. There were no cops, no first responders. It was just him and a bus that was no longer there. He gazed over at the skeleton of burning metal that had once been a large piece of transportation equipment and thought that, like a plane crashing nose first into the earth from a great height, there could be no survivors.

This area of D.C. was deserted at this late hour and there were no residences nearby. The only people wandering out to see what had happened were obviously homeless.

Robie watched as one old man dressed in ragged jeans and a shirt turned black by living on the street stumbled out onto the sidewalk from his home of cardboard and plastic trash bags inside a doorway. He looked at the bonfire that had once been a bus with passengers inside and called out between rotted teeth, "Damn, anybody got something good to grill?"

Robie slowly rose. He was bruised and sore and would be even more bruised and sore tomorrow. He looked around for the girl and found her ten feet from where he had landed.

She lay next to a parked Saturn whose side windows had been blown out by the blast. Robie raced to her and gingerly turned her over. He felt for a pulse, found it, and breathed a sigh of relief. He checked her over. No blood, a few scratches on her face from where her skin had collided with the rough pavement. She would live.

A few moments later her eyes opened.

Robie eyed the grenade that she still clutched in her hand.

"Did you leave a real one of those on the bus?"

She sat up slowly, looked toward the demolished bus.

Robie expected the sight to evoke some reaction from her, but she said nothing.

"Somebody really wants you dead," he said. "Any idea why?"

She got to her feet, spotted the knapsack lying a few feet away, and retrieved it, dusting off the outside and putting the strap over her shoulder. She looked up at Robie, who towered over her.

"Where's your gun?" she asked.

This caught him off guard. He didn't know where his gun had gone. He looked around, then squatted down and looked under a few cars parked on the street. There was a storm drain. It might have fallen in there when he'd gotten blasted off his feet.

"I'd find it if I were you."

He looked at her. She was watching him from a few feet away.

"Why?"

"Because you're probably going to need it."

"Why?" he asked again.

"Because you've been seen with me."

He rose. He could hear more sirens. Someone had finally called it in, because they were getting louder. The responders were heading this way. The homeless guy was now dancing around the bonfire yelling about wanting some "damn s'mores."

Robie said, "And why is that significant?"

She glanced at the destroyed bus. "What? Are you stupid?"

He gave up the search for his gun and came over to her.

Robie said, "You need to go to the police. They can protect you."

"Yeah, right."

"You don't think they can?"

"If I were you I'd get out of here."

Robie said, "There's no one left alive on that bus to tell the cops what happened."

"What do you think happened?" she asked.

"Over thirty people just lost their lives on that bus, including a guy who was trying to kill you."

"That's your theory. Where's your proof?"

"The proof is in that bus. Some of it. The rest is in your head, presumably."

"Again, *your* theory."

She turned and started to walk off.

Robie watched her for a few moments. "You can't do this alone, you know," he said. "You've already screwed up, or got ratted out."

She turned back. "What do you mean?" For the first time she sounded interested in what he had to say.

"They already followed you to the bus or they were waiting for you. If the latter, you were set up. They had advance intel. Knew the bus, the time, everything. So either you screwed up and let them follow you, somehow, or else someone you trusted turned on you. It's either one or it's the other."

She looked over his shoulder at the burning mass of metal and flesh.

He asked, "How did you spot the guy on the bus? Looked to me like he had a clean kill angle."

"Reflection in my window. Tinted glass, overhead light inside, dark outside equals a mirror. Simple science."

"You were reading a book."

"I was *pretending* to read a book. I saw the guy sit down behind me. He passed by three empty rows. Made me think, you know? Plus I saw him get on. He was doing his best not to let me see him."

"So you would've recognized him?"

"Maybe."

"I was behind you too."

"Too far behind to do you any good."

"So you spotted me too?"

She shrugged. "You just get used to checking stuff out."

"So he followed you to the bus. Did he chase you? I see the dirt on your hands and knees. Looks like you took a tumble before you got to the bus."

She looked down at her knees but didn't answer him.

Robie said, "But you still can't do this alone."

"Yeah, you already said that. So what do you suggest?"

"If you won't go to the police, you can come with me."

She took a step back. "You? Where?"

"Somewhere safer than here."

She eyed him coolly. "Why don't *you* stay and talk to the cops?"

He stared at her and listened to the sirens drawing uncomfortably close.

She said, "Did it have something to do with that gun and your being on that bus at this hour?" She eyed him more closely. "You don't look the type, you know?"

"Meaning?"

"You don't look like you have to ride in a crappy bus in the middle of the night to get to New York. And neither did the guy who was sitting behind me. That was his other mistake. You have to dress for the part."

"You want to go it alone, go. I'm sure you'll be able to hold them off for a few more hours. But then it'll all be over for you."

She looked once more over his shoulder at the burning mass.

"I didn't want anybody else to die," she said.

"Anybody *else*? Who else has died?"

Robie had the feeling that she wanted to dissolve into tears, but she said, "Who are you?"

"Someone who stumbled onto something and doesn't want to leave it."

"I don't trust you or anyone else."

"I don't blame you. I wouldn't either."

"Where do you want to go?"

"Someplace safe, like I said."

"I'm not sure there is such a place," she said in a voice that, for the first time, sounded like a kid's. Scared.

"Me either," said Robie.

17

Robie didn't just have an escape plan in case something went wrong on one of his missions. He had a safe house too. Now, with someone else in tow, he had opted for Plan C.

Unfortunately, Plan C was already getting complicated.

Robie's gaze swept the end of the alley. He'd put his goggles on. It was only a glimpse, but he clung to it, because he knew it was important: reflected light off a gun scope.

He removed the goggles, slipped back into shadows, looked down at the girl.

"What's your name?"

"Why?"

"Just something to call you. It doesn't have to be your real one," he added.

She hesitated. "Julie."

"Okay, Julie. You can call me Will."

"Is that your real name?"

"Is Julie *your* real name?"

She fell silent, looked past him, out into the darkness.

They had covered about ten blocks, so far in fact that the sound of the sirens had receded. She had not committed to go with him. They had silently agreed to leave the scene of the explosion by simply turning and walking away together.

Robie could visualize the activity surrounding the bus. The first responders would be trying to determine what had caused the explosion. Faulty gas tank? Or terrorist attack? But then he concentrated on that glimpse.

"There's someone out there," he told Julie in a low voice.

"Where?" she asked.

Robie pointed over his shoulder even as his gaze was running over her. "Any chance you have a tracking device on you? Because I'm good at getting away, and that was pretty fast to catch up to us."

"Maybe they're better than you."

"Let's hope not. Tracking device? How about your cell? I didn't notice one in your pocket. But do you have one? And is your GPS chip enabled?"

"I don't have a cell phone," she replied.

"Don't all kids have cell phones?"

"I guess not," she said stiffly. "And I'm not a kid."

"How old are you?"

"How old are *you*?"

"Forty."

"That's really old."

"Trust me, I'm feeling it. How old?"

She hesitated again. “Can I lie?” she asked. “Like with my name?”

“Sure. But if you say you’re over twenty I probably won’t believe you.”

“Fourteen.”

“Okay.”

He looked the way they had come. Something in his gut very clearly told him not to go back that way.

“What did you see that made you think there’s someone there?” she asked.

“Reflection, just like yours in the bus window.”

“It could be anybody.”

“Reflection of light off a rifle scope. It’s a pretty unique signature.”

“Oh.”

Robie studied the walls on either side of them. Then he looked up.

“You afraid of heights?”

“No,” she said quickly, perhaps a little too quickly. He hustled to a construction Dumpster parked in the alley and searched through it. He finally pulled out several lengths of rope and quickly knotted them together. There was a lenth of plywood in the Dumpster too. He positioned it so that it rested on top of the Dumpster’s rim, giving them a platform on which to stand.

“Strap your backpack down tight around you.”

“Why?”

“Just do it.”

She yanked the straps tight and looked at him expectantly.

"What are we doing?"

"Climbing."

Robie lifted her up and placed her on top of the plywood and hoisted himself on top of it.

"What now?"

"Like I said, we climb."

She stared up the brick face of the building.

"Can you really do this?"

"We'll find out." He motioned to her. "Come on. You need to stand on my shoulders." He pointed up. "We're aiming for that."

It was a fire escape ladder that in its up and locked position ended well above street level.

"I don't think I can reach it."

"We can try. Keep your legs rigid."

He lifted her up and onto his shoulders and then, grabbing her ankles, military-pressed her higher. Even with her arms stretched out fully she was still about a foot short of the goal. He set her back down.

Robie took the rope he'd gotten from the Dumpster and tossed it up and over the bottom rung of the ladder. He took one end, fashioned a knotted loop, and pulled the other end through it. He gripped the rope and quickly climbed up to the ladder, then freed the rope and passed one end back down to her.

"I'm not great at rope climbing. I flunked PE," she said doubtfully.

"You don't have to be. Tie the rope around your backpack straps. Make sure the knot is tight."

She did this.

Robie added, "Now cross your arms and hold them tight against your body. That'll keep the backpack from slipping."

She did so and he started pulling her up.

As soon as she reached him, Robie knew they were in trouble. Running feet were never a good sound.

"Climb, now," he said, the urgency clear in his voice. "As high as you can."

She struggled up the fire escape ladder while Robie turned back and focused on what was coming.

18

The man turned into the alleyway, stopped, cleared the lane by sight, and moved forward. Ten yards in he stopped again, looked left, right, and then ahead. He kept moving, his rifle swinging in precise, controlled arcs. He did this two more times. He was good, but not good enough, because he hadn't yet looked up.

When he finally did it was just in time to see the bottom of Robie's feet rushing at him.

Robie's size twelves smashed into the man's face and drove the rest of the attached body violently to the asphalt. Robie landed on top of the man, rolled, and came up in an attack posture. He kicked the rifle away and looked down. He didn't know if the man was dead. But he was certainly unconscious. He took a few seconds to search him.

No ID.

No phone.

No surprise.

But no official credentials either. No gold badge.

He did find an electronic device with a blinking blue light in the man's pocket. He crushed it underfoot and threw it into the Dumpster. He felt near the man's ankle and pulled out a .38 S&W throwaway. He slipped it into his jacket pocket, turned, and leapt on top of the plywood. He grabbed the rope, made his way up, snagged the rung of the ladder, freed and pocketed the rope, and climbed.

Julie was already near the top of the building when he reached her.

"Is he dead?" she asked, looking downward.

She had obviously been watching.

"I didn't check. Let's go."

"Where? We're at the top."

He pointed upward, to the roof. It was about ten feet farther up.

"How?" she asked. "The stairs don't go that far. They stop at the top floor."

"Wait here."

He found a handhold on a windowsill, and then another in a crack in the brick. He climbed. A minute later he stood on the roof. He lay on his stomach, uncoiled the rope, and fed it down to her.

"Tie it to your backpack straps, like before, lock your arms together again, and close your eyes."

"Don't drop me," she said, her voice panicky.

"I've already lifted you once. You weigh nothing."

A minute later she was beside him on the roof.

Robie led her across the flat, graveled terrain, reached the opposite side, and looked down and then around. There was another fire escape on this side. He used the rope to lower Julie down, then slipped over the side, hung from the building for a few seconds, and let himself drop. He hit the metal of the fire escape, grabbed her hand, and they started down.

"Won't we have the same problem if someone is out there?" said Julie.

"We would if we were going all the way down."

They reached the third floor of the building and Robie stopped and peered in. He used a knife he carried in an ankle holder to defeat the simple locking mechanism.

He lifted the window.

"What if someone lives here?" hissed Julie.

"Then we'll politely leave," answered Robie.

The apartment was empty.

They slipped through quietly and ran down the hall to the interior stairwell. A minute later they hustled down the street in the opposite direction from where they had come.

Robie finally pulled up and said, "They were tracking you. You must have a bug on you somewhere."

"How do you know that?"

"Piece of equipment I found on the guy. I busted it up, but we have to cut off the source. Open your bag."

She did and Robie quickly went through it. There were some clean clothes, a toiletry bag, a camera, some textbooks, an iPod Touch, a small laptop, notebooks, and pens. He popped the back off the iPod and examined the laptop but didn't find anything that shouldn't have been there. The pens were clean too. Robie looked through the toiletries methodically but found nothing. He closed the bag up and handed it back to her.

"Nothing."

"Maybe you've got a bug on you," she said.

"That's not possible," Robie said.

"Are you sure?"

He started to say yes, but then stopped. He pulled out the pinhole camera he'd thrown into his pocket. He popped the cover and underneath was the second blinking blue light he'd seen tonight.

"See, it *was* you. I was right," Julie said triumphantly.

He tossed it and the earwig and power pack in a garbage can.

"Yeah, you were," he conceded.

They did not see a single cab. In fact, a cab was not on his wish list right now. He didn't want a third party whom someone could interrogate to find out where his safe house was.

Robie broke into and then artfully sparked the ignition of an ancient pickup truck parked in front of a gas station. He got in the driver's seat. Julie did not follow. He looked at her across the width of the front seat.

"You decide to go it alone?" he asked.

She didn't answer. She fiddled with the straps on her backpack. He reached in his pocket, pulled out something, and handed it to her.

It was the pepper spray.

"You might need this, then."

She took it but then climbed in the truck, shutting the door firmly.

He put the truck in gear and drove off slowly. Squealing tires in the middle of the night could attract attention he did not want or need right now.

"Why the change of heart?" he asked.

"Bad guys don't give weapons back." She paused. "And you saved my life back there. Twice."

"Fair enough."

"So people are after me. Who's after you?" she asked.

"Unlike you, I know who they are," he said. "But I don't have to tell you. And I won't. It would not be good for your future."

"I'm not sure I have much of that anyway."

She settled back in her seat and grew silent, staring ahead.

"You thinking about somebody?" asked Robie quietly.

She blinked back tears. "No. And don't ask me again, Will."

"Okay."

Robie now drove fast.

As shockingly bad as tonight had been, he had a strong feeling it was only going to get worse.

19

Robie made one stop, at an all-night convenience store to get some groceries. A half hour after that the truck lights flickered across the face of the small farmhouse. Robie pulled the truck to a stop and looked across at Julie.

Her eyes were closed. She appeared to be sleeping, but after seeing her defend herself against the attacker on the bus, Robie was taking nothing for granted. He didn't want to get blasted with pepper spray so he didn't reach out to jostle her. He simply said quietly, "We're here."

Her eyes instantly opened. She didn't yawn, stretch, or rub her face, as most people would have. She was just awake.

Robie was impressed. Because that was exactly how he woke up too.

"What is this place?" she asked, looking around.

They had driven down a gravel road. Woods starting to turn color bracketed the gravel. The drive ended at the front of the white clapboard house. Painted black front door, two front windows, a small porch. In the back a barn rose high above the apex of the house.

"Safe," he said. "Or as safe as possible under the circumstances."

She stared at the barn. "Was this like a farm or something?"

"Or something. Long time ago. Woods have reclaimed the fields."

This was Robie's fail-safe. His employer provided other safe houses for Robie and people like him. But this place was his alone. Ownership under a shell company. No way to trace back to him.

"Where are we?"

"Southwest of D.C., in Virginia. Technical term would be the boonies."

"Do you own it?"

Robie put the truck back in drive and headed for the barn. He stopped, got out, unlocked the barn doors, and drove the truck inside. He got out again, grabbed the sack of groceries, and said, "Come on."

Julie followed him to the house. There was an alarm system. The beeping sound stopped when Robie put in the code. He was careful to not let her see the numbers he punched in.

He closed and locked the door.

She looked around, still clutching her backpack.

"Where do I go?"

He pointed up the straight set of stairs on one side of the small entrance hall. "Spare bedroom, second door on the right. Bathroom across the hall. You hungry?"

"I'd rather sleep."

"Okay." He lifted his gaze to the stairs in a prompting manner.

"Good night," said Robie.

"Good night."

"And make sure you don't shoot yourself with the pepper spray. It really stings the skin."

She looked down at her hand where the small canister was hidden.

"How did you know?"

"I saw you had it pointed at me the whole drive over. Don't blame you. Get some sleep."

She set off. He watched her trudge up the stairs. He heard the bedroom door open and close and then the lock engage.

Smart girl.

Robie went into the kitchen, put the groceries away, and sat down at the round table across from the sink. He set the .38 throwaway on the table and took out his cell phone. No GPS chip was in there. Company policy, because a chip could work both ways. But he had screwed up on the pinhole.

And they must have suspected he wouldn't fire on the woman tonight. They had the tracker on him in case he gave them the slip.

A setup from the get-go. Nice. Now he needed to figure out why.

He clicked some buttons on his phone and looked at the photos he'd taken at the dead woman's apartment.

Her driver's license stated that her name was Jane Wind, age thirty-five. Her unsmiling photo looked back at Robie. He knew she would be lying on the D.C. medical examiner's metal exam table shortly, her face not just unsmiling but badly disfigured by the rifle round. Her child would be autopsied too. Having taken the brunt of the round's kinetic energy, the boy would no longer really have a face.

Robie looked at the photos of her passport pages. He enlarged the screen so he could make out the ports of entry. There were several European countries on there, including Germany. Those were usual. But then Robie saw Iraq, Afghanistan, and Kuwait. Those were not so usual.

He next looked at her government ID card.

Office of the Inspector General, U.S. Department of Defense.

Robie stared at the screen.

I'm screwed. I'm totally screwed.

He used his phone to access the Internet and scrolled through news sites looking for any information on Wind's death or the bus exploding. There was nothing on Wind. They might not have found her yet. But the bus blowing up had already attracted attention. However, there were few details. Robie obviously knew more than any of the reporters out there trying to find out what had happened. According to the news accounts thus far, the authorities were not ruling out a mechanical cause for the explosion.

And that's where it might remain, thought Robie, unless they could find evidence to the contrary. Blowing up an old bus in the middle of the night and killing a few dozen people didn't seem like it would be high on a jihadist's bucket list.

His handler had not tried to contact him again. Robie was not surprised by this. They wouldn't have expected him to answer in any event. He was safe here for now. Tomorrow? Who knew? He glanced in the direction of the stairs. He was on the run, and he was not alone. Alone he might have a chance. But now?

Now he had Julie. She was fourteen, maybe. She didn't trust him or anyone else. And she was running from something too.

His mind and body tired, Robie could think of nothing else to do right now. So he did what made sense. He went upstairs to the bedroom across the hall from hers, locked the door behind him, laid the .38 on his chest, and closed his eyes.

Sleep was important right now. He wasn't sure when he would get another chance to do it.

20

The window opened and the tied-together sheets snaked down the side of the house. Julie looped the other end around the footboard of the bed and tugged on it to make sure it was secure. She slipped through the window, clambered quietly down the improvised rope, touched the ground, and darted off into the darkness.

She didn't know exactly where she was, but she had been following the truck's route while pretending to be asleep. She figured she could get to the main road and then follow that to a store or gas station where she could make a call to a cab company to come and pick her up. She checked her stash of cash and her credit card. She was good to go.

The darkness didn't frighten her. Sometimes the city during the day was far scarier. But she crept along silently, because as good as Will had seemed, she knew someone could still have followed them. She mapped out her plan in her head and decided that it was as good as she was going to come up with under the circumstances.

She knew her parents were dead. She wanted to lie down on the ground, curl up, and never stop crying. She would never see her mother again. She would never hear her father's laugh. Then their killer had come after her. And then he'd been blown up in that bus.

But she couldn't curl up and cry. She had to keep moving. The last thing her parents would have wanted was for her to die too.

She was going to survive. For them. And she was going to find out why someone had killed them. Even if the killer was now dead. She needed to know the truth.

The road was not much farther. She picked up her pace.

She had no time to react.

It just happened.

The voice said, "You know, I was going to make breakfast for you."

She gasped, turned, and gazed at Robie, who was sitting on a tree stump staring at her. He got up. "Was it something I said?"

She glanced back at the house. She was far enough away that all she could make out was a sense of powered light through the tangle of trees and brush.

"I changed my mind," she said. "I'm heading on."

"Where?"

"That's my business."

"You sure about this?"

"Completely sure."

"Okay. You need any money?"

"No."

"Want another canister of pepper spray?"

"You have some?"

He pulled one from his pocket and tossed it to her.

Julie caught it.

Robie said, "That one is actually more potent than the one you have. It has a paralytic built in. It'll lay down any assailant for at least thirty minutes."

She put it in her backpack. "Thanks."

He pointed to his left. "There's a shortcut through there to the road. Just stick to the path. Get to the road, turn left. There's a gas station half a mile up. They have a pay phone, maybe the last one in America."

He turned to go back to the house.

"So that's it? You just let me walk?"

He turned back. "Like you said, it's not my business. It's your decision. And, frankly, I've got my own problems. Good luck."

He started off again.

Julie did not move.

"What were you going to make for breakfast?"

He stopped but didn't look at her. "Eggs, bacon, grits, toast, and coffee. But I have tea too. They say coffee stunts a kid's growth. But then like you said, you're not a kid."

"Scrambled eggs?"

"Any way you like. But I do an exceptional over-hard."

"I can leave in the morning."

"Yes, you can."

"That's my plan."

"Okay."

"Nothing personal," she said.

"Nothing personal," he replied.

They walked back to the house, Julie trailing three feet behind Robie.

"I was pretty quiet getting out of the house. How did you know?"

"I do this for a living."

"Do what?"

"Survive."

Me too, thought Julie.

21

Three hours later Robie lifted his head off the pillow. He showered, dressed, and headed to the stairs. He heard gentle snores coming from the guest bedroom. He thought about knocking but decided to just let her sleep.

He glided down the steps and into the kitchen. He kept the alarm on. He would not turn it off until he left the safe house. In addition to the house alarm, he had perimeter alerts spread around the property. One of those had been triggered by Julie's escape. It had been easy for him to take a shortcut through the woods and intercept her.

Part of him was glad she had decided to come back. Part of him wasn't looking forward to the added responsibility.

But more of him was glad that she had returned.

Was it guilt over letting a little kid die right in front of me? Am I making amends this way, by saving Julie from whatever and whoever is after her?

A while later he heard a door open and feet padding across the hall. Later, the toilet flushed and the water in the sink started running. It kept going for a while. She was probably doing a "sink bath" to clean up.

When she came downstairs twenty minutes later, the meal prep was far advanced.

"Coffee or tea?" he asked.

"Coffee, black," she answered.

"It's over there, help yourself. Cups in the cabinet by the fridge, top shelf."

He checked the grits and then opened the carton of eggs. "Overhard, light or scrambled, or hard-boiled?"

"Who does hard-boiled eggs anymore?"

"Me."

"Scrambled."

He swished the eggs in a bowl and glanced up at the small TV sitting on top of the fridge. He said, "Check it out."

Julie pushed her damp hair back over her ears and glanced up as she sipped her coffee. She had changed clothes. It was still partially dark outside. But in the light of the kitchen she looked younger and scrawnier than she had last night.

At least she wasn't holding the pepper spray anymore. Both hands were cupped around her coffee mug. Her face was scrubbed clean but Robie could see her red, swollen eyes. She'd been crying.

"You have any cigarettes?" she asked, glancing away from his scrutiny.

"You're too young," he replied.

"Too young for what? To die?"

"I get the irony, but I don't have any cigarettes."

"Did you used to smoke?"

"Yes. Why?"

"You just seemed the type."

"What type is that?"

"The 'do things my way' type."

The sound on the TV was turned down low, but the scene on the screen that came on was self-explanatory. The still smoking bus, burned to a shell of metal. All flammable objects had pretty much disappeared: seats, tires, bodies.

Both Robie and Julie stared at it.

The bus had had a full tank of gas, Robie knew, for the trip up to New York. It had burned like an inferno. No, it *was* an inferno. There would be thirty-plus blackened corpses in that ride. Or at least parts of them.

Their crematorium.

The medical examiner would have his hands full with this one.

"Can you turn up the sound?" Julie asked.

Robie grabbed the remote and inched up the volume.

The TV newscaster, a grim-looking man, stared into the camera and said, "The bus had just departed for New York City. The explosion happened at approximately one-thirty last night. There are no survivors. The FBI is not ruling out a terrorist attack, though it doesn't seem clear at this point why the bus would have been targeted."

"How do you think it happened?" Julie asked.

Robie glanced at her. "Let's eat first."

The next fifteen minutes were spent chewing, swallowing, and drinking.

"Good eggs," Julie proclaimed. She pushed her plate back, refilled her coffee cup, and sat back down. She stared at his nearly empty plate and then up at him.

"Can we talk about it now?"

Robie crisscrossed his knife and fork over his plate and sat back.

"Guy who was after you might have set it off."

"What, like a suicide bomber?"

"Maybe."

"Wouldn't you have seen a bomb on him?"

"Probably. Most bomb packs are pretty prominent. Dynamite sticks lined together, wiring, battery, switches, and the detonator. But I tied him up, so it would have been impossible for him to set anything off."

"So it couldn't have been him."

"Not necessarily. You wouldn't need a lot of juice to blow up a bus. It could have been concealed on him. Some C-4 or Semtex and the full tank of gas will take care of the rest. Some explosive vapor in the tank plus a steady supply of fuel for the fire. And it could have been set off remotely. In fact, if that's what happened, a remote had to be used, since the guy was tied up. About half the suicide bombers in the Middle East never pull the trigger themselves. They're just sent out with the bombs and their handlers detonate from a safe distance away."

"I guess the handlers have the easy job, then."

Robie thought back to his own handler, a safe distance away calling the shots—literally.

"I wouldn't disagree with that."

"So if the guy wasn't the source of the explosion?"

"Then something else hit that bus."

"Like what?"

"Incendiary round into the gas tank is one possibility. Ignites the vapor, and boom. Then the gas-fed fire does the rest."

"Did you hear a shot? I didn't."

"No, but it could've been so close to the explosion that we might not have."

"And why would they blow up the bus?"

"How do you think the guy found you on the bus?"

"He came on fast and last," she said, adopting an analytical tone as she gazed at him.

Robie appreciated that tone. He used it often. "So he either just got the assignment at the last minute and was playing catch-up. Or more likely they lost you but then reacquired you." He paused. "Which do you think it is?"

"No idea."

"I'm sure you have some idea. Even a guess."

"How about the guy in the alley with the rifle?"

"He was after me."

"Yeah, that I know. You had the tracking device. But why was he after you?"

"Not something I can talk about. Like I said before."

"Then that's my answer too," Julie shot back. "So what now?"

"I can drive you to the gas station. You can call for a cab. Get another bus to New York. Or maybe the train?"

"Train tickets have names on them."

"Yours would just say Julie."

"And yours would just say Will," she replied. "But that's not exactly enough, is it?"

"No."

They sat staring at each other.

"Where are your parents?" Robie asked.

"Who says I have any?"

"Everybody has parents. It's sort of a requirement."

"I meant parents that were *living*."

"So yours are dead?"

She looked away, fiddled with the handle of her mug. "This arrangement is probably not going to work out."

"Do we go to the police?"

"Will that work for your situation?"

"I meant for you."

"No, it really wouldn't."

"If you tell me what's going on, I can maybe help you."

"You've already helped me, and I appreciate that. But I'm not sure what else you can do, realistically."

"Why were you going to New York?"

"Because it isn't here. Why were you going?"

"It was convenient."

"Well, it's not convenient for me."

"So you had to go. Why?"

"Need to know," she said. "And you don't."

"What? Are you a junior spy or something?"

He glanced at the TV when he caught it out of the corner of his eye. Two sheeted bodies on gurneys were being wheeled out of a condo building. One body was big, one very small.

Another reporter was out front talking to a spokeswoman from the D.C. Metro Police.

The spokeswoman said, "The victims, a mother and her young son, have been identified, but we're withholding their names until next of kin are notified. We have several leads that we are pursuing. We're asking for anyone who saw anything to contact us with that information."

"And it's been reported that the FBI is heading up the investigation?" asked the reporter.

"The deceased woman was a federal employee. The Bureau's involvement is standard operating procedure in those situations."

No, it really isn't, thought Robie. He kept staring at the screen, hungry for more information. It seemed like a year ago since he had escaped from the building, which was now surrounded by police and federal cops.

"And there was another child?" asked the reporter as she held the mike up to the spokeswoman's face.

"Yes. He was unharmed."

"Was the child found in the same apartment?"

"That's all we can say right now. Thank you."

Robie turned back to find Julie staring at him.

Her eyes were like acid, eating through any defense or façade he could muster.

"Was that you?"

He said nothing.

"Mother and kid, huh? And what? You help me to make up for that?"

"You want anything else to eat?"

"No. What I want is to leave."

"I can drive you."

"No, I'd prefer to walk."

She went up to her room and was back down a minute later with her backpack.

As he turned off the alarm and opened the front door for her, he said, "I didn't kill those people."

"I don't believe you," she said simply. "But thanks for not killing me. I've got enough shit to deal with as it is."

He watched her hurry down the gravel drive.

Robie went to get his coat.

22

Robie put on a helmet, slid the leather cover off the Honda street bike, fired it up, and drove it out of the barn. He parked the bike, closed and locked the barn, and then boarded the 600cc silver-and-blue motorcycle once more.

He reached the road in time to see Julie climb into the front seat of a big-as-a-boat ancient Mercury driven by an old woman whose head was barely level with the top of the steering wheel.

Robie let off on the gas and fell in behind the Merc, about fifty yards back. He was not surprised when the big car turned into the gas station he had told Julie about. He raced past, cut down a side road, and doubled back. He stopped the bike and killed the engine. He watched through a gap in a hedge by the road as Julie got out and went over to the pay phone. She hit three keys.

Probably 411, he deduced.

She put in some coins and dialed another number.

Cab company.

She talked, hung up, went inside the station, got the restroom key, and walked around the corner.

She'd have to wait for the cab, and so would Robie.

His phone rang. He glanced at the screen and drew a quick breath.

The number on the ID was known as a "blue" call. It came right from the top of his agency. Robie had never gotten one of those before. But he had memorized the number. He would have to answer it. But that didn't mean he had to be particularly cooperative.

He clicked the phone key and said, "You can't trace this call. You know that."

"We need to meet," the man said.

It wasn't his handler. Robie knew it wouldn't be. Blue calls did not come from handlers in the field.

"I had a *meeting* last night. I don't think I can survive another."

"There will be no repercussions for you."

Robie said nothing. He let his silence convey the absurdity of this statement.

"Your handler was wrong."

"Good to know. I still didn't complete the assignment."

"The intel was also wrong."

Robie said nothing. He had an idea where this might be going and wasn't sure he wanted to go there.

"The intel was wrong," said the man again. "What happened was unfortunate."

"Unfortunate? The woman was *supposed* to die. She was also an American citizen."

Now it was the other man's turn to say nothing.

"IG's Office," said Robie. "I was told she was part of a terrorist cell."

"What you were told is irrelevant. Your job is to execute the order."

"Even if it's wrong?"

"If it's wrong, it's not your job to deal with it. It's mine."

"And who the hell are you?"

"You know this is a blue call. It's above your handler. Well above. Let's leave it at that until we can meet."

Robie watched as Julie came back around from the restroom and went inside to return the key.

"Why was she targeted?"

"Listen, Robie, the decision on you can be changed. Is that what you want?"

"I doubt it matters what I want."

"Actually it does. We don't want to lose you. We consider you a valuable asset."

"Thanks. Where's my handler?"

"Reassigned."

"You mean he's dead too?"

"We don't play those games, Robie. You know that."

"I apparently don't know a damn thing."

"Things are what they are."

"Keep telling yourself that. You might start believing it."

"We're in damage control, Robie. We need to work together on this."

"I'm not feeling real good about working with you guys ever again."

"But you need to move beyond that. In fact, it's imperative that you do."

"Let's move on to this. Did you send someone to kill me last night? Guy with a rifle in an alley? Has my shoe prints on his face? Might still be lying unconscious, in fact, in an alley."

"He was not one of ours. I can promise you that. Give me the exact location and we'll check it out."

Robie didn't believe him, but it didn't really matter. He told the guy where it had happened and left it at that.

"What do you want from me? More missions? I'm not in the mood. Next, you might have me taking out a Boy Scout."

"There's an investigation going on in connection with the death of Jane Wind."

"Yeah, I guess there is."

"FBI is heading it up."

"I guess they are."

"We want you to act as an agency interface with the Bureau."

As many scenarios as Robie had thought through, that had not been one of them.

"You can't be serious."

Silence.

"I'm not going anywhere near this."

"We need you to be the liaison. And we need you to play it the way we want you to. That is essential."

"Why would we need a liaison to this case in the first place?"

"Because Jane Wind was working for us."

23

The meeting place and time was arranged and Robie slowly put away his phone. He looked through the gap in the hedge as the cab rolled into the gas station parking lot. Julie came out of the station with a pack of cigarettes and a bottle of juice.

She has ID showing she's eighteen.

She climbed into the cab and it immediately drove off.

Robie set off and took up a tracking position roughly fifty yards back in traffic.

He was not concerned about losing her. He had slipped a digestible biotransmitter into her scrambled eggs. It would be good for twenty-four hours and then it would wash out of her system. His tracking monitor was strapped to his wrist. He looked down at it and fell back even more. No sense letting her know she had a tail if he didn't have to risk it. She had already proven that she possessed better than average observation skills. She might be young, but she was not to be underestimated.

The cab turned onto Interstate 66 and headed east toward D.C.

Traffic was heavy at this hour. The morning commute into D.C. from the west was routinely abysmal. You rode in with the sun in your eyes and you rode out the same way in the evening along with thousands of other pissed-off commuters.

Being on the Honda allowed Robie to be more nimble than in a car, and he was able to keep within sight of the cab. It rode 66 in, crossed the Roosevelt Bridge, and hung a right at the fork, which took it over to Independence Avenue. They quickly moved from the touristy monument area of D.C. to less beautiful parts of the capital.

The cab stopped at an intersection where a number of old duplexes were located. She got out, but must have told the cab to wait. She walked down the street and the cab followed slowly. She stopped at one duplex, took out her small camera, and clicked some pictures of it. She took pictures of the surrounding area, then climbed back in the cab and it sped off.

Robie made note of the address of the duplex and took up his tail once more.

About ten minutes later Robie realized where she was headed, and part of him couldn't believe it. The other part of him could understand it, though.

She was heading back to the location of the bus explosion.

The cab had to let her out a couple of blocks from her destination because roads were closed off by police barricades. Robie looked around and saw cops and Feds everywhere. This blast had taken everyone by surprise. Robie could imagine lots of Tums were being dropped into federal mouths all over town.

He parked his bike, slipped off his helmet, and took up his pursuit on foot. She was a full block ahead of him. She never once looked back. That made him suspicious, but he kept on. She turned and he turned. She turned again, and so did he. They were now on the same street where the bus had ceased to be. One block over the street was closed to pedestrians as well. The police didn't want people traipsing through their evidence beds. Robie could see what was left of the bus, even though the police were in the process of erecting large metal frames with curtains on them to shield this sight from the public.

Robie looked at the spot where he had landed after the blast occurred. He still had no idea where his gun was. That was troubling. He looked up higher, at the corners of buildings. Were there surveillance cameras posted here? Perhaps on some of the traffic lights. He looked for ATM machines, which had cameras built in. There was a bank across the street. It would not have recorded him and Julie getting off the bus, because it was positioned on the wrong side of the street for that. Right now no one knew that they were the sole survivors of the explosion.

He spied a woman in her late thirties wearing an FBI windbreaker and FBI ball cap. Dark hair, pretty face. She was about five-six and slender, with the narrow hips and the fanned shoulders of an athlete. She had one-inch Bureau work shoes on, black pants, and latex gloves. Her badge and gun rode on her belt.

Robie saw both special agents and uniformed cops talking to her. He noted their air of deference when addressing her. She might be the special agent in charge of this thing. He pulled back into the shadow of a doorway and continued watching, first the FBI agent, and then Julie. Finally Julie turned and walked down the street away from the bus's remains. Robie waited a few moments and then followed.

24

Julie walked to a cut-rate hotel that was wedged between two vacant buildings. She went inside.

Robie pulled up on his bike and watched through a hotel window. She was checking in using a credit card. He wondered whose name was on it. If hers, it could send a marker through the system that would inform whoever was after her right where she was.

A minute later she stepped onto the elevator. Robie broke off surveillance at that point, but he was not done with her yet. He went into the hotel and up to the front desk. The man behind it was old and looked like he would rather be pouring road asphalt in August than holding down this job.

Robie said, "My daughter just checked in. I dropped her off for an internship on the Hill. I wanted her to use her American Express card because the card I gave her was corrupted, but I think she forgot. I tried calling her, but I guess she turned her phone off."

The old gent looked put out. "She just arrived. Why don't you go ask her yourself?"

"What room is she in?"

The old fellow smiled. "I can't give out that information. It's private."

Robie looked suitably irritated, like any father would. "Look, can you just help me out here? The last thing I need is for some cyber creep to screw up my credit by my kid using the wrong card."

The man looked at the records in front of him. "It's a lot of effort for me to do that."

Robie sighed heavily and pulled out his wallet. He slipped out a twenty. "Will this help ease your *effort*?"

"No, but two of them sure would."

Robie pulled out a second twenty and the man snatched them.

"Okay. Credit card used was a Visa. Name on the account was Gerald Dixon."

"I know that. I *am* Gerald Dixon. Now, I've got two Visa cards. Can I see the numbers?"

"You can for another twenty."

After exhibiting deep exasperation, Robie complied. He looked at the card and memorized the numbers. Gerald Dixon was now his.

"Great," said Robie. "That's the corrupted card."

"Already ran it through, sport. Nothing I can do," the man added gleefully.

Robie said, "Thanks for nothing."

He turned and left. He would find out who Gerald Dixon was. But he had to assume that Julie was safe for the moment. Now he had to get going.

He rode back to his apartment and checked out the

front and back of his building before going inside. He took the stairwell instead of the elevator. He passed no one. At this hour of the day everyone was at work. He opened the door to his apartment and poked his head inside. It was all as he had left it.

It took him five minutes to make sure the place was empty. He employed little traps—a piece of paper wedged into a door track, a thread that would be broken when a drawer was opened—to alert him if someone had broken into and searched his place. None of them were tripped.

He changed into slacks, sport coat, and white collared shirt and opened a wall safe that was behind a shelving unit holding his TV. His cred pack was in there. He hadn't used it in a long time. He slipped it inside his suit jacket and set off.

The meeting was in a public place at Robie's insistence.

The Hay-Adams Hotel was located across the street from Lafayette Park, which in turn was across Pennsylvania Avenue from the White House. The most protected ground on earth. Robie figured even his agency would have a hard time killing him here and getting away with it.

The Jefferson Room, an expansive eating area a short stack of steps up from the hotel lobby, was the actual site of the meeting. Robie got there early to see who might have arrived ahead of him.

Then he waited. One minute before the allotted

time a man in his sixties walked in. Modestly priced suit, red tie, polished off-the-rack shoes, the bearing and gravitas of a lifelong public servant who had accumulated far more power than wealth. Two tall young men were with him.

Muscle. Chest bumps revealed the weapons. Earwigs and wires revealed the communications.

They followed him into the Jefferson Room but did not sit with him. They took up positions on the perimeter, their gazes sweeping for threats. They did not let the man sit in the line of any window.

One of the men took out a slender device and set it on the piano that was parked in one corner of the restaurant. He turned it on. It emitted a humming sound.

White noise with a scrambler, Robie knew because he had employed one in his work. *If there are electronic surveillance devices in here, the recording will come out undecipherable.*

It was only then that Robie stepped out. He allowed himself to be seen, but did not approach until the older man saw him and nodded, which confirmed to his guards that Robie was the one he was meeting with.

The room was empty even though it was lunchtime. Robie knew this was not a coincidence. The wait staff was not in evidence. The restaurant had in effect been shut down. Robie would have to eat lunch afterwards if he was hungry. He doubted food was part of the agenda.

Robie sat catty-corner to the man, his back also to a wall.

"Glad you could make it," said the man.

"You have a name?"

"Blue Man will do."

"Creds, Blue, just for confirmation."

The man reached into his pocket and let Robie see the badge, the picture, and the position stated on the ID card but not the name.

This fellow was high up in the agency. Far higher than Robie expected.

"Okay, let's talk. Jane Wind? You said she was one of ours. I checked her ID. She's DCIS. Defense Criminal Investigative Service."

"Did you also see her passport?"

"Middle East trips, Germany. But DCIS has offices in all those places."

"That's why it made perfect cover."

"So was she a lawyer?"

"Yes. But she was more than that."

"What exactly did she do for you?"

"You know you're not read in."

"Then why ask me here?"

"I said you weren't read in. I'm officially reading you in now."

"Okay."

"But first, I need to know exactly what happened last night."

Robie told him. He figured at this point keeping

anything back was a stupid idea. However, he said nothing about Julie or the bus disintegrating. In his mind that was a separate matter entirely.

Blue Man sat back and took all this information in. He didn't break the silence and neither did Robie. He figured Blue Man had more to tell him than Robie had left to convey.

"Agent Wind worked in the field for years. She was a good agent, as I said. After she had her children she was reassigned to the IG's Office at DOD, but she still worked closely with DCIS in all of its investigation sectors. And of course she continued to work for us."

"How did that get her assigned to a hit list she wasn't supposed to be on?" asked Robie. "And how can something like this happen anyway? I know we're clandestine, but we're also part of an organization with checks and balances."

"Rogue traders lose billions of dollars of institutional money all the time. And those organizations are bigger and better funded than we are. And still it happens. If one person, or more likely a small group of people, are determined enough, they can accomplish the impossible."

"I saw her go into the building that night. She had no kids with her."

"Apparently they were with a sitter she's used before that lives in the building. This sitter took them to the apartment when Agent Wind returned home."

"Okay. What did Wind stumble on that got her killed?"

Blue Man looked curious. "How do you know she *stumbled* onto anything?"

"She lived in a crappy apartment with two little kids. There were legal docs on her table in the living room. You can't bring home classified stuff and leave it lying around. So her work wasn't classified. According to her passport her last trip out of the States was two years ago. She wasn't a field agent, at least not any longer, according to you. Her youngest child wasn't even a year old. She probably was pulled from the field because of that. But she was back working on something, probably considered routine. She found something. That's why she was targeted. I doubt it was directly related to her work."

Blue Man took this in, his head nodding approvingly. "You analyze well, Robie. I'm impressed."

"And I'm full of questions. Do you know what she had stumbled onto?"

"No. We don't. But like you we don't think it was tied to her official duties."

"Why do you want me to act as the liaison with the Bureau? That's a big risk, particularly if they find out what I've been doing the last dozen years."

"Which they won't."

"Like you said, one person or a group, if determined enough, can accomplish the impossible."

"Give me your theory."

"Someone found out what she had discovered and they ratted her. We have a mole on our side, as evidenced by the actions of my handler and others, and the hit was carried out. They weren't sure I would pull the trigger so they had a backup. He had no compunction about blowing the kid and his mother away. And you said my handler had been reassigned. That was a lie. I don't need lies from you."

"How do you figure it was a lie?"

"He ordered me to kill Wind. You said that wasn't authorized. So the guy's a traitor. You don't reassign traitors. If you had him in custody you wouldn't need me telling you what happened and theorizing why. That means the handler has disappeared. Along with whoever else he was working with. How many are we talking?"

Blue Man sighed. "We think at least three other people in the chain, but there might be more."

Robie just stared at him.

Blue Man looked down, fiddled with a silver-plated spoon on the immaculate white linen tablecloth. "It's not good, certainly."

"Understatement of the year. What exactly do you want me to do?"

"We have to keep tabs on the investigation without seeming to. So officially you will be a special agent with DCIS, but you will actually be reporting to me.

We'll provide you with all the cover and creds you need. They're being placed at your apartment as we speak."

Robie's face darkened. "You say you've got at least four traitors. What if you actually have more? And what if one of them is at my apartment right now?"

"These agents were pulled from an entirely separate division. They've had no contact with your handler. Their loyalty is above question."

"Right. Forgive me if I think that's bullshit."

"At some point you have to trust, Robie."

"No I don't. And everyone is okay with me joining the hunt?"

"DCIS is on board. Would you like to talk to the national security advisor? Or the deputy director of CIA?"

"Right now it wouldn't matter to me what they said. But why me?"

"Because you didn't pull the trigger, ironically enough. We trust you to do the right thing, Robie. There aren't many I can say that about right now."

Robie had thought of another possible reason why they wanted him involved.

I was there. Which means I'll make the perfect fall guy if this goes to hell.

But he said, "Alright."

His reasoning was straightforward. He would prefer to work the case himself and bring some sort of resolution and sense of justice to it, rather than wait for someone else to do it, and maybe screw it and him beyond repair.

If I go down, I go down by my own hand.

Blue Man rose and put out his hand. “Thank you. And good luck.”

Robie didn’t shake his hand. “It’s almost never about luck. We both know that.” He turned and walked out of the Hay-Adams, back into a world that seemed a little more unfamiliar and daunting than when he had walked in.

25

Everything was waiting for Robie when he got back to his apartment. That was not entirely comforting.

None of my traps were tripped.

He looked over the file, the creds, and his background information.

He had to come up to speed on this case as fast as possible. But fast-tracking something like this meant that mistakes could be made.

And probably will be.

Then it became a case of how fast his support from Blue Man would fade away.

Faster than the party and financial support of a candidate with plummeting poll numbers.

It was just how the town worked.

The name Will Robie stared back at him from the creds. Ironically, his real name was the safest one to use for this sort of assignment.

Robie picked up the badge and ID card pack and put it in his jacket. Also waiting for him was a fresh Glock G20 and a shoulder holster. He was glad to rid himself of the .38 throwaway. He strapped it on and buttoned his jacket.

As he headed out, Robie looked down the hall and watched as she unlocked her door. Annie Lambert turned to him. She was in a black business suit and sneakers with white ankle socks.

"Hello, Will," she said.

"Don't usually see you here in the middle of the day," he said.

"I forgot something. Lunchtime was the first chance I've had to come and get it. What are you all dressed up for?"

"Just a meeting. How did your chill session go?"

"What? Oh, it went fine."

The inquiries into Lambert triggered by her contact with Robie had turned up nothing. Not surprising. To work at the White House one had to be squeaky clean.

He said, "Sorry I left so abruptly. I was just tired."

"No problem. I was too, actually." She hesitated and said in a subdued voice, "But maybe we can have that drink sometime."

"Yeah, maybe we can," said Robie, who was thinking of all that lay ahead of him.

"Okay," she said uncertainly.

He started to walk off and then stopped, realizing that he'd once more been abrupt with her. He turned to her. "I appreciate the offer, Annie. I really do. And I want to have a drink with you."

She brightened. "That'd be great."

"And let's do it soon," he said. "Real soon."

"Why? Are you going somewhere?" she asked.

"No. But I've wanted to start getting out more. And I'd like to do that with you."

Her smile widened. "Okay, Will. You know where I live."

He walked off and wondered why he was suddenly so taken with the young woman. She was lovely and obviously smart and maybe she was smitten with him. But in the past that had not mattered to Robie. He turned and looked back at her apartment. She had gone inside, but he had the image of her standing there in the tennis shoes and the business suit. He smiled.

Robie drove his Audi to the crime scene. With his creds he was able to park within the security perimeter. On the way he had looked at his tracking device as he passed the hotel where Julie was staying. She was still there.

He walked to the apartment building's entrance feeling enormously uncomfortable. He was going to help investigate a murder at which he was an eyewitness.

There was a pack of cops and suits huddled in the lobby of the building. Robie made his way to them, thinking he would check in and introduce himself to the people running the case. The huddle started breaking up as he approached. Out from its middle stepped the same female FBI special agent he had seen at the bus bombing.

She came forward, looking at him inquisitively.

He pulled his cred pack, flashed first the badge and then ID card.

She reciprocated with her cred pack. It said she was FBI special agent Nicole Vance.

"Agent Robie, welcome to the show. I've got some questions for you," she said.

"I look forward to working on this case with you, Agent Vance."

She said, "I got a call from my supervisor about you. We're to associate you with the case, but purely for background information on the deceased and any other information that will help us solve the case. But the FBI has the lead, meaning *I* have the lead."

"I didn't mean to imply otherwise," Robie said smoothly.

Vance seemed to study him more closely. "Okay," she said cautiously. "Just so long as we understand the ground rules."

"What would you like my help on?"

"Any background you can give us on the victim."

Robie pulled a flash drive from his jacket pocket. "Her official background file is contained on here."

She took the drive and handed it to one of her associates. "Get it read and summarized ASAP."

She turned back to Robie. "We were just about to go over the crime scene again. Care to join us?"

"I'd appreciate that. My superiors want to know I'm earning my pay."

This comment earned him a smile. "I guess fed agencies all operate similarly," she said.

"I guess they do."

As they headed to the elevator Vance said, "Did you hear about the bus explosion?"

"I saw it on the news," said Robie. "I understand FBI is investigating that too."

"More specifically, I am."

"A lot on your plate," he commented.

"Might be a good reason to merge the investigations."

"Why is that?"

"We found a gun at the scene of the bus explosion."

Robie kept his gaze straight ahead even as his heartbeat quickened.

"Gun?" he said.

"Yeah. And we've already run ballistics. The Glock we found matches a slug we took from the floor of the apartment the deceased lived in. So in my mind, the two cases are definitely connected. Now we just have to find out how."

"The killer might have just thrown the gun away during his escape. Might just be a coincidence it was found near the bus explosion."

"I don't believe in coincidences. At least not ones like that."

As they stepped off the elevator and headed to the

condo where two people had been murdered right in front of him, Robie, despite the cool air, wicked a drop of sweat off his forehead.

He would take a hundred megalomaniacal Saudi princes and bloodthirsty cartel chieftains over this.

26

The apartment had changed since Robie had last been there. The cops were doing a thorough forensics search and fingerprint powder residue, evidence markers, and thirty-five-mil cameras flashing off were evident throughout the small space.

Robie eyed a sealed evidence box on the particle-board table.

"Is that Agent Wind's work papers? Laptop?"

Vance nodded. "It is. We've sealed it pending your agency's review. I'm cleared all the way on things like that, but I didn't want to step on your toes."

"Appreciate that."

"But we will need to be read in. If there's something in those docs and files that got her killed, the Bureau needs to know it."

"Understood. I can have the review done today and you can be read in directly after."

Vance's smile was guarded. "I never met a more cooperative agency liaison. You're going to spoil me."

"I'll do my best," Robie said.

Until I stop being cooperative, he thought.

"There were pick marks on the front door lock," Vance said. "They were subtle, so the person knew what he was doing. Follow me."

They walked into the bedroom.

Robie looked around. The bodies had been removed, but in his mind he still saw them on the bed, their heads pulverized.

"Wind and her son Jacob were found on the bed. She was holding him. One shot killed them both." She pointed to the shattered window. "We've run a trajectory. Shot came from that high-rise building, well over three hundred meters away. We're pinpointing the exact room. The building is abandoned, so it's doubtful anyone saw anything. But we're still following up. If we're lucky, the shooter left something behind."

You won't be that lucky, thought Robie.

"But you said you found a Glock round in the floor. How does that tie into a shot at that distance? It wasn't a pistol round that killed them. Had to be a rifle round."

"I know. That's what's so puzzling. If I have to speculate, there were two people involved. The person in this room last night fired a shot into the bed. It went through and lodged in the floor. That slug matched the gun we found underneath a car next to the bus explosion. But the kill shot came through the window, hit Jacob, passed through his head, and impacted his mother. Death was instantaneous for both. Or so the ME said."

Robie remembered the look on Jane Wind's face

and wondered how truly "instantaneous" her death had been.

"So two shooters? Doesn't make a lot of sense," he said.

"It makes no sense," replied Vance. "But that's because we don't have enough facts. We collect enough of those it will make sense."

"I appreciate your optimism." Robie stood in front of the bed, in nearly the exact spot from which he'd fired his weapon the night before. "So the shooter who presumably broke into the apartment fired into the bed. Where was the slug found?"

Vance motioned for one of her techs to move aside the bed. Robie saw the evidence marker next to a hole in the wooden floor.

Robie held up an imaginary pistol. He aimed and clicked his finger while Vance watched.

"He would have been standing about here," said Robie, who of course knew this for a fact. "The mattress and box springs seem really thin. I doubt they would have diverted the flight path of the round much, not at this close range."

"That's what I figured too," said Vance.

"No other wounds on the bodies? The round fired into the mattress didn't hit them?"

"Negative. No human residue on it and no other wounds on the victims."

"So he fired a shot into the mattress why? To get their attention?"

"Maybe," said Vance.

"Were they awake when they were shot?"

"Looked to be. The position where they fell on the bed leads me to believe they were awake when they were killed."

"So he fires, but doesn't hit them. He did it to get their attention, or maybe to get them to be quiet. Anyone report hearing any screams?"

Vance sighed. "If you can believe it, the only person who lives on this floor and was here last night is an old woman who's both deaf and blind. She, of course, heard nothing. The only other floor resident was working in Maryland at the time. The apartments above and below this one are vacant."

Oh, I believe it, thought Robie.

"But the round from outside killed them," he said. He went over to the broken window and examined it. He looked outside beyond to the building he could not see last night. The alleyway was down below. The one he had been supposed to use to make his escape. There were other buildings separating the two high-rise structures, but they were all one-story. The shooter would have had a clean shot.

"Okay, gunman inside. Shooter outside. Gunman fires into the bed. Shooter outside kills Agent Wind and her son." He turned back to Vance. "Wind had two sons."

"That's the other really puzzling piece. Her other son is less than a year old. His name is Tyler by the way. He was found by a woman on the third floor."

"Found how?"

"It's crazy, Robie. Someone knocked on her door shortly after the Winds were killed. At least according to the preliminary time of death the ME gave us. The woman opened the door and there was Tyler in his car carrier sound asleep. She recognized him as Wind's son and tried phoning her, then went to her apartment. No one answered so she called the cops. That's when the bodies were discovered."

"You have a theory for that?"

She shook her head. "I know this sounds unbelievable, but it might be that whoever broke into Wind's apartment took the kid down there."

"Why?"

"Why kill an infant? He can't testify against you."

"They had no problem killing the other son," countered Robie.

"Been thinking about that. Look at the hole in the window and then look at the bed. If Wind had grabbed up her other son, maybe to protect him against the intruder, he might have been on the left side—in other words, facing the window."

Robie finished this thought for her. "Shooter fires, really only aiming to hit Wind, but the shot hits the kid first and then her. Maybe he intended to kill them both, or at least wanted to kill Wind and if the kid was in the way, too bad."

"That's how I see it," agreed Vance. "So that sets up an interesting possibility."

"Such as?"

"How's this for a theory? Intruder comes in, just a standard burglary. He doesn't mean to but somehow awakens Wind and her son. He fires a shot into the bed to keep them quiet. At the same time, unbeknownst to him or Wind, of course, a shooter is targeting her from that other building at the exact same time. He fires, killing her and her son. The intruder is stunned. He could have ducked down, thinking he might be shot next. He sees the other kid in the carrier, grabs it up, and during his escape drops him off at another apartment. Then he gets away."

"I thought you didn't believe in coincidences," said Robie.

She smiled weakly. "I know. It's like the mother of all coincidences, isn't it?"

It's also exactly what happened, thought Robie.

27

They were in the other building, from where the kill shot had come. It was abandoned, filthy, full of junk, easy to get into and out of. In other words, it was perfect.

Robie and Vance had looked through several rooms that could have served as the shooter's sanctuary. When they entered the fifth one Robie said, "This is it."

Vance froze and, hands on hips, looked at him. "Why?"

Robie walked over to one of the windows. "Window is open a notch. None of the others were. The sight line is dead on." He pointed at the windowsill. "And the dust has been disturbed. Check the pattern. Muzzle mark." He pointed at a dark stain the size of a dime farther along on the sill. "Residue from the discharge." He looked down at the concrete floor. "Knee imprints in the dirt. He used the sill as his center of support, lined up his shot, and took it."

He knelt down, slipped out his gun, took aim through the window, lining up his iron sights with the window with the hole in it across the way. "There's a rack of lights on that taller building on the opposite side of the street where Wind lived. At night those lights would be on. A shooter would be looking right at them and that would screw his shot into the fourth floor over there. Except not from this spot. The angle is perfect." He rose, put his gun away. "This is it."

Vance looked impressed. "You have special forces in your background?"

"If I did I couldn't tell you."

"Come on. I know lots of former Delts and SEALs."

"I'm sure you do."

She looked out the window. "I also know some people at DCIS. I texted them about you. None of them have heard of you."

"I just came back into the country," said Robie, transitioning into his cover story. "If you really want to check me out, call DCIS. I can give you my direct superior's contact info."

"Okay. And I will," she said. "So my burglar theory and separate shooter theory looks sound. I can't see how the guy in the apartment last night could have known about the shooter over here."

You're right, I didn't, thought Robie.

Vance continued. "But now the question becomes, why kill Wind? What was she working on for your people? I'll need to know that."

"I'll check with my folks. But it could be something she stumbled onto," said Robie.

"Stumbled onto? How does that make sense?"

"Not saying it does. Only saying it has to be considered. Just because she worked for DCIS doesn't mean that was the reason she was killed."

"Okay, but forgive me if I take as my working hypothesis that her death was related to her work."

Robie said, "That's your prerogative. Has her ex been notified?"

"In the process. Her son is with Social Services for now."

"What's her former husband do?"

"You don't know?" she said in surprise.

"Not without looking at the file, no. I was just assigned to this case, Agent Vance. Cut me a little slack."

"Okay, sorry. Rick Wind. He's retired military but he has another job. We're in the process of tracking him down now."

"In the process of tracking him down? He'd have to have seen the news. He should've called you by now."

"Believe me, Robie, I thought of that."

"You have his home address?"

"Maryland. My agents have already been there. It's empty."

"You said he has a job. Where does he work?"

"He owns a pawnshop in northeast D.C. Bladensburg Road. Place called the Premium Pawnshop. Not the greatest part of town, but then you don't usually find pawnshops next to the Ritz, do you?"

"Premium Pawnshop? Catchy. Anybody tried to reach him there?"

"No one's there either. All locked up."

"So where is the guy?"

"If I knew that I would've told you."

"If he's not at home, and he's not at work, and he hasn't called the police, then there are only a few possibilities."

"He either doesn't watch TV, listen to the radio, or have any friends. Or he killed his soon-to-be ex-wife and kid and is on the run. Or else he's dead too."

"That's right. But you really think the guy killed his ex and kid using a sniper rifle? Domestic issues like that are usually face-to-face."

"Well, he was former military. And they *were* getting divorced."

"So it was not amicable?"

"I don't know. I'm making inquiries. Maybe you can help on that score. She's with your agency after all."

He ignored this. "Jane Wind have any family in the area that you know of?"

She looked at him quizzically. "Are you sure you two are from the same agency?"

"It's a big agency."

"Not that big. FBI dwarfs it."

"FBI dwarfs pretty much everybody. So, family in the area?"

"None. Neither apparently does her hubby. At least that we can find. But I've been working this case for less than eight hours."

Robie said, "Have you searched his home and the pawnshop?"

"Home, yes. Nothing that helped us. Pawnshop next. You care to tag along?"

"Absolutely."

28

The Bucars pulled up in front of the Premium Pawnshop and Robie and Vance stepped from one, while two other FBI agents climbed out of their vehicle. There were bars across the front door and windows of the pawnshop. The door had three serious locks. The businesses next to it were gutted, with blackened plywood nailed against their fronts. Trash littered the streets and Robie spotted a couple of druggies stumbling along.

Vance sent the other two agents to check the rear of the building while she and Robie approached the front. She shaded her eyes and peered inside. "Can't see anything."

"Can you knock down the door or do you need a warrant?"

"Rick Wind's house was less problematic. We suspected he might be hurt. This place is obviously closed."

"He could be inside, hurt or dead," said Robie, joining her at the front of the shop and peering between the bars into the darkened interior. "That should be enough."

"And if we find evidence he committed the crime

and his defense lawyer gets it thrown out because our search was determined to be unlawful under the Fourth Amendment?"

"I guess that's why you FBI agents get the big bucks."

"And the big career derailment."

"How about I kick open the door and search the place?"

"Still have the same evidentiary problem."

"Yeah, but it'll be my career that's derailed, not yours."

"I'm here with you."

"I'll tell them I did it all on my own, against your express instructions."

He examined the door and the framing around it. "Steel on steel. Tough stuff. But there's always a way."

"What kind of Fed are you?" she asked, her eyebrows hiked.

"Not the career-kissing type obviously. Stay here."

"Robie, you can't just—"

He drew his pistol, fired three times, and the trio of locks fell out onto the sidewalk.

"Holy shit!" exclaimed Vance as she jumped back. They heard running feet, as the other two agents were no doubt coming to find out what had happened.

"An alarm will probably go off," said Robie calmly. "You might want to call the cops and tell them not to bother." Before she could say anything, he opened the door and stepped inside.

No alarm went off.

Robie did not take that as a positive sign. He kept his gun out, felt for the light switch, hit it, and the pawnshop was quickly draped in weak light. Robie had been in pawnshops before and this looked pretty typical. Watches, lamps, rings, and an assortment of other items were stacked neatly in bins or inside glass cabinets. All had tags with numbers written on them. The man's military background, thought Robie. You never lost that precision. Or at least most didn't.

But the floorboards smelled of urine and the ceiling was blackened with decades of grime. Robie didn't know what the place had been before it was a pawnshop, but it had not worn well.

There was a cash register cage. Robie noted the bulletproof glass. There were scratches on the glass and what looked to be two dents from gunshots. Upset customers or people looking to rip the guy off. Ex-military Rick Wind probably dealt with that with his own hardware. Robie figured there were at least two guns in that cage somewhere.

He looked toward the ceiling corners and saw the camera mounted in one. It had a direct shot of the cage. That might come in handy.

Robie moved forward, doing visual sweeps. He heard nothing except the sounds of life outside. A breeze pushed through the open door, rustling lampshades and lifting tags on the merchandise. When he heard footsteps behind him he turned to see Vance there, gun out, her expression seriously pissed off.

"You're an idiot," she hissed.

"I told you to stay outside," he whispered back.

"You don't tell me to do anything. Not unless you want your ass—"

Robie put a finger to his lips. He'd heard it before her.

A squeak. And then another.

He pointed to the back of the shop. She nodded, her angry expression gone.

Robie led the way, turning down one aisle, and rode it back to a pair of swinging doors with a gap between. The doors were moving slightly, but that was not the source of the squeak.

He looked at Vance, pointed to himself and then the door, and then motioned to the right. She nodded in understanding and took up position on his right flank.

Robie lifted one foot, kicked one of the swing doors open and bulled inside, his gun making arcs and ready to fire as he stepped to the left. Vance followed on the right and cleared that part of the room.

Nothing.

She looked down and grimaced as the gray critter skittered into a darkened corner.

"Rats."

Robie looked down and saw the animal's tail before it whisked out of sight.

"I don't think rats squeak like that," said Robie.

"Then what?" she asked.

"That."

He pointed to one darkened corner of the room on the left side.

Vance looked that way and caught a breath.

The man was hanging upside down from the exposed rafter.

They approached. His body was swinging slightly. And the rope was squeaking against the wooden beam. Robie looked at the slit between the pair of swing doors.

"Acted like a funnel with the front door open," he said. "With the wind outside. Got the body to move a bit."

Vance looked at the dead man. He was black.

And green. And purple.

"Is that Rick Wind?" asked Robie.

"Who the hell can tell?" replied Vance. "He's been dead a while."

"Didn't kill himself. Hands are bound. Not strangulation." He touched the man's arm. "And he didn't kill his wife and kid. Condition of the body means he was dead before they were. Rigor's long since passed."

Robie bent over and looked at the man's open mouth. "And there's something else."

"What?"

"It seems they cut out his tongue."

29

Robie had left Agent Vance to deal with the new body in the pawnshop. They had confirmed that it was Rick Wind. The cause of death was not obvious and would probably require a medical examiner to figure out. They had checked the shop's surveillance camera. Someone had taken the DVD. Robie was now sitting in his apartment typing on his computer. He was not working the murders of Jane Wind and her ex-husband. He had his mind on something else, at least for now.

He typed in the name Gerald Dixon. He got too many hits, because it was too common a name. He switched tactics, going from Google to a more exclusive database to which he had access. The hits that came back were more manageable. He refined his search, utilizing other databases. It finally narrowed to one name. Robie looked at the street address. It did not match the one that Julie had gone to in the cab.

But one line on the man's record caught his attention.

Foster care provider.

The guy and his wife took in foster kids.

He wrote down the address and then checked his tracking device. Its range was long enough for it to reach here. Julie had not moved from the crummy hotel. That seemed unusual unless she was afraid of being spotted. In any event, she apparently was no longer interested in leaving town.

He wondered what had changed her mind. Was it the house where she had stopped? Robie was going to find out. But he had somewhere else to go first.

Gerald Dixon lived in a two-story duplex in a lousy neighborhood. When Robie knocked on the door it took a long time to get a response, and he heard noises inside that bespoke of frenzied activity. When the guy finally opened the door Robie noted the crimson patches on his cheeks, the bloodshot eyes, and the smell of breath freshener that shot like a cannonball from his mouth.

The idiot's been slapping himself to get sober and sucking on Listerine to hide the booze smell. The foster care standards must be plummeting in this country.

"Yeah?" the man said in an unfriendly tone.

"Gerald Dixon?"

"Who wants to know?"

Robie flashed his badge. "I'm with D.C. Internal Affairs."

Dixon took a step back. He was an inch shorter than Robie but unhealthily thin. Most of his hair was gone, though he couldn't have been much over forty. He had the pale, translucent skin and jerky manner of someone whose body and mind had been substance-abused to the point of no return.

"Internal Affairs. Ain't that for cops?"

"It's for a lot of things," said Robie. "Including your situation. May I come in?"

"Why?"

"To talk about Julie." It was Robie's gut instinct that the girl had used her real first name.

Dixon's face screwed up. "If you find her you tell her she better get her butt back here. If she ain't here I don't get paid."

"So she's gone missing?"

"That's right."

"Can I come in?"

Dixon looked put out, but he nodded, stepped back, and let Robie pass through.

The inside of the house looked no better than the outside. They sat on tattered chairs. Baskets of dirty laundry were piled everywhere, but Robie had a notion that before he knocked on the door all the clothes had been strewn on the floor. He also noted papers and the edge of a beer can sticking out from under a chair. He wondered what else was under there. His seat was very hard. He didn't think it was the cushion.

A small, curvy woman wearing tight jeans and an even tighter blouse came out of the back, wiping her hands on her pants leg. She looked to be at most thirty.

She had mousy brown hair, a heavily made up face, and the air of someone who was totally disconnected from reality. She lit up a cigarette and eyed Robie.

"Who's he?"

"Some dude from Internal Affairs," growled Dixon.

Robie flipped open his badge. "I'm here to talk about Julie. And smoking around our children is prohibited," he added.

The woman quickly stubbed the cigarette out on a tabletop. "Sorry," she said without sounding sorry in the least.

The woman snapped, "She's gone. Run off. Little shit never appreciated what we gave her."

"And you are?" asked Robie.

"Patty. Gerry and me are married."

"How many foster kids do you have currently?"

"Two not counting that shit Julie," said Patty.

"I would prefer if you wouldn't refer to one of the children under our responsibility as a shit," Robie said firmly.

Patty glanced at her husband. "Is he with the foster care people?"

"He told me Internal Affairs," said Gerald, looking betrayed.

"I'm with the government," said Robie. "That's all you two need to know. So where are the other kids?"

Patty adopted a loving matronly tone. "In school," she said, smiling. "We send those little angels to school every day, just like we're supposed to."

Robie heard a sound from upstairs. "You have kids of your own?" he asked, glancing upward.

Gerald and Patty exchanged a nervous glance. He said, "We got two of our own, little ones. Don't go to school yet. That's them up there probably reading. They're real advanced for their ages."

"Right. Now about Julie." He opened a notebook he drew from his jacket. Gerald Dixon's eyes widened as he saw the revealed weapon. "You're carrying a gun."

"That's right," said Robie.

"I thought this was about foster care," said Patty.

"This is about what I say it's about. And if you two want to stay out of serious trouble I suggest you cooperate fully."

Robie had decided he was done playing nice with these idiots. He didn't have the time or the desire.

Gerald sat up straighter and Patty sat down next to him.

Robie said, "Tell me about Julie."

"Is she in trouble?" asked Gerald.

"Tell me about her," repeated Robie firmly. "Full name, background, how she came to be here. Everything."

"Don't you already know that?" asked Patty.

Robie looked at her with a face of granite. "I'm here to confirm the information we already have, Mrs. Dixon. And please keep in mind the request I made for cooperation and then focus on the possible consequences of not cooperating."

Gerald sharply elbowed his wife and snapped, "Just shut up and let me handle this." He turned back to Robie. "Her name is Julie Getty. She came here, oh, about three weeks ago."

"Age?"

"Fourteen."

"Why was she placed in foster care?"

"Her parents couldn't take care of her."

"Yeah, that I get. Why couldn't they care for her? Were they dead?"

"No, don't think so. See, the agency people don't really tell you that much about that stuff. They just give you kids and you take care of them."

Patty added quickly, "Just like they were our own."

"Right. Like you said, not counting that shit Julie."

Patty colored and looked down. "Well, I didn't mean it exactly like that."

Gerald added, "Truth is, Julie could be a real piece of work. Speaks her mind too much for my taste."

"And so she's not here anymore?"

"Run off in the middle of the night."

Patty said, "We've been so worried."

"And you of course reported this, right?"

Gerald and Patty looked at each other. He said, "Well, we were hoping she'd come back."

"So we were waiting for a bit," added Patty.

"Has she run off before?"

"Not this time, well, except for last night."

Robie looked up from his notes. "This time? Was she placed with you before?"

"Three times."

"What happened those times?"

"Don't know exactly," said Gerald. "I think her parents got her back. Remember the caseworker telling me Julie's mom and dad would do that. But then there she'd be back in foster care."

"When was the last time you saw her?"

"Last night right after I served her a delicious dinner," said Patty in a syrupy tone that made Robie want to pull his gun and fire a shot just over her head.

"And when did you discover her missing?"

"This morning when she didn't come down."

"So you don't check on your beloved 'wards' at night?"

"She was very private," said Gerald hastily. "We didn't like to butt in."

Robie pulled the empty beer can out from under the chair. "I can see that." He waved his hand in the air. "And you might want to open some windows. Get the reefer smell out."

"We don't do drugs," said Gerald, feigning astonishment.

"And I don't know whose that is," added Patty, pointing at the beer can.

"Right," Robie said dismissively. "Have you heard from Julie since she left?"

They both shook their heads.

"Any reason to believe someone would want to hurt her?"

The Dixons looked genuinely surprised by this question. Gerald said, "Why, has something happened to her?"

"Just answer the question. Anybody come around here you didn't know? Suspicious cars?"

Gerald said, "No, nothing like that. What the hell has she got herself involved in? Gangs?"

Patty put a hand up to her ample bosom. "Do you think we might be in danger?"

Robie closed his notebook. "I certainly wouldn't rule out the possibility. Some folks don't care who they hurt." He had to fight back a smile.

He rose, lifted up the seat cushion, and pulled out a baggie of coke, some vials containing a brown liquid, two capped syringes, and elastic strips used to pop the blood vessels to the surface for ease of injection.

"And next time try locating your pharmacy somewhere more private."

They both stared down at the drugs and related paraphernalia but said nothing.

As Robie was walking down the street he saw a woman holding an envelope striding along with two police officers in tow.

"You heading to the Dixons'?" he asked as the woman neared.

"Yes. Who are you?"

"Just someone who wants you to make sure they never get foster kids again."

The woman waved the envelope. "Well, your wish has just been granted."

She steamed on with the officers right behind.

Robie walked on. Something on his wrist beeped. He looked down at the tracker.

Julie Getty was finally on the move.

And Robie was pretty sure where.

30

Julie clambered up the vine and slipped inside her bedroom window. She squatted on the floor listening. All she could hear were her own heartbeats. Her legs shaky, she moved down the stairs, holding on to the wall for support. She rounded the bend, closed her eyes, and then opened them.

It was all she could do not to scream.

Robie stared back at her.

"You get around," he said.

She looked quickly around the room. There was nothing there except furniture.

"Expecting to find something else?" he said, moving toward her.

She backed up a step.

"How did you get here?" she asked.

"Followed you."

"That's impossible."

"Nothing's impossible really. This is your home, right?"

She said nothing, just stared up at him, more in curiosity than fear.

He looked at a picture on a side table. "Your mom and dad were nice-looking. And there you are right in the center. Happy times, it seems."

"You don't know anything," snapped Julie.

"Correction, I know *some* things. Like you're in danger. People are looking for you. People who have a lot of money, muscle, and connections."

"How do you know that?"

"Because they covered up two murders right here."

Julie's eyes widened. "How did you know that?"

Robie motioned to the wall next to where she stood. "Fresh paint. But only in that spot. It was put there to cover something up." He pointed to the floor. "Used to be a square of carpet here. You can see where the wood is lighter. It's gone. Again, covering something up."

"How do you know it's about a murder? It could be anything."

"No, not anything. You paint walls and remove rugs to take away forensics. Blood, tissue, other bodily fluids. And they missed a spot of blood on the baseboard over there. Did you expect to find their bodies here? There would have been a smell by now, you know. An unmistakable one."

"You spend a lot of time around dead bodies?" she said warily.

"Ever since I hooked up with you."

"We're not hooked up in any way at all."

"I know about your foster parents, though calling them 'parents' stretches all credulity."

"I don't like that you've been snooping around my life," she exclaimed.

"The city busted them," he said. "The other kids there have been taken away by now. I think you had something to do with that."

Julie's angry look faded. "They didn't deserve to be treated like that. No little kid does."

"Now tell me what happened here."

"Why?"

"Like I said, I want to help you."

"Why?"

"Call me a Good Samaritan."

"There aren't any of those left," she said firmly.

"Not even your parents?"

"You leave my parents out of this," she said sharply.

"Did you see how they died? Is that why you were on the run?"

Julie backed up until she was against the wall. For a moment Robie thought she was going to run for it. And he wasn't sure what he would do if she did.

"Were they mixed up in something over their heads?" he asked. "Drugs?"

"My mom and dad wouldn't hurt anyone. And no, this had nothing to do with drugs."

"So they were killed? Just a simple nod will do."

She moved her head forward a notch.

"You saw that happen?"

Another nod.

"Then you need to go to the police."

"If I go to the police they'll put me right back in foster care. And then those people will find me."

"The guy on the bus, he was the one?"

"I think so."

"Julie, tell me exactly what happened. It's the only way I can help you. If last night showed you nothing else, it's that I'm someone who can get things done."

"What about those people on the TV. Did you kill them? A mom and her kid? You said you didn't do it, but I need to know the truth."

"Well, if I did kill them there's no way in the world I would admit it. But if I did do it why would I be here trying to help you? Give me a reason."

She let out a long breath, played with the straps on her backpack. "Do you swear you didn't kill them?"

"I swear I didn't kill them. I'm working with the FBI right now to try and figure out who did." He pulled out his badge and showed it to her.

Julie said, "Okay. I guess it's cool. I got away from the Dixons and came here last night. I hadn't been home very long when I heard someone come in. I thought it was my parents, but someone else was with them. He was yelling at them. Asking them stuff."

Robie drew a few steps closer. "Asking them what? Try to be as precise as you can."

Julie screwed up her face, thinking. "He said, 'How much do you know? What have you been told,' stuff like that. And then, and then . . ."

"He hurt one of them?"

Tears trickled down her face. "I heard a gunshot. I ran down the stairs. The guy looked at me. My dad was against the wall over there. He was all bloody. The guy pointed the gun at me, but my mom hit him and he fell down. I didn't want to leave. I wanted to stay and help her. But she told me to run."

Julie shut her eyes, but the tears eased out from under her eyelids. "I went back to my bedroom and climbed out the window. Then I heard another shot. And I ran hard. I was a coward. I knew that shot meant my mom was dead. But I just ran. I was a shit. I just left her to die."

She opened her eyes and stiffened when she saw Robie standing next to her.

"And if you hadn't run, you'd be dead," he said. "And that would have done no one any good. Your mom saved your life. She sacrificed her life for yours. So you did the right thing, because you did what your mom wanted you to do. Stay alive."

Robie handed her a tissue from a box on the table and she dried her tears and then blew her nose.

"So what now?" she asked.

"Do you think anyone around here heard the shots?"

"I doubt it. The place next door is empty. So is the duplex across the street. This used to be an okay neighborhood, but then everybody lost their jobs."

"Including your parents?"

"They worked at whatever they could find. My mom went to college," she added proudly. "My dad was a good guy." She looked down. "He just sometimes got down on himself. Felt like the whole world was against him."

"What were their names?"

"Curtis and Sara Getty."

"No relation to the Getty Oil folks, I guess?"

"If so, nobody ever told us."

He said, "Okay, here's my plan. We find out who killed your parents and why."

"But if it was the guy on the bus he's clearly dead."

"Did you leave from this house last night and go directly to the bus stop?"

"Yes."

"Then the guy wasn't alone. He couldn't have policed this place, gotten rid of two bodies, and made it to the bus. There have to be others."

"But why my parents? I loved them, but it's not like they were important or anything."

"You sure they weren't involved in drug dealing or gangs or anything?"

"Look, if they were drug kingpins do you think they'd be living in this place?"

"So no enemies?"

"No. At least not that I know of."

"Where did they work?"

"Dad at a warehouse in southeast. Mom at a diner a few blocks from here."

"So your dad would go over there for meals maybe?"

"Yeah. I spent a lot of time at the diner too. Why?"

“Just digging for info.”

“I want to leave here. Like right now. This isn’t my home anymore.”

“Okay. Where do you want to go?”

“I got a place I’m staying.”

“Yeah, I tracked you down there. And it was stupid to steal and use Dixon’s credit card. They’ll bust you for that. And more importantly, people can track you.”

“How did you—” She stopped and looked annoyed. “I have cash.”

“Save it for now.”

“So where do I go? Not back to your safe house. It’s too far out of town.”

“No, I’ve got another place. Why don’t you pack some things and come on.”

31

Robie waited until well after dark. They spent the time in between getting something to eat at a mom-and-pop restaurant on H Street. Robie asked more questions of the young woman, gently probing. She pushed back. She would make a good cop, Robie thought. Her tendency to give away as little as possible was remarkable, particularly for a generation that routinely posted the most intimate details about themselves on Facebook.

Robie drove Julie to his neighborhood in Rock Creek Park. Only he didn't take her to his building but to the observation post across the street. Like the farmhouse, no one other than Robie knew about it.

They walked in, he turned off the alarm system, and she looked around.

"This is your place?"

"Sort of," he said.

"Are you rich?"

"No."

"You seem rich to me."

"Why?"

"You have a car and two homes. That's pretty rich. Especially these days."

"I guess it is." He actually had another home right across the street, but she didn't need to know that.

He showed her how to use the alarm system and then let her look around. She picked out her bedroom from the two there. She dropped her backpack and a second bag she'd packed before leaving her house on the bed and continued to wander around the apartment.

"What's the telescope for?" she asked.

"Stargazing."

"That's not an astronomical telescope. And there's not really an angle here to point it skyward."

"You know about telescopes?"

"I do go to school, you know."

"I like to watch things," he said. "Especially to see if people are watching me."

"So are we going to be, like, staying here together?" She looked nervous by this prospect.

"No. I'm staying somewhere else. But it's close by."

"So you have three places?" she said incredulously. "What do you do for a living? I think I want to do it too."

"You should have everything you need." He took a cell phone out of his pocket. "This is for you. It's got my number loaded on speed dial. It's untraceable, so feel free to use it anytime."

"How far away will you be?"

"I thought you were nervous that we were going to be staying here together."

"Look, I know you're not some creep who gets off on underage girls, okay?"

"How do you know that?"

"Because I've had to deal with those sorts of jerks before. I know what to look for. You don't have the signs."

"Did you learn that in foster care?" he asked quietly.

She didn't answer him. And Robie thought about Gerald Dixon and wondered if he should have just shot the prick when he had the chance.

"You should have everything you need," he said. "I stocked up the kitchen last week. Anything else, give me a call."

"What about school?"

This caught Robie off guard.

Shows what a great parent I'd make.

"Where do you go to school?" he asked.

"At a G and T program in northeast D.C."

"G and T? That's a cocktail."

"Not gin and tonic. Gifted and talented."

"You're fourteen, so you're in ninth grade?"

"Tenth."

"How so?"

"I skipped a grade."

"Pretty smart, then."

"In some things. In other things I can be pretty stupid."

"Like what."

"I don't like highlighting my weaknesses."

"Considering what happened to your parents, I'm not sure I want you going back to school. Whoever killed them will know where you go. Or it'll be easy enough to find out."

"I can use the cell phone to text my program coordinator and feed her some bullshit."

"You think you're smarter than all adults?"

"No. But I'm smart enough to know how to lie and make it sound like the truth." She looked at him closely. "I think you're probably really good at that too."

"The foster care people will be looking for you."

"I know. Won't be the first time. They'll go to my parents' house. They'll think they skipped town and took me with them. Then they'll go to the school, find out I texted my coordinator, assume I'm okay, and that'll be a dead end. They've got too many kids in the pipeline a lot worse off to spend any more time on me."

"Thinking several moves ahead. That's good. You play chess?"

"I play life."

"I get that."

"So how close will you be?" she asked again.

"Pretty close."

"I'm not just going to sit in this place and do

nothing. I'm going to help you find the people who got my parents killed."

"You can leave that to me."

"Screw that! If you don't let me help, I won't be here when you come back."

Robie sat down in a chair and stared at her. "Let's get something really straight. You're a smart kid. You know the streets. But the people who are after you are at a whole different level. They will kill anyone who gets in their way."

"Sounds like you know the type real well," she shot back.

When Robie said nothing, she said, "The guy on the bus? The way you got us away from the dude in the alley? The way you analyzed the crime scene at my parents' house? The way you tracked me down? And you said you were working with the FBI. You're not just some guy in a cubicle working nine to five. You've got safe houses and guns and untraceable phones and telescopes pointed at who knows what." She paused and then added, "You kill people too, I bet."

Robie still said nothing.

Julie looked out the window. "My parents were all I had. I ran away when I could have stayed and helped them. Now they're dead. I know I'm young, but I can help you. If you just give me a chance."

Robie looked out the window too. "Okay. We'll do this together. But it'll be tricky."

"So what do I do first?" she said eagerly.

"You have a paper and pen in your bag?"

"Yes. And I have the laptop my school gave me."

"How long ago did you see your parents?"

"About a week."

"Okay, you write down everything you can remember about the last couple of weeks. I want you to try and recall anything you saw, heard, or suspected. Anything your parents said. No matter if it seemed insignificant. And anyone else around who they knew or were talking to."

"Is this busy work or is it really important?"

"Neither one of us has time to waste on busy work. This is stuff we need."

"Okay, I'll do it. I'll start tonight."

He rose to go.

"Will?"

"Yeah?"

"I'll make a good partner, you'll see."

"I have no doubt, Julie."

But his gut was ice. He much preferred to work alone. He didn't like having another life riding on him.

32

"Robie, got time for a cup of coffee?"

It was Nicole Vance on the phone.

Robie had answered the call on his way down the elevator after leaving Julie. He'd given the teenager a key to the apartment but asked her not to leave it without checking with him first. And he had told her to set the alarm.

"Anything break on the case?" he asked the FBI agent.

"There's a place open late near First and D southeast called Donnelly's. I can be there in ten minutes."

"Give me ten more than that."

"Hope I'm not interrupting anything."

"I'll see you there."

Robie grabbed his car from the street. The traffic across town was light at this hour. He parked on First and gazed up at the Capitol dome in the background. Five hundred and thirty-five members of Congress plied their trade near here in various buildings named after long-dead politicians. They, in turn, were surrounded by an army of lobbyists flush with cash who worked relentlessly to convince the elected officials of the unassailable righteousness of their causes. Such was democracy.

Donnelly's was busy for the lateness of the hour. Most of the patrons were drinking something stronger than coffee. When Robie hit the doorway, Vance caught his eye from the back of the main room.

He sat across from her. Her clothes were off-duty ones because she'd been home. Slacks, flats, light blue sweater, corduroy jacket. Good choices for the chill in the air. Her hair was down around her shoulders. It had been tied back earlier. Long hair and crime scenes were sometimes problematic. She smelled of a fresh shower with a light dusting of perfume. She must have scrubbed hard, thought Robie. The stink of death could get right into your pores.

Her cup of coffee was parked in front of her. With a wave of his hand Robie got the waitress's attention and pointed at Vance's cup and then at himself.

He waited until the woman came with a fresh cup and departed before he focused on Vance.

"So here I am."

"You're a hard man to find."

"You only called me once."

"No, I mean at DCIS. I called the number you gave me. They confirmed you worked there, but your file is classified."

"Nothing earth-shattering about that. Told you I

was out of the country for a while. That stuff was classified. Now I'm back." He took a sip of coffee and set his cup back down. "Please tell me that's not the only reason you asked for this meeting."

"It's not. I don't like to waste time, so here we go."

She pulled a manila folder from the bag sitting next to her. She opened the file and took out some photos and pages.

"Background on Rick Wind."

Robie leafed through the photos and written materials. One picture was of Wind in death, hanging above the urine-smelling floor of his pawnshop. The other photos were of Wind in life. Several of him in military uniform.

"Army, huh?"

"Career enlisted. Went in at eighteen. Did his full time and then he was out. He was forty-three."

"Their kids were little. Did they start late?"

"Jane and Rick Wind were married ten years. Lots of failed attempts at getting pregnant. Then they hit the jackpot twice in three years. Then they decide to end the marriage. Go figure."

"Maybe Rick Wind decided he didn't want to be a father."

"Not sure. They had joint custody of the kids."

"Where was he living?"

"In Prince George's County, Maryland."

"You find a cause of death?"

"ME's still working on that. No obvious wounds other than his tongue being cut out." She paused. "Isn't that what the mob would do to snitches?"

"Did Wind have ties to the mob?"

"Not that we know of. And he wasn't working with any federal or local police investigations as an informant. But he runs a pawnshop in a bad part of town. Maybe he was laundering dirty money and got his fingers caught in the cookie jar."

"And they kill his wife and kid too?"

"Maybe as a warning against other future skimmers."

"Seems a bit much. Particularly since they must've known Jane Wind was a Fed and her murder would trigger FBI involvement. I mean, why bring yourself the extra grief?"

"Thank you for your faith in the crime-busting prowess of the Federal Bureau of Investigation."

"Time of death?" he asked.

"About three days, the ME said."

"No one noticed him missing? His ex?"

"Like I said, they had joint custody. It was her week. They apparently didn't communicate much. He worked the pawnshop alone. Maybe he didn't have many friends."

"Okay, but this all could have waited until tomorrow."

"The gun we found near the bombed-out bus was the same gun that fired that round into Jane Wind's floorboard."

"I know. You already told me that." Robie picked up his cup and took another sip.

Never should have fired the round. Never should have lost my weapon.

"And the kill round for Wind and her son?" he asked.

"Different weapon entirely. Rifle round. Came through the window like we speculated."

"Again, all of this could have come over the phone."

"The rifle round was pretty special."

"How so?"

"Looks to be military-grade ammo," she said flatly.

Robie took another sip of coffee. Though his heart was beating a little faster, his hand did not shake even slightly.

"What was the specific round? Could they tell or was it too deformed?"

"It was jacketed. Came out in fine shape." She looked at her notes. "It was a 175-grain Sierra Match-King Hollow Point Boat Tail. That specific enough for you?"

"Lots of that kind of ammo around."

"Yeah, but our gun expert said this was different. Special Ball, long-range, and slight residue of a modified extruded propellant. I'm not sure what all that means, quite frankly. But he speculated it was U.S. military. Sound right to you?"

"Our guys use that ammo. But so do the Hungarians, the Israelis, the Japanese, and the Lebanese."

"You're just full of gun facts. I'm impressed."

"I'll give you some more. The U.S. military uses the M24 Weapon System. Our target was over three hundred meters from the shooter with a single pane of glass in between. And weather conditions last night were fine with very little wind. The round you're talking about is also called the 7.62 MK 316 MOD O. The components of the 175-grain round are the Sierra projectile, Federal Cartridge Company match cartridge case, Gold Medal match primer, and the modified extruded propellant. That round leaves the barrel at over twenty-six hundred foot-pounds per second. At three hundred meters, the Sierra would have plenty of juice to clear a child's skull with enough kill power to end another life in close proximity."

Robie had really been thinking out loud. But when he saw the look on Vance's face he wished he had kept these technical observations to himself.

"You know a lot about sniper stuff?" she asked.

"I'm with the DOD. But the Sierra ordnance is also available to the public. Too bad we don't have the casing."

"Oh, but we do. The shooter didn't police his brass. Or at least if he did he wasn't successful."

"Where was it? I didn't see it in the room the sniper was set up in, and I was looking for it."

"Crack in the baseboard. The casing was ejected, hit the concrete, probably bounced and rolled right into the crack. Completely invisible. The sniper was operating in the dark. No electricity in that building. Even if he tried to look for it before making his getaway he wouldn't have spotted it. My guys only found it later, when they were on their hands and knees with laser lights.

Robie licked his lips. "Okay, let me ask you something. Maybe you know the answer, maybe you don't."

"Okay."

"Was the casing shiny or dull?"

"I don't know. They found it after I had already left. But one phone call can answer that."

"Make the call."

"It's important?"

"I wouldn't be asking otherwise."

She made the call, asked the question, and received the answer.

"Dull, not shiny. In fact my guy said a little discolored. Do you think it was old ammo?"

Robie finished his coffee.

She tapped her fingernail impatiently against the tabletop. "Don't keep me in suspense, Robie. I made the call. Got the answer. Now tell me why it's significant."

"The military doesn't use seconds or rejects or old ammo. But manufacturers charge extra to buff up the casing to make it look shiny and pretty. The Army could give a crap about that; it has nothing to do with operational performance. A dull bullet flies as straight and true as a shiny one. And the Army buys millions of rounds, so it saves them a ton of money to go without the extra buffing. Now, the civilian rounds are typically shiny because those folks don't mind paying extra."

"So then we're definitely looking at military-grade ammo?"

"And that makes things more complicated."

"Is that all you can say?" she said in an incredulous tone.

"What do you want me to say?" he replied evenly.

"If this is a U.S. military hit on a government employee then this is not just complicated. This is a shitstorm. That's what I want you to say."

"Okay, this is a *potential* shitstorm. Satisfied?"

"By the way my boss was royally pissed that you shot your way into that pawnshop. He said he was going to be talking to DCIS."

"Good. Maybe they'll pull me from the case."

"Where the hell are you coming from, Robie? Do you even want to be an investigator?"

"Are we done here?" He started to get up.

She looked up at him. "I don't know, are we?"

He left.

She followed him outside.

Vance put a hand on his shoulder. "Actually, I'm not done with you."

Robie grabbed her arm, pulled hard, and they both fell behind some trash cans. An instant later a barrage of bullets shattered the front window of Donnelly's.

33

Robie rolled, lifted his gun from its holster, and aimed through a crevice between the toppled trash cans. His target was a black SUV with the rear side window down a crack. The muzzle of an MP-5 submachine gun was visible there and was currently spewing out a hail of bullets.

Right before the shots had started Robie had pushed Vance down and behind him. When she tried to rise up, he slammed her back down.

"Keep down or you'll lose your damn head."

The bullets from the MP shredded the trees, outdoor tables and chairs, and big umbrellas and pinged off the building's brick façade.

People inside Donnelly's and out on the street screamed, ducked, and ran for cover. Through all the chaos, Robie kept his calm and fired. His shots were dead-on. He hit tire rubber to disable the vehicle, the front and rear passenger windows to knock out the shooter and the driver, and the front-side metal of the SUV to kill the engine.

And nothing happened.

The MP-5 muzzle disappeared, the window slid up, and the SUV roared off.

Robie was up in an instant, slapping in a fresh mag and chasing the SUV down the street, firing at its backside and hitting it squarely in the ass. He nailed the rear tires.

Again, there was nothing.

But then Robie saw the windows of a Honda parked at the curb explode and the branch of a tree fall down, and he stopped firing. The SUV turned the corner and was gone.

Robie looked at the Honda's shattered glass, the car's alarm going off. And then he gazed over at the tree branch that had been shot off, probably by his ricochet.

He pulled out his car keys and was about to run to his Audi, which was parked two cars down from the Honda. But when he saw the shot-out tires on his car he put the keys away.

He heard running feet, turned toward them, knelt, and aimed.

"It's me!" screamed Vance, her gun out but held in a surrender position.

Robie stood, holstered his weapon, and walked toward her.

"What the hell was that?" exclaimed Vance.

"Call it in. We need to get that SUV."

"I already did. But do you know how many black SUVs are around here? Did you get a plate number?"

"They had it blacked out."

Sirens had started up. They heard more running feet. Down the block Capitol Hill police officers were rushing their way, guns drawn.

Robie looked back at the restaurant. People were slowly getting to their feet. But not all of them. He saw dark liquid pooling on the street. Inside the restaurant he heard screams and people sobbing.

There were casualties. Many. Bad ones.

"How many?" asked Robie.

She looked where he was. "I'm not sure. Two outside are dead. Three wounded. Maybe more inside. There were a lot of people behind that window. I called for ambulances."

Vance looked at the screeching Honda. "Did you do that?"

"Ricochet from my weapon," said Robie.

"Ricochet? Off the SUV? Your rounds should have easily penetrated."

"I hit it a total of seventeen times," said Robie. "Tires, windows, body. Ricochets, all of them. The Honda. The tree branch. I've probably got slugs all over the place here."

"But that means—" began a palefaced Vance.

Robie finished for her: "—that the SUV was armored and had run-flat tires."

She looked at him. "Those sorts of vehicles in D.C. aren't that plentiful outside certain circles."

"Mostly our own government's."

"So were they aiming to kill you, me, or both of us?" asked Vance.

"Shooter had an MP-5 set on full auto. That tends to be an indiscriminate weapon. Designed to kill everything in the zone."

She looked at his arm and flinched. "Robie, you're shot."

He looked down at the blood on his upper arm. "It didn't go in. Just a graze."

"You're still bleeding. A lot. I'll call you an ambulance too."

His voice was hard and fast. "Forget the ambulance, Vance. We need that SUV."

She said coldly, "I told you, I already called it in. I've got my guys and MPD looking for it. It must have some dings on it from your rounds. Maybe that'll help."

Robie and Vance jogged back to the restaurant. Ignoring the obvious dead, he went from one wounded to the next, quickly triaging and stopping the bleeding with whatever was handy while Vance assisted. The Capitol Hill police joined in his effort.

When ambulances showed up and paramedics poured out, Robie left the wounded to them and walked across the street to check out his Audi. He saw the holes in the body. MP-5 rounds. Not ricochets from his pistol. They'd had another shooter on this side. That was not good. That meant they knew his vehicle.

Had they followed him here? If so . . .

He turned and ran back to Vance, who was talking to two MPD officers.

Robie interrupted. "Vance, can I borrow your wheels?"

"What?" she said, looking at him.

"Your car. I need to go somewhere right now. It's important."

She looked flustered, while the cops eyed Robie with suspicion.

Vance must've noted this because she said, "He's with me." She pulled out her keys. "Parked around the corner. Silver BMW convertible. Obviously my personal ride."

"Thanks."

"So be careful with it."

"I'm always careful.

She dubiously eyed his shot-up Audi. "Right. But how am I going to get home?"

"I'll come back and get you. I shouldn't be long. I'll call you when I'm on my way."

He started to run off.

She called after him, "And please get your arm looked at."

She watched him for a few moments before one of the cops said, "Um, Agent Vance?"

She glanced back, embarrassed, and continued filling them in.

34

Robie slid into the Beemer, started it, and peeled off. As he drove he called the phone he had left Julie. She didn't answer.

Shit!

He punched it. Driving this fast in town, even at this late hour, was problematic. Traffic and lots of lights. And lots of cops.

But then he had a thought. Vance seemed the highly efficient type. That meant . . .

He looked over the dashboard. Then he saw the box under the steering column. It had been an add-on, obviously.

I love you, Agent Vance.

He hit the switch and blue grille lights were activated and a siren started blaring. He ran four red lights and shot across town so fast it would've made a kick-ass commercial for the German car company. Within minutes he found himself tearing down the street where his apartment was located. A couple of times he saw cops in cars glance suspiciously at the Beemer with police lights, but they let him go.

He parked on a side street, jumped out, and zigzagged his way on foot to the building where he'd left Julie. He took the stairs two at a time. He raced down the hall. He'd texted her twice on the way over and had gotten no response. He eyed the door. No forced entry. He pulled his gun, slid the key in the door, and eased it open.

The front room was dark. He did not hear the beep of the alarm. That was not good.

He closed the door behind him. He moved into the room, his gun swiveling in a defensive arc.

He didn't call out, because he didn't know who else might be in here.

He heard a noise and moved quietly into the shadows.

The footfalls were heading his way. He pointed his gun, ready to fire.

The light came on. He stepped out.

Julie screamed. "What the hell?" she gasped, holding her chest. "Are you trying to give me a freaking heart attack?"

She was dressed in pajamas and her hair was wet.

"You were in the shower?" he asked.

"Yeah. Am I the only person in the world who likes to be clean?"

"I called and texted."

"Water and electronics don't mix, so I've heard." She picked up her phone off the coffee table. "Do you want me to text you back now?"

"I was worried."

"Okay, I'm sorry. But I couldn't exactly take the phone in the shower."

"Next time, at least take it to the bathroom. Why wasn't the alarm on?"

"I went down to the lobby to get a newspaper. I was going to set it before I went to sleep."

"A newspaper? I didn't think your generation read old-fashioned newspapers."

"I like information."

"All right, but I want you to keep the alarm on all the time."

"Fine. But why were you so freaked about me?" She stopped and glanced at his arm. "You're bleeding."

He rubbed the spot. "I cut myself."

"Through your jacket?"

"Forget about it," he said sharply. "Did you notice anything suspicious tonight after I left?"

She noted the strain on his face and said, "Tell me what happened, Will."

"I think I was followed. But I don't know from what point. If from here, it's not good, for obvious reasons."

"I saw or heard nothing suspicious. If someone wanted to get me, they had their chance."

Robie looked down and saw that he still had his gun out. He holstered it and looked around. "Everything okay? You need anything?"

"I'm great. I did my homework, ate a healthy dinner,

brushed my teeth, and said my prayers. I'm good to go," she added sarcastically. She pulled a piece of paper from a pocket on her pajama top and handed it to him.

"What's this?"

"The assignment you gave me? Anything weird in the last couple weeks? I also put down the addresses of the places where my mom and dad worked. Things I know about their past. Friends they had. Things they used to do. I thought it might be useful."

Robie gazed down at the precise handwriting on the page and nodded. "It will be useful."

"Who shot you?"

He instinctively glanced at his arm and then at her.

"I've seen people shot before," she said matter-of-factly. "It's just sort of the world I grew up in."

"I don't know who did it," answered Robie. "But I intend on finding out."

"Does this have to do with that woman and her kid getting killed?"

"Probably, yeah."

"But then you strike me as the kind of guy who might have lots of enemies for lots of different reasons."

"Maybe I do."

"But you're still going to help me find out who killed my mom and dad, right?"

"I said I would."

"Okay," she said. "Can I go to bed now?"

"Yeah."

"You can stay if you want. It won't freak me out."

"I've got some things to do tonight."

"I understand."

"I'll set the alarm on my way out."

"Thanks."

She took her phone, turned, and walked down the hallway. He heard the bedroom door lock behind her. He set the alarm, locked the door behind him, and left.

Robie was pissed.

He was getting played. That he knew.

He just didn't know who was doing it.

35

Robie pulled to the curb and watched Vance finish up with the local cops and some of her people. Ambulances were everywhere and people were being loaded into the back of the rescue vehicles that would take them to local hospitals to treat their injuries.

They were the lucky ones. They were still alive. The dead stayed right where they had dropped, as people investigated their murders. The only act of privacy and respect was to drape a white sheet over the body. Other than that, people who an hour before were alive and enjoying a beer were now nothing more than pieces in a criminal investigation puzzle.

As Vance finished with the last cop, Robie honked the horn and she looked at him. She walked to the Beemer and checked it over as he rolled down the passenger window.

"If there's even one ding on this car your ass is mine," she declared but her expression showed she wasn't being serious.

"You want me to drive?" he asked. "Or you want the wheel?"

She answered by getting into the passenger seat. "I'm having your ride towed to the FBI garage. It's officially evidence."

"Great, then I don't have a car."

"DCIS has a motor pool. Get one from there."

"They probably have some Ford Pintos sitting around. I preferred my Audi."

"Ain't life a bitch?"

"What was the final count?" he asked quietly.

She exhaled a long breath. "Four dead. Seven wounded, three of them critically, so the death count could go higher."

"The black SUV?"

"Disappeared without the proverbial trace." She sat back against the seat and closed her eyes. "Where did you go that was so important?"

"I needed to check on something."

"What? Or who?"

"Just something."

"Need to know and I don't?" She opened her eyes and stared at him. He didn't answer. She looked down at the box under the steering column.

"I take it you found my grille light add-on."

"It came in handy."

"Who are you really?"

"Will Robie. DCIS. Just like the badge and ID card says."

"You handled yourself well back there. I was still fumbling for my gun while you emptied your mag at the shooters. Cool and collected with bullets flying past."

He said nothing, just kept driving. The sky was clear. Some stars were visible. Robie wasn't looking at them. He stared ahead.

She said, "That was basically a war zone back there and it didn't seem to have any effect on you. I've been in the FBI for fifteen years, right out of college. I've been in exactly one shootout during that time. I've seen my share of dead bodies after the fact. Caught my share of bad guys. Filled out my share of paperwork. Worn out witness chairs in courthouses."

He made a left. He had no idea where he was going. He just kept driving.

"And where exactly is this trip down memory lane going, Agent Vance?"

"After you left I threw up. Couldn't help it. Just upchucked into a trash can."

"Nothing unusual about that. It was pretty bad."

"You saw what I saw. And you didn't throw up."

He looked at her again. "You said it didn't affect me. You don't know that. You can't see inside my head."

"I wish I could. I'm pretty sure I'd find it fascinating."

"Doubtful."

"You triaged those people really effectively. Where did you learn to do that?"

"I just picked up some tricks over the years."

She glanced down at his arm. "Damn, Robie, you didn't even clean your own wound. You're going to get gangrene."

"Where are we going?"

"First stop, WFO," she said, referring to the Washington Field Office.

"After that?"

"Hospital for you."

"No."

"Robie!"

"No."

"Okay, we can drive to your place. But I insist on getting your wound cleaned up there. I can grab some stuff from WFO. Then I can head home and try to get a couple hours' sleep. Where do you live?"

He said nothing, but he hung a right and then another right and headed to the WFO.

"So you know the way to the Field Office?"

"No, I'm just making an educated guess."

"Where do you live? Or is that classified too?"

"We can part company at the WFO. I'll cab it from there."

"Do you *have* a place to live?" she asked.

"I'll find one."

"For Godsakes, what is going on with you?"

"I'm just trying to do my *job*."

The emphasis on the last word made her visibly react. "Okay," she said quietly. "Okay. Look, after WFO we can go to my place. I live in Virginia. Condo in Alexandria. You can get cleaned up there. And if you want you're welcome to the couch."

"I appreciate the offer but—"

"Careful. I'm not usually this nice to people, Robie. Don't blow it."

He glanced at her. She was smiling weakly at him.

He was about to decline again, but he didn't. For three reasons. His arm was aching like hell. And he was tired. Really tired. And he really had no place to go.

"Okay," he said. "Thanks."

"You're welcome."

36

The stop at WFO took longer than Robie had thought it would. He sat in a chair while Vance bustled around, filling out papers, briefing superiors, thumbing her phone and clicking computer keys and looking more and more tired with every passing minute.

Robie gave his official statement of events and then watched the ensuing activity. Part of him wondered if everyone was just running around in circles and accomplishing little.

"I'll drive," said Robie as they headed to the garage after they were finally done.

"Don't you ever get tired?" she asked with a yawn.

"I am tired. Really tired, in fact."

"You don't look it."

"I find things work better that way."

"What way?"

"Not showing what you're actually feeling."

She gave him directions and he took the GW Parkway south to Alexandria.

When they pulled into her condo building Robie said, "You have water views of the Potomac?"

"Yes. And I can see the monuments from my place too."

"Nice."

They took the elevator up and she unlocked the door to her place. It was small, but Robie immediately liked it. Clean lines, no clutter, and everything seemed to have a purpose, nothing was strictly for show. He assumed that matched the owner's personality.

Nothing for show. What I see matters.

"Reminds me of a ship's cabin," he said.

"Well, my father was career Navy. Apple didn't fall far from the tree. Other than I spend most of my time on dry land. Make yourself comfortable."

He sat on a long couch in the living room while she unpacked some medical supplies she'd taken from WFO. She kicked off her flats and sat next to him.

"Off with the jacket and the shirt," she ordered.

He looked at her awkwardly but did what she asked, setting his holstered gun on the coffee table.

When she saw the tats her eyebrows hiked.

"Red lightning, and what's the other one?"

"Shark's tooth. Great white."

"And why those?"

"Why not?"

She looked more closely and her eyes widened as she saw the old wounds the tats were obscuring.

"Are those—"

"Yeah, they are," he said tersely, cutting her off.

She busied herself with the medical supplies after this mild rebuke, while Robie stared at his hands.

"What are you, thirty-five?"

"Forty. Just."

"You've got to be former special forces right? Ranger, Delt, SEAL. They all have builds like you, although you're taller than most of those guys."

He didn't answer her.

She cleaned the wound, applied some antibiotics, and then wound gauze around it, taping it securely down.

"I brought some painkillers. Pill or syringe?"

"No."

"Come on, Robie, you don't have to play all macho with me."

"It's got nothing to do with that."

"What, then?"

"Knowing your pain tolerance is important. Pills and needles mask it. Not good. I could be slipping and I'd never know it."

"Guess I never thought of that."

She put her things away and looked at him. "You can put your shirt back on."

"Thanks for patching me up. I appreciate it."

He slipped his shirt back on, wincing a bit as he did so.

"That's nice to know," she said, watching him.

"What?"

"That you're human."

"I thought you could tell that from my ability to bleed."

"You need anything else? Hungry? Thirsty?"

"No, I'm good." He looked down. "This the couch?"

"Yes. Sorry, I've only got the one bedroom. But even though you're tall the couch is extra long."

"I've slept in a lot worse conditions, trust me."

"Can I?"

He folded his jacket over the arm of the couch. "Can you what?"

"Trust you?"

"You invited me here."

"That's not what I'm talking about and you know it."

He walked to a window overlooking the water. To the north he could see the lights of D.C. The triumvirate of the Lincoln, Jefferson, and Washington monuments were plainly visible. And rising above them all, the colossal dome of the Capitol.

She joined him.

"I like getting up in the morning and seeing that," she said. "I figure it's what I work for. Fight for. Defending what those buildings represent."

"It's good to have a reason," said Robie.

"What's your reason?" she asked.

"Some days I know, some days I don't."

"How about today?"

"Good night," he said. "And thanks for letting me stay here."

"I know we only just met today, but it feels like I've known you for years. Why is that?"

He looked at her. From her expression it wasn't an idle question. She wanted an answer.

"Looking for a killer bonds people pretty quickly. Almost dying together bonds you even more."

"I guess that's probably right," she said, though her tone spoke of disappointment with his answer.

She got him sheets and a blanket and pillow and fixed up the couch for him over his protests that he could do it himself.

Robie walked over to the window and looked at the monuments again.

Tourist sites, really. Nothing more.

But there could be more, if one thought about it. If one did something about it.

He turned to find Vance next to him.

"You can, you know," he said.

"I can what?"

"Trust me."

Robie couldn't look at her as the lie rolled off his tongue.

37

They rose the next morning, took turns showering, and had cups of coffee, orange juice, and buttered toast. While Vance was finishing dressing in her bedroom Robie sent Julie a one-word text.

Good?

He counted the seconds until she texted him back. There were only ten of them.

Her text was equally terse.

Good.

He stretched out his wounded arm and checked the bandage. Vance had done a good job rewrapping it after he'd finished showering.

A few minutes later he and Vance settled into her BMW. Neither spoke as they drove toward D.C. The traffic sucked, the horns blared, and Robie could tell that once or maybe twice Vance had been sorely tempted to trot out her fancy blue grille lights and maybe even her gun.

"Robie, I would appreciate if you didn't mention you stayed at my place last night. I wouldn't want people to get the wrong idea. And some of the guys I work with could really make something out of nothing with it."

"I don't talk to people about the weather, much less where I spent the night."

"Thanks."

"You're welcome."

She shot him a glance. "I hope you didn't think I invited you to stay for some reason other than a place to sleep."

"Never crossed my mind, Agent Vance. You don't strike me as the type."

"You don't strike me as the type either."

"I need to pick up a fresh set of wheels."

"You want me to drop you by DCIS?"

"There's a car rental place on M Street near Seventeenth. Drop me there."

"What, DCIS can't spring for fresh wheels for one of its own?"

"What they have is crap. Probably hand-me-downs from the Bureau. I'll get my own."

"FBI doesn't do things that way."

"FBI has a budget that allows for that. DCIS doesn't. You're the eight-hundred-pound gorilla. We're the underfed chimpanzee."

She drove to the rental place on M.

Robie got out.

"Do you want to meet me at Donnelly's?" she asked.

"I'll get there, I'm just not sure when," he said.

"Other things to do?" she answered in a surprised tone.

"Some things to think about," he said. "Some things to dig into."

"Care to share?"

"A mom and kid dead. A bus blown up. A shooter trying to take you or me or both of us down. I'll call you when I'm on my way to Donnelly's," he added.

He walked into the rental place and requested an Audi. They didn't have one, so he took a Volvo instead. The rental agent told him that Volvos were very safe cars.

Not around me they're not, thought Robie as he pulled out his license and credit card.

"How long will you be needing the car?" asked the agent.

"Let's just leave it open," said Robie.

The man blanched. "We actually need to have a turn-in date from you and the place where it will be returned."

"Los Angeles, California, two weeks from today," said Robie promptly.

"You're going to *drive* to California?" said the agent. "You know, a plane is a lot faster."

"Yeah, but not nearly as much fun."

Ten minutes later he sped out of the rental garage in his very safe silver Volvo two-door.

What had scared him the most about last night was

not nearly being killed or seeing others die. It was Julie. The feeling in his gut when he'd thought something had happened to her. He didn't like that. He didn't like someone else having that much power over him. He'd spent most of his life getting rid of those ties and avoiding any new ones.

He drove faster, pushing his nice, safe Volvo probably beyond its comfort zone.

That appealed to Robie.

He didn't much like comfort zones, his or anyone else's.

His phone buzzed. He glanced at the screen. Blue Man needed to meet with him again. Right now.

I bet you do, thought Robie.

38

No public place this time. No Hay-Adams with lots of witnesses.

Robie didn't have much of a choice. There were rules one had to play by or one was out of the game.

The building was sandwiched between two others in a part of D.C. that tourists would never tread. Even though the area was a high-crime one, none of the street punks ever bothered this place. It was not worth a bullet in their head or twenty years of their life in a federal cage.

Robie had to part with his cell phone before entering the secure room, but he would not give up his gun.

When the guard asked for it the second time, Robie told him to talk to Blue Man. The resolution was simple. Either he kept the gun or Blue Man could meet with him at the McDonald's across the street.

Robie went in with his gun.

Blue Man sat across from him in the small room. Nice suit, solid-color tie, neatly combed hair. He could be somebody's grandfather. Robie assumed he probably *was* somebody's grandfather.

"First, Robie, we have not found your handler. Second, there was no man with a rifle found in the alley you identified."

"Okay."

"Next," said Blue Man. "The attempt on your life last night?"

"The shooter was in a vehicle that looked a lot like a U.S. government ride."

"I don't think that is likely."

Robie pointedly tapped the tabletop. "You can't find my handler or a shooter I knocked out in an alley, but you think somebody gunning for me in a set of federal wheels is unlikely?"

"Who's the girl?" asked Blue Man.

Robie didn't blink, because he'd been trained not to. You blink, you lose. A blink was like a weak throw into triple coverage because you lacked the stones to wait for another receiver to break open as a three-hundred-pound lineman was about to plant you in the grass.

Robie had known Julie's presence in all of this might come out. His observation post was obviously not entirely secret, or else he'd been followed.

He said, "She's the linchpin. Anything happens to her we are screwed. So if you're telling me that my handler found her out, you better be prepared to do something about her safety."

The older man sat up straighter, adjusted his tie and

then his cuffs. "You'll need to explain that to me, Robie. The linchpin for what?"

"It won't take long, because I don't understand it all."

He took only a few minutes to describe the murders of Julie's parents, her escape attempt on the bus, the man attempting to kill her there, and the bus exploding.

"And you lost your gun at the scene. The one you had at Wind's apartment?"

"I didn't lose it. The bus exploding knocked me fifteen feet. I tried to find it before the cops showed up, but I was unsuccessful."

"But the FBI *did* find it. And now they believe there's a connection between the two cases."

"*Is* there a connection?" asked Robie.

"Actually, we don't know for sure. We'd like to talk to the girl."

"No. You go through me. No direct contact."

"That's not how we do things. And I'm not sure you're entirely clear on who's running this show, Robie."

Grandpa was showing some balls now. Robie was impressed. But just a little.

"You have a mole on the inside. Even if my handler is gone, he might not have been acting alone. If I were him I would have left somebody behind. You go pulling the girl in here, the mole gets wind of it, we lose her."

"I think we can protect her."

"You thought you could protect Jane Wind too, didn't you?" pointed out Robie.

Blue Man adjusted his cuffs again. "Okay, for now status quo," he said stiffly. "But I want a fuller debrief from you soon and follow-up reports."

"You'll get them," said Robie. "And I'd like the same."

"Do you go out of your way to rub people the wrong way?"

"I go out of my way to keep myself and those entrusted to me safe. Just as I go out of the way and above the call of duty to take out the people I'm assigned to eliminate."

"You didn't kill Jane Wind."

"And you really want to call that an error on my part?"

"Talk to me about Vance."

"Good agent."

"You spent the night at her place."

"I didn't have many options, did I?"

"Your place is safe."

"Is it?"

"I can confirm that your handler was not given that information."

"You can confirm that?" Robie said. *My ass you can*, he thought.

"Robie, we have assets deployed on this mission. Good assets. We're not leaving you out there by yourself. We have every incentive to see this through to the end. We have to find out what's going on. The motive behind this has to be worth the risks being taken. It's nearly impossible to turn one of our people like that. The payoff must be immense. And when the payoff is immense the target has to be of similar importance."

"That's the most sensible thing you've said so far," Robie replied.

Blue Man said, "I'm under no misapprehension that our relationship, such as it is, isn't strained. You have good reason to be skeptical, upset, and mistrustful. If I were in your shoes, I'd be reacting the same way."

"The second most sensible thing you've said so far."

Blue Man leaned forward. "Let me see if I can make it three for three." He collected his thoughts. "There are two possible reasons why Agent Wind and her husband were murdered. It either had to do with her, or it had to do with him."

"You know Jane Wind's work. Could it be related to her?"

"It's possible. I can't say definitively that it's not. Let's just say that I'm more interested in what you find out on Rick Wind's background."

"Former military. Retired. Owned a pawnshop in a bad section of D.C. Was hung upside down and his tongue was cut out."

"The last part has me concerned."

"I'm sure it had *him* concerned."

"You know what I'm talking about."

Robie leaned back. "Vance wondered if it was mob-related. Guy was a snitch and they symbolically cut his tongue out."

"Is that what you think?"

"No. I'm thinking what you're probably thinking."

"You cut off the hands of a thief."

"And the tongue of a traitor."

"If it involves the world of Islamic terrorists."

"If," said Robie. "But the guy was retired. What could he be involved in?"

"Terrorist cells are rarely obvious, Robie. At least the effective ones."

"Did he spend time in the Middle East? Could he have been turned and sent here as a ticking time bomb?"

"A time bomb that had a change of heart? Maybe, and yes, he did spend time in both Iraq and Afghanistan."

Robie thought about some of the missions he'd performed in the Middle East. The most recent one had not technically been there. Khalid bin Talal had been in Morocco when Robie had killed him. But there were many others from the desert that wished the absolute destruction of America. Too many, in fact, to narrow down easily.

"Then why don't I hit that angle while you work the other side?"

"But if anything occurs to you or you find out

something while working with Vance that has to do with Agent Wind?"

"You'll get it."

"Then we understand each other."

The two men rose.

Robie looked at him and said, "Is my place really safe? Because I could use a change of clothes."

Blue Man managed a rare smile. "Go and change your clothes, Robie. The ones you have on are looking pretty ragged."

"Well I'm feeling pretty ragged," admitted Robie.

39

Robie drove toward his apartment, parked a block away, and made his approach from the rear. He rode a service elevator up, got off, did a protracted observation of the hall, and then moved forward.

He bumped into Annie Lambert as she was coming out of her apartment with her bike. She had on a black skirt, pink parka, hose, and tennis shoes. A knapsack was over one shoulder.

"Late to work?" asked Robie as he approached.

She turned around, initially startled, but then she smiled.

"Doctor's appointment. Even White House staffers have to take them."

"Nothing serious?"

"No, just routine stuff."

He smiled. "So are you running the country into the ground?"

"The opposition would answer that with a big yes. But I think we're doing okay. Times are hard. Lots of challenges. How about you? Doing okay?"

"I'm fine."

If she noticed the bandage bulge under his jacket or the rumpled state of his clothes she didn't mention it.

"Still up for that drink sometime?" he asked. Robie seemed surprised by his own question.

I'm learning a lot about myself this week, he thought.

"Sure. How about tonight? You said you wanted to do it soon."

"If the president will let you off?"

She grinned. "I think he will. How about eight? W Hotel rooftop bar? The views arc great."

"See you then."

She left with her bike and Robie walked to his apartment. He had no idea why he had just done that. But he had committed and he would be there at eight. Ordinarily he disliked distractions while he was working. But somehow he was welcoming this one.

In his apartment he still checked his intruder traps even though it seemed his agency could easily circumvent them. Everything looked the same. They could have wired the place, but he had no intention of making any calls from here. In a way he was trapped right here at home.

He changed into fresh clothes and made up a small bag with other items he might need if he didn't come back here for a while.

He had the urge to check on Julie and pecked her a quick message, asking if that was okay with her.

The text came back seconds later: *Come on.*

He backtracked his way to her apartment and rode

the elevator up. He looked for elements of Blue Man's security force but didn't see any. Maybe that was good, he thought.

Maybe.

Julie unlocked the door only after peeping him through the hole. He also was gratified to hear her turning off the security system as well.

He closed and locked the door behind him.

"So you were talking to the bike chick," she said.

"What?"

She pointed to the telescope. "That thing is powerful. Works great night or day."

"Yeah, well, it's supposed to. But I don't want you using it to snoop on people."

"I'm just observing my perimeter, like you ordered me to last night."

"Okay, I guess I deserved that."

"So your other place is across the street?"

"Yeah."

"Normally people like to spread out their residences. You know, Paris, London, Hong Kong."

"I'm not normal."

"Yeah, that one I figured out on my own. So what have you found out? I've been watching the TV. Sounds like it was a real war zone down there last night. You're lucky you weren't killed. At least I'm assuming that's where you got shot. You never got around to telling me about your arm."

"Luck always plays a part," he said vaguely.

"They have any leads?"

"None they're sharing with me."

"How's working with the FBI?"

"It's working."

"She's pretty."

"Who?"

"Agent Vance. She was on the TV talking to reporters. She didn't mention you."

"That was a good thing."

"Where did you sleep last night? I know it wasn't across the street." She indicated the scope.

"I slept," he said. "That's all you need to know."

"Uh-huh," she said. "You slept with her, didn't you?"

This time Robie almost blinked. Almost. The kid was really getting to him.

"What makes you say that?"

She studied him closely. "Oh, I don't know. A certain glow. A woman can always tell."

"Well, you're wrong. Now I've got to get going."

"When are *we* going to get going, Robie?"

He stared at her.

"Partners, remember our deal? We find out who killed my parents?"

"I remember. And I'm working on it."

"I know you are. But *I* want to work on it too. I gave you that list. What have you done with it so far?"

"Going to run it down."

"Good," she said, pulling on her hoodie. "I'm ready to go."

"I don't think that's a good idea."

"And I don't think it's a good idea me just sitting here on my ass doing nothing except looking through a telescope. So either I go with you or I go on my own. Either way, I'm going."

Robie sighed and opened the door for her. "But you let me handle the questions," he said.

"I wouldn't have it any other way," she answered.

Liar, thought Robie.

40

They sat in Robie's rental and watched her parents' duplex.

Julie squirmed a bit and said, "Exactly how is this getting us anywhere?"

"We're seeing if anyone interesting shows up. I'll give it another half hour and we'll move on."

"This is busy work, right? You're trying to make me so bored I'll quit and go back and sit at the apartment, right?"

"Are you always so skeptical of everyone?"

"Pretty much, yeah. And are you telling me you're not skeptical?"

"Within reason."

"What the hell does that mean?"

"Forget it."

He looked out his window and watched as a stray cat skittered down the sidewalk. A few drops of rain started to fall and the animal picked up its pace, disappearing down an alley.

"How long had your parents lived here?"

"About two years. Longest we lived anywhere."

He glanced over at her. "So give me the short version of your life."

"Not much to tell."

"It might help the investigation."

"I just remembered something. Something my mom said when the guy with the gun was there."

"What?"

"When the guy started to come after me my mom said, 'She doesn't know anything.' "

Robie sat up straighter and his grip tightened on the wheel. "How did you forget to tell me that?"

"I don't know. Just being back here and seeing the house made me think of it."

"She told the guy that you didn't know anything," said Robie. "Which implies that your mom *did* know something. And before you said the guy asked your dad what he knew."

"I see where you're going with this. So now somebody thinks I know it too, despite what my mom said. But if the guy who was after me died in the explosion?"

"Doesn't matter. He would have communicated to whomever he was working for."

"Maybe he was a loner?"

"Don't think so."

"Why?"

"He wasn't the type. I can tell. And besides, someone removed your parents' bodies and blew up that bus. And it wasn't him. He wouldn't have had time or the opportunity."

"Why would they blow up the bus? If they were trying to kill me, I wasn't on it."

"But they might not have known that. Let's say someone fired an incendiary round into the tank on the side opposite from the door. The windows on the bus were tinted. They might not have known we had gotten off the bus. They were making sure of things just in case their guy on the scene failed, which he did."

"Do you think they still believe I'm dead?"

"Doubtful. These people apparently have a lot of resources. We have to assume they know you're alive."

Julie looked out the window. "What could my parents have gotten into?"

"Let's track their days a little bit and see if anything comes up."

"Where to first?"

"The diner where your mom worked. Give me directions."

Using Julie as the navigator, Robie drove over to the diner, which was only a short distance away. He pulled the Volvo to a stop at the curb about a block down and on the other side of the street from the diner.

He cut the engine. "They know you there, right?"

"Yeah, sure."

"So I'm not sure it's smart for you to be seen there."

"So I just sit in the car by myself? That was not part of the deal."

"The plan is ever-evolving depending on conditions on the ground."

He reached into the backseat and pulled out the bag he'd taken from his apartment. He slid out a pair of binoculars.

"Here's the plan. I go in and ask some questions. You keep a lookout. Anybody seems to be paying me too much attention, take his picture with your camera."

"How will you explain why you're asking questions in the diner?"

He reached into the bag again and pulled out two power packs, an earwig, and a headset. He handed the latter to her.

"You're command central. You speak into that, I'll be able to hear you in there but no one else will, okay? And you'll be able to hear everything from in there clearly. You feed me information as you see fit. Okay?"

Julie smiled. "Okay. Cool."

He put on his earwig, powered up his pack, and clipped it onto his belt, where it was covered by his jacket He got out and then leaned back in.

"Anything looks weird, you feel bad vibes, just say, 'Come,' and I'll be here in five seconds, okay?"

"Okay."

He shut the door, looked left and right, and then headed to the diner.

Through the binoculars Julie watched him every step of the way.

41

Robie dropped onto a free stool and picked up a dingy menu from a rack on the countertop. A waitress in a frayed blue uniform with a not overly clean apron over it faced him. A pencil was stuck behind her right ear. She was about fifty, wide in the hips, with gray roots running through her otherwise blonde hair.

"What can I get you?" she asked.

"Cup of black coffee to start."

"Coming up. I just put on a fresh pot."

In Robie's ear Julie said, "Her name is Cheryl Kosmann. She's my mom's friend. She's a good person."

Robie nodded slightly to show he'd gotten the info.

Cheryl brought his cup of coffee and set it down. "You look like you could use some meat on your bones. Our meatloaf is really good. Sticks to your ribs. Lord knows I've had enough of it. Haven't seen my ribs for about twenty years." She laughed.

"You're Cheryl Kosmann?"

The laugh caught in her throat. "Who wants to know?"

Robie pulled out his cred pack, flashed first the badge and then the ID card.

Cheryl stiffened. "Am I in trouble?"

"Should you be?"

"Not unless working your ass off for pennies is a crime."

"No, you're not in trouble, Ms. Kosmann."

"Just make it Cheryl. I know this is a four-star fancy place, but we try to keep things informal."

"How long you worked here?"

"Too long. Came here out of high school to work one summer and here I am all these years later. If I think about it too much I start to cry. I know where my life went. Right in the crapper."

Robie pulled out the picture of Julie and her parents, which he'd taken from the duplex.

"What can you tell me about these folks?"

Kosmann glanced at the photo. "You're interested in the Gettys? Why? Are they in trouble?"

"Again, any reason you know of why they should be?"

"No, they're just good people who got into some bad stuff and never could find their way back out. That little girl of theirs is something, a real piece of work. Now, I mean that in a good way. If she had half a chance in life she'd make something of herself. Smart as a whip she is. Gets real good grades in school. She works hard at it. Many the times she's been here with books piled high. Tried to help her once on a math problem. That was a joke. I can barely add up numbers on a customer's bill. But Julie is special. I love that girl."

"But she's in foster care."

"Well, she is and she isn't. Sara, that's her mom, does all she can to get her back each time."

"And her dad?"

"Curtis loves her too, but the man is a mess. Too many coke snorts, if you ask me. After a while how much brain do you have left, right? Even Einstein would be a dumbass with that much white stuff up there."

"When was the last time you saw any of them?"

Kosmann folded her arms across her chest. "Funny you should ask that. Sara was supposed to work today, but she never came in. Never called. Not like her either, well, unless something had happened."

"Like a binge maybe?" suggested Robie.

"Or Curtis couldn't get out of bed and she had to take care of him. I expect she'll be in tomorrow."

No she won't, thought Robie.

In his ear he heard Julie sniffle.

"Does the owner put up with that?"

"The owner is a three-time loser who's done his share of drugs. He understands the mindset. He lets her slide. But when she's here, nobody works harder."

"So the last time she was here?"

"Day before yesterday. She had yesterday off. Her

shift was over at six. She'd pulled twelve hours at that point. On your feet all day is a real bitch. Curtis came to walk her home."

"From his job?"

"Right, a warehouse about five minutes from here. He walked her home a lot. Didn't think the streets around here were safe, and sometimes they're not. I thought it was sweet. He really loved her and she really loved him. They had absolutely nothing. Lived in a dump. No car. No savings. No retirement. Well, they did have Julie. That's something for sure. They wanted the best for her. Didn't want her to end up like them. Paid every last penny they had and then some to get her into a gifted and talented program at a really good school. Sara worked extra hours here all the time to help pay for the tuition. We had lots of chats about that when we were working the same shift. And Curtis pulled extra hours at the warehouse. He was a druggie, but he could work hard when he wanted to. And for his little girl he wanted to."

In his ear Robie heard Julie breathing fast and hard.

His hand reached down to the power pack on his belt and he turned it off.

"You see Julie a lot?" he asked.

"Oh, yeah. Like I said, she'd sit at a booth or here at the counter and do her homework while her mom finished her shift. Then the three of them would walk home together."

"When she wasn't in foster care?"

"Right. I know. It seems like she was more in foster care than not."

"You see anybody hanging around here the last few weeks you didn't recognize?"

Kosmann frowned. "Look, has something happened to Sara, or Curtis or Julie?"

"I'm just here collecting information."

"Your badge said DCIS."

Robie was surprised at this. Most people never focused on the actual insignia.

"You know the agency?"

"We got some veterans who are regulars here. One was with DCIS, so I know the symbol. But what's the connection to the Gettys? Neither Curtis nor Sara was in the service, at least that I know of."

"Again, I'm just collecting information. Did either of them seem edgy or concerned when you saw them lately?"

"Something has happened to them, hasn't it?" Kosmann looked like she might start crying. Several patrons at other tables glanced at them.

"Cheryl, I'm just here doing my job. And if you don't want to answer my questions, that's fine. Or we can do it another time."

"No, no, it's okay." She wiped her eyes with a napkin and collected herself. "But I think I'm going to have some coffee too, to steady my nerves."

He waited while she poured herself a cup and returned to stand in front of him.

"Edgy, or concerned?" prompted Robie.

"Now that you mention it, yeah. At least Sara. I don't know about Curtis. He's always edgy and looks ready to jump out of his skin all the time. But that's just the drugs talking."

"Did you ever ask Sara what was bothering her?"

"No, I never did. I figured it was either Curtis or maybe losing Julie to foster care again. There was nothing I could do about any of it."

"She mention any names? Take any phone calls here that seemed out of the ordinary?"

"No."

"Her last day here did anything unusual happen?"

"No, but the night before they had some friends in here for dinner."

"What friends?"

"Just buddies of theirs. They took that booth over there. Sara was off duty, and she had her meal free and discounts on everybody else's. When you don't have much money, every little bit helps."

"Did you know them?"

"Another couple. Leo and Ida Broome."

Robie took a sip of his coffee and then wrote this down.

"Tell me about them."

Some more customers came in and Robie waited while Cheryl seated them at a booth and took their drink orders. After she delivered them and took their food requests she came back over to Robie. He'd eyed the new folks and saw nothing threatening. While Cheryl was doing her duties he'd turned the power pack back on and immediately heard Julie's voice.

"Don't turn it off again. I'm not going to start crying. Okay?"

He nodded slightly.

Cheryl said, "Sorry about that."

"No problem. We were talking about the Broomes?"

"Not much to tell, really. They're in their late forties, nice couple. I think Ida works in a hair salon. And Leo does something with the city, not sure exactly what. I don't know how they met. Maybe they were all in rehab together. Who knows? I only know them from when they come here to have a meal with Sara and Curtis from time to time."

"You have an address or phone number for them?"

"No."

In his ear Julie said, "I do."

Robie said, "Cheryl, did you notice anything unusual while they were together that night?"

"Well, I served them. I was working the late shift that night. I just caught snatches of conversation. Nothing really important, but they all looked . . ."

Robie waited patiently until she found the words she was looking for.

"Well, they all looked like they'd seen a ghost."

"And you didn't ask them what was bothering them?"

"No. I just figured it was either drugs or Julie was back in foster care or it was something to do with the Broomes. Look, I'm a waitress at a crummy diner, okay? If people want to talk, I'll listen, but I'm not into poking around things that don't concern me. I have enough of my own problems. If that makes me a bad person, then I'm a bad person."

"You're not a bad person, Cheryl," said Robie. But he was also thinking something else. "You got any time off coming up?"

She was clearly surprised by this question. "Got a week of vacation left."

"You have family out of town?"

"In Tallahassee."

"I'd go see your family in Tallahassee."

Kosmann stared at him as Robie's meaning sank in.

"Do you, do you think that I'm . . . ?"

"Just take the vacation, Cheryl. Take it now."

Robie laid a twenty down for the coffee, rose, and left.

42

Robie climbed back in the car and slid out his earwig and power pack, stashing them in the console between the front seats. He looked over at Julie, who gazed straight ahead.

"You okay?"

"I'm okay." She stared over at the diner. "That place was almost more of a home for me than my real home. Certainly more than any of the foster places."

"I can see that," replied Robie.

"I liked to do my homework there. My mom would get me pie and let me drink coffee. I felt really grown-up."

"And I guess it was nice being with her."

"I liked to watch her work. She was good at it. Juggled all these orders. And she never wrote anything down. She had a great memory."

"Maybe your brains are genetic."

"Maybe they are."

"The night your parents were killed they left the diner at around six. But they didn't show up at their house until hours later, and with the gunman. I wonder where they were in the meantime?"

"I don't know."

"Okay, how about the Broomes?"

"They live in an apartment in northeast."

Robie put the car in drive. "What can you tell me about them?"

Before she could answer, Robie's phone buzzed. He put it up to his ear. "Robie."

"Where the hell are you?"

It was Vance.

"Doing some digging, like I told you."

"You need to get over here."

"What's happening?" he asked.

"First, I've got the press all over my ass. Second, I've got MPD, a joint terrorist team, and Homeland Security trying to tell me how to run my investigation. Third, I'm just pissed."

"Okay. Give me an hour and I'll be there."

"Is that really the best you can do?"

"It really is."

He clicked off and hung a left, working his way over to Union Station. He abruptly pulled off, parked, and undid his seat belt.

"What are you doing?" asked Julie.

"Give me a minute."

Robie stepped outside and shut the door behind him. He made the call.

The office of Blue Man answered. He was patched directly through.

Robie told him what Vance had told him. "You might want to pull some strings at DHS, the joint terrorist squad, and MPD to get them off her back," he said. "Otherwise this might get even more complicated real fast."

"Consider it done," said Blue Man.

Robie slid back in the car and started it up.

"Top-secret stuff?" said Julie, looking at him with an unfriendly gaze.

"No, I was just checking on my dry cleaning."

"So have you slept with her?" asked Julie.

Robie kept his eyes straight ahead. "I already told you. No! Not that it's any of your business who I sleep with."

"Well, she wants to have sex with you."

He shot her a glance. "How the hell do you figure that?"

"She's pissed off at you now. I heard her voice over the phone. She wouldn't get that upset unless she had a thing for you."

"She's FBI. She's probably reamed lots of guys who give her trouble."

"Maybe, but this is different. I can just tell. It's a woman thing. Guys wouldn't understand."

"You're fourteen. You shouldn't know about woman things."

"Will, what century are you living in? Five girls in my old school are pregnant. And none of them are older than me."

"I guess I'm just old-fashioned."

"Sometimes I wish I could be old-fashioned too. But that's not the world I live in."

"So, the Broomes?" asked Robie again.

"My parents have known them for years. Like Cheryl said, Ida works in a hair salon. I've gone there with my mom. Ida would cut my hair for free and my mom would bake stuff for her. My mom is a good cook." She paused. "*Was* a good cook."

"And her husband?" Robie said quickly, hoping to move her off this thought. "Cheryl said he had some job with the city."

"Not sure about that," answered Julie.

"Anything unusual about them?"

"They seemed pretty normal to me, but I didn't know them all that well."

"Then I'll guess we'll just have to ask them." *If they're still alive*, he thought. "How did they meet your parents?"

"I think Mr. Broome was a friend of Dad's. I'm not sure what the exact connection was."

"You think they could have anything to do with what happened to your parents?"

"I wouldn't think so. I mean, she works in a hair salon and they eat in crummy diners. It's not like they're international spies or anything."

"Not that you know."

"Are you kidding?"

"Spies don't usually look like spies. That's sort of the point."

"You look like a spy."

"That's good, because I'm not."

"So you say."

They drove in silence for a few seconds.

"So are you sleeping with her?" she asked again.

"Why the hell do you care?"

"I'm just naturally curious."

"Yeah, that I get. But even if I were sleeping with her I wouldn't tell you."

"Why?"

"Something called being a gentleman."

"Now you really sound old."

"Compared to you I'm ancient," replied Robie.

43

The apartment building had been built in the sixties but had been rehabbed. Robie could tell this from the new awning out front, the cleansed brick, and the fresh paint on the trim. As he watched from the car with Julie, a man opened the door by touching a plastic key card against an electronic receiver housed next to the entrance. The door clicked open and he walked inside. The door clicked shut behind him.

Julie glanced at Robie.

"What now?"

"You know the apartment number?"

"No, I just passed the place one time with my mom. She told me the Broomes lived there. I've never been to their apartment."

"Okay. Give me a sec."

He slipped out of the car and hustled across the street to beat some oncoming traffic. He gazed at a call box set in the wall next to the door and pushed the button.

A voice came on. "Yes?"

"I'm here to see Leo and Ida Broome."

"Hold on."

The voice came back on about twenty seconds later. "Called their apartment. No answer."

"You sure you called the right apartment? Number 305?"

"No, it's 410."

"Oh, okay, thanks."

Robie looked around to see if there was a surveillance camera, but saw none.

A couple was approaching him. Elderly. The woman had a scarf and a cane. In her free hand was a plastic grocery bag. The man was skimming along with the use of a walker that had tennis balls stuck on the ends of the front poles.

Robie watched as the woman pulled out a key card.

"You need any help, ma'am?" asked Robie.

She looked at him suspiciously. "No, we're just fine by ourselves."

"Okay." Robie stepped back, waiting for her to open the door with the card.

She stopped and stared at him. "Can I help you, young man?"

Robie started to say something when he heard her voice.

"Dad, I told you to wait for me."

Robie turned and watched Julie run up to him. She had her knapsack slung over her shoulder. She looked at the elderly couple and smiled.

"Hi, I'm Julie. Do you live in this building? My dad and I are thinking about moving here. We came to see one of the apartments. My mom's supposed to meet us here." She turned to Robie. "But she called and said she's running late. And she has the key card the rental agent gave her. We'll just have to wait outside." She turned back to the couple. "This'll be the first time I'll have a bathroom to myself. You promised, right, Dad?"

Robie nodded. "Anything for my little girl."

The old man smiled. "Nice to have some young blood in the place. I'm feeling old."

"You *are* old," said the woman. "Really old." She looked at Julie kindly. "Where are you moving here from, honey?"

"Jersey," said Julie promptly. "I hear it's warmer down here."

"What part of Jersey?" asked the woman. 'That's where we're from."

"Wayne," said Julie. "It's nice there, but my dad got transferred."

"Wayne is very nice," said the woman.

Julie looked at Robie. "Mom said about forty-five minutes. She's stuck in traffic."

"Everybody's stuck in traffic in this area," said the old man. "Hell, you can be a pedestrian in this town and get stuck in traffic."

"Come on, we'll let you in," said the woman. "No sense you standing around out here."

Robie took the woman's bag of groceries and they

rode the elevator up to the sixth floor, where they left the old couple. The woman gave Julie a cookie from the bag and pinched her cheek.

"You look just like my great-granddaughter. Hope we see a lot of you if you move in here."

Robie and Julie rode the elevator back down to the fourth floor and got off.

"Nice work back there," said Robie. "They might have tripped you up, though, being from Jersey too."

"I've been to Wayne. First rule, don't say you're from someplace you've never been."

"Good rule."

They found Apartment 410. It was at the end of a hall with no other door facing it. Robie scanned the hall for a surveillance camera but found none. He knocked on 410 three times without an answer.

'Turn around and face out into the hall," he told Julie.

"Are you going to pick the lock?"

"Just turn around."

It took Robie all of five seconds. The lock was not a deadbolt. One slender piece of metal did the trick as opposed to two.

They stepped inside and he closed the door behind them.

"I guess this makes us felons," said Julie.

"It might."

The place smelled of fried foods. It was furnished

sparingly, the rooms were few, and there was no one there. They stood in the middle of the living room. Robie surveyed the area.

"It's a little too clean, don't you think?" he said.

"Maybe they're neatniks."

He shook his head. "This place has been scrubbed."

Julie looked up at him. "You mean?"

"I don't know if anything happened to the Broomes, Julie. Maybe they're okay. But someone has wiped this place down, and whoever did it knew what he was doing."

Julie gazed around the space. "Should we check for prints or something?"

"Waste of time. We need to find out what Leo Broome did."

"We can go to the hair salon and ask around."

"I have a better idea. *You* can go to the hair salon and ask around. I don't want to tip anyone off to what we're doing. Folks are less likely to suspect a kid."

"I'm not a kid. I'm practically old enough to drive."

"But they'll open up to you. They know you, right?"

"Yeah. I've been there lots of times."

They left the building and drove off in the Volvo.

"You think the Broomes are dead, don't you?" she asked.

"Based on what happened to your parents and the condition of the Broomes' apartment, yeah, I think they're probably dead. But then again, if Ida Broome is at the hair salon, I'll be proved wrong."

"I hope you're wrong, Will."

"Me too."

44

While Robie waited outside in the car, Julie entered the hair salon. It was full of customers and her gaze darted around, noting the stylists working there today.

Ida Broome was not among them.

The smells of hair care products and perming solutions filled her lungs as she walked over to the reception desk. A constant chatter also permeated the place as stylists and patrons discussed the latest gossip.

"Julie, right?" said the young woman behind the counter. She looked college-age and wore black slacks and a low-cut top that revealed a flower tat near the top of her left breast. Her haircut, understandably, was very hip.

"Yep. Is Ida in today? I was hoping to get my bangs trimmed."

Julie was praying that Ida was in the back, or maybe taking a smoke break in the alley behind the salon, but the woman shook her head. "She was supposed to be in at ten, but she never showed. I called her place, but no one answered. Really put us behind. She had seven cuts, two perms and a coloring scheduled today.

Her clients were not happy when I called them to cancel."

"I wonder what happened," said Julie.

"Maybe some emergency came up."

"Maybe it did," said Julie slowly.

"I might bc able to get Maria to do your bangs. She has an open slot after the lady she's working on now."

"That would be great."

Maria was a Latina in her mid-twenties with short dark hair that was cut in precise lines around her angular face. She greeted Julie with a toothy smile.

"Look at you girl. You need your bangs cut, right?"

"How'd you know?"

"I'm a professional, okay?"

The stylist next to her chuckled as she clipped away at the thinning hair of a young man.

"No school today?" asked Maria.

"Teacher conference."

"How's your mom?"

Julie didn't blink. She'd been expecting this question.

"She's fine."

Julie settled in the chair and Maria swept a black smock over her and tightened it down around her neck.

Maria said, "You know, you'd look real cute with, like, a Zooey Deschanel cut. It's so chic with glasses."

"My eyesight is perfect," said Julie.

"That's not the point. It's the look."

"Have you seen Ida lately? The girl at the front told me she didn't come in today."

"I know. Surprised me. She never misses work and she had a full slate today. The boss is pissed. The economy still sucks and every dollar counts."

"Business looks pretty good today."

"Yeah, but it's not like this every day."

Julie said, "*Apreciar todo lo bueno que viene su manera.*"

Maria laughed and bopped Julie lightly on the head with her scissors. "You know I don't speak Spanish."

"I wonder where Ida is?" asked Julie.

"Don't know. She was acting kind of funny day before yesterday."

"Funny ha-ha or funny weird?"

"Definitely funny weird. She messed up a lady's perm and then took two inches off a client instead of the one inch she wanted. Talk about a lady being pissed. You know how we women are about our hair. It's like a religion. That and shoes."

"Did you ask her what was up?"

"Yeah, but she wouldn't say much. Just that it had something to do with Leo."

"Her husband? Did he lose his job or something?"

"I doubt it. He works for the government. They don't lose their jobs."

"I don't know about that. Lots of governments are cutting back now."

"Well, anyway, I don't think Leo got canned."

"What does he do?"

"Something with the government, like I said."

"Yeah, but what? And what government? D.C.? Feds?"

"Well, aren't you just the nosy one today?"

"Just naturally curious. All teenagers are."

"Right. My youngest sister is seventeen and she could give a crap about anything or anybody other than herself."

"I'm an only child. We tend to be more observant."

"Well, I'm not sure where Leo works. But Ida told me one time that his job was pretty important. Down on Capitol Hill somewhere."

"Then maybe he works for the federal government."

"Maybe he does."

"So Ida wasn't in yesterday either?"

"Nope, but that's okay. It was her day off. But today is a whole different story."

Maria had been working this whole time and said, "Okay, we are done and looking sharp. But think about those glasses, okay?"

Julie admired her hair in the mirror. "Thanks, Maria."

Maria took the smock off and Julie pulled out some cash. Maria waved it off.

"No, this one is on me."

"But you should get paid."

"I tell you what, you can start teaching me some Spanish when you come in. My mother is really ragging me to learn it."

Julie smiled. "Deal."

45

Robie had not stayed in the Volvo the entire time he was waiting for Julie. He was roaming. And watching. He knew there were eyes out there somewhere. He just wanted to find them before they found him.

And he had things to think about.

He had two cases going simultaneously.

Jane Wind was dead along with her young son. She was with the Defense Department. She'd traveled to Iraq and Afghanistan and probably other hot spots. Robie's handler had been turned and had ordered Robie to kill her. Now the handler was missing and Robie was investigating murders that had occurred when he'd been present. Nicole Vance was sharp and Robie had to be extra careful he didn't slip up around her. Rick Wind had been found with his tongue cut out and hanging upside down in his pawnshop. No leads there either.

And then he had Julie Getty. Parents murdered and the crime scene policed. Killer on the bus to finish the job. Bus blows up. Robie's gun was found at the scene, which made the Feds believe the cases were connected. And the guy who'd attacked them in the alley had disappeared. The Broomes' apartment had been scrubbed too, and Robie didn't know where they were. Or if they were still alive.

He glanced at the salon and saw through the window that Julie was getting ready to leave. If he were a betting man he would wager that Ida Broome had not been in there.

He met her at the car and they both climbed in.

"Talk to me," he said.

Julie spent a few minutes filling him in.

"So we still don't know what Leo does," said Robie.

"Can't you find that out on some government database?"

"Probably. I'll check it out."

"The Broomes are most likely dead," she said.

"Or they could be in hiding," said Robie. "That would be best case."

"If Mr. Broome has some important job in the government do you think he's the reason for all this?"

"It's certainly a possibility."

"But why would that involve my parents?"

"They were friends. They met for meals. He might have let something slip."

"Great," she said, her voice catching slightly. "My parents might have been killed because they had a meatloaf dinner with the guy?"

"Stranger things have happened."

"What now?" she asked.

"I drop you back off. I have to get going."

"Right. To see special super agent Vance."

"Just Special Agent Vance."

"But she was super, wasn't she?"

"You won't let it rest, will you?"

"Does this mean I go back to the apartment and die of boredom?"

"Don't you have homework to do?"

"Going from investigating murder to doing calculus, wow."

"You're only fourteen and you're already doing calculus?"

"G and T, Will, like I said. I actually don't like math very much. But I'm good at it."

"Education is the key to success."

"You sound like somebody's grandfather."

"You disagree?"

"I'm just taking it one day at a time."

"Not a bad philosophy."

"My classmates' parents have their whole lives planned out for them. Top colleges. Top graduate programs. Wall Street, medical school, law firms. The next Steve Jobs, the next Warren Buffett. Makes me want to gag."

"Nothing wrong with getting ahead."

"You mean there's nothing wrong with making as much money as possible at the expense of everyone else? The planet has over seven billion people and too many of them live in poverty. Me coming up with an algorithm to make a fortune on Wall Street and tank the economy in the process, which in turn creates a lot more poor people, doesn't exactly rock my career boat."

"Then do something else. Something that helps people."

She gave him a sideways look. "You mean like you?"

He glanced away.

No, not like me, he thought.

46

After dropping Julie off, Robie navigated traffic until he arrived at Donnelly's about twenty-five minutes later. The bodies were gone but the street was filled with police cars, forensics vans, and Bureau sedans. Smack in the middle of the sidewalk was a mobile FBI command post that had probably been dropped off last night.

On the other side of the wooden police barriers was an army of reporters. Media trucks with communication masts raised to the sky lined the street behind the jostling journalists. Robie flashed his creds and was passed through the barriers as the reporters with deadlines and a never-ending news cycle to service screamed questions at him.

Vance met him out front. She seemed hassled and harried. As he looked around at the chaos of the First Amendment slamming head-on into the right of the government to solve the murders of several of its citizens, Robie could hardly blame her.

"Got everything under control?" he asked.

"Don't make me shoot you."

He followed her into Donnelly's, where federal techs

and FBI agents in dark blue windbreakers were working the crime scene hard. Evidence markers were placed throughout denoting the position of victims. Colored pieces of plastic with numbers on them, they seemed grossly inadequate to symbolize the death or wounding of a human being.

"What's the latest?" Robie asked.

"Two more of the victims died last night at the hospital," she said grimly. "That makes the total count six. And chances are we might lose more."

"You said DHS and MPD were hassling you?"

"That's quieted down now actually. They pulled up their tents and went home."

"Good to know."

She glanced sharply at him. "Did you have anything to do with that?"

He held up his hands. "I don't have that kind of pull. If the FBI can't move the mountain, don't expect little DCIS to do it."

"Right," she said, looking unconvinced.

"Any clues?"

"Black SUV was found abandoned about a mile from here. It had bullet pocks on it. You were right, it was heavily armored."

"Who was the owner?"

"The U.S. government."

So I was right, thought Robie. *And Blue Man was wrong*. This did not make him feel any better. In fact, it made him feel worse.

"Which part?"

"Secret Service."

Robie stared blankly at her.

"It went missing from one of their motor pools."

"How? Those places are monitored twenty-four/seven."

"We're running that down now."

"That is not good if they have someone on the inside. They protect the president."

"Thanks, Robie. I wasn't aware of that," she snapped.

"What does the Secret Service say?" he asked, ignoring her tone.

"They're concerned. And they've tightened up security even more."

"Anything else?"

"MP-5 casings all over the street. Hope we find a gun we can match them to."

"No one saw anything? No faces?"

"We've been canvassing the area all night and day. Nothing so far."

"Are we sure we were the targets? Not someone else in the restaurant or on the street?"

"We're not sure about that. We're profiling all victims and all persons who were in the restaurant last night. Maybe we get lucky and one of them provides a motive for this level of carnage."

"But if we *were* the target?" said Robie. He thought, *If* I *was the target.*

Vance shook her head. "Why would they waste time taking us out? Just because we were investigating the bus blowing up or Jane Wind's murder? They kill us, other investigators take our place, and the case goes on. And like you said before, killing Feds brings a lot of extra grief. I just don't see it."

"Latest on Rick Wind?"

"They're doing the posts today. I asked for a rush on the results."

"The bus?"

"Just going through the bodies—or body parts, rather—will take a long time. We're transporting the remains to an FBI evidence facility. We'll comb it to see if we can find what caused the blast. We've called in ATF to assist. Those guys are the best. They can usually find the detonation source. But it'll take time."

Robie cleared his throat and asked the question that had been hammering in his gut for too long now. "Any surveillance cameras in the area? They might show what happened. Give your guys a shortcut."

"There were some. We're collecting those now. Don't know what they'll show, but they might give us something to go on."

"Where are you collecting them?" he asked.

"The mobile command post outside. We should have them all there later today or tonight. We wanted to make sure we were thorough in gathering them all. One I know is from an ATM, and another was posted on the corner of a building, but its sight line might be obstructed. And I've been told there are others."

Robie nodded, thinking how he was going to phrase it. "I know that technically I'm not deployed on the bus case, but since it seems the two cases might be connected, you mind if I go over it too?"

She thought about this for a few moments. "Never turn down a fresh pair of eyes."

Vance signed off on some documents handed to her by a tech while Robie glanced through the window at the portable command center.

If I show up on one of those videos? Or Julie does?

"Penny for your thoughts."

He turned to see Vance watching him.

"So what can I do to help?" he said, ignoring her question.

"You can noodle all this. And we can follow a few leads down."

"What are they?"

"Wind's employment at DCIS, for one. You're of course uniquely positioned to follow up on that. And then there's her husband. Was there something in her background that led to his death?"

"From the condition of the body, he was killed before her."

"Which leads me to believe the reason might lie with Rick Wind," said Vance. "Anything else you know about him?'

"He was deployed to both Iraq and Afghanistan while in the military," said Robie.

"So was everybody in uniform the last ten years."

"He apparently left the military with a clean record. His wife, in her capacity with DCIS, also visited Iraq and Afghanistan on several ocassions."

"At the same time as her husband?"

"No, afterwards."

"You said Wind left the Army clean, but could there be something else? How long was he in the Middle East? Was he wounded or captured? Or did he have a change of heart?"

"You want to know if he was turned somehow? Became an enemy of his own country?"

"Yeah, I would."

"I can't answer that."

"Can't, or won't?"

"I don't know the answer."

"They cut out his tongue."

"I was there, Agent Vance."

"I did some research on the computer last night."

"That can be dangerous."

"And I also emailed some of our Middle East experts. Islamic fundamentalists sometimes cut out the tongues of people who they believe have betrayed them."

"Yeah, they do."

"That could be the case here."

"We need to know a lot more before we can confirm something like that."

"Tongues cut out, a bus blown up. This is starting to look like international terrorism, Robie."

"Why the bus?"

"Mass casualties. Throws the country into a tizzy."

"Maybe."

"Rick Wind was somehow involved. He got cold feet. They took care of him. And then killed his wife because they were afraid he might have told her something."

"His ex-wife. And she works for DCIS. If he had told her something she would have told us. And I can tell you that she didn't."

"Maybe she never got the chance."

"Maybe she didn't."

"It's a workable theory."

Robie scratched his cheek. "I guess."

"You don't sound convinced."

"That's because I'm not."

47

Robie walked outside an hour later after going over the details of the mass shooting. The air was warmer today and felt warmer still as the sun rose higher. It was one of those cloudless days in D.C. that you knew would not last. Not at this time of the year. The capital city was like a bull's-eye on a weather map. Systems from north, south, and west regularly crossed the line of the Appalachians and hit the area, and their confluence could cause severe weather.

Yet today was good, weather-wise. But that was the only good thing about it.

Robie looked over at the numbered markers for the dead on the sidewalk. *Yeah, the weather is the only good thing.*

He mulled over what Vance had told him.

A Secret Service SUV had been the shooter's platform.

It had gone missing.

Things did not go missing from the Secret Service.

Robie had worked with that agency years ago to clean up a mess in a country he had never wanted to go back to. The agency was small in comparison to the behemoths of the FBI and DHS. But its people were excellent, loyal, really the only federal agents who systematically trained to take a bullet for their protectee.

He glanced to his left and saw the FBI mobile command post.

He approached, rapped on the door. He flashed his creds to the agent who answered his knock. He mentioned Vance's name, and was allowed in. It was filled with high-tech gadgetry and investigation equipment. There were four other people present. In his mind Robie split them up between special agents and tech support. The two techs were hammering on computer keyboards, and data obediently flowed across the multiple computer screens stacked on the long table.

Robie said, "Vance told me about collecting surveillance camera footage from the scene of the bus explosion. You got any of it uploaded yet?"

The agent who had let him in the command post nodded. "Hang on a sec."

He texted something on his phone. Robie knew exactly what.

He's getting the okay from Vance to show me the pictures.

Robie would have expected nothing less. The FBI did not employ stupid people.

Robie heard the sound of a text shooting back to the agent. The man glanced at the screen and said, "Over here, Agent Robie."

He led him to one corner and indicated a blank screen.

"Here's what we have so far."

The agent punched some keys and the file uploaded to the screen.

Robie sat in a swivel chair, folded his arms across his chest, and waited.

"Have you looked at it yet?" Robie asked.

"First time for me too."

Robie felt his pulse quicken.

This might truly be enlightening for everybody, he thought.

The door opened and he saw Vance. She closed it behind her and walked over to them.

"Am I in time for the show?" she asked.

"Yes, ma'am," said the other agent respectfully.

She sat down next to Robie, their knees nearly touching. She focused on the screen that was now coming to life.

The bus came into view. It traveled a few hundred yards. Robie was relieved to see that the camera shot was not on the side of the bus with the door. A few seconds later the bus exploded.

Robie tensed again. With the bus destroyed, there would be nothing to block the camera's view across the street, where Robie and Julie's pixeled figures were now rolling and eventually coming to rest. In a few seconds they would both rise and then . . .

The screen went black.

Robie looked at the agent controlling this process. "What happened?"

"Blast must've knocked out the camera. That can happen. It's not like bank cameras are built for that stuff."

He tapped more buttons on his keyboard and finally called a tech over. The tech executed more keystrokes and five minutes later they still had nothing.

Robie sat through two more video feeds that were very much like the first two. Opposite side of the bus and the cameras went down after the explosion.

"Any cameras around the bus depot showing the passengers getting on?" asked Robie. He had searched his memory but could not recall any such surveillance.

"Not that we can find right now," said Vance. "But it's early days yet. And we're trying to locate more footage. Particularly from the other side of the street. And everybody has cell phones and most cell phones have camera and video features, so we're trying to find anyone who was there last night who might have seen or even photographed or filmed something in the aftermath. Though if they did it probably would be on all the news shows or YouTube by now. I'm going to have my guys go check for more surveillance cameras along the bus route this afternoon, after we get this crime scene under better control."

Which means I have to find it first, Robie thought.

48

Robie stood near what was, for him, ground zero.

The remains of the bus were being sifted through by a dozen forensics techs, with an FBI evidence truck waiting nearby to take these items away to the lab. Just like at Donnelly's, roadblocks were everywhere, holding back the reporters who wanted to see and know everything right now.

He looked left and right, up and down. Vance was correct; nothing obvious that he could see. The bank video across the street was already in the database but thankfully also had been knocked out by the blast. He gazed upward. Surveillance camera about ten feet off the ground at the corner of one intersection. It was pointing downward and had gotten a shot of the bus as well. If it had been pointed a bit differently, it might have captured on film both him and Julie as they escaped.

Like football, a game of inches. Some things were just beyond your control. Then you counted on luck.

But how much more luck can I count on?

His attention turned to the troublesome part of the

street, the side he and Julie had been on. He started to walk. With the angle of coverage a camera might have on the street, he gauged what his box of concern should be and added ten percent on each end just to be safe. He covered this ground methodically.

He quickly registered on a camera posted on the wall about twenty feet to the left of where the bus had gone down. It seemed to be pointing directly at the spot of the explosion. He looked at the business located there.

Bail bondsman. Of course. In this neighborhood the owner probably had a ready group of customers. He looked through the plate glass window with rusted iron bars in a crisscross pattern fronting it.

The sign to the right of the door said, "Ring Bell."

Robie rang the bell.

A voice came out of a small white box set to the door.

"Yeah?"

"Federal agent. Need to talk to you."

"So talk."

"Face-to-face."

Robie heard footsteps approaching. A short, wide man in his fifties with more white hair in a mustache over his lip than on his head looked out at him through the window.

"Let me see your badge."

Robie pressed it against the glass.

"DCIS?"

"Part of DOD. Military."

"What do you want with me?"

"Open the door."

The man pulled the heavy door open. He was dressed in black slacks and a white shirt with the sleeves rolled to his elbows. Above his loafers Robie saw pink skin.

Robie stepped through and closed the door behind him.

"So what do you want?" the man asked again.

"The bus that blew up across the street?"

"What about it?"

"You have a surveillance camera."

"Right, so?"

"FBI been by to see you about it yet?"

"No."

"I'm going to have to confiscate the film or DVD or whatever you use to house the images captured by the camera."

"That would be nothing."

"What?"

"That camera hasn't worked for a year. Why do you think I had to come to the window to see who it was at the door, smart guy?"

"So why leave it up?"

"As a deterrent, why else? This is not exactly a safe area."

"I'll still need to see for myself."

"Why?"

"Smart guys like to cover all the bases."

However, it turned out the man was telling the truth. The system had evidently been broken a long time, and when he examined the camera Robie saw that the cable running to it inside the building wasn't even connected.

Robie left and continued his walk.

He had nearly gotten to the end of the sector he'd outlined when he saw the homeless guy from the night the bus had exploded, the one who'd been dancing around yelling about wanting some s'mores to grill on the bonfire of metal and flesh. It looked like he and his fellow homeless had been evicted from the crime scene and were huddled on the other side of the police barriers. There were three of them, each with their trash bags filled, no doubt, with everything they possessed.

The homeless guy looked like he'd been on the streets for a long time. His clothes and body were filthy. His fingernails were long and blackened and his teeth rotted. Robie could see that the reporters were giving the three a wide berth. He wondered if it had occurred to any of the journalists that the people of the streets might have seen something that night. Even so, Robie wondered how successful the reporters might have been in getting any reliable information out of them.

And then he wondered if the FBI had attempted to interview them. Vance's folks might not have even known they were there that night. Might not know that they could possess valuable information. And also some information that could be quite damaging to Robie.

Robie cleared the police barrier and was immediately engulfed by reporters. He looked at none of them, made no attempt to answer their shouted questions. He pushed mikes and notepads out of his face and kept going until he reached the three street people.

"You hungry?" he asked.

The s'mores fellow, wild-eyed and looking as though reason had left him long ago, nodded and laughed. "Always hungry."

At least he can understand me, thought Robie. He eyed the other two. One was a woman, small, bloated, blackened by the street. Her garbage bag bulged with blankets and what looked to be recycled trash. She might have been twenty, she might have been fifty, Robie couldn't tell under the layers of grime. "You hungry?"

She just looked at him. Unlike S'mores, she apparently didn't understand English.

He led them farther away from the sea of reporters and then glanced at the third person. She looked more promising. About forty, she did not have years on the street grafted onto her. And there was both intelligence and terror behind her eyes. Robie wondered if the recent economic crisis had left her as one of the new millions who were once working- or middle-class, but now were neither. "Can I get you something to eat?"

She took a step back, clutched the canvas bag. It was monogrammed. That was another clue as to her background. Longtime homeless did not have such bags. Over the years they rotted away or were stolen.

She shook her head. Robie understood her trepidation. The next thing he did would confirm his suspicions of her.

He took out his badge and held it up. "I'm a federal agent."

The woman stepped closer to him, looked relieved. S'mores's grin faded. The other woman just stood there, looking out at a reality that had clearly left her behind.

Robie had his answer. Recent homeless still respected authority. They in fact craved the law and order they had recently left for the anarchy that awaited them on the concrete. People long on the streets, after years of being told to move, get off their ass, clean up their crap, get the hell out of here because they were not wanted, did not. They feared and loathed the badge.

To S'mores Robie said, "There's a café down this way. I'm going to get you some food and bring it back. For her too," he added, indicating the woman who stared off at nothing. "Will you wait until I get back?"

S'mores slowly nodded, looking suspicious. Robie took a ten-dollar bill out of his pocket and handed it to the man for reassurance. "You want coffee, sandwich?"

"Yeah," said S'mores.

"And her?" Robie said, pointing to the other woman.

"Yeah," said S'mores.

Robie turned to the third homeless person. "Will you come with me to the café? And wait there while I get their food?"

"Am I in trouble?" she asked. Now she did sound like a longtime streeter.

"No, not at all. Were you here the night that bus blew up?"

S'mores tapped his chest and said, "Me."

Robie almost said, "I know," but caught himself. S'mores was actually starting to concern him. He sounded reasonably sane.

If he remembers seeing me?

"Have any other agents talked to you?" asked Robie, looking at the three.

S'mores glanced away when the sounds of a siren started up. He pulled his lips back. He looked like he was snarling. Then he started to howl along with the sirens.

"We all were there," the second woman said. "But we left after it happened. I don't think the police are aware that we saw anything."

Robie focused on her. "What's your name?"

"Diana."

"Your last name?"

The fear sprang up again in her features.

Robie said quietly, "Diana, you're not in any trouble. I promise you. We're just trying to find out who blew up the bus and I'd like to ask you some questions. That's all."

"My last name is Jordison."

S'mores gabbed his arm. "Hot eats?"

"Coming up." Robie escorted Jordison to the café. When they walked in, the man behind the counter started to shoo Jordison away, but Robie flashed his badge. "She stays," he said.

The man backed off and Robie seated Jordison at a table in the rear. "Order anything you want," he said, handing her a menu from a stack on the next table.

He walked up to the counter and said, "I need some food to go." He placed the order. While it was being prepared he sat down across from Jordison. A young waitress came over to take their orders.

Robie said, "Just coffee." He glanced at Jordison.

She flushed and looked unsure of herself. Robie wondered how long it had been since she had ordered anything in a restaurant. A simple process for most people, it was astonishing how quickly simple processes became complex when you slept in alleys, parks, or over steam grates and gathered your daily bread from trash cans.

Robie pointed to an item on the menu. "The American has just about everything: eggs, toast, bacon, grits, coffee, juice. How about that one? Eggs scrambled? Orange juice?"

She looked like she could use a boost of vitamin C and protein.

Jordison nodded meekly and handed the menu back to the waitress, who seemed disinclined to accept it.

Robie looked at her. "My *friend* will have the American," he said. "And could you please bring the coffee and juice out now? Thanks."

The waitress walked off to fill the order. She brought back the coffees and juice. Robie drank his black, but Jordison doused hers with cream and several sugars. He noted that she slipped most of the sugar packets into her pocket. He looked over and saw the owner giving him the high sign and pointing to two bags he was holding and a carrier with two coffees riding in it.

Robie said, "I'm going to take the food to the other two and then I'll be right back, okay?"

Jordison nodded but wouldn't meet his eye.

Robie paid the check, grabbed the bags, and headed out.

49

When Robie got back to S'mores and the other woman, a male reporter he'd seen earlier was circling the pair like a shark after shipwreck survivors.

The reporter looked at Robie. "Playing the Good Samaritan?" he asked, eyeing the bags and beverages.

"Your tax dollars at work," replied Robie. He handed one bag and coffee each to S'mores and the woman. The latter snagged her food and coffee, grabbed her plastic bags, and disappeared down the street. Robie let her go because he didn't think she would be able to tell him anything.

S'mores stood there sipping his coffee.

The reporter said, "Can you answer a few questions for me, uh, Agent . . . ?"

Robie hooked S'mores by the arm and walked off.

The reporter called after him, "I'll take that as a 'no comment.' "

When they had reached the next intersection Robie said, "Tell me what you saw the night the bus blew up."

S'mores had opened the bag and dug greedily into

the bacon, egg, and cheese sandwich. He crammed a handful of hash browns into his mouth and chomped down.

"Take it slow, friend," said Robie. "Don't want to choke."

The man swallowed, took a slurp of coffee, and shrugged. "What you want?"

"Everything you saw or heard."

S'mores took another, smaller bite of his sandwich. "Boom," he said. "Fire. Holy shit."

He took another sip of coffee.

"Anything more detailed than that?" Robie added slowly. "Did you see anyone around the bus? Maybe get off or on?"

S'mores crammed another handful of hash browns in his mouth and chomped. "Boom," he said again. "Fire. Holy shit." Then he laughed. "Grilling out."

Robie decided that his first impression of S'mores's sanity was the correct one. He wasn't sane. "You didn't see anyone?" he asked halfheartedly.

"Grilling out." Then he laughed and finished his sandwich in one bite.

"Good luck to you," said Robie.

S'mores gulped down the hot coffee.

Robie left him there and fast-walked back to the café.

Jordison had gotten her food and was eating it slowly. There was none of S'mores's energetic desperation. Robie hoped that boded well for her being able to tell him something useful, or at the very least intelligible.

Robie sat down across from her.

"Thanks for this," said Jordison quietly.

"No problem."

He watched her eat for a few seconds and then said, "How long you been out there?"

"Too long," she said, wiping her mouth with a paper napkin.

"I'm not here to grill you about that. It's none of my business."

"I had a house and a job and a husband."

"I'm sorry."

"Me too. Surprised me how fast it all went to hell. No job, no house, no husband. Nothing but bills I can't pay. I mean, you hear about it happening, but you never think it'll happen to you."

Robie said nothing.

Jordison continued, "He's probably homeless too for all I know. My ex, I mean. Well, I call him my ex. He never even bothered to file for divorce. He just up and left. And it wasn't like I could afford a lawyer to get it done." She paused and added, "I went to college. Got my degree."

"It's been really bad times the last few years," said Robie.

"Worked hard, did all the right things. The American dream. Right."

Robie was afraid she might start crying.

She took a quick sip of coffee. "What do you want to know?"

"The night the bus blew up? What can you tell me?"

She nodded. "I've been sleeping behind a Dumpster the last couple of weeks. Nights haven't gotten too cold yet. Last winter was a bitch. Didn't think I was going to make it. January was my first month on the street."

"That's rough."

"I thought something or someone would come through. Half my friends are like me. The other half will have nothing to do with me."

"Family?"

"None that are in a position to help anymore. It's just me now."

"Where did you work before?"

"Admin support for a construction company. Like the worst possible job to have in this economy. I was just an expense item, generated no revenue. I was one of the first to go even though I'd been there twelve years. No severance, no health care, nothing. Salary stopped but the bills sure didn't. Then my unemployment benefits ran out. I fought to keep my home for a year. Then my husband got sick. That sucked what little savings we had and left a whole ton of bills. Then he gets better and off he goes. For better pastures, he told me. Can you believe that shit? What happened to the marriage vows for better or worse?"

She glanced up at him, looking ashamed. "I know you don't need to hear this."

"I can understand how you might need to get it off your chest."

"I've already vented plenty, thanks." She finished her breakfast and pushed the plate away.

She took a few moments to collect her thoughts. "I saw the bus come down the street. It was really noisy so it woke me up. I don't sleep well on the street. Concrete isn't too comfortable. And it's just not . . . well, safe. I get scared."

"I can see that."

"And then the bus stopped, right there in the middle of the street. I remember sitting up and leaning around the Dumpster and wondering why it had stopped. I've been over to that bus terminal going through the trash cans. It wasn't a city bus. It goes up to New York. Leaves same time every night. Seen it before. Sometimes I wish I were on it."

Not that night you don't, thought Robie.

"What side of the street were you on? Side facing the bus door or the other side?"

"The door was on the other side."

"Okay, go on."

"Well, it just blew up. Scared the hell out of me. Saw stuff flying everywhere. Seats, body parts, tires. It was horrible. I thought I was in the middle of a war zone."

"Did you see anything that might have caused the bus to explode?"

"I just assumed it was a bomb on the bus. You mean it wasn't?"

"We're still trying to figure it out," said Robie. "But if you saw something, anything impact the bus, that could be important. A shot fired into the gas tank, maybe? Did you see or hear anything like that?"

Jordison shook her head slowly. "I know I didn't hear a shot."

"Did you see anyone?"

Robie stared directly at her but hid the tension he was feeling.

"After the bus blew up, I saw two people on the other side of the street. Before the bus was blocking my view. But then there wasn't any more bus. A man and what looked to be a girl, maybe a teenager."

Robie sat back but kept staring at her. "Can you describe them?"

Better it come out now, he thought.

"The girl was short, wearing a hooded coat, so I didn't see her face."

"What were they doing?"

"Getting up. Well, the guy was. The blast must've knocked them both down. Maybe knocked them out. I guess I was far enough away and the Dumpster I guess acted as a barrier. But they must've been closer. They were on the other side of some parked cars."

"What happened next?"

"The guy came to first and then he went over and helped the girl up. They spoke for a few moments and then the guy started looking around the parked cars. That's when the old guy back there started dancing around yelling about s'mores. Then the guy and girl took off."

"Any idea where they came from?"

"No."

"What did the guy look like?"

She stared at him pointedly. "He actually looked a lot like you."

Robie smiled. "I guess I look like a lot of people. Can you be more specific?"

"I've got great eyesight. Had eye surgery done before my life fell apart."

"But there were flames and smoke between you and the man. And it was dark."

"That's true. I couldn't pick him out of a lineup, if that's what you mean. But the fire really turned night to day."

"But my height, build, age roughly?"

"Yeah."

"And you're sure you saw nothing hit the bus before it blew up?"

"Well, I was pretty wide awake by that time. But I didn't see or hear anything that would have made that bus detonate."

"Thanks, Diana. If I need to get back in touch with you, will you be around here?"

"I really don't have any other place to go," she said, her gaze downcast.

Robie handed her a card. "I'll see what I can do to get you off the streets."

Jordison's voice shook as she looked down at the card. "Whatever you can do, mister, I'd really appreciate it. There was a time when I didn't take charity. Figured I could get it done by myself. Those days are long gone."

"I understand."

Robie drove back to Donnelly's and was getting out of his car when Vance spotted him.

"We got a break in the case," she said after hurrying over to him.

"What?"

"ATF guys found the source of the detonation."

"Where?" Robie asked sharply.

"Wheel well of the bus, left side. Had a motion sensor. Bus starts going, engages the timer. A few minutes later, boom."

Robie stared at her, his mind racing.

The guy after Julie certainly wouldn't have gotten on a bus he had just rigged to explode.

That left only one explanation.

I was the target.

50

Robie spent an hour with Vance going over the ATF findings and then he slipped away and made a call to Blue Man.

"Her name is Diana Jordison." Robie described her. "She'll be hanging around the area where the bus detonated. She was very helpful and I think she might be more helpful down the road. But she needs to get off the streets. Too risky otherwise."

Blue Man said he would take care of it and Robie had to trust that he would. At least for now. He planned to check on that later. At the end of the day Robie could not trust anyone.

"I also want you to run down whatever you can find on a Leo Broome. Works somewhere on Capitol Hill."

"How does he figure into this?" asked Blue Man.

"I don't know if he does. But I have to cover that angle."

"That briefing, Robie. I want it soon."

Blue Man clicked off.

I want a lot of things, thought Robie. *I want a way out of this nightmare.*

An hour later he was back at his apartment. He took a shower and changed his clothes. He put his gun in a belt holster centered on his back and climbed in the Volvo, then texted Julie and received a response a few seconds later confirming that she was okay. He sent her another text saying he would be by to see her later and would probably stay at the apartment with her tonight.

He drove across town and pulled into a parking garage around the corner from the Old Ebbitt Grill, a Washington landmark that sat facing the east side of the Treasury building, which was located next to the White House. He snagged a space near the entrance.

Robie was here to keep his eight o'clock drink date with Annie Lambert. He entered the W Hotel and rode the elevator up to the rooftop outdoor bar, which was actually covered. Up here one could enjoy views from the White House all the way up to Arlington Cemetery in Virginia.

It was a weeknight so the tables weren't full, but there were about twenty people cradling drinks, munching snacks, and ordering off the bar menu. Robie glanced around but did not see Lambert. He checked his watch. He was about two minutes early.

He took a seat at a table next to the railings and gazed out over the cityscape. The buildings here were impressive. Anyone would think so. Well, probably not the people who were doing their best to blow them up. The waiter came over and Robie ordered a ginger ale. He sipped on it and constantly checked the door into the bar. On his fifth rotation he glanced at his watch. Fifteen after. Lambert might turn out to be a no-show. She might have wanted to call him, but he hadn't given her his number and he didn't have hers. Maybe late duties at the White House had interrupted her plans.

He was about to get up when she walked in, spotted him, and rushed over.

"I am so sorry," she said. She draped her coat over the back of the chair and sat down, setting her bag next to her. She had kept on her heels, he noted. Her sneakers were probably in the bag. Her hair was down around her shoulders and proved to be an attractive backdrop for her long neck.

"You fast walked over?"

"How'd you know?" she gasped.

"You wouldn't ride your bike with heels on, and you're pretty breathless for a short walk followed by an elevator ride."

She laughed. "Good deductions. Yeah, I left my bike at work and ran over. I got caught up in something right at five to eight. Had to get it done. And I did."

"Then that deserves a reward."

Robie waved the waiter over and Lambert ordered a vodka tonic. The waiter brought it back, along with a bowl of nuts and pretzels, and set it down between them.

Robie bit into a nut and took a swallow of his drink.

Lambert sipped her cocktail and snagged a handful of the snack mix and gobbled it down.

"Hungry?"

"No time for lunch today," she explained. "Or breakfast either, actually."

"You want to order off the menu?"

She ordered a cheeseburger and fries while he went with some spring rolls.

"My diet is not the healthiest in the world," she said. "Sort of an occupational hazard."

Robie settled farther back in his chair and prepared himself to engage in small talk. He had wanted to have a drink with Lambert. But now that he was here with her, it seemed crazy given all that he was confronting right now.

I can't be normal, no matter how much I want to be.

"I can understand that. You do much traveling in your job?" he said, trying to sound excited to hear her answer.

"No. I'm not officially high enough in the pecking order to ever be considered for a ride on Air Force One or even in any of the secondary planes. But I'm working hard and making a name for myself, and maybe one day, who knows, right?"

"Right. So you enjoy politics?"

"I enjoy *policy*," she replied. "I don't really get into the campaigning or election stuff. Energy is my specialty and I do white papers and briefing documents and I help write speeches for the administration in those areas."

"So energy is your background?"

"My undergraduate degree is in engineering. I have a Ph.D. in biochemistry with an emphasis on renewable energy resources. And we are running out of the fossil fuel stuff. Not to mention wreaking great harm through climate change."

Robie grinned.

"What?" she asked.

"Now you sound like a politician."

She laughed. "I guess the place rubs off on you."

"I guess it does."

Their food came and she bit eagerly into her burger and followed that up with several fries awash in ketchup.

Robie put duck sauce on one of his spring rolls and bit into it.

"So what about you?" asked Lambert. "You said investments and that you worked on your own."

"Actually, right now I'm doing as little as possible."

"You don't strike me as that sort. You seem way too intense to just sit around."

"I don't just sit around. I've traveled quite a bit, done some interesting work, made enough to take some time off, and that's what I'm doing now. As little as possible. But at some point that will end. You're right, I am too intense."

"Sounds nice, though. Just enjoying life."

"It can be. Or it can be really boring."

"I wouldn't mind trying it at some point."

"I hope you can."

She said, "How'd you end up in D.C.? Or are you from here?"

"I haven't met many people who are from D.C. I came from the Midwest. How about you?"

"Connecticut. My parents were from England. I'm actually adopted. Only child."

"You don't have an accent."

"I only lived in England until I was five. Now the only accent I have is a New England one, and not much of that, actually. Do you have any brothers or sisters?"

"No, just me. Wouldn't have minded some siblings."

"But kids don't really have any say in the matter."

"You sound like you wanted some brothers and sisters too," said Robie. He glanced over her shoulder after he heard a siren.

She looked at him resignedly. "It feels like we're just going through the motions, doesn't it?"

Robie didn't process this right away. When he finally did he looked at her. "What?" he said.

"Look, I know you said you wanted to get out more, and it was nice to have a drink together. But I'm not sure you're really here. If you know what I mean." She bit into a fry and looked down. She continued, "I mean, I'm just a policy geek. I'll never make much money. I'll spend my life at a desk writing well-researched papers that no one will ever read. And even if they do they'll spin them in ways I never intended. You've made a lot of money, probably traveled the world. I must seem pretty boring to you." She nervously picked up another fry but didn't eat it. She just stared at it like she wasn't sure what it was.

Robie hunched forward, coming out of his protective shell in more ways than one. He took the fry from her and bit it in half.

"I wanted to have a drink with you. If I didn't want to I wouldn't. And if I was going through the motions I apologize. I really do. I don't find you boring."

She smiled. "Did you like the fry?"

"Yeah. You want some of my spring roll?"

"I thought you'd never ask."

As they ate from each other's plates she said, "You probably don't usually eat fatty foods. I've seen you work out, of course. Do you run too?"

"Only when someone is chasing me."

She laughed. "My metabolism must be really high. I eat crap and never gain an ounce."

"A lot of people would like to have that problem."

"I know. Some of the women I work with say that too." She held out her burger. "Would you like a bite? It's really good."

He took a bite of the sandwich and wiped his mouth with his napkin. When he finished chewing he said, "I guess being at the White House is long hours, little exercise, eat when you can, and crazy schedules."

"Did you ever work there? Because you've summed it up pretty well."

"I don't think I'm White House material. Best and the brightest, you know."

"At least half the country would disagree with you on that."

Robie smiled and watched her munch away on her fries. He took in the view of the city.

Lambert followed his gaze and said, "Even though I work there it's still weird to see the snipers on the roof of the White House."

"Countersnipers," said Robie automatically and then regretted the slip. He smiled. "I watch a lot of *NCIS*. That's where I learned that word."

"I DVR it," said Lambert. "Great show."

They lapsed into silence again.

Robie finally broke it. "I'm sorry I'm not a good conversationalist. Has nothing to do with intent. Just tends to ebb and flow."

"Neither am I, so maybe we're very compatible."

"Maybe we are," said Robie. But now he found himself really wanting to talk. He looked out again, toward Arlington Cemetery on the Virginia side, up a hill. "When the Union took over Robert E. Lee's land and turned it into a military burial ground, they said General Lee could have his property back if he paid the back taxes. But the catch was he had to pay them in person. He understandably never took Lincoln up on his offer."

"I never heard that one."

"Don't know if it's true or not, but it's a good story."

"And you just disproved your point. You *are* a good conversationalist."

"I guess I have my moments."

"Do you like the investment business?"

"I used to," he answered. "But after a while simply making money doesn't seem like enough. More to life, you know."

"There's always more to life than money, Will," she said. "Money is just a means to an end. It shouldn't be the goal."

"For a lot of people it is."

"And there are a lot of people with screwed-up priorities. Especially in this town."

"Politician again," he said, making her face flush. "Want me to be your campaign manager?"

"Yeah. I can run on a platform of caring for others more than you care for yourself. That'll go over really big with the powers that be."

"Hey, screw them. Take your message to the people."

He watched her as she finished her meal. "So, really, what's next for you after the White House?"

She shrugged. "Just about everybody there has his life planned out forty years. They know exactly what they want and how to get it. Overachievers, I guess."

"Over-something," replied Robie. He was thinking

about Julie's similar answer when talking about the future.

Lambert added, "And when you work at the White House you're really dedicating your life to someone else, the president you serve. Your whole identity is connected to the success of someone else."

"Must be tough living your life that way."

"Frankly, I never thought I'd ever get this far."

"You must have done something right. Ivy League? Connections?"

"Guilty on both counts. My parents are pretty well-off and they're active politically, so I know they pulled strings to get me here."

"I think to get to the big white house you have to do it mostly on your own, because everybody at that level has strings to pull."

"Thanks for saying that. It's not usually what I hear." She pressed her napkin against her lips and studied him. "So what's next for you?"

"Maybe a change in direction. I've been doing the same thing too long."

"Change is good."

"Maybe. And maybe we can talk about it some more another time."

She beamed. "Are you asking me out?"

"Is there an interim step I missed? Can't go from drinks to date?"

"That's okay in my rulebook," she said quickly.

Later, when the check came, Robie picked it up

despite her protests. "It'll equal out," he said. This comment made her smile.

He walked her back to the White House. She'd explained that she needed to finish up a few things and retrieve her bike. Along the way Lambert slipped her arm through his.

When they arrived at the gate she held out a card. "All my relevant info is on here, including my desk at the White House."

Robie took the card. "Thanks."

"Is there a way I can get in touch with you?"

Robie gave her his cell phone number, which she inputted to her phone.

She leaned forward and kissed him on the cheek. "Thanks for a really nice time, Will. And let's work on that 'date' thing together."

"Count on it," said Robie.

A few moments later she had hurried through the White House gate.

Robie walked off, trying to put aside their encounter yet feeling the warmth of her lips on his face.

It was strange days indeed.

51

Robie stood in front of the terminal from where the doomed bus had left. In his mind he went over once more the events of that night. He had failed to kill Jane Wind and the backup shooter had done his job for him. Robie had executed his escape plan and come to this bus terminal to catch a ride out of the city. He had told no one. He had left no trail of any kind.

But I did reserve a bus ticket for that day and for that bus using an alias that only I was supposed to know existed. But someone else knew. And they were willing to kill all those people just to get me.

He glanced around. There was no way anyone could have planted that wheel-well bomb on the bus here. It had pulled into the terminal and people had boarded. As soon as the door closed after the last passenger, the bus had sped off. But there were other people around the terminal. Another bus was leaving soon to take people south to Miami. The bomber would have been seen. No, the explosive was not placed on the bus here.

Robie walked over to the terminal building. He glanced through the plate glass window and made sure the woman behind the counter was not the same woman who had sold him his ticket. It wasn't. He had confirmed earlier that there were no surveillance cameras either inside or outside the building. The company probably didn't have the money to spend on such things.

He went inside the terminal. It was as dingy as the buses used by the company. He walked toward the counter and stood in line behind a large woman with a baby clinging to her chest. Another child was in a car seat, which the woman was swinging back and forth. This image made Robie think of Jane Wind and her two kids.

When Robie got up to the counter the young woman looked back at him with a bored expression. It was nearly eleven and she probably wanted to get out of this place.

"Can I help you?" she mumbled.

He held up his creds. "I'm looking into the bombing of one of your buses."

She sat up straighter and looked more attentive. "Okay."

"I need you to tell me where the buses come in from before they arrive here and load up passengers."

"We have a maintenance and prep center two blocks from here. The driver checks in there, goes over the trip schedule, and then does a bus safety inspection. It gets fueled and cleaned there too, stuff like that."

"Give me the exact address."

She wrote it down and passed the piece of paper to him.

"Thanks," said Robie. "What time do you get off?"

She raised her eyebrows as though she thought he was hitting on her and was not pleased by it. "Midnight," she said warily. "And I've got a boyfriend."

He said, "I'm sure. You go to school?"

"Catholic University."

He looked around the depressing interior of the cinder-block building. "Study hard," he said. "And never look back."

He climbed into his Volvo and headed two blocks south.

The gate to the maintenance and prep yard was shut and locked. Robie finally got the attention of a security guard who was making rounds. The guy was suspicious until Robie flashed his badge. The guard unlocked the gate.

"Had some FBI agents in here already," the man said. "And some NTSB guys too, to see if the bus had something wrong with it."

"Did it?"

"Beats me. So what can I do for you?"

"Walk me through the prep for the buses."

"I don't really know that much about it. I just get paid to walk around with a gun looking for trouble. And in this area you usually find it."

"Who does know? Is that person here?"

The guard pointed to the old brick building. "Two dudes in there. They work until two a.m."

"Names?"

"Chester and Willie."

"They been here a while?"

"I've only been here for a month. They've been here longer. Don't know how much longer."

"Thanks."

Robie swung the door open and looked around at a cavernous space with high ceilings, rows of tube lighting, five parked buses, rolling toolboxes, generators, and work lights in grill cages. Everything was drenched with the odor of oil, grease, and fuel.

He called out, "Anybody here?"

A tall, thin black man dressed in work overalls walked around the front of a bus rubbing his hands on a dirty cloth.

"Can I help you?"

Robie held up his cred pack. "Need to ask you some questions."

"Cops already been by."

"I'm just one more cop coming by," replied Robie. "Are you Chester or Willie? Guard outside told me," he added when the man looked suspicious.

"Willie. Chester's under a bus pulling a transmission."

"So run me through how the buses are processed."

"They come in maybe six hours before they're

scheduled to head out. We go over them in here. Got a checklist of maintenance items. Check the engine, coolant, tire tread, brakes, steering fluid, clean the inside of the bus, pick up all the crap people leave behind. Then we take it behind the building to the washing shed. Clean the outside. Then we gas it up at the fueling station near the front gate. Then it sits until the driver checks in and takes it to the terminal."

"Okay."

"Look, I showed all them dudes the maintenance records. Ain't nothing on that bus made it blow up. I know we don't look like much, but we take our work seriously here. Had to be something like a bomb."

"Could you show me where the bus would sit?"

"Look, man, I got a ton of shit to do on three buses."

"I'd really appreciate it," said Robie, motioning to the door.

Willie sighed and led him out and around the building. He pointed to a spot near the fence. "They're parked right there until the driver shows up."

"How many buses were sitting here the night the one blew up?"

"Two. Side by side. The one heading to New York and one heading south to Miami."

"Okay, somebody looking to put a bomb on a particular bus. How would they know which was which?"

"You asking me to think like some maniac?"

"Nothing on the bus exterior to tell them?"

"Oh sure, there's a number on the front of the bus. The 112 goes to New York. The 97 bus goes to Miami."

Robie said, "So whoever put the bomb on there would be able to tell which bus was which if they had the bus schedule or checked online?"

"I guess that's right."

"Or if they worked here."

Willie took a step back. "Look, man, I ain't got no idea how somebody put a bomb on one of our buses, if that's what happened. And I sure as hell didn't help them do it. I knew two of the people got blowed up. One was a friend and the other knew my momma. Went up to New York once a month to visit her granddaughter. Wore a damn robe on the bus. I used to think it was funny. Don't think it's funny no more. Almost gave my momma a heart attack when she found out."

Robie thought back to the bus ride, to the old lady in her robe who had been screaming.

"So the 112 goes to New York." He eyed the fence. Easy enough to get over. The bomber could have hopped the fence when the guard was on the other side of the property. Plant the bomb and then be gone. Less than a minute.

He looked at Willie. "That night, how long was the 112 bus sitting out here before the driver showed?"

Willie thought about this. "Didn't have much work

to do on it. It got in early from the last trip. Chester did the checklist, vacuumed the interior. I did the outside wash, fueled and then parked it. Maybe two-three hours."

Robie nodded. "Did you notice anyone suspicious around?"

"I'm inside most of the time working on the buses. Guard might have seen something, but probably not."

"Why's that?"

"He does more eating in his little guard shack than walking, you get my drift. Why he's so fat."

"Okay."

"Can I get back to work now?"

"Thanks for the information."

Willie left him and walked back into the building.

Robie stood there in the dark and eyeballed the spot the 112 bus had been in. Bomber did the bus. Robie got on the bus. Robie got off the bus. Bus blew up. They sent a shooter into the alley to finish the job. Someone really wanted him bad.

Another thought occurred to him. *But maybe not that bad.*

"Doing some private sleuthing on your off time?"

He turned and looked through the chain-link fence.

Nicole Vance was staring back at him.

52

Robie walked through the open gate.

"Where have you been all this time?" asked Vance.

"Let's go back to Donnelly's," said Robie.

"Why?"

"I want to check something I should have already checked."

Fifteen minutes later Robie stood in the same spot he had on the night an MP-5 had tried to rip his life away. He eyed where the SUV had been, then his defensive position behind the trash cans, and then over his shoulder at the shattered plate glass window. He walked back and forth and framed, in his mind's eye, the shot pattern of the attackers.

"Total number of dead and wounded as of right now?" he asked Vance, who was watching him.

"Six dead, five wounded. One's still in the hospital but looks like he'll make it."

"But not us," said Robie.

"What?"

"We're not dead."

"A somewhat obvious deduction," Vance said dryly.

"Eleven people shot, six fatally, and yet the shooter misses us? We were the closest target, right out in the open. Aluminum trash cans the only thing between us, thirty-round clips, and a cooler bed at the D.C. morgue."

"You're saying the shooter missed us on purpose?"

He looked over to find Vance staring at him, a perplexed look on her face.

"How does that make sense?" she asked.

"How does it make sense that the guy missed us at basically point-blank range with a weapon that is designed for mass destruction in narrow fields of fire? There should be at least eight dead, including you and me. Look at the shot pattern. He was firing *around* us."

"Then are you saying they killed all those people for what? A warning? Something to do with the Wind case? The bus bombing?"

Robie didn't answer her. His thoughts were racing ahead, taking him in a direction he had never expected to go.

"Robie?"

He turned to her.

Vance said slowly, "I guess looking at it that way, what you're saying makes sense. I guess we should be dead. Then it has to relate to the Winds, or the bus, or maybe both."

"No it doesn't."

"But Robie—"

He turned back away from her to stare at the spot

on the street again from where the SUV had launched its attack.

Someone has tagged me. Someone is playing mind games with me. Someone close is trying to get to me, screw with me.

"Robie, do you have any other enemies?" asked Vance.

"None that I can think of," he said absently.

Other than a few hundred, he thought.

"Is there something you're not telling me?" she asked.

He broke off his thoughts and rubbed the back of his neck. "Do you tell me everything?"

"What?"

He faced her. "Do you tell me everything?" he demanded.

"I guess not."

"Then you have your answer."

"But you told me I could trust you."

"You can, but you have your agency and I have mine. I'm assuming you'll tell me everything you can and I'll do the same. I've got people to report to and so do you. It all has limits. But that doesn't mean we can't work together to get the job done."

Vance glanced down at her feet, poked a cigarette butt lying on the street with the toe of her shoe. "So you find anything over at the bus maintenance shop that you *can* tell me?"

"That bus was parked there a long time, long enough for someone to plant the bomb on it."

"So the bomber knew the target was going to be on the bus."

"Do we have a passenger list?"

"Only partially. For those who paid with a credit card, not for those who paid with cash, unless a family member or friend came forward and told us a person was on the bus."

"So how many people on the bus?"

"Thirty-six plus the driver. We're doing background checks on all known persons that were on the bus. That's twenty-nine people. That leaves eight unaccounted for. They were probably walk-ups that night who paid cash for the tickets."

Robie thought, *That includes Julie and the hit man.*

"Can I see the list?"

She slipped out her phone and hit some buttons. She held the screen out to him.

He ran his gaze down the list. Julie wasn't on it. And thankfully neither was Gerald Dixon, which meant Julie had not used his credit card to buy her ticket. But no other name on the list meant anything to him, other than the alias Robie had reserved his ticket under.

Okay, he had been the target, not Julie. But then why really try and kill him on the bus and then miss him on purpose when the MP-5 had him in the kill zone?

The plan changed, that's why. They wanted me dead. Now they want me alive. But why?

"Robie?"

He looked up from the screen to find Vance gazing at him.

"I don't recognize anyone on that list." His lies to her were piling up quickly.

"So we still don't know the target."

Robie did not want to lie to her again so soon, thus he said, "Anything new on Rick Wind?"

"ME did the post. Cause of death was suffocation."

"How?"

"Petechial hemorrhaging was the main clue. But he wasn't initially sure how it was accomplished. No pillow over the face, nothing like that."

"Why hide the manner of the killing?" asked Robie as he drew in a long breath.

"Harder to find out who did it."

"Maybe, maybe not."

"But he did find out the manner of killing eventually."

Robie looked at her. "And you couldn't tell me that first why?"

"I like melodrama."

"How was he killed, Vance?" Robie said sharply.

"They forced his severed tongue down his throat and wedged it there. They used his own cut-out tongue to kill him," she said just as sharply.

"Thanks," he said tersely.

"Look, Robie. If the killing of Jane Wind and her husband and the bus exploding are connected, there have to be some common denominators."

"The only reason you think they're connected is

because of the gun. That gun wasn't used to kill Jane Wind and her son. As I said before, whoever was in that apartment could have just flung it away after he got out of the apartment. It could have nothing to do with the bus exploding."

"Or it could."

"You really believe that or do you just want to have a terrorist bust and a murder conviction on your résumé?"

"My résumé is doing just fine with or without this case," she snapped.

"All I'm saying is don't have tunnel vision on this. If the cases aren't connected then trying to hook them together is not smart. You make assumptions and decisions based on those assumptions that you otherwise wouldn't make. And you pound round pegs into square holes in the process. You get an answer but it'll be the wrong one. And it's doubtful you'll get a second chance to make it right."

She folded her arms across her chest. "Okay, what would you do?"

"Work both cases, but in parallel. You don't cross the streams unless you have solid evidence of a connection. And that means something more than a gun near the scene."

"Okay, that makes sense, actually."

Robie checked his watch. "I'm going to grab a few hours' sleep. Anything shakes loose you can wake me up."

"You have a place to sleep now? If not, you're welcome to crash at my place."

Robie glanced at her. "You sure about that?"

"Why wouldn't I be?"

"You were afraid people might give you shit, even though I'm on the couch."

"You don't talk. I don't talk. And even if it gets out, it was all professional, so screw them. So I can do you the favor."

"I've got a place. That changes, I'll let you know. Thanks."

He walked to his car. He had turned her down for a specific reason.

In his line of work favors were almost never free.

And he wanted to check on Julie.

53

Robie unlocked the door and turned off the alarm system. He shut and locked the door behind him and reset the alarm.

"Julie?"

He moved down the hall, his hand on the butt of his weapon.

"Julie?"

He cleared three rooms before reaching her bedroom. He eased the door open. She was asleep in the bed. Just to be sure, Robie watched the steady rise and fall of her chest three times. He closed the door and walked down the hall to his bedroom.

He sat on the bed but did not undress. He felt hot and cold at the same time.

His phone rang. At first he thought it might be Vance, but it wasn't.

It was Blue Man.

He answered. "Got anything for me?" he asked.

"Leo Broome's a Fed. Works as a public liaison officer."

"For what agency? DOD?"

"No. DOA."

"The Agriculture Department?" exclaimed Robie. "You're kidding me."

"No, I'm not."

"What else in his background?"

"It's being emailed to you right now. Take a read. And see what hits you."

"There has to be something there," said Robie.

"Then find it."

Robie's email inbox buzzed. He hit the requisite keys and brought up the story of Leo Broome's professional life. He read it over carefully. Then he read it again, putting in order certain elements that seemed most promising.

"What are you doing up?" he said, without looking at her.

Julie stood there in sweatpants and a long-sleeved T-shirt and looking sleepy. "How did you know I was even standing here? I made no noise."

"Everyone makes noise regardless of what they're doing."

"I think you have eyes in the back of your head, Will."

"I wish I did, actually."

She sat in a chair across from him. "Find out anything?"

"Yes. But not much makes sense."

"Tell me the part that does."

"I think I was the target of the bomb, not you."

"That's comforting. So I only had one person trying to kill me?"

"Leo Broome works for the Department of Agriculture."

"Any spies work there?"

"Doubtful. While lucrative, corn subsidies don't really get bad guys all that excited."

"So what's the connection?"

"Might not be any. Then again, there might."

Robie held his phone screen up. "Broome was also in the army. Gulf One."

"So?"

"The woman and child who were killed? Her ex-husband was also found murdered. He was in the military as well. Maybe he and Broome knew each other."

"And if they did, what would they know that would get them killed? And how does that tie into my parents being murdered?"

"I don't know. I'm still working on the possible theories."

"And whoever blew up the bus, you said they wanted to kill you. Why?"

"For things I can't talk about with you."

She sat there looking at him. Robie wasn't sure what her next question would be, but he doubted he could answer it truthfully. He glanced around the confines of the room. For a long moment he felt acutely claustrophobic.

"What do you think they did with my parents' bodies?"

This was not one of the questions Robie had been anticipating, but it was certainly an understandable one. He studied Julie, trying to read something deeper in her question than was probably there. She was still just a kid, despite the street cred, despite the brains. She was grieving for her parents. She wanted to know where they were. He got that.

"Probably in a place we'll never find," said Robie. "Remember them as you knew them. Don't think about where they are now, okay? It won't do you any good."

"Easy to say."

"Yes, it is easy to say, but I think it needed to be said."

Robie waited for her to break down and cry. Kids were supposed to do that, or so he'd been told. He had never done it when he was a child. But his childhood had not been normal in any possible way.

But Julie did not break down. She did not sniffle. She did not cry. She glanced up at him and the look on her face was cold.

"I want to kill whoever did this."

"The guy who did it was on that bus. He's just ash. Stop worrying about him. He's over."

"I'm not talking about him and you know it."

"Killing someone is not as simple as it sounds."

"It would be for me."

"You kill someone you leave a piece of you with them."

"That sounds like a line from some stupid movie."

"It may sound like it, but that's exactly how you feel."

"You know a lot about that?"

"What do you think?" he said stiffly.

She glanced away and rubbed her hands nervously together.

She said, "Could it be that this Wind guy told something to the Broomes, who told something to my parents?"

"Yes, it could. In fact, that's my most promising line of investigation."

"And you're doing this part with super agent Vance?"

Robie didn't answer her.

"So you're not working with her on this?"

"I'm working with her on *part* of this."

"Okay, I get that."

"Do you?" Robie asked.

"I want to be part of it too."

"You are. You've been helping me."

"But I want to help more."

"You mean you want to find the people responsible and kill them?"

"Wouldn't you?"

"Maybe. But you have to think it through."

"Will you help me kill them? I know you can."

"You need to go back to bed," he said quietly.

"The kid gets in the way, right? That's what you're figuring, isn't it? Put me in that box?"

"I'm not going to be a part of putting you in any box, least of all a coffin."

Julie visibly stiffened at this comment.

He said slowly, "What you have to get is that this is not a game, Julie. It's not a movie, TV show, or PlayStation crap. You want to kill them. Fine, I get that. It's natural. But you're not a killer. You hate them, but you won't be able to kill them when it comes to it. But keep one thing in mind."

"What's that?" she asked in a strained voice.

"They want you dead. And when they get the chance, they won't hesitate for a second. You'll be dead. And there's no reset button to hit."

"What if I told you I don't care?"

"I'd say you're young and think you're immortal."

"I know I'm going to die one day. The only question is when and how."

"And the answers should be eight decades from now and peacefully in your sleep."

"That's not how life works. At least not my life."

"It's not smart to be thinking that way."

"Look who's talking. You don't exactly lead a cautious life."

"My choice."

"That's my point. It is a choice. *My* choice."

She got up and walked back to her room.

Robie just sat there, staring at the spot where she'd been.

54

It was two a.m. and Robie had been asleep for exactly one hour and then his eyes opened. He knew from long experience that it was useless to just lie there. He got up, padded into the living room of his home away from home, and went over to the window. D.C. was asleep now, at least the ordinary citizens of the city. However, there was a vast world here that never slept. They were highly trained, highly motivated people who rose to the occasion during the night-time to keep their fellow citizens safe from harm.

Robie knew this because he happened to be one of those folks. It was not always so. He'd grown into the job over the years. That did not mean he liked it.

He put his eye to the telescope. The building across the street came into tight focus. He maneuvered the scope up to his floor. There were no lights on except for one.

Annie Lambert was on the move. Robie watched as she walked from her bedroom to the kitchen. She was dressed in black tights and a football jersey that came down to her mid-thighs. A New England Patriots jersey, he noted. That would not be too popular in D.C., where the Redskins were the favorite NFL team. But she was from Connecticut and the woman was in the privacy of her own home.

Some privacy, he thought guiltily. But he continued to watch.

She pulled out a book from a shelf against the wall, sat down, and opened it. She read and spooned yogurt into her mouth.

He was not the only one tonight with insomnia.

He felt embarrassed to be watching her again. He told himself it was for professional reasons. But that wasn't true.

He pulled out the business card she had given him. Before he could reconsider his decision he called her cell phone. He watched through the telescope as she put the book down, reached over, and snagged her phone off a table.

"Hello?"

"It's Will."

He watched as she sat up straighter and put the spoon down. "Hey, how are you doing?"

"Can't sleep. Hope I didn't wake you."

"I wasn't asleep. I'm just sitting here eating yogurt."

"Fast metabolism? Cheeseburger's already worn off?"

"Something like that."

Robie paused and gazed at her through the scope. She was twisting one strand of hair with her finger, her feet curled up under her. He felt his palms moisten and his throat get crusty. He felt like he was back in high school about to talk with the girl he had a crush on.

He said, "You know, there's a nice view from the top of our building. Ever been up there?"

"I didn't think you could get up there. Isn't it locked or something?"

"No problems with locks if you have a key."

"You have a key?" she asked. Her voice was tinged with the girlish glee of having been told a cool secret.

"How about I meet you at the stairwell in ten minutes?"

"Really? You're serious?"

"I don't call people at two a.m. unless I'm serious."

"You're on."

She clicked off and Robie watched in amusement as she leapt up and raced down the hall, presumably to change her clothes.

Nine minutes later he was standing at the entrance to the stairwell when she hurried up to him.

She had changed into a knee-length skirt and blouse and sandals. She had brought a sweater too, because it was a little chilly outside.

She said, "Reporting for duty, sir."

"Let's do it," replied Robie.

He led her up the stairs. When they came to the locked door to the roof he pulled out his pick tools and in a short time the door swung open.

"That wasn't a key," she said, smiling in admiration at his skill. "You just picked the lock."

"A pick is a key by another name. That's as close to poetic as I'll ever get."

She followed him up a short flight of stairs and through another doorway. The rooftop was flat and coated with a sealed asphalt top coat. It radiated a slight warmth.

Robie pulled out a bottle of wine from under his jacket.

"Hope you like red."

"I love red. Are we going to take turns chugging from the bottle?"

From his pocket he produced two plastic wineglasses.

He uncorked the bottle and poured out the wine.

They stood by the edge of the roof and rested their arms and glasses on the chest-high wall of the building.

"It is a beautiful view," said Lambert. "I guess I never thought about there being one from here. I just look out my window and see the building across the street."

Robie felt a pang of guilt as he thought about his vantage point from that building into her apartment. "Every place has a view," he said hesitantly. "Some are just better than others."

"Hey, that was poetic," she said nudging him with her elbow.

The wind blew gently across them as they sipped their wine and talked. The conversation was innocuous and yet helped to deliver a bit of a respite, of peace, to Robie. He had no time to be doing something like this, which was one reason why it was so important *to* do it.

"I've never done anything like this before," said Lambert.

"I've come up here before, but not with anyone else."

"I feel honored, then," she said. She looked out once more at the surrounding area. "It seems like this would be a good place to come and think."

"I can show you how to pick a lock," he said.

She smiled. "That might come in handy, actually. I'm always forgetting my keys."

Another thirty minutes passed and Robie said, "Well, I guess we should call it a night." He looked at his watch. "And you might as well shower and get ready for work. I guess you don't need much sleep."

"Look who's talking."

He walked her back to her apartment. She turned and said, "I really enjoyed this."

"So did I."

"I haven't met many people since I've been here."

"It'll happen. Just takes time."

"I meant that I'm really glad I met you."

She kissed him on the lips, letting her fingers linger against his chest.

"Good night," she said.

After she went inside Robie stood there. He wasn't

sure what he was feeling. Well, maybe he only hadn't felt it in a really long time.

Finally, he turned and walked off, more confused and unsure of himself than ever.

55

Robie got back to the other building a few minutes later. Part of him wanted to look at Lambert through the telescope, to see what her reaction had been to tonight. Although her kiss probably told him all he needed to know. He imagined her showering and getting ready for work. But maybe she would think about him today too as she went about the important work of the country.

And after that thought Robie refocused on what lay ahead for him. It was time for him to go back to work too.

He checked on Julie and found her sound asleep.

He showered, dressed, and left, setting the alarm.

He drove through the empty streets. His wandering was not aimless. He had places to go, more things to think through.

He passed an MPD cop car going the opposite way, its rack lights blasting blue streaks into the dark. Someone was in trouble. Or dead.

Robie's first stop was Julie's home.

He parked a block away and approached the house

from the rear. A minute later he was in the duplex. He navigated with a penlight through the dark interior. He knew what he wanted to look at.

Two people being murdered here had set Julie's flight in motion. The bodies had been removed and the place sterilized. To what degree precisely was the reason Robie was here tonight. At some point the Gettys' disappearance would prompt calls to the police. They would come here and find the place empty. They would connect that Julie was or at least had been in foster care. They would try to find her. They would fail. They would assume that the Gettys had gone off together for some reason—perhaps to escape accumulated debt or unpaid dealers who wanted payment for the drugs the Gettys were known to have used.

The police would put some time in, but not a lot. Without any evidence of a violent end to the lives of the Gettys, the investigation would be put on the back burner. Big-city police departments did not have the luxury of expending time and resources on cases like this one.

Robie stooped and studied the mark on the wall. Blood, to his eye, but the police might not even notice it. Even if they noticed it they wouldn't test it. That meant paperwork, tech hours, and lab time. And for what?

But that little smudge was telling Robie something.

Blood spatter. They got all of it except this spot. This spot is not hidden. It's in plain view. They should've cleaned it off, or painted over it like they did on the other section.

Robie straightened. That mark was a message.

The Gettys were dead. He had never doubted that.

But who was the message meant for?

They knew that Julie was aware her parents were dead. She had seen it happen.

Was it for one of the Gettys' friends? Who might want to talk to the police, but wouldn't if they knew they'd been killed?

That was a stretch, thought Robie. The friend might never see this mark or know what it was if they did spot it.

But I would find it. I would know what it is.

He searched the rest of the house, ending in Julie's bedroom. He shined his tiny light around. He saw a stuffed bear in a corner lying on its side. He picked it up, put it in the knapsack he'd brought with him. There was a photo of Julie and her parents next to her bed. He put that in the knapsack too.

He'd give them to Julie when he saw her again.

His next stop was Rick Wind's. Not his place of business where someone cut his tongue out and then stuck it down his throat. He was heading to Rick Wind's house in Maryland.

But he would not get there. At least not tonight.

His phone buzzed.

It was Blue Man.

"We found your handler. You can come and see what's left of him."

56

There was no stench. A burned body doesn't give off much odor. The flesh and bodily gases, the twin engines of forensic malodor, had been burned off. Charred remains carried a scent, but it was not a disagreeable one. Anyone walking into a fast-food burger place or the aftermath of an inferno had experienced it.

Robie looked down at the mass of blackened bone and then stared two feet over at Blue Man. His white shirt was crisply starched, his tie point dropped right at six o'clock. He smelled of Kiehl's facial fuel. It was a little after five o'clock in the morning and he looked ready to make a presentation to a Fortune 500 board.

Blue Man was staring down at the black husk that used to be a man. A man who had ordered Robie to kill a woman and her child.

"Hard to feel sorry about it, I know," said Blue Man, seemingly reading Robie's thoughts.

"Sorry doesn't really enter the equation, does it?" said Robie. "What do we know?"

"His name, position, and employment history. We

do not know his recent whereabouts, why he was turned, or who killed him."

They were standing in the middle of a park in Fairfax County, Virginia. To Robie's left was a Little League baseball diamond. To his right, tennis courts.

"I'm assuming he was toasted and left here recently," Robie said.

"Since no parents reported seeing this pile of detritus while attending their kid's baseball game last evening, I think we can assume that," replied Blue Man.

"How'd you find out?"

"We received an anonymous phone call with explicit information."

"We sure it's the guy? You can't get DNA off charred bone, can you?"

Blue Man indicated the left pinky of the body, or at least where the pinky had once been. "They very helpfully covered that finger with fire-retardant material. We removed the finger and made the match off that, both prints and DNA. It's him."

"Phone call, pink pinky. That was very helpful of them."

"I thought so."

"You said you don't know why he switched sides?"

"We're checking all the obvious ones: secret bank accounts, threats to family members, a change in political philosophy. Nothing definitive yet. The truth is we may never know."

"They're taking care of loose ends," said Robie.

"You think this guy would have understood his chances of survival were basically zero."

"All traitors should ultimately recognize that, and yet they do it anyway."

"Did you come up with any thoughts on Leo Broome?"

"Not yet."

Blue Man pointed to an SUV parked at the curb. "I think it's time for that briefing."

"I don't have much to tell you."

"I'm awake. There's fresh coffee in there. Whatever you can tell me will be more than I know right now."

As they walked to the vehicle Robie said, "You ever think about retiring or doing something else for a living?"

"Every day."

"And yet you're still here."

Blue Man opened the door of the SUV. "I'm still here. And so are *you*."

And so am I, thought Robie.

Robie eased into the backseat. There was a space between him and Blue Man. He closed the door and pointed to two coffee cups in the holder between them. "They're both black. I don't like to cut perfectly fine coffee with cream or sugar."

Robie nodded. "Same with me."

Robie lifted the cup on his side and put it to his lips. Blue Man did the same with his.

Blue Man said, "Leo Broome?"

Robie could tell the man everything and probably should. But he had a natural disinclination to tell anyone everything. Actually, he had a natural disinclination to tell anyone anything.

"My handler is lying out there barbecued," began Robie.

"I wouldn't trust anyone either," replied Blue Man, again reading Robie's thoughts. "I can't force you to tell me what you know."

He let that statement sit there.

"What about heightened interrogation techniques?"

"Don't believe in them."

"Is that the agency's official position now?"

"It's my personal one."

Robie mulled things over for a few seconds.

"Like I said, the girl was on the bus. Her name is Julie Getty. A guy on there tried to kill her. I took him out. We got off, and the bus blew up. I lost my gun in the blast. We got away from the shooter in the alley and she's staying at my other place."

"Ties to Leo Broome?"

"A friend of Julie's parents, Curtis and Sara. I don't know why the guy on the bus killed them, maybe they knew something and had to be silenced. We need to check out their backgrounds. Whoever killed them probably thought Julie knew the same thing her parents did. She gave me the names of friends of her parents.

The Broomes were on that list. I went to their apartment. They were gone. And the place had been scrubbed."

"So they're either on the run or dead too," commented Blue Man.

"Looks to be."

"Broome was with the DOA. Not exactly the epicenter of espionage."

"He was also in the military, in Gulf One," replied Robie.

"That does open up some possibilities."

Robie eased forward in the seat, making the leather squeak slightly. Outside, the investigation continued as the techs tried to find any clue as to who had taken a human being and turned him into a kabob. Robie did not like their odds of success. Killers who guided you to the bodies didn't usually leave useful clues behind.

He took another sip of the coffee, let it warm his throat, get it lubricated to talk some more. Robie did not normally like to talk. About anything. But tonight he would make an exception to that rule. He needed help.

"There's something else," said Robie.

"I thought there might be," answered Blue Man.

"I thought initially Julie was the target on the bus. Now I believe that I was."

"Why?"

"Principally it's a question of timing. The bomb had to have been put on that bus hours before it left. Julie spontaneously decided to get on the bus after the bomb had already been placed. I had reserved a seat using an alias, an alias someone knew who shouldn't have known. They couldn't have known she would be on the bus. But they knew I would be. And that bomb had to be placed on the bus before I even got to the Winds' apartment."

"But why kill you? What do you know that can hurt them?"

Robie shook his head. "I can't figure that one out. At least not yet."

Blue Man said, "You should be dead, you know."

"You mean from the bomb blast?"

"No, from the shooting at Donnelly's."

"I know. They let me live."

"So they wanted to kill you before, but now they want to let you live?"

"Change in plan."

"Why? Do they need you for something?"

The way Blue Man said it made Robie look at him.

"You think I've been turned too?"

Blue Man stared over Robie's shoulder at where the forensic work lights were illuminating the remains of what had once been a man.

"Well, if you have been you can certainly see there's no future in it."

57

Robie drove north into Prince George's County, Maryland. Prince George's was largely working- and middle-class, with cops, firefighters, and midlevel government types making their homes there. Its more affluent neighbor, Montgomery County, had more than its share of lawyers, bankers, and CEOs who lived in massive houses on relatively small plots of land.

Rick Wind had lived on a narrow street in a neighborhood where people parked their cars and trucks at the curb and filled their garages with things their small homes couldn't contain.

There was a police presence here, though no crime scene tape was strung, for the simple fact that no crime had been committed here. Blue Man had had his people call ahead, and the officer on duty let Robie pass by after he showed his cred pack.

Since there might technically be usable evidence here, Robie put on latex gloves and shoe covers before entering the house. He passed through the front door and shut it behind him. He turned on the lights and gazed around. Wind's pawnshop business had obviously not been doing that well. The furniture was old and shabby, the rugs stained and worn. The walls needed painting. The smells that hit Robie were all deep-fried foods. Wind hadn't been here in a while to cook anything, so Robie assumed these aromas were buried deeply in the bones of the place, never to be eliminated until the house was knocked down.

There was a shelf against one wall. On it were a few books, mostly military thrillers, and a number of framed photographs. Robie picked them up one by one and saw Rick and Jane Wind and the couple's two sons, only one of whom was still alive.

The family looked happy in the pictures and Robie let his thoughts wander for a moment and wondered what had caused the marriage to break down. He put down the last photo and kept moving. Affairs of the heart were beyond his expertise.

He worked his way from the main floor to the top floor. And found nothing.

He searched the basement and again struck out. All he found was damp and mold and boxes filled with junk.

He stepped outside and entered the single-car garage through the side door. He assumed the police had thoroughly searched inside here, as well as the house, but they might not have been looking for the right things.

As I if I know what I'm looking for either.

A half hour later he sat down in a lawn chair in the

middle of the garage and gazed around. Staring back at him was a push mower, cardboard boxes, power tools, a workbench, a weed whacker, lawn and plant food, some sports equipment, and a combat helmet that Wind had obviously kept from his time in the Army.

Hanging from the helmet were Wind's dog tags. Robie rose and picked them up, read off the information. It was not very useful to him. He set the helmet back down.

This had been a wasted trip. But at least he could check it off his list.

He looked at his watch. It was after eight now. He called Vance.

"Got time for some coffee?" asked Robie. "I'll buy."

"And what exactly do you want for that?"

"How do you know I want anything?"

"I've finally figured you out. Nothing comes before the mission for you."

Maybe she does have me figured out.

He said, "Okay, how about the medical examiner's report on Rick Wind?"

"Why do you want that?"

"It's a piece of the investigation."

He heard her sigh. "Where and when?"

He told her, making the location close by for her and not too distant for him.

Robie drove back south, crossing over the Woodrow Wilson Bridge, where he ran into rush-hour traffic, but did a decent job threading his way through it.

Vance was already there when he arrived at the café on King Street in Old Town Alexandria.

He sat down and noted that she had ordered a coffee for him.

"I know how you like it," she said, spooning some sugar into her cup. "From when you were at my place," she added unnecessarily.

"Thanks. Do you have the report?"

She slid a file out of her bag and passed it to him. It was filled both with photos of Wind's body from every angle and a detailed analysis of his physical condition and cause of death. Robie studied the pages while he drank his coffee.

Vance said, "You look like you've been up all night."

"Not all night. Just most of it."

"Don't you need to sleep?"

"I get three solid hours a night just like everybody else."

She snorted and sipped her coffee. "Find anything interesting?"

"Wind wasn't in the greatest shape. Heart disease and a bad kidney, and report said his liver and lungs were suspect too."

"He fought in the Middle East. You know all the crap they used over there? It can do stuff to you."

"Can it?" asked Robie.

"My older brother fought in the First Gulf War. He died at forty-six. His brain looked like Swiss cheese."

"Gulf War syndrome?"

"Yep. Never got much traction in the news. Too many defense dollars stacked against it. Truth could never get out."

"I'm sorry about your brother."

Robie put the file down.

She said, "So, you find anything useful?"

"Interesting tattoo on his left forearm."

He slid the photo of the arm out and showed it to her.

"I know. I wondered what that was," said Vance.

"You don't have to wonder anymore. It's a Spartan warrior in a hoplite battle stance."

"What?"

"Did you ever see the movie *300*?"

"No."

"It depicted a battle between the Greeks and the Persians. Persia had a far bigger army, but the Greeks used a bottleneck in the terrain to hold off the superior force. A way around this was provided to the Persians by a traitor. The Spartan king sent the vast part of the Greek army away while he stayed back with a small contingent of Spartans to take on the Persians. They were the three hundred depicted in the movie. They used the hoplite battle formation. Close ranks, many rows deep, shields up, spears out. They were killed to a man, but it took the Persians a long time to do it. By then the Greek army had escaped."

"Interesting history lesson."

“Makes sense for Wind to have a tattoo like that. He was in the infantry. You mind if I keep this file?”

“Go ahead. I have copies. Anything else?”

“Not really, no.”

Her phone buzzed.

“Vance.”

She listened and Robie noted her eyes widened considerably.

She clicked off and looked at him. “I think we just got the break we needed.”

“Really?” Robie took a sip of coffee and looked casually at her.

“We just had someone come forward. An eyewitness to the bus blowing up. She apparently saw everything.”

“That’s great,” said Robie. “Really great.”

58

"You want to follow me over?" Vance asked, rising from the table in the café.

Robie looked up at her. "I've got a meeting at DCIS I have to get to. Where are you going to be questioning the woman? WFO?"

"Yes."

"I can hook up with you there later. What's her name? What was she doing there? And why is she only coming forward now?"

Robie was thinking, *Did the homeless woman Diana Jordison get past Blue Man's guys and go to the FBI? If so, she might tell Vance about her meeting with me.*

"Her name is Michele Cohen. I don't have the other information yet, but I will soon enough. Give me a call when you're on your way."

They parted company at the door. Robie hustled back to his car and drove off. He got on the phone to Blue Man and filled him in.

The man's remarks were terse. "I would stay away from this eyewitness if I were you."

"I think I had that one covered on my own. But

find out what you can about her. Do you have Jordison?"

"She's doing fine and eating quite well. She's cleaned up and has new clothes. Does our help include finding her suitable employment?"

"Yes, it does, preferably somewhere other than here. And make sure she gets a nice bump in salary over what she was making."

Robie clicked off and sped up. Something had just occurred to him. He needed to talk to Julie. And he didn't want to do it over the phone.

She was waiting for him when he opened the door.

"I'm not sure how much longer I can just sit in this place and do nothing, Will."

He closed and locked the door behind him. He sat across from her. She wore jeans, a sweatshirt, lime green Converse tennis shoes, and an exasperated attitude.

"I'm juggling lots of balls," he said. "I'm doing the best I can."

"I don't want to be one of the little balls you're juggling," she shot back.

"I've got a question for you. Depending on how you answer might change the complexity of everything."

"What is it?"

"Why the bus? More particularly, why that bus on that night?"

"I don't understand."

"It's a simple question, Julie. There are lots of ways

you could've gotten out of town. Why did you choose that way?"

If her answer was what he thought it would be, things were going to get more complicated than they already were. His head started to throb at that possibility.

"My mom sent me a note."

"How? You said you didn't have a cell phone."

"She sent the note to my school. She did that a lot. They put it in your mailbox and they send an email to your advisor that a student has a note. I went to the office and got it."

"When did she send it?"

"I guess the day I left the Dixons'. It was hand-delivered."

"Did the office say your mom had delivered it?"

"No, I just assumed."

"What did the note say?"

"It said to come home that night. That my mom and dad were going to make some changes. Get a fresh start."

"Sounds like they were moving."

"I wasn't sure about that, but I knew that could be a possibility. All I know is as soon as I got the note I wanted to get out of the Dixons' house. I dropped off those photographs of them at the foster care agency that night."

"But what about the bus?"

"That was in my note too. Mom said if they weren't

home when I got there I was to go to the Outta Town bus station and take the 112 bus to New York City. They would meet me at the Port Authority Bus Terminal the next morning. They put cash in the envelope that came with the note."

"Did you recognize your mom's handwriting?"

"It was typed."

"Did she often send you typed notes?"

"Sometimes. She used the computer at the diner. They have a printer too."

"Why not just come to the school and talk to you directly?"

"She wasn't allowed to. I was in foster care. They wouldn't have let her in to see me. But she could drop off a note at the office."

Robie sat back.

She stared pointedly at him. "You think my mom didn't write that note?"

"I think the odds are very high she didn't."

"Why would someone else send me that information? And the cash?"

"Because they wanted you on that bus. And it was a pretty big coincidence that the moment you walk in the house, the guy comes in with your parents and starts shooting. And think about it, Julie. The man who killed your parents, do you really think he would've let you get away?"

"You mean it was all a setup? And he let me escape? So I'd get on that bus?"

"Yes. We wondered where your parents were from the time your mom got off work to when they showed up at their house. I think they were abducted and held until they saw you sneak in the house."

"But the bus was rigged to blow up. If they were going to kill me why didn't he just do it at the house?"

"I don't think that bomb was set on a motion timer to blow up. I think the plan was if we got off the bus they would detonate it remotely. If we didn't get off the bus, the bomb wouldn't have been triggered. We would have ended up in New York City. But that wouldn't have happened."

"Why?"

"The man who killed your parents was instructed to get on that bus and kill you. He obviously didn't know about the bomb or else he never would have gotten on. Loyalty is one thing, a death wish is something else. They were counting on the fact that I would have intervened when the guy made his move against you. Then the most likely result is we both get off the bus."

Robie thought, *Especially if they knew what I was running from.*

"You say 'we' as though we were paired together."

Robie said, "I think that's exactly what happened. We were supposed to team up."

"But why? Wouldn't they want us dead?"

"Apparently not."

"I could've gone to the police about my parents.

And you're investigating the case. Why would they have wanted that?"

"They might have correctly guessed you wouldn't have gone to the police. And maybe they *want* me to investigate."

"That makes no sense."

"If I'm right it makes sense to someone."

"But wouldn't they be afraid my parents had told me something? If they killed those other people because of that, why not me?"

"You already answered that question. You were in foster care, no access to your parents. No cell phone. When your mom told the guy you didn't know anything, I think they knew that was true."

Robie unzipped his knapsack and pulled out her stuffed bear and the photo he'd taken from her home. He handed them across to her.

"Why did you go back there?" she asked, looking down at the objects.

"To see if I missed anything."

"Did you?'

"Yeah. They wanted me to spot the blood. They wanted me to know that your parents were dead."

"I could have told you that."

"That's not the point. They also want me to know I'm being played."

"What about that guy in the alley with the rifle? If they wanted us to get away, why send him after us? The bus had already blown up."

"At first I thought it was a change of plan on their part. They didn't want me to live, but then they did. But now I think their plan all along was for me to walk away. But they knew I'd get suspicious if they made it look too easy."

"Easy!"

"I have higher standards than most people, at least when it comes to survival. They had to send someone else after me. It was probably the shooter from the Winds' apartment."

"But if they wanted you to live and me too, that means they need us for some reason," Julie said slowly.

"That's exactly what I was thinking."

"But why?"

"Nobody puts this much effort into something, kills that many people, without a damn important reason."

"And we're caught right in the middle of it," she said.

"No, we're caught right in the *front* of it," replied Robie.

59

Robie was on the move with Julie. He'd had her pack up most of her stuff in her knapsack without really giving any explanations.

He glanced at her from time to time as he steered the Volvo through traffic. She caught him doing it more than once and said, "Why do you keep staring at me?"

Why do *I keep staring at her?* wondered Robie. The answer was actually easy, if unwelcome. *I have somebody other than myself I'm responsible for and it's driving me nuts.*

His phone buzzed. It was Vance.

"Robie, you need to get down here," she said.

"What's up?"

"The eyewitness, Michele Cohen. She saw a man and a teenage girl get off the bus right before it blew up. She also said the man's gun flew away and landed under a car. That's the gun we found that ties into the Wind killing. So there is a definite connection. I was right."

"Where was she while all of this was going down? And why is she only coming forward now?"

"She's married and she was leaving a hotel in the

area after spending some time with a man other than her husband."

"Okay," said Robie slowly.

"We're having one of our techs put together a digital image based on her description of the man and girl. It should be ready shortly."

"Did she see where they went?"

"They were knocked out for a few seconds. But then they fled into an alley."

"And your witness just went home to her hubby?"

"Cohen was scared, disoriented. When she got home and thought about it, she finally decided to come forward."

"What's the background on her?"

"What does that matter?"

"We have to verify that what she's saying is true."

"Why would she lie about something like this?"

"I don't know. But people do lie. All the time."

"Just get down here. I want you to hear her story, and you might have some questions for her I haven't thought of."

"I'll be there as soon as I can."

"Robie!"

He had already clicked off. He slid his phone back into his pocket. It buzzed again, but he ignored it. He knew it was Vance calling back. And his answer would be the same.

"Problems?" asked Julie.

"A few."

"Insurmountable?"

"We'll see."

Julie picked up the file folder that lay between them. "What's this?'

"Not something you want to look at."

"Why not? Is it classified?"

"Not really. But it's an autopsy report on a guy."

"What guy?"

Robie glanced over at her. "What's it to you?"

"Is it connected to what happened to my parents?"

"Doubtful."

"But you're not sure?"

"I'm not sure of anything right now."

She flipped it open and looked at the glossies. "Gross. This is disgusting."

"What did you expect? The guy's dead."

Julie's hands began to shake.

Robie slowed. "Don't get sick in the car. I'll pull over."

"It's not that, Will."

"What then?"

She held up a photo from the file. It was a full-on shot of Rick Wind's right arm.

Robie was about to explain about the tattoo. But Julie broke the silence first.

In a quavering voice she said, "It's a Spartan warrior in a hoplite battle stance."

He looked at her in amazement. "How'd you know that?"

"Because my dad had a tattoo exactly like it."

60

Robie pulled the car to the curb, slipped the Volvo into park, and turned in his seat to stare at her.

"You're sure your dad had the same tattoo?"

She held the glossy up. "Look at it, Will. How many tattoos like this do you think I've seen in my life?"

Robie took the photo from her and studied it.

"Okay. His name is Rick Wind. That ring any bells with you?"

"No."

"You're sure?"

"Yeah, I am."

Robie looked down at the photo again. What were the odds?

"Was your dad in the military?"

"I don't think so."

"But you don't know for certain?"

"He never talked about being in the military. He didn't have any medals or stuff like that around."

"But he has that tattoo. Did you ever ask him where he got it?"

"Sure. It was really unusual. He said he was into

ancient Greek history and mythology. That's where it came from. He explained to me what it was."

"When did your dad start using drugs?"

Julie shrugged. "As long as I can remember."

"You're fourteen. How old was he?"

"I saw his driver's license once. He was forty-five."

"So thirty-one or so when you arrived on the scene. Lot of time before that he could have been doing something else. How long were he and your mom married?"

"I'm not sure. They never talked about it."

"They never celebrated anniversaries?"

"No. Just birthdays. In fact, just mine."

"But they were married?"

"They had wedding bands they wore. They signed stuff 'Mr.' and 'Mrs.' Other than that I don't know."

"Never saw any wedding photos? Never talked to any of your other family members?"

"No and no. They didn't have any family around. At least that they told me about. Both of them were from California—at least that's what they told me."

"When did they move to D.C.?"

Julie didn't answer. She gazed out the window.

"What's the matter?" Robie asked.

"Your questions made me realize I knew shit about my parents."

"Lots of kids don't know much about their parents."

"Don't lie to try and make me feel better."

"I'm not," Robie said evenly. "I didn't even know my parents."

She looked over at him. "So you were adopted?"

"I didn't say that."

"But you said—"

"So you don't know if your dad was in the military or not? I need to find out for certain."

"Why?"

"If he was in the military and has the same tattoo as Rick Wind it might be that they served together. Lots of grunts from the same unit did similar body art. If we can track that down, things might start making sense."

Julie said, "Can you find out if my dad was in the military?"

"Shouldn't be a problem. The Pentagon is great at keeping track of who served."

Robie slid his phone out, hit a speed-dial key, and was soon talking to Blue Man. He relayed his request and clicked off.

"We'll know soon enough," he told Julie.

"Why did you ask me when my dad started doing drugs?"

"No reason."

"That's crap. You have a reason for everything you do."

"Okay, he might have started using drugs in the military."

"Why? Do all soldiers use drugs?"

"Of course not, but some of them do. While they're in the military, and they keep it up after they leave.

And if he served abroad, he might have had access to them more readily."

"So this is all about drugs?"

"I didn't say that."

"You're not making much sense," she said irritably.

"Do you know how your parents met?"

"At a party. In San Francisco. And, no, I don't think it was a drug party," she added bitterly.

Robie put the car back in gear and continued driving. His phone buzzed again. He glanced at the screen. It was Vance.

Julie saw it too. "Sounds like super agent Vance really wants you to go and see her."

"Well, super agent Vance will just have to wait," replied Robie.

"An eyewitness to the bus explosion?"

Robie shot her a questioning glance.

Julie said, "Super agent Vance has a loud voice. Pretty easy for me to overhear."

"Yeah, that I got."

"Did the eyewitness see us?"

"Would seem so."

"I don't remember seeing anybody around that night."

"I didn't either."

"You think the person is lying?"

"It's possible."

"But if the person sees you? Big problem."

"That's right," replied Robie.

"How are you going to get around that?"

"I'll get around it."

Julie looked away from him and rested her chin on top of her knapsack. "If my dad was in the military why wouldn't he have talked about it?"

"Lots of people don't talk about their military service."

"I bet heroes do."

"No. A pretty accurate rule of thumb is the people who did the most talk about it the least. The blowhards are the ones who did squat."

"You're not just saying that?"

"I wouldn't lie to you about something like that. There would be no reason to."

"To make me feel better."

"Would it make you feel better if I lied to you?"

"I guess not."

He glanced over to see her staring at him.

"How's your calculus coming? I guess you're falling behind on your homework."

"I used the phone you gave me to go online and get my assignments. The teachers post them each day. I downloaded some files I needed and texted two of my teachers with some questions I had. And I emailed the school office and told them I have the flu, that I'll be out for a few days, but I'll email in my homework assignments and keep on top of things that way."

"You did all that online with a phone?"

"Of course. No big deal. I have a laptop, but I don't have Internet service on it. That costs money."

"In my school days we still used erasers and hard-line phones."

They drove in silence for a few more miles.

"If my dad was in the military, do you think he was maybe a hero or something?" Julie asked quietly.

This time Robie didn't look at her. He knew the answer she wanted by her wistful tone.

"Maybe he was," Robie said.

61

"Will, where are we going?" Julie asked.

They had driven across Memorial Bridge and were in northern Virginia. The day was crisp and clear. The sun drenched the area in a wash of intense light.

"Change of location for you."

"Why?"

"Never a good idea to stay in one place too long."

He peered in the rearview mirror just as he had been doing every sixty seconds.

There's no way anyone could have followed me. And if they have it won't do them any good.

He turned off after driving a few more miles and reached a gate. A man in uniform holding an MP-5 on a leather strap strode toward the car. Behind him Robie could make out another man, similarly armed, who was covering his partner.

Robie rolled down his window and held out his cred pack. He told the guard, "I'm on the list." The guard checked on this statement using his cell phone.

While they waited, two other armed men came forward. One looked inside the car. Next, the trunk of the car was searched and the underside examined. Julie's bag was looked through and a machine that could detect pulses behind metal and leather gave the Volvo the once-over. It confirmed that only two beating hearts were in the car.

The gate rose and Robie pulled forward, drove down a straightaway, and slipped into an empty parking spot.

He unbuckled his seat belt, but Julie just sat there.

"Come on," he prompted.

"Where?" she said. "What is this place?"

"Safe. For you. That's all you need to know."

"Is this like the CIA?"

"Did you see a sign saying that it is?"

"They wouldn't have a sign, would they? I mean, it's secret."

"If they didn't have a sign, how are the spies supposed to be able to find it?"

"You're not funny," she snapped.

"No, this is not the CIA. I wouldn't have brought you to Langley. In fact, I couldn't have brought you to Langley without getting into a lot of trouble. This place is a couple steps down but it's secure."

"So you're just going to drop me here?"

"Come on," he said again. "We need to do this, Julie."

She followed him across the parking lot and they were buzzed through the glass doors of a two-story building. They were met in the lobby by an armed guard and led back to a long, narrow conference room.

Julie sat while Robie paced.

"Are you nervous?" she asked finally.

He looked at her and finally realized that she was scared. And why wouldn't she be? he thought. This was a lot to deal with, precocious teenager or not.

He sat down next to her. "Not really." He looked around the room. "It's just better for you to be here."

"So is this like prison?"

"Nothing like it. You're not a prisoner. But we do need to keep you safe."

"You promise?"

"I'm telling you the truth, Julie, nothing more and nothing less."

She unzipped her knapsack. "Can I do some of my homework here? I've got some math problems to do."

"Yes, but just don't expect any help from me. I topped out at pre-cal."

Five minutes later the door opened and Blue Man entered. Tie knotted, slacks pressed, shirt starched, shoes polished. His features were impassive, but Robie could sense the irritation in the older man. He was carrying a manila file.

He looked first at Julie and then at Robie.

"Is this a good idea?" he asked Robie, indicating Julie with his free hand.

"A better idea than leaving her where she was."

"I told you it had not been compromised."

"I know what you *told* me."

Blue Man sighed and sat down across from Julie, who stared at him with interest.

Robie, sensing that some introduction was necessary, said, "This is Julie Getty."

Blue Man nodded. "I deduced as much."

"What's your name?" asked Julie.

Blue Man ignored her question and turned to Robie. "And what do you hope to accomplish by this?"

"I hope to accomplish keeping her safe. I hope to accomplish getting to the truth. I hope to accomplish getting to them before they get to me."

"Paranoia setting in?" asked Blue Man.

"You're late by about ten years on that," replied Robie.

"Do you two work together?" asked Julie.

"No," said Robie.

"Sometimes," amended Blue Man.

She looked around the room. "Am I supposed to stay here somewhere? This isn't, like, a house or anything."

Blue Man stared at Robie, who looked away. Blue Man turned to Julie.

"We can accommodate you here. Comfortably. We have certain quarters for, uh, guests."

"And Will's going to be here too?"

"I'll have to let him speak to that," said Blue Man.

Robie ignored this and said, "Anything on my queries?" His gaze flitted to the file sitting in front of Blue Man.

"Quite a lot actually. Do you want to hear it now?"

Robie glanced at Julie and then back at Blue Man with an inquiring look.

Blue Man cleared his throat. "I see no reason why she can't hear this. It's not classified." He opened the file. "Miss Getty, your father had a very distinguished military career in the Army."

Julie sat up straighter. "He did?"

"Yes. A Bronze Star with valor, a Purple Heart, and several other impressive commendations. He was honorably discharged, leaving the service with the rank of sergeant."

"He never talked about it."

"Where did he serve that he got the Bronze with the V-device?" asked Robie.

"Gulf One," answered Blue Man.

Robie spoke up. "Was his discharge based on anything other than him not re-upping?"

"There were some medical issues."

"Like what?" asked Julie.

"PTSD," replied Blue Man.

"That's post-traumatic stress disorder," noted Julie.

"Yes, it is," said Blue Man.

"Anything else?" asked Robie.

Blue Man glanced down at the file. "Some cognitive issues."

"My dad's brain was messed up?" Julie said.

"It was alleged that he had exposure to some materials that might have adversely affected him."

"DU?" said Robie.

Julie shot him a glance. "DU? What's that?"

Blue Man and Robie exchanged a look.

Julie saw this and hit the table with her fist. "Look, you guys can't just keep speaking this code crap and expect me to just sit here and take it."

"Depleted uranium," said Robie. "DU stands for depleted uranium. It's used in artillery shells and also on tank armor."

"Uranium? Isn't that bad for you? I mean if you're exposed to it?" asked Julie.

"There have never been any conclusive studies done that demonstrated the truth of that statement in a battlefield environment," Blue Man said matter-of-factly.

"Then where did my dad's 'cognitive issues' come from? And why did they discharge him if there was no problem?"

"I understand that he was a heavy drug user."

Julie glared at Robie. "Did you tell him that?"

Blue Man held up pages from the file. "He didn't have to. I could read the arrest and conviction reports for myself. All small-time, petty stuff. All quite stupid."

Julie stood and said defiantly, "You didn't know my dad, so you have no right to judge him."

Blue Man glanced at Robie. "She always this shy and unassuming?"

Robie didn't answer.

"And none of that happened while he was in the Army," added Julie. "Or he wouldn't have left just for medical reasons. They would have kicked him out or arrested him. So why did they discharge him?"

"As I said, cognitive issues."

"But not related to drugs. So it had to be something else," countered Julie. "And you read from the file. It said that he'd been exposed to this DU stuff and it had adversely affected him. That's what *you* said."

"Those were *his* claims. They were never substantiated. But I do see your point. I guess the Army thought there might be some validity to his claims."

"Did they run any tests on him?" asked Robie. "To see what the cognitive issues stemmed from?"

"No."

"They probably didn't want to prove that this DU crap messed with his mind," said Julie, glowering at Blue Man.

He said, "When you graduate from college, why don't you apply for a position in the intelligence field? From what I've seen you might have what it takes to be a first-rate field agent."

"I think I'll pass on that. I'd prefer to use my life in a more positive way."

Robie pulled out the glossy of Rick Wind showing the tattoo. "This is from Rick Wind's autopsy. Julie confirmed that her dad had a tat just like this one."

Blue Man looked at her. "Did they know each other?"

"I've never heard of Rick Wind and I've certainly never seen him before," said Julie.

Robie said, "Can we find out if they ever served together?"

Blue Man rose, went to a phone on a credenza, and made a call, while Julie looked down at the tattoo and Robie looked at her.

"You okay?" he asked in quiet voice.

"Should I be okay?" she snapped.

Blue Man returned to them. "We will have an answer shortly."

"Anything on this eyewitness?" asked Robie.

"Michele Cohen? Not yet. We're checking. She's definitely in FBI custody as we speak."

"If she can ID me and Julie?"

"That would be slightly more than catastrophic," Blue Man said.

"Maybe she's lying," said Julie.

"Maybe she is," agreed Robie. "But if so we need to find out her motivation."

Blue Man said, "How will you handle this with Vance? You can't keep ducking her."

"I'll figure something out."

But right now Robie had no idea what.

His phone buzzed. He looked at the screen.

"Super agent Vance?" said Julie.

Robie nodded. The text message was clear: *Come now or I'll come and get you wherever the hell you are.*

He phoned her back. "Look, I told you I was in a meeting," he said.

"Cohen gave us enough to get a BOLO on the two people from the bus."

"That's great."

"Might be a father and his daughter."

"Okay," said Robie. "You said the girl was a teenager?"

"Right. Light-skinned. The guy was much darker, according to Cohen."

"Come again?" said Robie.

"African American, Robie. Can you get your butt over here?"

"I'm on my way."

62

Robie sat across from Michele Cohen. She was in her late thirties, with soft dark hair coiled around a long neck. She was petite, about five-two, with a narrow build. She seemed nervous, and Robie would have been surprised if she weren't.

Vance sat next to Robie in the small conference room at WFO. She was making some notes on her electronic tablet while Robie stared across at Cohen. She had told him her story in great detail. Coming out of a nearby hotel seconds before the explosion occurred. Seeing the man and young woman get off. Being stunned and blown back against a wall when the bomb had detonated. Running down an alley to her car. Driving home to the suburbs where her cuckolded hubby was waiting for her and accepted her story of forgetting the time over dinner with a girlfriend.

The hotel had confirmed that Cohen had come in at the time she said she had. A man was also with her. His story had checked out. He was unemployed and had been for a year. There was no reason why either he or Cohen would lie about this.

And yet of course Robie knew they had lied.

She had given detailed descriptions of two black people getting off that bus before it had exploded, and Robie knew that had never happened. But he couldn't tell Vance that without revealing his own secret.

These people are playing me and Cohen is part of it. They've got me screwed between two packs of Semtex and I have no wiggle room. They're counting on that. They want to make me sweat and they're doing a good job.

He wondered if Cohen knew that he was the man who had gotten off the bus. Would she have been told that? Or did she simply have her part to play? Robie wondered where they had found her. Maybe she was a former actress who needed some fast money, and that was her limited role in all this. Yet she knew she was lying to the cops. To the FBI. That would not be done lightly. She had to be very sure that the truth would not come out. And there had to be a very large incentive for her to do this.

Well, if they want to play with me, then I'll smack some of it back at them and see how they like it.

"Have you ever cheated on your husband before, Ms. Cohen?" he asked.

This question got a stare from Vance, but he ignored it.

Cohen pressed a tissue to her right eye and said, "Twice before. I'm not proud of it, but I also can't change it."

"Have you told your husband the truth?"

This time Vance didn't simply stare. "What does that have to do with anything, Robie?" she exclaimed.

Again, he ignored her. "Could you pick the guy and teen out of a lineup?"

"I'm not sure. There was so much going on. And their backs were to me for some of the time."

"But you're sure they were African American? Even though it was dark, there was distance between you and them, and as you said, there was a lot of stuff going on?"

"They were definitely black people," she said. "I'm not wrong about that."

"But initially you didn't go to the police. You only did days later."

"I explained that to Agent Vance. I was worried about being exposed."

"You mean your affair being exposed?" amended Robie.

"Yes. I love my husband."

"Right. And I'm sure you're very sorry for being an adulteress, but your hubby probably doesn't understand you," said Robie.

This comment drew another hard look from Vance.

"I'm not proud of what I did," Cohen said stiffly. "But I did come forward. I'm trying to help your investigation."

"And it's much appreciated," cut in Vance, with another incredulous glance at Robie. "And despite my partner's comments he appreciates it too."

"Will that be all? Can I go now?" asked Cohen.

"Yes. I can have one of my people show you out. Agent Robie and I have some things to discuss."

As soon as Cohen had departed Vance whirled around on Robie.

"What the hell was that about?" she demanded.

"I was questioning a witness."

"You mean you were *interrogating* her."

"Same thing in my book. And for the record I think she's lying."

"What possible motivation would she have for lying? She came to us. We didn't even know she existed."

"If I knew that the case would be solved."

"Why are you so sure she was lying?"

Robie thought back to the passengers on the 112 bus. There were a number of black men. And at least two black teenage girls. They had been on the bus when it blew up. But the bus had turned into an inferno with the full fuel tank. Everybody had been hurled from their seats, burned beyond recognition, many of them down to bone. It would be nearly impossible to match remains with the passenger list.

Vance said, "There were at least six black men on the bus and three black teenage girls. The clerk in the depot that night remembers them. Cohen's story fits the facts."

"Doesn't matter, I still think she's lying."

"What, based on your gut?"

"Based on something."

"Well, I have to conduct my investigation on evidence gathered."

"You've never gone with your instincts?" he asked.

"Yes, but when cold, hard facts trump them, it's a different story."

Robie rose.

"Whcre are you going?" she asked.

"To find some cold, hard facts."

63

Robie knew a quick way out of the WFO and was in his car and waiting out front when Michele Cohen pulled out of the parking garage and raced down the street in her BMW coupe. He slid into traffic behind her. She cleared three yellow lights and he narrowly avoided being trapped behind the last of them. Ten minutes later they were heading up Connecticut Avenue toward Maryland.

Robie was keeping his eye on the Beemer and thus failed to see the two police cars converging on his Volvo. The cops hit their rack lights and the officer in the cruiser on Robie's left motioned him over. Robie watched the Beemer accelerate and pass through yet another yellow light. A few moments later it was out of sight.

Robie slowed his car and pulled to the curb. He wanted to jump out and start reaming the guys in blue, but knew that might get him shot. He sat there fuming as four cops cautiously approached, two on each side.

"Let me see your hands, sir," called out one of them.

Robie held his left hand out the window, with his federal badge in it.

He heard one of the cops mutter, "Shit."

A second later two cops appeared at his window.

Robie said, "I'm sure you guys have a terrific reason for pulling me over while I was tailing someone."

The first cop pushed his hat back and stared down at Robie's cred pack.

"Got a call from Dispatch that said a woman was being followed in her car by some guy. She was scared and requested we roll on it. She gave us your car description and plate number."

"Well, that's a good way for a perp to evade the police," said Robie. "Just call in more cops."

"I'm sorry, sir, we didn't know."

"Can I go now?" asked Robie.

"Is she really a suspect? We can help you run her down," offered the second cop.

"No, I'll catch up to her later. But in the future, don't be so quick to hit the panic button."

"Yes, sir."

Robie eased the Volvo away from the curb and pulled back into traffic. In his rearview mirror he watched the cops congregating around their cruisers, no doubt wondering if this screwup was going to cost them career-wise. Robie had no interest in derailing them professionally. It had actually been a clever, if ballsy move by Cohen. She could always claim she didn't know who was in the car, only that someone was following her. And she could tack on the completely true facts that she had just been to visit the FBI and was a valuable witness in a horrific crime and was understandably afraid for her safety.

No, Robie would have to go after her another way. Fortunately, it would not be that difficult to track Cohen down. Her home address was in the file Vance had let him read.

He crossed over into Maryland and worked his way through a number of surface roads until he reached the one he wanted.

Michele Cohen didn't live in a McMansion, but she did live in an upscale neighborhood. Yet according to Cohen she was unemployed. Her most recent job had been with a financial planning firm that had gone belly up. Robie didn't know what her husband did. Vance had not mentioned it, if she even knew.

Cohen probably could use the money, thought Robie. But he wondered if they had some other dirt on the woman. Money alone, he thought, would not get an otherwise innocent person to go along with lying to the FBI in a possible terrorist case.

Unless she isn't otherwise innocent.

He wondered if Vance had run a criminal check on Cohen. Or her husband. Or her alleged boyfriend. Possibly not, since Vance clearly did not think she was lying. Like she had said, why would the woman have come forward? Robie could think of at least one reason.

To screw with me.

He pulled his car to the curb and phoned Blue Man.

"Anything on Michele Cohen yet?"

"No, but you'll be the first to know."

"I need everything you can find on her husband too."

"Already doing it. So she lied to the FBI? Said it was two black people instead of you and Julie?"

"Yes."

"Her motivation?"

"Hopefully we can find it."

"Tricky move for the other side. They've exposed a pawn for us to exploit."

"I was thinking the same thing. That's why I'm nervous."

Robie eyed the end of the street where Cohen's Beemer was parked in the driveway of a two-story stone and siding home. "I'm going to check some things out. I'll call back in later. How's Julie?"

"Safe and sound and doing her homework. The calculus problem she was working on looked far beyond my pay grade."

"That's why we're in the intelligence field," said Robie. "We suck at math."

He put his phone away and checked his watch. Cohen would know he had been following her and would also know that he had her home address. His sitting out here would produce nothing useful.

But he had a better idea anyway.

He wasn't necessarily afraid of pawns. But nobody who knew what they were doing would leave one hanging out there without a good reason.

And now I need to find out what that reason is.

64

Michele Cohen poured herself a cup of coffee and carried it into the family room where the TV was on. She was alone. She set her cup down, picked up the remote, and changed the channel.

"I preferred the other program, actually."

She screamed.

Robie sat down in the chair opposite her.

"What the hell are you doing in my house? How did you get *in* my house?" she demanded.

"You should lock your doors, even while you're home," said Robie.

"I don't know who you think you are. But I'm calling the police. You were very rude to me today at the FBI. And I think you were following me earlier. I don't have to stand for this. It's harassment, plain and simple."

She stopped talking when Robie held the item up.

"Know what this is, Michele?"

She stared at the flat square box.

"Should I?"

"I don't know, should you?"

"I'm not going to sit here and play stupid mind games with you."

"It's a DVD. From a security camera."

"So?"

"It was pointed right at the spot where the bus exploded."

"If that was the case, why didn't the police know about it?"

"Because it was from a webcam a guy had set up in his apartment overlooking the street. I found it because I went door-to-door before the cops did. This guy had had some problems with burglars. Wanted to catch them in the act. It was on a rotation program. Clean sweep of the street. And it has a time and date stamp. Would you like me to tell you what it didn't see?"

She said nothing.

"It didn't see you, Michele, or your boyfriend, at the spot you said you were."

"That's ridiculous. Why would we lie about something like that? And the motel clerk backed up our story."

"I'm not saying you weren't at the motel. I'm just saying you're lying about what you saw. In fact, you saw nothing."

"You're wrong!"

"You said you saw the bus explode."

"I did."

"And you also said you saw the guy's gun fly off and land under a car?"

"That's right."

"That bus explosion would have blown thousands of pieces of debris all over the air. It would've been a shitstorm of stuff. And you, all whacked out from seeing a bus explode and lots of people die, you saw one little gun fly through the air, and you were able to follow its path, with all the other stuff going on, until it landed under a car?" He paused. "That is total and complete bullshit."

She jumped up and raced to the phone on the table next to the doorway into the kitchen. "I want you out of here. Now. Or I will call the police and have you arrested."

Robie held the DVD up higher. "And we both know that you didn't see two black people get off that bus, Michele. And the DVD will confirm that. So you lied to the FBI. That will get you at least five years in a federal prison on about three different felonies. No more working in the financial industry for you. And you'll be early forties when you get out. And prison is not easy on the body or the psyche. You'll come out looking closer to fifty. Maybe sixty if they're rough on you in there. And it's not just the guys who have the bitches inside, Michele. The ladies get lonely too in there. You'll be easy fresh meat. You're small and soft. You won't stand a chance."

"You're just trying to scare me."

"No, I'm trying to enlighten you on just how serious your situation is."

Robie set the DVD down on the coffee table. "Two people did get off the bus. But they weren't black."

"How do you know that?"

"Because I saw it on here, Michele. Now why don't you sit down and we can talk about this and maybe come up with a way out of it for you."

"Why would you do that?"

"Because I'm a nice guy, that's why."

"I don't believe that for a second."

"Believe what you want to believe. If I believed for one second that you weren't just a patsy in this whole thing I would've already arrested you. But if I can use you to get to the people I really want, then that's valuable. That's something you can negotiate with, Michele. Don't walk away from this deal, because you won't get another one."

He inclined his head to the spot she had occupied on the sofa.

Cohen sat, her gaze downcast.

"Drink your coffee," said Robie. "It'll help calm your nerves."

She took a sip and set the cup back down, her hand shaking.

Robie sat back, studied her. "Who told you to lie?"

"I can't talk to you about this."

"You'll either have to talk to me or the FBI. Which do you prefer?"

"I can't talk to the FBI."

"Why?"

She exclaimed, "Because they'll kill him, that's why."

"Kill who?"

"My husband."

"What's he got to do with this?"

"Gambling debts. He's way over his head. But someone approached him and told us there was a way out. All debts forgiven if we did this."

"Lie to the FBI?"

"Yes."

"Big risk."

"Prison over death?" she said incredulously.

"What does your husband do?"

"He's a partner in a law firm. He's a good man. A pillar in the community. But he has a little problem with betting. And he used some client trust funds to make up a shortfall. He'll be ruined if it comes out."

"Who were the people who got you to do this?"

"I never met them. My husband did. He said he was taken to a room, sat in the dark, and given an ultimatum. They told us everything we needed to do."

"Why were you chosen to do it instead of your husband?"

"I guess I'm cooler under pressure than he is. We didn't think he would be able to lie to the FBI."

Robie thought about this. Respectable couple, believable witness. No motivation to tell an untruth. Made sense.

"Who was the guy you were supposed to be having an affair with?"

"They supplied him. We just sat in the motel bedroom staring at the floor. Then we left at the time we'd been given. I didn't actually see the bus explode. I was told to say it was a black man and black teenager who got off the bus. And then the rest that you heard today."

"Where is your husband now?"

"Confirming that his gambling debts have been taken care of."

"You really think it will be that easy?"

"What do you mean?"

"You're a liability to these folks, Michele. Do you think they were going to let you and your husband live?"

Her face flushed. "But we don't know anything."

"What you just told me disproves that."

"You think they'll try to kill us?"

"What time is your husband supposed to be back?"

She looked at her watch and her face turned whiter. "About twenty minutes ago."

"Call him."

She grabbed the phone and punched in the number. She waited, the phone pressed to her ear.

"It went right to voice mail."

"Text him."

She did. They waited for five minutes and no text came back.

"Call him again."

She tried twice more, with the same result.

"Where was he going to confirm that the debts were canceled?"

"At a bar over in Bethesda."

Robie thought quickly. "Let's go."

"Where?"

"To the bar in Bethesda. We might be in time to save his life."

65

On the way Robie called Blue Man and requested backup. They would meet him at the bar.

Robie gunned the Volvo and glanced over at Cohen. Her face was tear-streaked and her breaths only came in short gasps that might have caused Robie to feel sorry for her under different circumstances.

She glanced at him, her look of misery deepening. “You think he’s dead, don’t you?”

“I don’t know, Michele. But that’s why we’re here. To prevent it if we can.”

“It seems so stupid now. Of course they wouldn’t just let him walk away. But it was the only chance we had. We were desperate.”

“Which made you the perfect people to approach.”

He made a left, a quick right, and pulled the car to the curb. “That the place?” he said, indicating a bar farther down the street with the sign “Lucky’s” above it.

She nodded. “Yes, that’s it.”

Well, I hope it’s lucky for us.

Robie looked around for his backup. He texted Blue Man. The reply came back almost immediately.

Sixty seconds away.

Cohen blurted, "That's Mark's car over there." She pointed to a gray Lexus sedan parked a half block down.

A few moments later an SUV pulled up behind Robie. He signaled to the driver. The man signaled back. Robie got out and escorted Cohen to the SUV. There were three men inside. Cohen got in the backseat.

"Stay put," he told her. "No matter what you see or hear, these men will take care of you, okay?"

"Please bring my husband back to me."

"I'll do my best."

Robie looked at the man in the passenger seat. "You want to come with me?"

The man nodded, racked his pistol, and put it back in the holster.

The pair moved down the street, their heads rotating side to side, looking for anything threatening. When they got to the bar Robie saw that it was closed.

He looked at his watch and eyed the other man. "Late opening time for a bar."

"You're right about that. How do you want to do this?" asked the other man.

"Give me two minutes to access the back. Then hit the front. We'll meet in the middle."

The man nodded and Robie skirted down an alley leading to the rear of this cluster of buildings.

He quickly found the back entrance to the bar. He didn't know if the door was alarmed and didn't really care. If the cops came, so be it. They might have to come anyway, depending on what Robie found inside.

He used his pick tools to beat the lock, pulled his gun, and slowly pushed the door open. It was nearly dusk outside, and totally dark inside. Robie wasn't going to risk a light. He was already a target enough without helping anybody to see his position better.

He let his eyes adjust to the low level of light and moved forward. As he stepped he listened. He checked his watch. His partner should be coming through the front door right about now.

Robie passed through the kitchen and saw nothing except pots and pans, rows of clean glasses and mugs, and a line of mops. The next room had to be the bar area. He would meet his guy there.

Only his guy wasn't there.

But someone else was, and Robie's attention was immediately captured by the person. He ducked down behind the bar and took in the room grid by grid, noting all possible shooting points. He waited another thirty seconds and then came out from behind his cover. The room was empty. Except for him and the other guy.

Robie approached the man sitting in the booth to the left of the front door. He was leaning back against the leather seat.

There was enough light coming in from the front

windows for Robie to see what he needed to. He thumbed 911 on his phone and spoke briefly.

He clicked off and eased over to the man.

Single gunshot wound to the head. Robie touched his hand. Cold.

He'd been dead a while.

Robie grabbed a napkin off a table and covered his hand with it. He snaked his hand inside the man's jacket and pulled out his wallet, flipped it open.

The name on the license was Mark Cohen. The man's picture, minus the bloody wound to his head, stared back at Robie.

He put the wallet back, looked at the front door.

Shit.

He raced to the door, unlocked it, and stepped outside. There were people walking up and down both sides of the street. Robie noted them and then his gaze went across the street.

His Volvo was there.

The black SUV was not.

He ran across the street and slid into his Volvo as he heard sirens coming.

He got on the phone to Blue Man. "Mark Cohen is dead and your guys took off with Michele Cohen. Want to explain that to me?"

Blue Man said, "I don't understand. They were two of my best men. My most trusted people. They were supposed to follow your orders."

Robie said, "There were *three* guys in the SUV."

"I only sent two."

"Then one of them tagged along, and I guess now I know why."

"This is unprecedented, Robie."

"I'll be there in twenty minutes. Go right now and check on Julie. Take a bunch of guys with you. They can't have bought off all of them."

"Robie, are you saying—?'"

"Just do it!"

66

When Robie raced into the secure building the first person he saw was Blue Man.

The second person he saw was Julie.

Robie's gut unclenched and he slowed his pace.

Blue Man said tersely, "Follow me, both of you."

They walked quickly down a hall. Robie saw that Blue Man had a gun in a belt holster.

Robie looked at Julie striding next to him.

She said anxiously, "Is something wrong, Will? What's going on?"

"Just a precaution. Everything will be cool."

"You're lying to me, aren't you?"

"Pretty much, yeah."

"Thanks for being honest about your dishonesty."

"Seems to be the best I can do these days."

Blue Man closed and locked the door behind them. He motioned for Robie and Julie to sit.

Robie gazed at the pistol. "You don't usually carry a weapon."

"We don't usually have traitors in the ranks."

"Michele Cohen?" Robie asked.

“Dead. Along with two of my men. The two I officially sent.”

“Where and how?”

“They just found the bodies in the SUV about ten blocks from the bar. Gunshot wounds, all of them.”

“Who was the third guy?”

“Malcolm Strait. Worked here for ten years. Impeccable record.”

“Not anymore. Describe him to me.”

Blue Man did so.

Robie said, “He was the guy who was supposed to come through the front door of the bar. Any sign of him?”

“Not so far. He no doubt had an escape plan in place.”

“What are we talking about?” asked Julie. “Who are these people?”

Robie looked at Blue Man and said, “I think she deserves to know.”

“Go ahead, then.”

Robie took a few minutes to fill Julie in.

She looked puzzled. “Why would they get this lady to tell an obvious lie? They had to know you would track her down, find out the truth. They would have had to kill her and her husband anyway to shut them up.”

Robie said, “You’re right. What did they gain by having Michele Cohen come forward with her story?”

Blue Man said, “Exactly. What did they gain by it?”

Julie said slowly, "Otherwise it was a big risk for them."

"Michele Cohen had no idea who had approached her husband," said Robie. "She said he'd gone to the bar to confirm that his gambling debts had been paid off. Instead he got a hole in the head."

"And so did his wife," added Blue Man.

"Who else did this Malcolm Strait work with here?"

"Lots of people."

"You need to talk to all of them. At the very least we need to learn if he left behind anybody."

"Agreed."

"So this guy might have somebody else here?" said Julie. She looked straight at Blue Man. "Not so safe a place."

Blue Man glanced at Robie and said, "We will find that out as quickly as possible. This sort of breach is highly unusual," he added, looking back at Julie.

"Well for me, it's one out of one," Julie shot back.

Robie said, "We can't stay here now. We have to move."

"Where?" asked Blue Man.

Robie rose. "I'll be in touch. Let's go, Julie."

Blue Man said, "Where are you going?"

"Someplace safer than this," said Robie.

Robie piloted the Volvo through the gate and turned left. "This is the spot where we could pick up a tail," he told Julie. "We're in a funnel here. Only one way in or out. So keep your eyes peeled."

"Okay," said Julie. Her gaze swiveled from side to side and then she turned her head and checked the rear.

As they pulled onto the main road and sped up, she said, "I don't see any car lights."

"How about a satellite overhead, can you see that?"

"Are you kidding? They could be tailing us with a satellite?"

"The fact is I don't know."

"So what do we do?"

"Hope for the best and prepare for something a lot less than that."

"Where are we going?"

"The only place I've got left. The little house in the woods."

"Pretty isolated if someone wants to ambush us."

"And far easier to see someone coming at us. Trade-off. Weigh the pros and cons. I say the pros win in this case."

"What about satellites?"

"They can't use a satellite to harm us. They have to have boots on the ground for that."

"They might send a lot of guys."

"They might. And then again they might not send anybody."

"But why wouldn't they?"

"Think about it, Julie. What's their endgame? This Malcolm Strait guy was inside that facility with you.

He could've killed you there. And they could've popped me a couple of times already, but conveniently missed."

"So they want to keep us alive, like you said before. With the bus and everything. But we still don't know why."

"No, we don't. But we will."

67

"Will, this isn't the way to your place," said Julie.

"Slight change in plan."

"Why?"

"Getting a little needed help and making a big confession."

Robie had made a decision, an unusual one for him. He had been a loner most of his life. He did not normally seek help from others, preferring to solve his own problems. Yet he had finally realized that he could not do this alone. He needed help.

Sometimes asking for help showed strength, not weakness.

Whether the decision would turn out to be the right one or a disaster, Robie couldn't know. Yet right now it was *his* decision.

He pulled into the condominium complex and got out of the Volvo. Julie trailed him inside the building. They rode the elevator up, got off, and walked down the hall.

Robie knocked on the door of 701.

He heard footsteps. They stopped. Robie sensed an eyeball looking at him through the peephole.

The door opened.

Vance wore black jogging shorts, a pale green Marine Corps T-shirt, and white ankle socks. She stared first at Robie, and then her gaze fell to Julie.

Julie exclaimed, "You're getting super agent Vance to cover your ass?"

Vance looked back at Robie. "Super agent Vance? What the hell is going on? Who's the kid?"

"That's why I'm here," said Robie.

Vance stepped back and let them pass through. She shut the door behind them.

Robie said, "Got any coffee? This might take a while."

"I just put some on."

"I like mine black," said Julie.

"Oh, really?" said a bemused Vance.

"Michele Cohen and her husband are dead," said Robie.

"What?" exclaimed Vance.

He sat on the sofa and motioned Julie to take a seat. Vance stood in front of him, hands on hips.

"Cohen is dead? How?"

"She was lying, like I said. The truth caught up to her."

"Why would she lie?"

"Her husband had gambling debts. This was a way out, or so they thought."

"How do you know they're dead?"

"I saw him with a third eye at a bar in Bethesda. She died later along with two federal officers."

Vance gaped. "What in the hell is going on? What federal officers?"

"Maybe that coffee first? I'll help you."

He walked into the kitchen and Vance was right on his butt.

She gripped his shoulder. "You better start talking and making sense, and you better do it now, Robie."

"Okay. First, I don't technically work for DCIS."

"Big surprise. What else?"

"This needs to be off the record."

"The hell it is."

"You want that cup of coffee now?"

"What I want are some straight answers from you."

Robie poured out two cups of coffee and handed one to her. He looked out the window at the lighted monuments in D.C. He pointed to them.

"What's it worth to you to keep that place safe?" he said, turning to Vance.

She said incredulously, "What's it worth? Hell, it's worth everything."

Robie took a sip of his coffee. "Now, what's it worth to keep that girl in there safe?"

"You haven't even told me who she is."

"Julie Getty."

"Okay, how does she figure into any of this?"

"She was on the bus that night, but got off before it blew up."

"How the hell do you know that?" Vance asked sharply.

"Because I got off with her. That's why I knew Cohen was lying. As you can see, Julie and I aren't black."

Robie took another sip of coffee and turned to look back at the monuments.

Vance stood there rocking back and forth on her heels, obviously trying to process this stunning revelation. Finally, she stopped rocking.

"*You* were on that bus," yelled Vance. "Why? And why am I just finding out now?"

Julie said, "Because it was a need to know and you didn't need to know. At least back then."

They both turned to see Julie standing in the doorway.

Vance looked from her to Robie. "Need to know? So you're in intelligence? I swear to God, Robie, if this is some CIA bullshit that we've been running around in circles on, I will seriously consider shooting somebody, starting with you."

"There's something off with this whole case, Vance, and there has been from the start."

"Robie, you have a ton of explaining to do, starting now. What were you doing on that bus? And what happened there? And who blew it up?"

"I don't know who blew it up. But it had to be done remotely. Not a timer."

"Why?"

"They didn't want to kill either of us, that's why."

"Again, why?"

"Don't know. I just know that they want one or both of us alive, for some reason."

Vance turned to Julie. "What were you doing on the bus?"

"Can I have my coffee first?"

"Jesus, here." Vance handed Julie her cup. "Now, what were you doing on the bus?"

"Some guy murdered my parents. My mom sent a note to me at school, or at least I thought it was from my mom. The note told me to get on that bus and meet them in New York. When I did, the same guy who killed my parents got on and attacked me. Will helped stop him. We got off the bus. And that's when it blew up. Knocked us both off our feet."

Vance snapped, "It was *your* gun we found near the bus. You were in Jane Wind's apartment. You were going to kill her."

"Just listen to him, Agent Vance," pleaded Julie.

"Why should I?"

"Because somebody killed my parents. And Will saved my life, more than once, actually. He's a good guy."

When Vance looked back Robie was sipping his coffee, staring out the window, his back to her.

Vance calmed and said, "I think I'll take a cup of coffee too."

Julie poured one and handed it to her.

Vance glanced at Robie. "Is the rest of what you're going to tell me just as bad?"

"Probably worse," he replied.

"You've put me in an awkward situation. I should report all of this."

"Agreed. You should. I did with my people, only to find out we had a traitor or two in the ranks. I wonder what the odds are of there being more?"

She hiked her eyebrows. "You mean at the Bureau?"

"You never had any bad apples?"

"Not many," she said defensively.

"It only takes one," noted Julie.

"It only takes one," repeated Robie.

Vance sighed and slumped against the counter. "What do you want me to do?"

68

Robie turned the Volvo in at Dulles Airport and took the shuttle bus to the main terminal. He bought a ticket on a United Airlines flight leaving for Chicago in about two hours, went through security, and hit the restroom along with a dozen other guys. He went into a stall with his duffel bag and came out later with a collapsible roller and wearing a warm-up suit, glasses, and a ball cap. He walked to an exit, rode the bus back to the car rental outlets, leased a new set of wheels using a credit card under an alias—an Audi this time—and sped west on the toll road.

He peered in the rearview mirror. If anyone could keep up a tail after that, they deserved to win.

An hour later he pulled into his hideaway in the woods. He drove the car into the barn and closed the doors. Using a rake to shove straw out of the way on the floor of the barn, he revealed a metal hatch. He removed the hatch and hoisted himself down through the opening. He flicked a switch and old fluorescent tube lighting blinked on. He skipped down the metal steps and put his feet down on a solid concrete floor.

He had not built this place. The farmer who'd originally owned the property had grown up in the thirties. When the fifties had come along he'd decided to build a bomb shelter under his barn, thinking that some wood, straw, and inches of concrete could protect him from any thermonuclear shenanigans the Soviet Union might decide to throw at America.

Robie moved down a short hallway and stopped. In front of him was a wall of firepower that he had drawn on in the past to accomplish his work. It included pistols, rifles, shotguns, and even a surface-to-air missile launcher. It seemed James Bondish, but was actually just the typical stock-in-trade for people in Robie's field. He took down what he thought he might need and stacked it against one wall.

He opened a drawer of a workbench and pocketed a couple of electronic transmitters. He spent another ten minutes picking out various other items that might come in handy and packed everything up in a large duffel bag. He carried it up the steps, closed the hatch, spread the straw back over it, and put the duffel in the trunk of the Audi.

Five minutes later he was speeding back east. He checked in at an extended-stay motel and unloaded his equipment. He changed clothes and called Julie. Robie had left her in the care of Vance and the FBI. Vance had only told her superiors that Julie was a possible witness and needed protection. Two agents from out of town had been called in to assist with the protection detail. Right now Robie didn't really trust anyone in D.C.

Julie sounded excited. "I got an idea. I called the Broomes on the phone you gave me. And I got a text back," she said. "They want to meet."

"You know it's probably *not* the Broomes, right?" said Robie in a calming tone. "They could have had the Broomes' phone, and when they got your call, they just texted back to your number. If it were the Broomes they probably would have simply called."

"Do you always have to be a downer?" asked Julie.

"Where and when?"

She told him.

"Can you come and pick me up?" she asked.

"Julie, you're not going anywhere near that place."

He could almost see her face falling across the digital ether.

"What?"

"This is most likely a setup. You're not going. I'll handle it."

"But we're a team. You said so."

"I'm not putting you in any more danger than you already are. I'll handle it and then report back to you."

"That sucks."

"I'm sure from your point of view it does suck, but it's the smart thing to do."

"I can take care of myself, Will."

"Under most circumstances I would agree with that. This is not one of those circumstances."

"Thanks for nothing."

"You're welcome."

But she had already clicked off.

Robie put the phone back into his pocket and mentally prepared for the upcoming meeting. At some point whoever was behind this would no longer be interested in keeping him alive. He wondered if that time was about to come.

He gunned up and slipped a few other items into his jacket pocket, then called Vance and filled her in.

"I'll come with you," she said.

"You sure?" he asked.

"Don't ask me again, Robie. Because my answer might just change."

69

The Martin Luther King Jr. Memorial's official opening had been delayed because of a hurricane that had exhibited incredibly bad timing as it swept up the East Coast. But now the memorial was open. The centerpiece was the Stone of Hope, a thirty-foot-high statue of Dr. King, comprised of 159 granite blocks fashioned to look like a single chunk of stone. Its official address was 1964 Independence Avenue, after the 1964 Civil Rights Act. The memorial was roughly equidistant between the Lincoln and Jefferson memorials, and sited along the "line of leadership" between the other two memorials. It was adjacent to the FDR Memorial and was the only memorial on the National Mall dedicated to a person of color, and a non-president.

Robie knew all of this and had even attended the opening ceremony for the memorial. But tonight he was only interested in survival.

He spoke quietly into his headset as he eyed the memorial. "You in place?"

Vance's voice came into his ear. "Roger that."

"See anyone?"

"No."

Robie kept moving and kept looking. He had on night-vision goggles, but they couldn't see what wasn't there.

"Julie?"

The voice was to his left, near the memorial.

It was a man. Robie tightened the grip on his pistol and spoke into his headset again. "Did you hear that?"

Vance said, "Yes, but I don't have a visual on the source yet."

A second later Robie did.

The man stepped clear of the memorial. In the wash of moonlight and with the aid of his special goggles Robie could see that it was indeed Leo Broome. He recognized him from a photo he had seen in the man's apartment.

Vance's voice came into his ear. "Is that Broome?"

"Yes, sit tight and cover my back."

Robie moved forward until he was within ten feet of the other man.

"Mr. Broome?"

The man immediately ducked back behind the memorial.

"Mr. Broome?" Robie said again.

"Where's Julie?" Broome said.

"We didn't let her come," called out Robie. "We thought it might be an ambush."

"Well, that's exactly what I'm thinking," said

Broome. "Just so you know, I've got a gun and I know how to aim and hit what I'm aiming at."

Vance spoke up. "Mr. Broome, I'm Special Agent Vance with the FBI. We just want to talk to you."

"You saying it doesn't mean you are with the FBI."

Vance came out into the open and held her weapon up and her shield out. "I am with the FBI, Mr. Broome. We just want to talk. To try and find out what's going on here."

"And the other guy?" said Broome. "What about him?"

Robie said, "I know that Julie's parents are dead, Mr. Broome. I've been trying to help her find their killers."

"Curtis and Sara are dead?"

"So are Rick Wind and his ex-wife. Both murdered."

Broome appeared around the edge of the memorial. "We've got to put a stop to all this."

"Couldn't agree with you more," said Vance. "And with your help maybe we can. But first we need to get you to a safe location. And your wife too."

"That won't be happening."

"Did they get to your wife?" asked Robie.

"Yes. She's dead."

Robie said quickly, "Were you with her when it happened?"

"Yes, I barely got out in—"

Robie was running full tilt toward Broome. "Get down, now. Down!"

But he knew he was already too late.

He heard the crack of the shot. Broome whipped around and then fell where he had stood. He hit the dirt hard, twitched once as his heart gave a final pump, and then lay still.

Robie reached him, ducked down, and surveyed the area. The shot had come from the left. He called this out to Vance, who was already on her phone.

Robie realized this had been a setup from the start.

He was never intended to get any information from Leo Broome. They were still just playing him. Giving him a tantalizing piece of gold and then jerking it away when he got too close. Whomever he was confronting knew far more about everything than he did. They had assets on both sides, something he didn't.

Vance knelt down next to Robie. "Is he dead?"

"Round blew right through his head. He won't be talking to anyone anymore."

She let out a long breath and stared down at the dead man. "They're always one step ahead, it seems."

"It seems," said Robie.

"You were telling him to get down before the shot. How did you know?"

"They killed his wife, but he got away? I don't think so. Same thing happened with Julie. They don't let people just get away."

"But what purpose did it serve letting Leo Broome live? He could have told us something."

"They weren't going to give him the chance, Vance."

"So why let him come here at all? If they were following him they could have killed him at any point."

"This seems to be a game to them."

"A game! People are dying here, Robie. Some game."

"Some game," he replied.

70

Robie sat in his apartment in the dark.

Vance and a quartet of FBI agents were keeping watch over Julie. He had told the teenager about the Broomes' murders. She had taken it stoically, hadn't cried, but apparently just accepted it as a fact of life. Maybe that was worse, thought Robie. It didn't seem right that a fourteen-year-old should have her emotions so hardened that violent death didn't shock anymore.

He had come back here because he needed somewhere to go that didn't involve other people being around. And though he had a room at the extended-stay residence, he had come back here instead. He wasn't concerned about killers coming for him, at least not yet.

They want me alive, for something. And then they'll want me dead.

He had strained his mind going back over missions he'd performed in the recent past. It would seem that in his line of work there would be many people who would want revenge against him, too many to plausibly investigate. But he had never failed on a task, and that meant his target always had died. And he had exited successfully each time, which meant that his identity should have remained a secret. But his handler had been turned, which meant that Robie had been exposed to anyone with the ability to pay.

He rose and looked out the window. It was two a.m. There were few cars moving down the street, no people. But then he caught sight of someone and he moved closer to the window for a better look.

Annie Lambert brought her bike to a stop outside the apartment building, got off, and rolled it into the lobby.

When she got off on her floor Robie was waiting for her. She looked surprised to see him, but then apparently noted the pain in his features.

"You okay?" she asked anxiously.

"Had better days. Long one for you, obviously?"

She smiled and struggled with her bag. Robie took it from her, slung it over his shoulder.

"Thanks," she said. "I messed up today," she admitted. "Had to work overtime to repair things."

"What happened?"

"Blew official protocols. I bypassed my direct supervisor to get a question answered because my direct supervisor wasn't around. Got called on the carpet for it."

"That doesn't seem right. In fact it seems fairly petty."

"Well, when you don't get paid much to handle

important issues, folks stand more firmly on titles and lines of authority than maybe they should."

"I think you're being overly generous."

"Maybe I'm just tired," she said wearily.

"Here, I'll help you to your door and you can get some sleep."

As they walked down the hall she said, "You don't seem too good either."

"Like you, a long day."

"Petty rules too?"

"A little different."

"Life can suck sometimes," said Lambert.

"Yes, it can."

They reached her door. She turned to him. "When I said I was tired, I didn't mean I needed to go to sleep. Would you like to come in for a drink?"

"You sure you're up for it?"

"We both look like we could use one. Nothing fancy like your wine. I can only afford beer."

"Okay."

They went inside. She put her bike away and pointed Robie to the kitchen, where he got out two beers and came back into the living room. He felt guilty that he knew the layout of her apartment from looking at it through the telescope.

It fit the image of a young government worker whose salary was in no way commensurate with her brains or ability. Everything was on the cheap, but Robie noted one oil painting of a harbor scene and a couple pieces of good-quality furniture that had probably come from Lambert's parents.

When she came back out of her bedroom she wore loose-fitting jeans and a long-sleeved T-shirt and her hair was pulled back in a ponytail. Her feet were bare. He handed her a beer and she plopped down in a chair and curled her feet up under her.

Robie sat opposite on a small faux leather love seat.

Lambert said, "Nice to get out of the professional armor."

"Until tomorrow morning, which is almost here."

"I actually have the day off tomorrow," she said. "Or today, as you pointed out." She took a sip of beer. Robie did the same.

"Why's that?"

"The president is out of town with most of his personal staff. When he gets back there's a big White House dinner. I have to work the event. So I'm going to enjoy my day off."

"I would too."

She smiled resignedly. "Especially since I've been working weekends for the past month. And staff morale is a little low."

"Why's that?"

"The president isn't doing very well in the polls. The economy is awful. The next election is not shaping up to be easy or pleasant."

"Country's split right down the middle. No election is easy anymore."

"True," she said. "I could never be a politician. It just hurts too much, you know? Every second of every day someone is judging you. And not just for your positions on issues. But for how you talk, look, walk. It's ridiculous."

"So have you given any more thought to what life will look like for you after the White House?"

"I'm in a phase of life right now where I just take each day as it comes."

"Not a bad thing, actually."

"Some would call it lazy."

"Who cares what some think?"

"Exactly."

"Great minds think alike, in fact."

She reached over and clinked his beer with hers. "To great minds."

"To great minds," he agreed with a grin.

"So is this officially our first date?"

"Technically I wouldn't think so," replied Robie. "It was more spontaneous. But we can make it anything we want. It's a free country."

"I really enjoyed drinks at the W."

"First time I've done something like that in a while."

"Me too."

"At your age you should be out a lot."

"Maybe I'm older than I look," she teased.

"I doubt that."

"I like you, Will. I like you a lot."

"You don't really know me yet."

"I'm a good and quick judge of people. Always have been." She paused, took a swig of beer. "You make me feel, I don't know, good about myself."

"You have a lot of reasons independent of me to feel good about yourself, Annie."

She set her beer down. "Sometimes I get depressed."

"Hell, we all do."

She rose and sat down next to him. She touched Robie's hand with hers. "I've had a couple of bad experiences with guys."

"I promise you won't have one with me." Robie had no way to guarantee this, but as he said it he believed it to be the truth.

At the same moment they each leaned toward the other. Their lips touched gently. Then they drew apart,

When Lambert opened her eyes he was looking at her.

"Did you not like that?" she asked.

"No, I liked it a lot, actually."

They kissed again.

"I'm a lot older than you," he said as they pulled apart once more.

"You don't seem a lot older."

"Maybe we shouldn't do this."

"Maybe we should do exactly what we both obviously want to do," she murmured in his ear. They kissed once more. Not gently this time, but hungrily, both breathing hard.

Robie's hand slipped to her thigh and he caressed it.

She edged her arms around his back and squeezed. Her mouth touched his ear.

"The bedroom might be more comfortable."

He rose, lifting her into the air as he did, and carried her to the bedroom door. She hit the door lever with her foot and pushed it open. Robie kicked the door shut behind them. They took their time disrobing each other.

She looked at his tats and scars and the wound on his arm. She lightly touched it. "Does it hurt?"

"Not anymore."

"How did you do it?"

"It was just something stupid." He pulled her to him.

A minute later they slid between the sheets, their clothes in a commingled pile on the floor.

71

It was six in the morning and Robie was on the move again. His rental glided down the dark street.

As soon as he left Annie Lambert still lying in her bed, he had regretted sleeping with her. The sex was wonderful. It had left him shaky and warm and completely out of sorts. It had been a liberating feeling.

And yet it still had been a mistake.

He had essentially left a man dead on the National Mall to go and screw a White House staffer. He hadn't been thinking about the case while in bed with her. Well, that would change right now.

He called Vance. Despite the early hour she picked up on the second ring.

"I'm in the office," she answered. "Actually I never left the office. Where are you?"

"Driving."

"Driving where?"

"Not sure."

"What happened to you last night? You just sort of disappeared after we got Julie squared away."

He didn't answer.

"Robie?"

"I just had to step back for a bit, get my head straight."

"Is it straight now? Because we have a case to work."

"Yeah."

"I didn't have dinner. And I haven't had breakfast. There's a twenty-four-hour place around the corner from WFO. You know it?"

"I'll meet you there in ten minutes," said Robie.

He beat her there and had already ordered them both mugs of coffee when she walked in.

"I thought you said you hadn't been home. You're wearing fresh clothes," he said.

"I keep a set at the office," she replied as she sat down and picked up her coffee and took a sip. "You don't look good," she said.

"Should I look good?" he shot back. He wondered for a moment if she could tell he had been with another woman.

They sat in awkward silence drinking their coffees until Robie said, "How's Julie?"

"Fidgety, depressed. I think she believes you've abandoned her."

"How did you explain things to your boss about all this?"

"I skirted the line. Told him some things, didn't tell him others."

The waitress came over and they ordered. After she had refilled their coffees she left.

Robie studied Vance. "I'm not looking to derail your career over this, Vance."

"You know, you can call me Nikki, if you want."

This offer seemed to deepen Robie's guilt. "Okay, Nikki, at the end of the day you need to be able to walk away from this with everything in your life intact."

"I don't think that's possible, Robie."

"My point is you don't have to cover for me. It was unfair to ask it of you."

"And my point is if I don't cover for you the FBI will come down like a ton of bricks. Too many questions, not enough answers."

"I've got some professional cover."

"Not enough. And quite frankly, I'm not just doing it for you. If everything does come out, my butt is probably off this investigation and it'll get so muddled we'll probably never figure it out. And I obviously have a real problem with that happening."

"Just so we understand each other," said Robie.

"I'm not sure I completely get you, but that's neither here nor there. I'm not your shrink. I'm just working with you to see if we can put away some killers."

"Leo Broome," he said. "Anything found on him that would help? He said they had gotten to his wife?"

"He had nothing on him. We're trying to trace where he came from. There was no car parked nearby that was unaccounted for. That late at night we can rule out the Metro probably. We're checking with cabbies to see if we can determine where he was picked up."

"Or else he could have walked," pointed out Robie. "But there was no hotel room key card, nothing else to show where he was staying?"

"Nothing like that. But we did find one thing."

"What was that?"

"A hoplite tattoo on his forearm identical to the one on Rick Wind's arm. And it has to match the one Julie said her dad had on his arm."

"So they must've known each other in the Army, then," said Robie.

"What if this isn't connected to you after all? They were in the Army together, maybe had some secret. Now it's come back to haunt them."

"Still doesn't explain me and Julie walking off that bus. Or them missing you and me in front of Donnelly's."

"No, I guess it doesn't. You said they *let* him escape after they killed his wife. Part of the game, you said. They might be screwing with you, but there has to be some purpose to it all."

"I'm certain there's an excellent purpose. I just don't know what it is."

"If this is a contest of sorts between you and them, there must be something in your past to account for it. Given that any thought?"

"Some. But I have to give it a lot more."

"What line of work were you in, Robie? DCIS isn't

your real home, but somewhere else in the federal government obviously is."

He drank his coffee, said nothing, because there was nothing he could say.

"I'm not read in, is that why your lips aren't moving?" asked Vance.

"I don't make the rules. Sometimes the rules suck, like now, but they're still the rules. I'm sorry, Nikki."

"Okay. You don't have to answer, but hear me out, okay?"

Robie nodded.

"I think you were at Jane Wind's apartment to kill her as some sort of sanctioned hit. Only you didn't pull the trigger for some reason. But someone else did, from long range. You took her youngest child to safety and then got out of there. Then you got roped into investigating a crime you were present at under the cover of a DCIS badge." She paused, studied him. "How am I doing?"

"You're an FBI agent, I would've expected no less."

"Tell me about the hit on Wind."

"It wasn't really sanctioned. I never should have been dialed up, but I was. Person who did it is now a burnt pile of bone."

"Cleaning up loose ends?"

"How I see it, yeah."

"So someone is playing with you, digging you in deep. Seems like the start of it was your going after

Jane Wind. Her hubby was already dead. So she dies. The Winds are out of the way. Point one."

Robie finished his coffee and sat up, looked more attentive. "Keep going."

"Point two. Julie's parents are killed. We know they were friends with the Broomes. And Rick Wind and Curtis Getty had the same tattoo on their arms. It must be from them serving together in the military. Have your people connected them up yet?"

"Still working on it."

"Point three. So Getty, Broome, and Wind, including their spouses—or, in Wind's case, ex-wife—are all dead."

Robie nodded and took up the thread. "I try and make my escape on that bus. They knew that I would. Julie gets routed to the same bus by a message supposedly from her mother. We get off, the bus blows up."

"The attack outside of Donnelly's where you and I should have been killed?"

"More window dressing, more playing with my mind."

"Some playing. A lot of innocent people were killed, Robie."

"Whoever's behind this could care less about collateral damage. They're chess pieces to them, nothing more."

"Well, I'd love to slap a pair of cuffs on people who think like that."

"But what's the endgame? Why do all of this?"

She took another sip of coffee. "So where'd you spend last night?"

The image of a naked Annie Lambert sitting astride him flashed into Robie's mind before Vance had even finished her question.

"I didn't sleep much," he admitted truthfully.

Their plates of food came and they spent some time digging their way through eggs, bacon, toast, and hash browns.

When they were through, Vance pushed her plate away and said, "How do you want to attack this?"

"Priority one is keeping Julie safe. We obviously had a mole in our operation and I have to count on the Bureau."

"We will do all we can to make sure no harm comes to her, Robie. What's the second priority?"

"I have to find out who in my past wants me this bad."

"You have lots of possibilities."

"Too many. But I have to narrow it down and I have to do it fast."

"You think this thing is on a timer?"

"Actually, I think the timer is just about up."

"So what are you going to do?"

"Take a trip, far away from here."

Vance looked astonished. "You're leaving?"

"No, I'm not."

72

Robie sat in the small room that he had used as an office for the last five years. No chubby middle-aged man in a rumpled suit came to bring him yet another flash drive. He was not here for another mission. He was here to see what had come before.

The trip he had referred to with Vance had been one taken in his mind. He stared at the computer screen in front of him. Staring back at him were the reports on his last five missions that had carried him back a full year in time.

He had eliminated, at least for now, three of them. The last two had captured his attention for a couple of reasons: They were the most recent ones, and they involved targets with long arms and many friends.

He clicked a few computer keys and an image of the deceased Carlos Rivera appeared on the screen. The last time Robie had seen the Latino, he had been screaming obscenities at Robie in Underground Edinburgh. Robie had killed Rivera and the man's bodyguards and made what he thought had been an undetected escape.

Rivera had a younger brother, Donato, who had taken over much of his brother's cartel operations. The book on Donato was that he was every bit as ruthless as his late brother, but with far less ambition. He was content to run his drug empire without inserting himself into the political situation in Mexico. Perhaps this was also due to what had happened to his big brother. Still, he might want to avenge Carlos's death. And if he had found out Robie's identity through Robie's handler, he might have the necessary information to do so.

In his mind's eye Robie went through the events leading up to the killing of Carlos and company. After completing this process he thought, *Do I fly to Mexico and attempt to kill Donato?*

Something deep in his gut told Robie that the man's relations could care less who had gunned Rivera down. Little brother was alive and doing very well without big brother around.

So Robie moved on to the next target of interest.

Khalid bin Talal, one of the Saudi princes, a fixture on the Forbes 400 list, richer even than Rivera.

Once more Robie closed his eyes, and this time transported himself back to the Costa del Sol.

On the third night the target had walked right into his crosshairs along with the Palestinian and the Russian, geopolitically an odd couple. Talal had exited his motorcade, walked up the steps to the hulking plane. Robie had lost visual on him for a few seconds. But then Talal had sat down across from his fellow conspirators.

Robie's shot had hit the man dead center in the head. No possibility of survival. Robie had gunned down two bodyguards, disabled the plane, executed his escape, and been on the slow ferry to Barcelona within the hour.

Clean kill, clean exit. And the truth was, bin Talal was not popular in the Muslim world. His ideas were too radical for the moderates. The ruling family was well aware that he desired to overthrow it, and it was largely at the family's behest that Robie had been sent out on this mission. And even the Islamic fundamentalists tended to give Talal a wide berth because they did not trust his close business ties to Western capitalists.

He sat back in his chair and rubbed his temples. If he still smoked he would have lit up right now. He needed something to take his mind off a deep sense of failure. Something was staring him in the face. Perhaps it was the truth, the answer he needed. But it wouldn't come.

He went back through the three missions previous to Rivera and bin Talal. Every step, like he had with the Latino and the Muslim. Clean executions, clean exits, all of them.

And yet if not one of them, who?

He took out his pistol and laid it on the desk in front of him, the muzzle facing away from him. He stared down at the Glock. A fine weapon, it almost always performed flawlessly. This was not a mass-produced piece. This was customized to fit his hand, his grip, and his way of shooting. Every piece was meticulously crafted to make success a foregone conclusion. But it wasn't just about aiming straight. There were a million parts to every mission, and if any one of them failed, so did the mission. For Robie the easiest part was the actual killing. He was good at it, and had some semblance of control over events. The other parts of the puzzles often came down to others doing their job, totally outside of his control.

He had not always killed on behalf of the U.S. government. He had worked for others, all allies of the Americans. That's what had gotten their attention. The pay was better on this side of the Atlantic, but if it had solely been about money Robie would have moved into another line of work a long time ago.

There was a reason he kept taking these assignments, kept pulling the trigger on one monster after another. He had never talked to anyone about it, and doubted he ever would. It wasn't that the memories were too painful. It was that he had frozen that part of his mind. He was incapable of articulating a single sentence about it. That was the way he wanted it. Anything less would not allow him to function.

He rose from behind the desk, the sense of failure now profound.

His phone was buzzing as he reached the door of his car.

It was Blue Man.

They had tracked down the military ties among Curtis Getty, Rick Wind, and Leo Broome. They had all served together.

"I'm on my way," said Robie.

73

"Same squad," said Blue Man.

He and Robie were sitting in Blue Man's office.

"They fought together for the entire campaign, along with other assignments post-Gulf One."

"It was no wonder Julie didn't know about it," remarked Robie. "She wasn't even born yet."

"And her father was tight-lipped about his service," said Blue Man. "Maybe he didn't even tell his wife."

"I know some soldiers don't talk about their time on the battlefield, but they don't usually keep the fact that they actually served secret. Anything in his records to warrant such secrecy?"

"Maybe."

Blue Man pulled out another manila folder from a stack he had on his desk. "As you know, during Gulf One allied forces never actually went into Baghdad. The mission was to drive Saddam Hussein from Kuwait, and that mission was accomplished."

"Hundred days," said Robie. "I remember."

"Right. Now, the Iraqis had reportedly looted much

of Kuwait, which is one of the richest Gulf states. Cash, gold, precious jewels, that sort of thing."

"Is this going where I think it is?"

"Nothing could be proven, but Getty, Wind, and Broome might have had sticky fingers when they were in Kuwait. They were each given general discharges Under Honorable Conditions."

"You told Julie that her dad got an *honorable* discharge based on medical reasons."

"That's right. I did."

"If they were involved in the thefts, do you think they were able to get their loot back to the States? None of the three showed any signs of wealth," pointed out Robie. "The Gettys worked at crap jobs and lived in a crappy duplex. The Winds weren't wealthy. And I saw the Broomes' apartment. Nothing special."

"Curtis Getty probably put most of it up his nose. Rick Wind's finances showed that he never earned much money, but he owned a home and had the pawnbroker's business. Again, we could find no record of how he was able to buy the business."

"But he stayed in for the full ride. How would that be possible if he was believed to be a thief?'

"'Believed to be' is the operative phrase. Lack of evidence, I suppose. But the general discharge he did receive speaks volumes, because there was nothing else in his service record that would have warranted anything other than an honorable discharge."

"So they got him in the end?"

"And he apparently didn't contest it. Again, speaks volumes. If he did steal the stuff and still got his full ride and pension and no jail time, and the fruits of his larceny, Wind probably thought he got a great deal."

"And if he was rich from the thefts, why stay in?"

"We don't know how much they might have gotten away with. Maybe he saw it as his nest egg and decided to keep drawing his government check."

"And Leo Broome?"

"Hit the jackpot there. His apartment in D.C. wasn't much to look at, but they had an oceanfront home in Boca Raton and we tracked down an investment portfolio he'd hidden under another name. Had about four million in it."

"Okay, at least it seems he stole from the Kuwaitis. So you think someone's coming for them after all this time? And why stick me in the middle of it?"

"You're the worrisome piece, Robie. The three ex-soldiers maybe fit a pattern. You don't." Blue Man closed the file and looked across the desk at him. "You went back over your recent missions?"

"Five of them. They're cookie-cutters. No clear reason why someone would want to come after me. And no clear reason why they wouldn't. So I wasn't able to narrow down the possible suspects." He brooded for a few moments. "Julie said her mother told her killer that Julie didn't know anything."

"What of it?"

"Didn't know what? About her dad's military service? I can tell you right now that that guy on the bus going after Julie was not Middle Eastern."

"Means nothing. You're not Middle Eastern either, and yet you've worked on their behalf before. They could have hired local talent to do the job. Makes it easier than trying to slip one of their own into the country, especially these days."

Robie glanced up at him. "So why didn't you tell Julie about these allegations of theft?"

"I decided to focus on the medals. And nothing was ever proven against Curtis Getty. He might be innocent."

"But still?"

"What would have been the point?"

"Why?" Robie asked again.

"I have granddaughters."

"Okay," said Robie. "I can understand that."

"But we don't seem to be any closer to the right answers," said Blue Man.

"No, maybe we are."

"How so?"

Robie stood. "They want me involved in this somehow, whatever it is."

"Granted, but how does that help us?"

"I need to make them try a little harder to engage my attention."

"What do you mean?"

"I'm going to make them push harder. When people push harder they make mistakes."

"Well, make certain you don't push them so hard that you end up dead."

"No, I *want* them to focus on *me*. There's been way too much collateral damage on this already."

Robie turned and walked out of the room.

He was going to see Julie. He had nothing really to tell her. And like Blue Man had said, no good could come from informing her of things her father might have done in the past. Robie was convinced that whatever the three soldiers had done more than twenty years ago was irrelevant to the present situation. They were just convenient pieces on the chessboard.

This is about me, thought Robie. *It started with me and it has to somehow end with me.*

74

"So, Mr. Broome and Rick Wind served with my dad in the Army?" said Julie.

Robie was sitting with her in the FBI safe house. How safe it was Robie wasn't sure, but he had few options left. The FBI agents guarding Julie looked professional and alert, and yet he kept his hand near his Glock and was prepared to gun them down if they made a move to harm the girl.

"They fought in Gulf One. They left the Army at separate times after that. Apparently, a number of soldiers in their squad got that tattoo on their arm."

"I still can't believe my dad was like a hero."

"Believe it, Julie, he was."

She fingered the zipper on her jacket. "Did you find out anything else?"

"Not really," said Robie.

"My dad must've been young when he left the military. I wonder why he didn't stay in."

"No way to tell," said Robie quietly. "Some guys do their stint and go on to other things."

"Maybe if he'd stayed in he might've, you know . . ."

"Well, he might not have met your mother either, if he'd stayed in."

"That's true," said Julie slowly. She eyed Robie closely. "Why do I think you're not telling me everything?" There was something in her look that Robie recognized. It was the same look he gave people who were simply telling him things they knew he wanted to hear.

"Because you're naturally suspicious, just like me."

"Are you holding something back from me?"

"I hold lots of things back from lots of people. But always for a good reason, Julie."

"That's not really an answer."

He locked his gaze on hers, figuring that not to look at her now would be simply an exclamation point on his underlying deceit. "It's the only one I have to give. I'm sorry."

"So you haven't figured out what's going on, then, have you?"

"Not really."

"Do you need my help? And don't say you have to keep me safe. There's no such place, not even here with super-duper FBI guys all over the place."

Robie was about to turn her offer down using this very safety issue, but stopped. Something had just occurred to him.

"Your mother said that you didn't know anything, right? When she was talking to the guy in your house?"

"That's what she said."

"So that implies that your parents did know something. That your mother, in fact, probably knew why the guy was there. Why he wanted to kill them."

"I guess that's right. But we've already covered this ground, Will."

"And Leo Broome, right before he died, implied that he knew something too."

Julie wicked a tear from her right eye. "I didn't know him all that well, but he seemed like a nice guy. And I really liked Ida. She was always nice to me."

"I know. It's a tragedy all around. Now, Cheryl Kosmann said that the day before your parents were killed they had dinner with the Broomes at the diner. She said they looked like they had seen a ghost."

"That's right."

"When was the last time you talked to your parents before you went back to your house that night?"

"Just before I was put back in foster care. I never got a chance to sneak over and see my mom at the diner."

"And how did your mom seem when you did see her last?"

"Fine. Normal. We just talked about stuff."

"And then later a guy is at their home looking to kill them and your mother is not surprised by it?"

Julie blinked. "You mean something had to happen after I last saw her and before the guy showed up at our house?"

"No, it had to be between you seeing her last and your parents having dinner with the Broomes where they all looked like they had seen a ghost, according to Cheryl."

"But we don't know what that something is."

"But narrowing it down to a specific time period helps. The way I see it, either something happened with your parents, they found out something and told the Broomes. Or the Broomes found out something and told your parents."

"What about the Winds?"

"That's sort of the wild card. They weren't at the dinner, but they must be involved somehow too, otherwise why would they have ended up dead?"

"Do you think it has something to do with their time in the military?"

"My gut tells me that it should. But all the facts don't point to that. Namely, my involvement in all this. If I'm right and I'm the reason why this whole thing has been orchestrated, why involve your parents, the Broomes, and the Winds? I didn't know any of them."

"So you really think all of this is tied to you somehow?"

Robie could sense the question left unspoken.

Was I the reason her parents were killed?

"Yes, I think it does. Too many coincidences otherwise."

Julie pondered this. "So either the Winds, my parents, or the Broomes found something out. Because they were in the military together the guys might have told each other about it. The bad guys found out and they had to kill them."

"That makes sense."

"Yeah, I guess it does," Julie said, looking away from Robie.

He let a few tense moments pass by before he spoke. "Julie, I don't know what's going on. If this is really all about me, and your parents and the others were caught up in it, I'm sorry."

"I'm not blaming you for what happened to my parents, Will," she said, though her voice held no conviction.

Robie stood and paced. "Well, maybe you should," he said over his shoulder.

"Blaming you isn't going to bring them back. And what I want hasn't changed. I want to get whoever did this. *All* of them."

Robie sat back down and looked at her. "I think there was no more than a twenty-four-hour window when whatever got your parents killed was communicated among Wind, Broome, and your dad. If we can trace a call, or a movement, or any type of communication among that group, we might be able to get a better handle on all this."

"Can you do that?"

"We can at least give it a hell of a shot. The problem is, so far nothing in their background suggests they were involved in anything that could have been the catalyst for all this."

"Well, they weren't the only ones in the squad, right? A squad consists of nine or ten soldiers, with a staff sergeant in command."

"How do you know that?"

"American history class. We're studying World War II. So my dad, Wind, and Broome are three guys. That means you have six or seven more to track down."

Robie shook his head, wondering how he'd missed something that obvious. Then he looked down at Julie's chest.

The laser dot was centered right over her heart.

75

Robie made no visible reaction to the laser dot. He knew it was from a sniper rifle. He didn't look to the window, where he knew the blinds must be partially open. The rifle and the shooter were out there somewhere, probably within a thousand yards of a house that had just become as unsafe as it was possible to be.

He inwardly chastised himself for not earlier noting the open blinds.

He put his hands under the table separating him and her. He smiled.

"What's so funny?" she asked quizzically.

"You ever play a game called Whac-A-Mole?"

"Uh, are you feeling okay, Will?"

He felt along the underside of the table. Solid wood, not cheap composite. That was good. About an inch thick. That might be good enough. It would have to be good enough. He would have to perform two movements, one with each hand. He drew a breath and his smile deepened, because if Julie made any sudden movements it would be over.

"I was just thinking about something that happened to me a long time ago—"

He flipped up the table with one hand so it was shielding Julie from the sniper, and drew his Glock with his other hand.

Julie screamed as Robie fired, killing the overhead light. The rifle shot shattered the window and drove into the wood and passed through it, but the barrier had served to throw off the line of fire. It struck the wall to the left of Julie.

"Get down," snapped Robie. Julie immediately went to her belly. Robie heard footsteps rushing down the hall.

Robie moved behind the table.

He turned to Julie, who lay flat on the floor with her hands over her head.

"Are you okay?"

"Yes," she said in a trembling voice.

"Did you open the window blinds?"

She peered up at him. "No, they were like that when I got here."

The door started to open. A voice called out, "Robie, you okay?"

Robie recognized the voice as belonging to one of the agents guarding them. He called out, "Put your gun down on the floor and slide it in the room with your foot."

One of the men yelled, "What the hell is going on, Robie?"

"Just what I was about to ask you. Who opened the blinds in this room?"

"The blinds?"

"Yeah, the blinds. Because a sniper just took a shot right through that opening. So unless you have an answer I'll shoot the first person that comes through the door. I don't care if it's you or anybody else."

"Robie, we're the FBI."

"Yeah, and I'm one seriously pissed-off guy with a Glock. Where does that get us?"

"There's a sniper outside?"

"That's what I said. Didn't you hear the shot?"

"Hang tight."

He heard the feet running away again.

Robie looked down at Julie and back over at the window. He wasn't hanging tight. He pulled out his phone, thumbed Vance's number. She answered.

He said, "Sniper at the safe house. Mole somewhere. Need backup. Now."

He clicked off and took Julie's hand. "Keep low," he warned her.

"Are we going to die?"

"Just keep down and follow me."

He led her out of the room, cleared the hall, and they ran, not to the front or back doors, but to the opposite side of the house from where the shot had come. They crouched down in the room while Robie did a turkey peek out the window. There was no way he could do a clean sweep of the area with his naked eye, but he didn't see a scope reflection, although the high-end equipment they had out there now wouldn't necessarily have such a signature wink of light. He had no idea if the guy who had told him to hang tight was an ally or foe, and he didn't think it was a good idea to wait and find out for certain.

They would be expecting them to go out either the back door or the window on the side opposite from the sniper fire.

So Robie planned to go out the front door.

But first they had to get there.

They moved back into the hall, and with Robie leading they made their way slowly toward the front of the house. The house was in a neighborhood with one road in or out. There were no houses close by. You had to really want to get to the place. Someone evidently had. And he had done so with help from the inside.

When Robie looked around the corner into the front room he saw the body of one of the agents lying there, feet closest to the front door, blood around his neck. Not a bullet wound. Robie would have heard the shot, and only a shotgun would have made a gash that big. Had to have been a knife. Hand over the mouth, knife slash to the neck, not much sound. Death would come fast.

Hand over the mouth. Killer would've had to get real close for that.

Another traitor in the ranks.

"Oh my God."

He looked back at Julie. She had just seen the body.

"Look away," said Robie.

He thumbed his phone keypad again. Vance picked up. Robie could hear the sound of her engine. She must've had it revved to over a hundred.

"Got one dead agent. Don't know where the others are. Dead guy has up-close wound. Whoever nailed him he thought was a friend."

"Shit!" exclaimed Vance.

"How far away are you?"

"Three minutes."

He put away the phone and turned to Julie.

"We're going to go out that front door, but we need to draw attention somewhere else."

"Okay," she said, her gaze darting between Robie and the dead man. "How?"

Robie cleared the chamber on his pistol, popped the mag, pulled out the two top rounds, inserted the two rounds he'd taken from his jacket pocket, and smacked the clip back into place. He racked the slide, which pushed one of the new rounds into the chamber.

He edged to the door and used his foot to move it open.

"What are you going to do?" asked Julie. "Shoot your way out of here?"

"Cover your ears."

"What?"

"Cover your ears and look away from the door."

Robie waited while she did so. Then he aimed and fired.

The first round hit the gas tank on the Bucar parked in the driveway. The incendiary round ignited the gasoline vapor and the explosion lifted the sedan right off the asphalt.

His second shot was aimed at the second Bucar, parked next to the first. A second later it joined the fireball of the first.

Robie grabbed Julie's hand and they sprinted through the doorway. Keeping the wall of flames and smoke between them and, hopefully, whoever had just tried to kill Julie, they turned away from the house and ran down the street. Robie had debated trying to reach his car but decided that that would be akin to painting a target on their heads.

A car turned onto the street and accelerated. Robie saw the blue grille lights. He flagged Vance down. She hit the brakes and the Beemer skidded to a stop. Robie threw open the door, pushed Julie into the back, and jumped into the front passenger seat.

"Go, now!" he told Vance.

She put the car in reverse and smoked her tire tread backing down the street. She hit a J-turn, and as soon as the hood of her car was pointing in the other direction she gunned it. She reached the end of the street and turned left.

She looked at Robie and then glanced at Julie huddled in the back.

"You both okay? Nobody hurt?"

"We're okay," said Robie tersely.

"So tell me what the hell happened."

Robie said, "Just keep driving."

76

Robie rode shotgun and he kept rotating his gaze to look behind and then over at Vance. His gaze was suspicious and his hand gripped the butt of his Glock. That had been unbelievably close. If he hadn't looked down and seen the dot, Julie would have joined her parents among the dead. It was apparent to Robie that the other side no longer required either or both of them to continue living.

He settled back in his seat, but his posture was rigid, coiled. He did not think the danger was over just yet.

Vance kept her gaze on the road mostly. Every once in a while she would glance at Robie's gun and then her gaze would travel to his face. When their eyes occasionally met, she would quickly look away.

They had traveled about two miles when she finally spoke.

"You have a particular reason keeping your gun out with the muzzle pointed in my direction?"

"I have about a dozen reasons for it, but you've probably thought of them all."

"I didn't rat you out, Robie. I'm not the one behind all this."

"Good to know. I'll take that into consideration."

"I can understand why you don't feel you can trust anyone, including the FBI."

"Again, good to know." His voice was flat, dead. Robie didn't even recognize it as his.

"Where do you want to go?"

He looked at her, his expression inscrutable. "Why don't you pick a place? We'll see how it goes."

"Is this a test?"

"Why shouldn't it be?"

"Will you guys stop? This is not helping."

They both glanced in the rearview mirror to see Julie staring at them.

"Someone just set us up while in FBI custody," said Robie, his voice calm and even. He said again, "So pick a place, Agent Vance. Take us there and we'll see what happens."

"How about WFO?"

"How about it?"

"Robie, I'm on your side!"

He glanced out the window. "The guys you called in from out of town?"

"*I* didn't call them in. They were called in by others at the Bureau."

"What others?"

"I don't know specifically. I put in a request for agents from out of town." She gave him a hard stare.

"At your insistence. They were the ones who were sent."

"One was killed," said Robie. "I doubt he came down here to die. So we can rule him out. But someone left the blinds open in the room where Julie was placed." He looked at her. "Which agent sent you back there?"

Julie said, "The one who came to the door after the shot was fired. I recognized his voice."

"The one who never came back. The one who killed his partner," added Robie. "The one who told us to hang tight." He glanced at Vance. "Just like you told me to. Hang tight."

Vance slammed the Beemer to a stop in the middle of the road. She turned and faced him.

"Okay, shoot me, then. If you don't trust me I'm no use to you anyway. So put the gun against my head and pull the damn trigger."

Robie said, "Histrionics really won't get you anywhere on this."

"So what exactly do you want me to do?"

"I already told you. For now, just drive."

"Where?

"Pick a direction and stick to it."

"Shit," Vance muttered in a shaky voice. She put the car in gear and sped off.

She said, "I heard explosions before I turned onto the street. Your doing?"

"I blew up two Bureau cars. Be sure to bill me for that."

"You blew them up?"

"We needed a diversion," chimed in Julie. "It was the only way we got out of the house alive."

Robie sat back in his seat. "So I've got traitors in my own organization. Traitors in the FBI. A puzzle I'm not close to solving. And time is running out."

"So what are you going to do?" Vance asked nervously.

"Regroup and rethink. The three of us are going to stick together. But we need new transportation."

"What's wrong with my car?"

"Principally, that people know it's your car."

"Are you going to steal another car, Will?" asked Julie.

"Another?" asked Vance in a raised voice.

"He's really good at it," added Julie. "Makes it look easy."

"And I hope you're just as good at driving," said Robie to Vance.

"Why?" asked Vance.

He had his gun up and he hit the button to bring his window down.

"Because we have an SUV on our six and it's coming fast."

77

Vance looked in the rearview mirror. An SUV, black, big, and gaining on them way too fast. It looked like a bulky jet barreling down the runway just prior to liftoff.

She punched the gas and the Beemer leapt forward.

"Wait a minute," she exclaimed. "Do you think they're cops or Feds?"

The shot shattered the Beemer's rear glass. Julie shrieked and ducked down as the bullet passed between Vance and Robie and cracked the windshield.

"No," said Robie tersely. "I don't think they're cops or Feds."

Vance cut the wheel to the left and screeched the Beemer into a ninety-degree turn, racing down a side street.

"Well then *do* something!" she snapped.

He turned, looked at Julie, who was hunkered down in the seat. "Undo your seat belt and get on the floorboard," he said.

"What if the car wrecks and I don't have a belt on?" she said.

"I think that'll be the least of your worries."

Julie undid her belt and dropped into the space between the front and rear seats.

Robie took aim with his Glock and fired once through the shattered back window. His shot hit the front of the SUV. Robie had aimed to take out the radiator. His shot had hit dead center. He could hear the round ping off.

"Armored," he said to Vance.

He fired next into the left front tire. The rubber should have shredded. It didn't.

"Run-flat tires," said Robie. "Cute. Really cute."

"If they're armored we should be able to outrun them," said Vance.

"Depends on what kind of horsepower they've got."

He fired again, at the windshield. It cracked part of the glass, but the SUV did not slow down.

"Well, at least they're not perfect," said Robie.

He saw the gun appear from the passenger-side window. Robie observed instantly that it wasn't just any gun. If it hit them it would be over.

He grabbed the wheel from Vance and slammed the car into a hard right turn that took it off the road, over the curb, and into someone's front yard.

A split second later the gun pointing from the SUV roared a dozen automatic times. The rounds missed the Beemer, but behind them the car that was parked nearest the intersection exploded.

The SUV couldn't make the turn and continued to

speed down the road. Then came the screech of brakes and gears reversing.

Robie worked the wheel and the Beemer jumped the curb and landed back on the road. He took his hands off the steering wheel and looked back.

"What the hell was that?" demanded a shaky-looking Vance.

"It's called a Sledgehammer," said Robie. "Assault combat shotgun. I recognized it from the big ammo drum. It must've ignited the fuel tank on that car back there."

He pointed up ahead. "Take the next left and then a right and then hit the gas hard. By the time they get back on our tail we'll be gone."

Vance did as he instructed and they were soon alone on a road leading west away from all the shooting. They could hear sirens seemingly coming from all directions.

Julie sat up and buckled her seat belt after wiping shards of automobile glass off the seat and out of her hair.

Robie glanced at her. "You okay?"

She nodded but didn't say anything.

He looked around. "You left your backpack at the safe house?"

She nodded again.

Vance said, "What changed, Robie?"

He looked at her after easing his gun back into its holster.

"Come again?" he said.

"They didn't want to kill us before, just scare the shit out of us or intimidate us or who the hell knows what. But now it seems pretty clear they want us gone. So what changed?"

"Could be lots of things," he answered. "Without knowing the endgame it's hard to know what makes these folks tick. Or what part any of us play in all of it."

"So we need to figure out the endgame," said Vance.

"Easier said than done," replied Julie.

"What changed?" This time the query came from Robie.

Vance and Julie looked at him. "That's what I just said," replied Vance.

He didn't answer. He just stared straight ahead.

He would've smiled, only he didn't because it might lead to nothing.

But finally, *finally* Robie might have something.

78

Robie directed Vance to his hideaway farmhouse. At his demand she had turned off the GPS chip in her phone. Vance had called in to her supervisor on the drive over and reported what had happened. One FBI agent was dead on the scene, the man Robie and Julie had seen. The other agent was nowhere to be found. In fact, the Bureau could not confirm that he was in fact the agent that had been sent to Virginia to protect Julie.

Vance dropped the phone into her lap with a grimace of disgust. "Dammit! Get the little shit right and the big shit doesn't happen."

"You have to go off grid," said Robie. "You okay with that?"

"Does that mean you actually trust me?"

"They were willing to kill you back there too."

"I have no problem going off grid so long as there's a plan."

"It's evolving. But I need some information."

"What kind?"

He looked at Julie, who sat in the backseat staring at him.

"What changed was Julie came up with the right answer."

"What answer?" Julie asked.

"It was a timing issue, really. As soon as you said it the red dot appeared on your chest. That's when we both might've become expendable."

Vance looked at Julie. "What did you say?"

She said, "That my dad and Mr. Broome and Rick Wind were part of a squad. And a squad has nine or ten soldiers in it. So maybe they talked to someone else in the squad. And that's where all this started. I mean, if the three of them kept in touch, maybe some others did too."

Robie nodded and looked at Vance. "So the safe house wasn't just unsafe. It was also bugged. They could hear everything we were saying. And the second Julie said that, the dot appeared."

Vance said, "You really think that might be it? The other members of the squad?"

"I think we need to find out whether it is or isn't, and we need to do it fast."

"You can get that info pretty quickly from DCIS."

"I could. But since DCIS has been infiltrated I don't want to tip my hand."

Vance slumped back as she drove and thought about this. "And the Bureau might have been infiltrated too."

"Might have been!" exclaimed Julie. "What part of tonight did you miss super agent Vance?"

Vance grimaced. "Okay, *was* infiltrated." She looked at Robie. "So what do we do?"

"I know someone who might be able to help," he said. "An old friend."

"You sure you can trust this person?"

"He's earned that trust."

"Okay."

"But I have to leave you to go see him," said Robie.

"Do you think it's a good idea to split up?" asked Vance nervously.

"No," he replied. "But it's the only way this will work."

"How long will you be gone?" asked Julie anxiously.

"Only as long as I have to," he replied.

Robie got them settled in the house, showed Vance where things were, set the alarm and perimeter security, and then strode out to the barn. He climbed on his motorcycle, slipped on his helmet, and started the bike. The powerful pulses of the engine soothed him, gave him something else to focus on besides what he had to do later.

He rode his bike east and then north. He reached the Beltway and followed that long curve north. He raced over the Woodrow Wilson Bridge, the winking lights of D.C. to his left, the green sweep of Virginia running to Mount Vernon to his right.

The building he arrived at nearly thirty minutes later

was brick, small, and had a high fence running around it. There was a guard in uniform posted out front. Robie had called ahead. He was on the list. He had his proper creds. The guard let him pass through after doing a thorough search.

A few minutes later he was walking down the only hall the building had. Doors on the left and right led off from this main artery. They were all closed. The hour was late. There wouldn't be many people here.

But there was at least one. The one he wanted. The man who had held Robie's position before Robie had.

He stopped at one door, knocked.

Footsteps came his way. The door swung open.

A man in his mid-fifties with white close-cropped hair stood before him. He and Robie were about the same height. The man was trim, his shoulders broad; he seemed to have retained much of the strength of his youth.

When he shook Robie's hand, that strength was clearly evident. He ushered him in and closed the door, but not without first taking a look down the hall, ostensibly for any threats. Even here, Robie would have done the same thing. It was just a part of you at this level.

The room was small, efficiently laid out. No personal mementos were evident. The man sat behind his desk, on which was a small laptop. Robie sat across from him, settled his hands over his flat stomach.

"It's been a while, Will," said the man.

"I've been kind of busy, Shane."

Shane Connors said, "I know you have. Good work."

"Maybe, maybe not."

Connors cocked his head to the left. "Explain that."

Robie took ten minutes to walk him through the recent developments. When he was done the other man leaned back in his chair, his gaze solidly on Robie.

"I can get the squad makeup right now. But once you get that, what are your plans?"

"To follow it up. There's a maximum of seven of them left. Local ones will be the focus, of course."

"I can see that."

Connors leaned toward his laptop, hit some keys, and then sat back. "Give it ten minutes." He continued to look at Robie. "It's been twelve years for you."

"I know. I've been counting too."

As though on cue, Robie could hear the tick of a clock coming from somewhere in the office.

Connors said, "Looked down the road?"

"I've been looking down the road since the first day."

"And?"

"And there are certain possibilities. But nothing more than that."

Connors looked disappointed by this, but he said nothing. His gaze went to the laptop. For the next eight minutes both men stared at it.

When the email fell into the electronic mailbox,

Connors hit a few keys and a printer resting on the edge of the desk whooshed. Some papers slid out. He picked them up but did not glance at the pages before passing them to Robie.

"I need a fresh car. Untraceable," said Robie. "I can leave my bike as collateral."

Connors nodded. "It'll take two minutes."

"Thanks."

He made a call. Two minutes passed. The computer dinged. Connors nodded again.

"Done."

They rose.

Robie said, "I appreciate this, Shane."

"I know."

Robie shook his hand. As he turned to leave Connors said, "Will?"

Robie turned back.

"Yeah?"

"When you look down the road next time, look farther than a place like this."

Robie glanced around the office, settled his gaze back on the man, and gave a slight nod. Then he was walking down the hall, the papers clutched in his hand.

79

Before starting up the car, a trim, tan Chevy, Robie looked at the pieces of paper. There were only three names on them, because of the seven squad members other than Wind, Getty, and Broome, four had died, all of them years ago. That made Robie's job a little easier. At least potentially. There was something else that made it easier still. All lived locally. Also included were their current addresses and a brief military history of each. The military kept impeccable records.

He slipped the papers into his pocket, started up the car, and raced past the guard on his way out of the small government complex. As he retraced his route back to Virginia, he thought about Connors in his little cage back there. Connors had taught Robie pretty much everything he knew. The man was a legend in the field of sanctioned assassinations. When he'd officially retired and Robie had gone full throttle, operating all over the world, he and Connors had lost contact. Yet Robie could still vividly remember the first mission the two had performed together. After the kill was done, Connors had kissed the barrel of his rifle. When

Robie asked him why he had done that, Connors had replied simply, "Because it's the only thing standing between me being here and me not being here."

There were a few men who could not be bought under any circumstances. Shane Connors was one of them.

Robie made sure he wasn't followed and zigzagged the last ten miles of his trip just to be certain.

He got back to the farmhouse early in the morning. Vance was awake with gun in hand and a serious expression on her face. Julie was asleep on a couch in the back room of the first floor.

Vance had seen the car pull up. "Where'd you get it?" she asked when he came into the house.

He held up the pieces of paper. "Same place I got these."

As they stood in the doorway gazing at the sleeping Julie curled up like a cat on the couch, Vance said, "She didn't want to go upstairs. I don't think she wanted to be that far away from me."

He walked into the kitchen. Vance followed.

They sat, looked over the names and current addresses.

"Three individuals. Two guys and one woman," said Vance. "How do you want to do this? Split up again?"

"Don't think so. They've been warned by Julie's comments. They probably know what we're going to do."

"So they'll anticipate we'll go after these folks and they'll be waiting?"

"Maybe something a little more efficient."

"Like what?"

"Like maybe they'll make all three disappear."

"You mean kill them?"

"If they kill two, then they've done our work for us. They left the one who really matters. If they make all three go away, we're in the same boat as before."

Vance set her gun on the table and rubbed her eyes.

"You need to get some sleep," said Robie.

"Look who's talking," she shot back.

"I'll take the first watch. You can catch a few hours."

"It'll be eight a.m. You won't go to sleep then."

"I actually feel pretty rested."

She squeezed his arm.

"What was that for?" he asked.

"Just checking to see if you're actually human. Despite your ability to bleed."

He said, "So we go after these people one by one, knowing that they'll be waiting."

Vance added, "So they really have the upper hand. Like you said, they could just make them disappear."

"They could, except for one thing."

"What's that?"

"If they need one of them for some reason to do something."

"Like what?"

"If I knew that I wouldn't be sitting here trying to figure it out."

"What do we do with Julie? We can't leave her

here. And it would be really stupid to take her on something like this."

"It might be stupid, but I'm going anyway."

They glanced over to see Julie standing in the doorway looking at them with sleepy eyes that still managed, at their edges, to look angry and even betrayed.

Vance said, "Boy, you're really good at eaves-dropping."

Julie retorted, "It's the only way I find out anything with you two."

Robie said, "It's dangerous."

"What else is new?" Julie replied in an even tone. She sat at the table. "I've been shot at, nearly blown up, seen my parents killed. Chased on foot, chased by car. So really, your 'dangerous' argument falls pretty flat."

Vance glanced at Robie and a smile tugged at her lips. "At certain levels her logic is awfully compelling."

"So the logic is, since you've nearly been killed a few times, the smart thing is to put you in another situation where you'll probably get killed?" said Robie.

"Don't feel you're responsible for me, Will, because you're not," replied Julie. She tucked her hair behind her ears and glared at him.

Vance's smile faded. "Okay, you two, the last thing we need is to turn on each other."

Robie said, "I am responsible for you. I've been responsible for you ever since we walked off that bus."

"Your choice, not mine. I'm a victim of circumstance."

"But you'd still be a victim."

"I want to find out why my parents were murdered. That's all. Anything more than that I don't care." She looked at Vance and then at Robie. "So don't feel you have to care about what happens to me. Because you don't."

"We're just trying to help you, Julie," exclaimed Vance.

"I'm not your little do-gooder project, okay? Foster kid off the street you want to make all well and good. Forget it. That's not what this is about."

"You're stuck with us, Julie, whether you want to be or not. And if it weren't for us you'd be dead," added Robie.

"I feel like I'm already dead."

"I can understand that. But feeling dead and actually being dead are two totally different things."

"Why should I trust anybody?" she retorted.

"I think we've earned your trust," Robie snapped.

"Well, think again," Julie shot back.

She stood and left the room.

Robie said to Vance, "Can you believe that crap?"

Vance stared across the table at him. "She's just a kid, Robie. She's lost her parents and she's scared."

Robie immediately calmed and looked guilty. "I know."

"We have to stick together to get through this."

"Might be easier said than done."

"Why?"

"Events might conspire to tear us apart."

"Events?"

"Your loyalty should be to the FBI, Vance. Not me."

"Why don't you let me decide that for myself." She put a hand over his. "And me being here shows exactly where my loyalties lie, Robie."

Robie stared at her for a moment and then got up and walked out, leaving a surprised Vance staring after him.

80

Robie went out into the barn, uncovered a box on the workbench, and took out a pack of Winston cigarettes. He popped one out, lit it up, and put the filter to his mouth. He drew in the carcinogens and then exhaled them.

Lung cancer slow or bullet fast. What's the real difference? Time? Who gives a shit?

He took another pull on his smoke, stretched out his neck. He took one final puff, ground the cigarette out on the workbench, and left the barn, locking the door behind him.

He stared up at the small farmhouse. There were two lights on inside.

One room where Julie was.

One room where Vance was.

He was separated from them by about fifty feet.

He was actually separated from them by about fifty light-years.

I am a killer. I pull triggers. I end lives. I do no more than that.

He turned and pulled his gun so fast she threw up her hands to shield her face.

Vance slowly lowered her arms and gazed at him.

He eased down his gun and said, "I thought you were in the house."

"I *was* in the house. But I decided to come and check on you."

"I'm just fine."

She eyed the gun. "Fine, if a little edgy?"

"I prefer to call it being professional."

She folded her arms across her chest, took a breath, exhaled, and watched it turn into mist in the chilly air. "We all are in this together, you know."

He holstered his weapon but said nothing.

She moved closer. "You know, I understand guys who keep it all bottled up inside. The silent, stoic warrior. The FBI sure as hell has enough of them. But it does get old after a while. And a little grating, particularly at times like these."

Robie looked away. "I'm not like anybody at the FBI, Vance. I kill people. I'm ordered to do it. But I carry out those orders. No remorse. No nothing."

She said, "So why didn't you kill Jane Wind and her son? Why did you take the time to get her other child to safety? And you did it while people were trying to kill you. Explain that to me."

"Maybe I should have just killed them."

"If I thought you believed that I'd shoot you right now."

He turned to see Vance pointing her pistol at his chest.

"So are you just a killer, Robie? Don't give a damn about anything or anyone else?"

"Why do you care?"

"I'm not sure why. It just seems that I do. Maybe I'm just stupid. I just swore an oath of loyalty to you back there. But it didn't seem to register with you. I wasn't expecting you to jump up and cheer when I put you above the FBI and my professional career, but I did expect some type of positive reaction. Instead you just walked out."

Robie turned and started to walk back toward the house.

"Do you always just walk away when the questions get tough?" she snapped. "Is that your way of handling things when the going gets shitty? If so, it sucks. I expected better from you."

He turned back around, settled his hands in his pockets, and rocked back and forth on his heels. He took several shallow breaths and stared at a spot directly over Vance's shoulder.

She walked toward him, sliding her gun back into its belt holster. "I thought I came here to be part of something. Please don't tell me I was wrong about that."

Robie glanced at the house. "She's only a kid. She's in way over her head. She shouldn't be involved in this at all."

"I know that. But she's also a tough kid. And smart. And determined."

Robie's mouth twisted. "This isn't some scrape-up on the playground. Or some chemistry test you either pass or fail. One or both of us probably won't make it through to the end. So what chance does she have?"

Vance said, "But you're just a killer, Robie. You said that's all you are. So why do you care what happens to me or her? It's just another job. If we die, we die."

"But she shouldn't die. She deserves to have a life."

"Pretty weird statement for a cold-blooded killer to make."

"Okay, Vance, I get your point."

She pointed toward the house. "Let's go work on the plan. *All* of us."

Robie didn't say anything, but he started to walk toward the house. Vance fell into step beside him.

He said, "Whatever happens, Julie is going to survive this."

Vance said, "And for what it's worth, I'll do all I can to make sure you do too."

81

Jerome Cassidy.

Elizabeth Claire Van Beuren. Her maiden name was Elizabeth Claire and she had incorporated that into her married name, Van Beuren.

Gabriel Siegel.

Those were the three names on the list.

Robie stared down at them as he drank his coffee at the kitchen table of the farmhouse.

It was eight-thirty. The sun was well up. He could hear the shower running upstairs and figured Vance had just stepped into it. Julie was already up. She was in the back room, no doubt brooding about their last encounter.

Fifteen minutes later Vance was seated across from him, her hair still wet, her pants and shirt wrinkled but presentable.

"If we have to be off grid much longer," she said, "I might have to get a few things."

He nodded, rose, and poured her a cup of coffee.

She spun the pieces of paper around and eyed the list of names.

"Who do we go after first?" she asked.

Robie handed her a cup of coffee right as Julie walked in. Her eyes were puffy and her clothes were even more wrinkled than Vance's. She obviously had not bothered to undress when she had gone back to sleep.

Robie held up the cup. "Want some?"

"I can get it," she said irritably.

She took down a cup and poured out her coffee. They sat at the table, not making eye contact.

Robie pushed the pieces of paper at Julie and said, "Recognize any of these names?"

She took her time looking at the list.

"No. My parents never mentioned any of them to me. Do you have pictures of them?"

"Not yet," answered Robie. "You sure, though? None of them ring a bell?"

"None."

He took the list and eyed it.

"Gabriel Siegel is closest distance-wise. Lives in Manassas. We'll go there first, find out what we can."

Vance said, "If we're doing it geographically, Van Beuren will be next and Cassidy last. But they might be at work. I'm assuming these are the home addresses."

"I thought about that too. But if they're not at home and someone else is, we can flash our creds and get the work addresses."

"Once we hit one of these addresses we could pick up a tail, Robie," said Vance. "And they could follow us right back here."

"Well, we just have to make sure they don't do that."

"How about we call the people on the list first?" said Julie. "That way we don't have to expose ourselves."

"Or how about I call the Bureau in and get them picked up for questioning?" said Vance. "They can't have bought off everyone at the FBI."

"That's what we thought last time," noted Robie. "It didn't work out too well."

"Come on, you know what I mean."

"I'd prefer we do this alone," he said.

"Okay, so we go with this Siegel guy first," said Vance. "I've looked at his military history. What does that tell us about him?"

"He was the staff sergeant. The leader of the squad. Fifty years old now. Out of the service for years. Don't know what he does now. My source didn't have that info."

Julie pulled out the phone Robie had given her. "Let me plug in his military history and address and see if Google can tell us anything."

She looked at Robie's sheet and then typed away on her miniature keyboard. She waited for the data to load.

"Mr. Siegel has a Facebook page." She turned the phone around so they could see it. An image of a jowly man with graying hair stared back at them.

"Do we know it's the right guy?" asked Vance.

Julie said, "His Facebook says he was in the Army during Gulf One, and he's even listed the name of the Army squad he was in."

She showed this to Robie, who nodded. "He's the right Siegel."

Julie continued. "According to his profile he works at SunTrust Bank as a branch manager."

"Lots of SunTrust branches around here," said Vance. "Does it say which one?"

"No. But his likes are guns, football, and chili cook-offs. He has twenty-nine friends, which isn't a lot, but I don't know how long he's been on Facebook either. And he's a really old guy."

"He's only fifty," Vance pointed out.

Julie shrugged. "Like I said, he's a *really* old guy. And I don't see anything on his page that would explain why all these people are dead."

"What about Cassidy?" said Robie.

Julie hit some keys and the page loaded. "Quite a few Jerome Cassidys." She ran her eye down the page and hit the scroll key. "Offhand I don't see any that list military service or the address you gave, at least on the Google summary page. I can go more in-depth on each of them."

"Try Van Beuren. That's not such a common name," said Vance.

Julie did so. The page loaded. "A lot more than one would think," she said. "It'll take a while to go through these."

"We don't have a while," said Robie. "We need to hit this now."

He had pulled the car into the barn. He had earlier loaded the vehicle up with gear he thought they might need from the bunker underneath the barn. He showed Vance the firepower in the backseat. She touched an MP-5 and gazed at a Barrett rifle that could punch a hole in an armored Hummer.

"Where'd you get stuff like that?" she asked. "Never mind, I don't want to know," she added quickly.

Robie took out from the trunk three armored vests and put one on Julie while Vance slipped one on, Velcroing it tightly to her torso and putting her jacket on over it.

Julie said, "Is this really necessary?"

"Only if you want to survive," said Robie.

"It's heavy," she said.

"Better than taking the bullet it'll stop," replied Vance.

Robie drove, Vance rode shotgun, and Julie sat in the backseat. Robie had backed the car into the barn, so he pulled it straight out. He got out and closed and locked the barn door.

When he got back in Vance said, "Might be the last time we can come here."

"It'll be what it'll be," replied Robie. "Now, let's see what Mr. Siegel can tell us."

He gunned the engine and drove toward the road.

82

It was a quiet tree-lined street with modest-sized houses with attached garages, houses that would sell for two or three times what they would fetch in most other parts of the country. The lots were small and poorly landscaped, the bushes around the cookie-cutter homes overgrown enough to hide most of their fronts. Cars were parked along the streets and in a few of the yards small kids played under the watchful eyes of their mothers or nannies.

Robie slowed his car and checked the addresses. Vance saw it first.

"Third one on the right," she said. "There's a van in the driveway. Hopefully, someone's home."

Robie eased over to the curb and killed the engine. He took off his sunglasses, picked up a pair of binoculars from the front seat, and surveyed the area. There were multiple attack points, too many for them to adequately cover.

"We're way out in the open here," he said.

"No surprise," replied Vance. "I'll go knock on the door. You cover me from here."

“How about the other way around?” said Robie.

“I’ve got my FBI creds, Robie. They trump yours.”

“A federal shield is going to intimidate anyone.”

Vance already had the door open.

“If someone starts shooting, make sure you shoot back,” she said. “And shoot straight!”

Robie and Julie watched as Vance walked up to the front stoop and rang the doorbell.

Robie pulled his pistol from its holster, hit the button to roll down the passenger-side window, and kept his gaze sweeping in long arcs but always returning to an imaginary three-foot box around Vance.

“She’s pretty brave to just walk up there,” noted Julie.

“She’s a super-special FBI agent; it comes with the territory.”

“Don’t try to make nice with me, Robie.”

“So I’m Robie now? What happened to Will?”

She didn’t answer.

The front door opened and Robie fixed his gaze on the woman standing there. Vance flashed her cred pack and then took a few minutes explaining to the woman what she wanted. The look on the woman’s face—Robie assumed she was Siegel’s wife—was one of astonishment. The two women spoke for about a minute longer, and then the door closed and Vance walked quickly back to the car.

Robie saw the curtain on the front window of the house move to the side and the woman peer out.

Vance got back into the car and Robie started it up.

"Gabriel Siegel works at a SunTrust branch about ten minutes from here. Got the address from his wife."

"She looked surprised," said Robie.

"She *was* surprised. I think she thought it had to do with some problem at the bank."

"Maybe her husband is stealing money," piped up Julie. "Maybe he's laundering it for terrorists. And my parents and the others found out."

"Maybe," said Robie. He looked at Vance. "The lady was watching you as you walked back to the car."

"I'm sure she was. She's probably calling her husband as we speak. So let's get going."

"I'll take the meeting with him," said Robie. "You stay in the car with Julie."

"And when do I get to do something other than sit in the car?" she asked.

"Your time will come," said Robie. "Before this is over everybody's time will come."

They reached the bank branch in less than ten minutes. Robie left them in the car and walked into the small brick building right off a busy road in Manassas. He asked for Gabriel Siegel and was shown back to a glass-enclosed cubicle about ten feet square.

Siegel was about five-eight, stocky and pale. To Robie, he had looked much better in his Facebook photo.

Siegel rose from the chair behind his desk and said, "What's this about?"

His wife obviously had called him.

Robie flashed his badge and said, "You were in an Army squad in Gulf One?"

"Yeah, so? Does the Army want me to reenlist? Not going to happen. I did my stint. And I'm too out of shape to carry a rifle in the desert."

He sat down in his chair, while Robie remained standing. "I'm more interested in the people you served with. Keep in touch with any of them?"

"Some, yeah."

"Who exactly?"

"*Exactly* what is this about?"

The banker was showing some balls, thought Robie.

"It's a national security issue. But I can tell you that it might be tied to the bus explosion and the deaths of those people at the restaurant on Capitol Hill."

Siegel turned paler still. "Jesus. Somebody from my old squad was involved in that? I can't believe it."

"So you know them all, well?" Robie asked pointedly.

"No. I meant that, well, we all fought for our country. And to turn against it . . ." His voice trailed off and he just sat there, pudgy hands on his cheap desk, looking like a little boy who'd just been told his puppy had been run over by a car.

"Which of them have you kept in touch with?"

Siegel came out of his trance and said slowly, "Doug

Biddle, Fred Alvarez, Bill Thompson, and Ricky Jones died. Years back."

"That I know. But they didn't live in the area. They were all spread out."

"Yeah, but we would call each other. Exchange emails. Doug came here once and I took him around to some of the monuments. Fred got killed in a car accident. Billy put a damn gun in his mouth and pulled the trigger. Doug and Ricky both had cancer. Younger than me. I think it was all the crap we were exposed to over there. You know, Gulf War syndrome. I could be dying and not even know it. Every time I get a migraine I think it's all over."

He sank back in his chair.

Robie sat down opposite him and said, "Any of your old buddies locally that you hang with?"

"I saw Leo Broome a few times. That was a while back."

"How far back?"

"Over ten years ago. Ran into him at a bar in Seattle, of all places. He was out there on business and I had just changed jobs and was at a seminar. He seemed to be doing okay. Think he worked for the government or something like that. Don't remember exactly."

"Anyone else?"

"In the Middle East I was closest to Curtis Getty. But I haven't seen him since we got back stateside. Don't even know where he is now."

That would be dead, thought Robie.

"Leo Broome ever mention Getty?"

"Don't remember. For some reason it didn't seem like they had kept up. But like I said, that was a decade ago."

Ten years ago, that might have been the case, thought Robie. "Anyone else? Rick Wind, for instance?"

"I read that he had been murdered. Is that what this is about?"

"Had you been in contact with Wind?"

"No. Not for years. Used to see him. But he'd gotten strange. Bought that pawnshop in that crummy neighborhood. I don't know. It was just different."

"How about Jerome Cassidy?"

"Nope. Haven't heard from him since we left the Army."

"He lives in the area. Not that far from here."

"Didn't know that."

"How about Elizabeth Van Beuren? That's her married name. Her maiden name was—"

"Elizabeth Claire. I know."

"It was unusual having a woman in the ranks back then, wasn't it?"

"Yeah. Things are different now, of course. But I always thought the combat exclusion rule for women was crap. They can fight just as good as men. And in a unit they really let their strengths shine. Guys are more macho. Women build a team perspective. And I gotta tell you, even though women were deployed in combat support positions, but technically weren't supposed to shoot back, they sure as hell did. At least in Gulf One. And Lizzie was one of the best. She was a better soldier than I was, I can tell you that."

"But she's no longer in the Army," said Robie.

"Well, there's a good reason for that," replied Siegel.

"You've been in touch with her?"

"I have."

"So what's the reason she's no longer in the Army?"

"Cancer. Started in her breasts and then it spread. It's in her brain, lungs, liver now. She's terminal, of course. Once that stuff metastasizes, it's over. They don't have any magic bullets for that. She's at a hospice center in Gainesville."

"You've seen her?"

"Went regularly until about a month ago. She was in and out of it. Mostly out. Morphine. I'm not even sure if she's still alive. I should have kept up, but I guess it was just too hard to see her like that."

"What's the name of the place?"

"Central Hospice Care. It's off of Route 29."

"Okay."

Siegel exclaimed, "I'm telling you, it's all the crap we breathed in over there. Depleted uranium, toxic cocktails from all the artillery blasts. Fires burning all over the damn place, painting the sky black, burning crap we didn't know what the hell it was. And there we all were, just sucking it in. That could just as easily be me in that bed waiting for the end."

Robie handed Siegel a card. "Anything else occurs to you, give me a call."

"What is this really all about? How can somebody from my old squad be involved in all this stuff?"

"That's what we're trying to find out." Robie paused. "Did your wife give you a heads-up we were coming?"

"She did," admitted Siegel.

"She worried about something?"

"She's worried I might lose my job."

Robie thought back to Julie's theory of money laundering for terrorists. "Why? Problems here?"

"I haven't done anything wrong, if that's what you're implying. But who comes into banks anymore to do stuff? It's all online. I'll be here for about eight hours today and I'll see maybe two people. How much longer do you think they're going to pay me to do that? There's a reason banks have all the money. They're cheap as hell. Writing's on the wall. World has changed. And I guess I haven't changed fast enough. Maybe I will end up carrying a rifle in the desert. What else is there for a guy my age? I can be a fat mercenary. But I'll die the first day out there."

"Well, thanks for your help."

"Yeah," Siegel said absently.

Robie left him there looking like he'd already received a death sentence.

83

They pulled into the parking lot of Central Hospice Care twenty minutes later. There were about fifteen cars in the parking lot. As they drove through the lot, Robie examined each one to see if they were occupied.

He pulled into a space and looked at Vance. "You want to do this one or should I?"

Julie said, "I want to go in."

"Why?" asked Robie.

"She fought with him. Maybe she knew something about my dad."

"She's probably not in much condition to talk," said Vance.

"Then why are we even here?" asked Julie.

Robie said, "I'll take her in with me. You keep watch."

"You sure?" asked Vance.

"No, but I'm doing it anyway."

He and Julie walked into the hospice building, a two-story brick structure with lots of windows and a cheery atmosphere inside. It did not look like a place where people would come to see their lives end. Maybe that was the point.

The flash of Robie's creds got them escorted back to Elizabeth Van Beuren's room. It was as cheery as the rest of the place, with flowers grouped on tables and on the windowsill. Light streamed in from outside. A nurse was checking on Van Beuren. When she moved away, Robie's hopes for any personal information from the critically ill woman sank.

She looked like a skeleton and was on a ventilator, the machine inflating her lungs via a tube inserted down her throat, with another tube bleeding off that to carry away toxic carbon dioxide. There was also a feeding tube inserted into her abdomen, and multiple IV lines running to her. Bags of medication hung from an IV stand.

The nurse turned to them. "Can I help you?"

"We just came to ask Ms. Van Beuren some questions," said Robie. "But it doesn't look like that's possible."

"She was put on the ventilator six days ago," said the nurse. "She comes in and out. She's on heavy painkillers." The nurse patted her patient's hand. "She's a real sweetheart. She was in the Army. It's just awful it's come to this." She paused. "What sort of questions did you have?"

Robie pulled out his creds. "I'm with the DOD. We were just making some inquiries into a military matter and her name came up as a possible source of information."

"I see. Well, I don't think she'll be of much help. She's in the last stages of her disease."

Robie studied the ventilator and the monitoring systems hooked up to the shriveled woman lying in the bed. "So the ventilator is helping to keep her alive?"

"Yes."

He looked at Julie, who was staring at Van Beuren.

"But she's in hospice," said Robie.

The nurse looked uncomfortable. "There are many levels of hospice. It's all in what the patient or their family want." She looked down at the woman. "But it won't be long, ventilator or not."

"So the ventilator is what the family wanted?" asked Robie.

"I'm really not at liberty to say. Those matters are private. And I can't see what this would have to do with any military inquiry," she added with some annoyance.

Julie had wandered over to the windowsill and had picked up a photo. "Is this her family?"

The nurse looked curiously at Julie and then at Robie. "You said you were with DOD. But why is she with you?"

"I'm really not at liberty to say," answered Robie, causing the nurse to purse her lips.

Julie brought the photo around to show Robie. She

said to the nurse, "My dad was in the same Army squad as Mrs. Van Beuren. I was hoping to find out some things about his past from her."

The nurse's stiff expression vanished. "Oh, I see, sweetie. I didn't realize. Yes, that's her and her family. There used to be more pictures in the room. But her daughter and husband have been slowly taking them. They know the end is almost here."

Robie took the photo. It showed Van Beuren in healthier days. She was in her dress greens, her chest awash in medals. A man was beside her, presumably her husband. And there was a girl about Julie's age.

"So that's her husband?" asked Robie.

"Yes. George Van Beuren. And that's their daughter, Brooke Alexandra. She's older now, of course. That photo was from a number of years ago. She's in college now."

"So you know her?"

"She's been in to visit her mother quite often. That's how I know her. Brooke's a lovely girl. She's very torn up about her mother."

"And her husband?"

"He comes here regularly. I know he's devastated too. They're barely fifty and they have to face this? But who ever said life was fair."

"Anybody else come to see her?"

"A few people. At least that I know. I'm not assigned to this wing all the time."

"You have a guest log?"

"It's out front by the receptionist. But not everyone signs in."

"Why not?"

"This is not a high-security facility," bristled the nurse. "People who come here to visit friends and family are usually very emotionally upset. Sometimes they forget to sign in. Or one person signs in for the group. As you can imagine, we're a bit flexible on that. They come here to show love and respect and support. But it's just not the sort of place anyone wants to *have* to visit."

"Understood. How long has she been here?"

"Four months."

"Isn't that a long time to be in hospice?"

"We have people here for longer and shorter periods. It's not a one-time-period-fits-all sort of place. And until a couple of weeks or so ago Ms. Van Beuren wasn't like she is now. The drop-off came relatively quickly."

"But the ventilator will keep her alive so long as it's on, right? I mean, even if she can't breathe on her own?"

"I really can't talk to you about this. Federal and state law prohibits me from doing so."

"I'm just trying to understand the situation."

The nurse once more seemed uncomfortable. "Look, normally the use of a ventilator would decertify a person for hospice care. Hospice is to allow a patient to pass with dignity. We're not a place where someone goes to be cured of her disease, or to artificially sustain life."

"So the use of the ventilator in a situation like this is unusual?"

"It could be grounds for decertification and the transfer of the patient back to a hospital or other care facility."

"So why the ventilator?" asked Robie. "Does she have a chance of pulling through?"

"Again, even if I knew, I couldn't tell you. What I can tell you is that sometimes families reach a point where they have false hope. Or where they made a decision to come to hospice and then reconsider that decision."

"I see," said Robie.

Julie added, "It's hard watching someone you love die."

The nurse said, "Yes, it is. Very hard. Now, unless you have any other questions I have some things to do for my patient."

"You said her husband visits regularly?"

"Yes. But at odd hours. Brooke goes to college out of state so she doesn't get in as often."

"Do you have any idea where her husband works?"

"No, I don't."

"I can probably find that out easily enough."

The nurse looked at Julie, who was staring at Van Beuren. "I'm sorry that she couldn't tell you anything about your father."

"Yeah, me too."

Julie reached over and touched Van Beuren's hand. "I'm sorry," she said to the dying woman.

Then she turned and left. Robie handed his card to the nurse. "If her husband comes in can you have him give me a call?"

Robie glanced once more at the terminally ill former soldier, turned, and followed Julie out.

84

Robie held the door open for Julie and then climbed into the car after her. He buckled up and looked at Vance.

"Don't see anything with Elizabeth Van Beuren being helpful. She can't talk. And she won't be alive much longer."

"And what about Siegel? You didn't say much after you left the bank."

"He said he spoke to Leo Broome, but over a decade ago. Said he didn't know Curtis Getty or Jerome Cassidy were in the area. He seems to just be waiting to see if he'll get cancer too, or lose his job. Unless he's hiding something really well, I'm not sure how he figures into this either."

"So that leaves Jerome Cassidy," said Vance.

"He's in Arlington, right?"

"What the paper says."

"Note anything suspicious out here?"

"Not a thing."

"Let's go."

*

It took over an hour to get to Arlington because traffic was bad, or, in other words, traffic was normal heading toward D.C. It was nearly lunchtime when Robie found a parking space and pulled into it. He turned to Vance. "You sure this is the space?"

She held up the page and he read off it.

All three of them turned to look at the building.

"It's a bar and grill," said Julie.

Robie looked upward. "But there seem to be rooms above it. Maybe Cassidy lives in one of them."

Vance undid her seat belt. "My turn."

Robie looked across the street and then back at her. The area they were in was congested, like much of Arlington. There were too many homes and businesses with not enough land to put them on. That resulted in tight streets with not much parking, and lots of hidden spots from which they could be watched.

"Let's all go in on this one," said Robie.

Vance shook her head. "What about the car? We can't leave it unattended. I'm not looking to get back in here with a bomb under the chassis."

"I got this car from a special source. Which means it has special defensive devices."

"Like what?"

"Like if someone tries to break into it or booby-trap it, it will not be a fun time for them and we will most certainly know about it."

They all climbed out of the car. Robie's gaze was shifting in every direction.

"What is it?" asked Vance nervously. "You see something?"

"No, but that doesn't mean they're not out there."

"You didn't seem this tense at the other places."

"That's because this is the *last* place."

Vance took a quick breath and nodded. "Right. I see your point."

The name of the bar was the Texas Hold 'Em Saloon. At ten minutes to noon it already had about twenty people inside. It was decorated in a western theme, heavy on saddles, bridles, cowboy hats and boots, and with murals of horsemen, cattle, and the flat Texas plains. At the far end of the space was an enormous bar that spanned the entire width of the interior. Barstools with faux bull's horns as seatbacks lined the space in front. Behind the bar a large Texas flag hung on the wall. All around the flag were stacked hundreds of libations designed to wet the whistle, lighten the wallet, and dull the senses.

"Somebody spent a lot of cash on this place," commented Robie.

A young woman dressed all in black except for her white cowboy hat and white boots and holding a menu approached them.

"Party of three?" she asked.

"Maybe," said Robie. "We were given this address for a friend of ours. Jerome Cassidy. You know him?"

"Mr. Cassidy is the owner."

Robie and Vance exchanged a quick glance.

"Is he here?"

"Can I tell him who's asking?' said the woman politely.

Vance held out her cred pack. "FBI. Could you take us back to where he is?"

The woman looked uncertain. "Can you let me just check to make sure he's here?"

"So long as you check while we can see and hear you," said Robie.

The woman's polite features vanished. She looked at them nervously. "Is Mr. Cassidy in some sort of trouble? He's a great boss."

"We just want to talk to him," said Robie. "So he *is* here?"

"Back in his office."

"Lead the way," said Robie.

She turned and started off hesitantly. She walked past the bar and down a short hallway and turned right. Passing through a door marked "Authorized Personnel Only," she continued on. There was another short corridor down here with two doors on either side. She stopped at one marked "Office" and timidly knocked.

They heard noises coming from inside this room.

Robie's hand ventured toward his gun. Vance saw this movement and mimicked him.

A voice from inside the room called out, "Yeah?"

"Mr. Cassidy? It's Tina. I have some people here who want to talk to you."

"Do they have an appointment?"

"No."

"Then tell them to make one."

Robie moved past Tina and tried to open the door. It was locked.

"Hey!" Cassidy called out. "What the hell is going on? I said to make an appointment."

Robie pounded on the door. "Cassidy, it's the FBI. Open the door. Now!"

Robie heard more noises, shuffling, and a drawer slamming. He moved back and then drilled his right foot against the doorknob. The door flew inward as Tina screamed and jumped back.

Robie and Vance had their guns out. Vance moved Julie to the side. "Stay back," she ordered.

Robie moved into the room first, with Vance covering him.

Cassidy was standing behind his desk staring at him. He was about Robie's height, but thinner, with broad shoulders and narrow hips. His hair was longish, gray-and-brown. His face was slender but good-looking, with a few days' worth of stubble. He had on faded jeans and an untucked white shirt.

As Robie moved forward, Cassidy said, "You want to tell me why you just broke my door and are pointing a gun at me?"

"You want to tell me why you didn't open it when we asked you to?"

Cassidy glanced at Robie's gun. Then he stared over

at Vance as she moved into the room. "Let me see your creds, right now."

Robie and Vance held them out.

Cassidy read them carefully and picked up a pen and wrote their names and badge numbers down on the white blotter on his desk. "Just want to get the info right for my lawyers when they sue your ass."

"You didn't open the door, Mr. Cassidy," pointed out Vance.

"I was just fixing to when you broke it open. And I didn't know if you really were the Feds."

"Your employee told you that we were FBI."

"I pay her ten dollars an hour to look cute and seat people. I don't trust her to know the FBI from a postal worker or some guy looking to rob me." He eyed Tina through the open doorway. "It's okay, Tina. Just go back to work." She hurried off and Cassidy looked at Robie, who had holstered his gun. "And you're not even FBI. You're DCIS."

"You know DCIS?"

"I was in the Army. So what?" He sat down behind his desk, pulled a slender cigar from his shirt pocket, and lit up.

"You can't smoke in a restaurant or bar in Virginia," said Vance.

"While it's true that the good commonwealth of Virginia has seen fit to deprive its citizens of the right to smoke in an establishment like this—even though the health department, which enforces said law, has no real enforcement powers and lots of places still light up to their heart's content—this is my personal space and it has a special ventilation system, so I can smoke myself into late-stage lung cancer if I want to. Care to sit and watch?"

"We have some questions for you," said Robie.

"And my lawyers will have *no* answers to your questions." He pulled a card from an old-fashioned Rolodex and handed it to Robie. "Their contact info is right on there, Mr. DCIS."

"You always that quick to call in the legal beagles?" asked Robie.

"I've found they're worth every penny of their outrageous fees."

"So you have a lot of need for legal services?" asked Vance.

"Ma'am, this is America. If a businessman wants to wipe his ass he better have a lawyer on retainer."

Robie looked around the office. It was high-dollar decorated. And there was a shelf full of business awards against one wall.

"You look to be pretty successful. Bar must do well."

"This bar is one of twenty businesses that I own. And all of them are highly profitable, and I don't have one dime of debt. How many of the Fortune 500 jerk-offs can say that? I've even got my own damn plane."

"Good for you," said Robie. He put the business card for the law firm down on Cassidy's desk.

"We're here to ask you about your old Army squad."

Cassidy looked genuinely surprised by this. He took the cigar out of his mouth.

"What the hell for?"

"You keep in touch with any of them?"

Cassidy looked past him and saw Julie peering around the corner of the doorway.

Cassidy slowly rose and said, "Come on in here, girl."

Julie eyed Robie, who nodded. She stepped into the office.

"Closer," said Cassidy.

Julie drew nearer to the desk.

Cassidy stubbed out his cigar in an ashtray and rubbed his chin. "Damn."

"What is it?" asked Vance.

"You're Julie, aren't you?" said Cassidy.

"I am. But I don't know you."

"I knew your parents real well. How they doing?"

Robie said, "How do you know them?"

"Like you said, the squad. Curtis Getty and me served together. Saved my ass a couple times in Gulf One."

"I didn't even know my dad was in the Army until just recently," said Julie.

Cassidy nodded, but didn't look surprised by this. "He wasn't much of a talker."

"How did you know I was Julie? I don't think we've ever met."

"Because you look just like your mother. Same eyes, same dimple, everything. And we *have* met. Only you were just a baby. Diapered you a couple of times myself. Probably botched the job. Not great with little kids."

"So you kept in touch with them?" asked Robie.

"Not for a long time. I haven't seen them since Julie turned one."

"What happened?"

Cassidy looked away and shrugged. "Folks get busy. Drift apart." He eyed Julie. "Your mom doing okay?"

"No, she's dead."

"What?" Cassidy said quickly. "What the hell happened?" He put one hand on the desk to steady himself.

Robie said, "She and Curtis were murdered."

"Murdered!" Cassidy dropped back into his chair. The questions tumbled out. "Why? How? Who did it?"

"We were hoping you could help us answer those questions," said Robie.

"Me?"

"Yeah, you."

"Like I said, I haven't seen the Gettys in a long time."

"Didn't you know they lived in D.C.?" asked Robie.

"No. They didn't use to live around here. They were in Pennsylvania last time I saw them."

"Pennsylvania?" exclaimed Julie. "I didn't know that. I thought they were from California."

"Curtis might've been. But when we got back to the States they lived over near Pittsburgh. That was the last time I saw them, you understand. Didn't know they'd moved down here."

Vance said, "So you were living in Pennsylvania too back then?"

"Yeah. In fact, I lived with them for a while. Long time ago. Trying to get back on my feet. I actually knew your mom before she met your dad. They got married while he was still in uniform. I was at the wedding."

Robie glanced at Julie and noted her wide-eyed look at all this new information about her parents.

Cassidy continued. "Anyway, after Gulf One I didn't do too well. Got into some bad stuff. They helped me out."

"Drugs?" asked Robie.

"I wasn't the one into the drugs," said Cassidy quietly, looking away from Julie.

"I know my parents had drug problems," said Julie. "Especially my dad."

"He was a good man, Julie," said Cassidy. "Like I said, he saved my butt over in the desert. Earned himself the Bronze with valor. A Purple too. When we were in uniform he never touched even a drop of liquor. But after we came back we were all changed. The war wasn't that long. Not like Nam or WW II. But we saw some serious stuff over there. Lots of deaths, mostly civilians, women, kids. And lots of guys came back messed up or sick. Anyway, your daddy started using. Pot. Coke. Meth. Your mom tried to get him straight, but never really could. And then she fell into that crap too. Hard as hell to get out of that hole once you're in it."

"And what was your vice?" Vance asked.

"I was a drunk," said Cassidy frankly.

"And yet you own a bar?" said Robie.

"Best way to test yourself on a daily basis. I'm surrounded by the best stuff, and I haven't touched a drop of it in over a decade."

"Julie's fourteen. So about thirteen years ago was the last time you saw the Gettys?" asked Vance.

"That's what I said."

Robie looked around the spacious office. "The Gettys were pretty down on their luck. Might've been good if you'd returned the favor and helped them out."

Cassidy said, "Would've been glad to do it. If I could've found them." He opened his desk drawer and pushed a button located on the inside of it. A portrait of a woman on a horse on the wall behind his desk clicked open, revealing a safe.

He opened the safe, pulled out a stack of letters, and held them up. "Letters I wrote to your parents, Julie, over the years. All returned unopened, addressee unknown. I spent a lot of time and money trying to find you all. Never thought to look in my own backyard."

He tossed the letters down on his desk and sat back in his chair. "I can't believe they're dead," he said, his voice quavering. He wiped at his eyes and shook his head.

Robie looked at the letters. "Lot of effort went into those."

"Like I said, they were my friends. Curtis saved my life. They helped me when I needed it." He looked at Julie. "If your parents are gone, who are you staying with? Who's taking care of you?"

"Them, for now," said Julie, indicating Robie and Vance.

"Is she in protective custody or something?" asked Cassidy.

"Or something," replied Robie.

Cassidy looked at Julie. "I can help you. I would like to help you, just like I wanted to help your parents."

"We can talk about that later," said Robie. "Is there nothing else you can tell us about Getty, or the other members of the squad?"

"Like I said, I haven't kept in touch."

"Do you remember Gabriel Siegel and Elizabeth Claire?"

"Yeah, I do. How are they doing?"

"Not so great, actually. How about Rick Wind?"

"Yeah, he was a good guy. Fine soldier."

"He's dead now too. So is Leo Broome."

Cassidy stood and slapped his desktop. "All these people from my old squad have been killed?"

"Not all of them. But the mortality rate is higher than we'd like to see," said Vance dryly.

"Should I be worried?" asked Cassidy.

"I think everyone should be worried," replied Robie.

85

As they walked back to the car Robie said, "We've visited all three and nothing happened."

"Meaning they didn't tip their hand as to which one was important," said Vance.

"Smart move, actually."

"Maybe it didn't matter. Siegel didn't know anything except that Van Beuren was in a hospice. Van Beuren couldn't tell you anything because she's terminal. Cassidy was a little strange, though."

Julie said, "I liked him. He sort of reminded me a little of my dad."

Robie said, "He'd definitely tried to locate your family. But it was odd that he never knew any of the others were in the area. If the guy could afford to look for the Gettys, why not some of the others?"

"My family helped him, like he said," replied Julie. "And my dad saved his life. The other ones were just soldiers in the same squad."

"Maybe," said Robie. "But I'm not convinced."

Vance eyed his car. "You think it's okay to get in it?"

"I told you about the special features. But if it makes you feel any better I'll get in first and start it up."

"Robie, you don't have to do that. We're in this together."

"And because we're in this together, I do have to do it. No sense in all of us going up in the same flame ball."

They waited at the corner while he unlocked the car and got in. Vance and Julie tensed noticeably when he started the engine. When nothing happened, they both let out long breaths at the same time.

He drove to the corner and they climbed in.

"Now where?" asked Vance.

"Back to our little HQ, compare notes, think it through, and come up with new leads."

"I don't see anything *to* think through," grumbled Julie.

"You'd be surprised," replied Robie.

"Well, let's hope we're surprised," said Vance. "Because I don't see any daylight in all this either."

Traffic was just as bad heading west and it was well over ninety minutes later before they were seated at the table in the farmhouse kitchen staring at each other.

They'd grabbed some burgers and fries on the way back and had eaten in the car. But while their bellies were full, their heads were still empty of any promising leads.

"Okay, let's go through it again," said Robie.

"Do we have to?" said Julie. "It seems like a waste of time."

"Most of investigative work can be a waste of time. But you have to do it to get to the parts that actually mean anything," shot back Vance.

Robie looked at Vance. "Your turn."

Vance said, "Okay, we've gone down some scenarios that petered out. Let's retool and start by ruling out some people. From what you said about Van Beuren I don't see how she can be involved in any of this. She's been in hospice for months. She's got a machine breathing for her. Her husband and daughter are just watching her die, basically."

Robie nodded. "And Siegel seems to be just as clueless. He's more concerned about losing his job. And he seemed genuinely surprised when I told him why I wanted to talk to him."

"So maybe you were wrong, Robie," remarked Vance. "You said it was what Julie mentioned, about the other squad members, that caused them to try and kill her. It just doesn't appear to be the case."

Robie said, "But what about Cassidy?"

"What about him?"

"He knew the Gettys. I don't personally buy the fact that he couldn't find them. Or that he didn't know that any of his other squad members were around. The guy has cash, and cash gets you results. And while he seemed genuinely surprised that Curtis and Sara were dead, it just seems pretty odd."

Julie said, "My mom and dad never mentioned him. That's pretty odd too, considering how close he said they were. I mean, why didn't they answer his letters?"

"It doesn't make sense," agreed Robie.

Vance was about to say something when her phone buzzed. She looked at the number.

"Don't know that one. But the area code is northern Virginia."

"Better answer it," said Robie.

"Hello?" said Vance into the phone. The person on the other end of the line started speaking fast.

"Wait a minute, slow down." Vance clamped her phone against her ear with her shoulder, pulled out a notepad and pen, and started scribbling.

"Okay, okay, I'll be right over."

She clicked off and looked up at Robie.

"Who was it?" he asked.

"Maybe you were right after all," said Vance.

"About what?"

"That was Gabriel Siegel's wife. I left my contact info with her."

"Why was she calling?"

"Her husband got a phone call just after you left him. He walked out of the bank right afterwards and never came back. He missed a meeting with a client and a luncheon the bank was holding. He's just disappeared."

86

They didn't drive to the bank but instead went straight to Gabriel Siegel's house. His wife was waiting at the door as they pulled into the driveway. Robie led them up to the front porch. The woman looked at him strangely until she saw Vance behind him.

"We're partners," Vance said curtly. "Robie, this is Alice Siegel."

"Mrs. Siegel, we're here to help find your husband."

Alice Siegel nodded, her eyes brimming with tears. When she caught sight of Julie she once more looked confused. "Who is she?"

Robie said, "It's not something we can go into right now, ma'am. Can we go inside?"

Alice stepped back and let them pass through into the house. They settled in chairs around the living room.

Robie looked around. The interior had been done mostly on the cheap. But it was neat and clean and functional. The Siegels were clearly frugal. The bank probably didn't pay that much. But the Siegels obviously stretched dwindling dollars as far as they could go, just like millions of other families were doing right now.

Vance opened the conversation. "So you said he received a phone call and then walked out. Any idea who called him?"

"No one at the bank knows. I was hoping the call could be traced."

"Did it come to his line at the bank or his cell phone?"

"His office line. That's how they knew he had gotten the call."

"But if it came to the office didn't someone at the bank ask who was calling your husband?"

"I think they just put the calls through. It's a business, after all. I guess the person who answered just assumed Gabe would want the call. They don't have a formal receptionist or anything. Banks don't really do that anymore. They've scaled back."

"So your husband told me," said Robie. "Did the person at the bank say it was a man or a woman?"

"A man. Are you going to go there? I mean, isn't the trail getting cold?"

"We'll cover that end, Mrs. Siegel," said Vance. "But no crime has been committed. And your husband isn't technically missing. He went off apparently of his own free will."

"But he didn't come back. He just walked out. That's not normal."

"Could he have had an accident?"

"His car is still in the parking lot."

"So he might have walked off," said Robie. "Or gotten a ride from whoever called him. Have you tried calling his cell phone?"

"Twenty times. I texted him too. Nothing back. I'm very worried."

Robie eyed her closely. "Is there a reason why he would have just walked off like that?"

"The phone call. It must be."

Vance added, "But we don't know that the two events are connected. He might have been planning to walk off anyway. The timing of the call might just be a coincidence."

"But why?"

Robie said, "He mentioned to me that you were both worried he might lose his job at the bank."

"Well, walking out like that is a pretty good way to ensure that he *will* lose his job," snapped Alice.

"And you're sure he didn't try to contact you? On your cell? Maybe on your hard line?"

"We don't have a hard line. We cut that out when Gabe's pay was reduced last year."

"Can you think of any reason why your husband would just up and walk off like that?"

She eyed him suspiciously. "Well, *you* came to talk to him. And then he disappeared. Maybe you can tell me the reason."

That was fair enough, thought Robie.

"Your husband was in the Army during Gulf One," he began.

"Is that what this is about? But he's been out of the military for years."

"He was a member of a squad," continued Robie. "We were interested in that squad."

"Why?"

Robie hesitated and glanced at Vance. She said, "We were just interested, Mrs. Siegel. We wanted to ask your husband if he'd been in touch with anyone from his old squad."

"I know that he knew Elizabeth Claire Van Beuren. They had kept in touch."

"We know about her."

"She's dying."

"We know that too," said Vance. "Anybody else he ever mention?"

"A few names from time to time. Hard to remember."

"Leo Broome? Rick Wind? Curtis Getty? Jerome Cassidy?" prompted Robie.

"Getty, yes, that name I recall. Gabe said they had been close, but he hadn't seen him since he'd come back. Rick Wind sounds familiar. The thing is, Gabe didn't talk much about his military time. He was terrified that he was going to die because of the toxic conditions they fought in over there. There are soldiers dropping left and right and the Army won't even acknowledge there is a thing such as Gulf War syndrome. After Elizabeth got sick he went into a deep depression. He thought a lot of her. He was convinced he would be next."

Julie said, "You mentioned he and Curtis Getty were friends. Did he have any pictures of them together?"

Robie and Vance looked at Julie. Robie felt immediate guilt. He had never stopped to consider how all of this must have been affecting the teenager.

Alice looked momentarily flustered, but the earnest look on Julie's features prompted the woman to stand up. "I believe he does. Hold on for a moment."

She left the room and a couple of minutes later came back holding an envelope. She sat next to Julie, opened, the envelope, and took the photos out.

"Gabe brought these back from overseas. You're welcome to look through them."

Vance and Robie crowded in closer and they looked through the photos. Julie said, "There's my dad!"

Alice looked at Robie and then at Vance. "Her dad?"

"It's a long story," said Robie.

He took the photo from Julie and studied it.

The group was standing in front of a burned-out Iraqi tank. Someone had spray-painted the words "Saddam Kabob" across the blackened shell of the armored vehicle.

Curtis Getty was on the far right, dressed in combat

fatigues with his shirt unbuttoned, a pistol clenched in his right hand. He looked very young and very happy, probably to be alive. Next to him was Jerome Cassidy. His hair was brown and cut military short. His shirt was off and he looked tanned, lean, and muscular. Next to him was Elizabeth Claire. Shorter than the others, she looked tougher than all of them. Her uniform was sparklingly clean, with every button where it was supposed to be. Her sidearm was in its holster and she stared at the camera with a very serious expression.

As Robie looked at her image he thought it probably would never occur to her that she would be lying in hospice waiting to die just twenty years later.

Alice said, "That's Gabe on the far left there."

Siegel was thinner, with more hair. He seemed confident, even cocky, as he looked at the camera. These days he was a shell of the man who was depicted in the photo, thought Robie.

Alice pointed at two other men, standing next to each other in the middle of the group. They were taller than the others. "I don't know who they are."

"Rick Wind and Leo Broome," said Robie. "We know about them."

"Do you think they might know something about why my husband has disappeared?"

"They might," said Robie. But he thought, *We won't have much luck asking them.*

Vance, obviously reading Robie's thoughts, said, "We'll check into that angle."

"I don't know why my husband's military service would come up now, after all these years."

"Does your husband have anything else connected to his time in the Army?"

"Not that I know of. He had brought some things back. His helmet, boots, and some other things. But he got rid of them."

"Why?" asked Vance.

Alice Siegel looked surprised by the question. "He thought they were toxic, of course."

87

When they returned to the farmhouse, Vance called in to the FBI and got an earful from her superior for going off grid without authorization. After the man finished his tirade Vance was able to ask him to trace the phone call Gabriel Siegel had received at the bank.

He called back twenty minutes later with the answer.

Disposable phone, dead end. He ordered Vance to come in to the office, right that instant.

Robie overheard this part of the conversation. When Vance started to refuse he grabbed her arm and said, "Go, and take Julie with you."

His gaze went upward where Julie had gone to use the bathroom.

"What?" said Vance.

"Things are going to get really hairy very shortly."

Vance put her hand over the phone. "How do you know that?"

"I just do."

"All the more reason for us to stick together."

"But not Julie. We can't have her in the middle of this. Take her to WFO and surround her with firepower. Then you can come back and hook up with me."

She studied him warily, distrust in her eyes.

The voice squawked from the phone.

"Yes, sir," said Vance into the phone. "I'll be in directly. And I'll be bringing Julie Getty with me. I hope we can do a better job of protecting her than we did last time."

She clicked off and gazed at Robie with a searching look. "If you're screwing with me . . ."

"Why would I do that?"

"Because you seem to have a propensity for it. If you have this noble idea that you're the only one in the world who can tackle this thing. Or that you're somehow protecting me from danger—"

"You're an FBI agent. You signed up for this. I have no noble thoughts in my head. All I've ever tried to do is my job and then survive. If I engage in any sort of fantasy it's that I keep on believing those goals are not mutually exclusive."

"Don't try to confuse the issue."

"Take your car and take Julie. Get her settled and then come back here."

"And you'll just be here waiting for me?" she said skeptically.

"If I'm not here you have my phone number."

"I don't believe this, Robie. You're shutting me out at the very moment—"

Robie turned and walked away.

"Is that your answer? Ignoring me? Walking away again?" she called after him.

"What's going on?" Julie peered over the stair rail at them.

Vance looked at Robie and then sighed. "Come on, Julie. We need to get out of here."

"Where are we going?"

"To run down a lead."

"What's Will going to do?"

"Run down another lead."

"Why are we splitting up?"

"Because our fearless leader wants it that way. Don't you, Robie?" she added in a louder voice.

He was in the next room now and said nothing in response.

Robie watched as the Beemer with the cracked windshield and shattered rear window backed away from the house. Vance slammed it into drive and did a doughnut in the dirt and gravel before careening down the road away from him.

Robie took a deep, cleansing breath. He had never played well with others. For the last dozen years he had worked in almost total isolation. He preferred it that way. He was better alone than with a team. That's just how he was built.

He felt an immediate freedom. A washing away of responsibility.

He drove from his mind the promise that he had made to Julie to let her help find out what had happened to her parents. It was a false promise anyway. He'd had no business making it. Fulfilling it, he told himself, would only end up getting the girl killed.

Yet it didn't really matter one way or another to Robie. He kept telling himself that as he prepared to finish what he had started.

His mind had not changed on one thing. This was about him. Despite their detour down to the squad Curtis Getty had been in.

This is about me. And it's also about something bigger.

Now he had to find out what that was.

This was once more a chess match. The other side had just made a move.

Robie had to decide if it was a legitimate move or something else.

He gunned up and set out to do just that.

88

The first stop was the bank. Robie talked to the employees, but they had no helpful information. Gabriel Siegel had left his briefcase behind but it contained nothing helpful. Yet its presence did tell Robie that Siegel's hasty exit had been unplanned and not related to the business of the bank. He was pretty certain of that already, but in his mind it was now confirmed.

As Alice Siegel had indicated her husband's car was still in the parking lot. It was a decade-old Honda Civic. Robie picked the lock and searched it but found nothing useful. He drove off in his car, wondering what had prompted Siegel to simply leave his place of business.

Next stop was the hospice. He had forgotten something when he was there before.

The guestbook.

The receptionist let him look at it. While she was attending to other business he took photos of the pages for the last month or so. Then he walked down the hall to Elizabeth Van Beuren's room.

Nothing much had changed. She was still lying in the bed with a big pipe stuck down her throat. The sun was still coming in the windows. There were flowers. The photo of the family.

And she was still dying. Hanging on to life, probably because she was a soldier and it was just part of her psyche. And the ventilator didn't hurt. At some point the family would have to make a decision about that.

Like the nurse had said, this place wasn't designed to cure or even prolong life. It was to let folks die with dignity, in comfort, in peace.

As he stared at Van Beuren, Robie decided she didn't look too peaceful.

They should just let her go. Just let her pass to a place better than this one.

He picked up the photo and stared at it. A nice family. Alexandra Van Beuren was pretty, with soft brunette hair, a playful smile. Robie liked how the camera had captured the energy in her eyes, the life there. The dad looked rugged, but weary and haunted, as though he might have predicted the fate that would befall his wife in the not too distant future.

At some point in his life Robie had supposed he could have had a family like this. He was long past that, of course. But sometimes he still thought about it. Right at that instant, Annie Lambert's face appeared in his thoughts. He shook his head clear. He just didn't see how something like that was possible.

He walked back out into the fading sunshine and set off for Arlington.

To the bar that Jerome Cassidy had built.

He made good time and pulled to a stop in front of the bar at around five o'clock.

He walked in, ordered a beer, and asked for Cassidy. The man came out a few minutes later and approached Robie, an uncertain look on his face. He eyed the beer like it was a stick of TNT about to go off.

"Like to talk to you," said Robie.

"What about?"

"Julie."

"What about her?"

"You planning on telling her you're her father?"

"Let's go sit."

Cassidy led him over to a booth in a corner. There were about fifteen customers in the place.

They settled in their seats and Cassidy said, "Early drinking crowd comes in around five-thirty. Place will be full by seven. Standing room only by eight. Empties out around eleven-thirty. D.C. plays hard and works hard. Folks get up early. Especially the ones in uniform."

Robie cradled his beer but didn't drink it. He waited for Cassidy to pull the trigger on answering his question.

The man finally sat back, slid his palms along the top of the table, and looked at Robie.

"First, how the hell did you know?"

"Guys don't write bundles of letters to 'friends.' Especially guy friends. You don't spend time and money tracking them down. And I saw how your face lit up when Julie walked in. You hadn't seen her since she was a baby, but you instantly knew who it was. Not that hard to figure out, actually. And I recently saw a photo of you when you were in uniform twenty years ago. There may be a lot of her mother in Julie, but there's some of you too."

Cassidy blew out a long breath and nodded. "Think she knows?"

"No, I don't. Would it matter to you?"

"Probably."

"So you thinking of telling her?"

"Do you think I should?"

"Why don't you first tell me what happened?"

"Not much to tell, really. And I've got nothing to be ashamed of. I cared for Sara. This was before she was married to Curtis. And she cared for me. And then Curtis came along. She and him just hit it off right from the first minute. Love at first sight. Stronger than anything we had. I didn't feel bitter about it. I didn't love Sara like Curtis did. And like I said, he saved my life. He was a good guy. Why not let him have some happiness?"

"But Julie?"

"Stupid one last roll in the bed. Curtis thought Julie was his. Sara knew better. I knew better. But I never said a word."

"You seem to be an impossibly good person on that score," remarked Robie.

Cassidy said, "I'm not a saint, never claimed to be. Done lots of people wrong in my life, especially when I'd been drinking. But Sara and Curtis, well, they just belonged together. And there was no way I could take care of a kid. It was an easy out for me, you see. Nothing noble about it."

"Not so easy now?"

Cassidy eyed the full beer.

Robie said, "You want it?"

Cassidy rubbed his palms together. "No, no I don't. I do want it, but no."

Robie took a sip of the beer and set it back down. "Not so easy now?" he said again.

"Older you get the more regrets pile on you. I never had any intention of trying to take Julie away. Never! I just wanted to see her. See what sort of person she'd become. But by then I'd left Pennsylvania. By the time I got around to trying to find them they'd left too. Looked everywhere except for right here." He paused and eyed Robie. "What's going on here? Feds involved. People getting killed. Julie in the middle of it."

"Can't tell you. What I can tell you is that Julie will need a friend after all of this is over."

"I want to help her."

"We'll just have to see how it plays out. I can't make any promises."

"I am her dad."

"Her biological dad, maybe."

"You don't believe me?"

"I don't believe anybody anymore."

Cassidy started to say something but then stopped and smiled. "Hell, me either, Robie." He gazed out the window. "So I told you my side. You think I should tell Julie?"

"I'm not sure I'm the best person to advise you on that. Never been married. Never had any kids."

"Well, let's assume you are the best person. What would you advise?"

"She loved her parents. She wanted their lives to be better than they were. She wants to find out why they were killed. She wants to avenge them."

"So you're saying not to tell her?"

"I'm saying my answer might be different tomorrow than it is today. But you're the only one who can really make the call."

Robie stood and eyed the beer. "You're going to make it."

Cassidy stared up at him. "Why?"

"You turn down a perfectly good beer under these circumstances, you can turn it down under any circumstances. I'll be in touch."

89

Robie didn't know why he had come back here.

It was the apartment across the street. He opened the door, turned off the alarm, and stood looking around. He had this place. He had his apartment across the street and the farmhouse. Each place was supposed to be safe, secure, and yet they weren't. So Robie felt homeless. He half expected someone to walk down the hall and ask him what he was doing here.

He looked at his watch. It was almost seven o'clock.

He'd called Vance but it had gone straight to voice mail. She was probably enduring some difficult times with her boss for going off grid. He doubted she would be getting back to him anytime soon. And he was actually relieved about that. He'd texted Julie and received a terse response. She no doubt was furious that she'd been snookered into going into protective custody again. At least she would get to grow up, do something wonderful with that big brain of hers.

After leaving Cassidy he had driven around. He'd ridden to the scene of the bus explosion, then over to Donnelly's, which was still closed. Indeed, Robie doubted it would ever reopen. Who would want to grab a drink or have a meal in a place where so many people had lost their lives?

Now he was here and he wasn't sure why.

He looked at the telescope, drew closer to it, and finally bent over slightly and gazed through it. His condo building immediately came into focus. He shifted the viewing angle slightly and looked at the line of windows representing his space. It was dark. It was supposed to be. He moved the telescope to the left and his gaze flitted over the lighted hallway running past all the apartments on that floor.

His gaze shifted, as he knew it would, to Annie Lambert's place. Her windows were also dark. She was probably still at work. He wondered if her day off had gone well. He hoped it had. She deserved it.

As he watched he saw her come down the street on her bike. He continued to watch as she walked her bike into the building. Counting off the seconds in his head, he positioned the telescope so that it was right on the elevator bank on his floor. The doors opened a few seconds later and Lambert got off, rolling her bike next to her. She unlocked the door to her apartment and went inside.

Robie moved the telescope and watched as she parked her bike against the wall, took off her jacket and tennis shoes, and padded down the hall in her socks. She made a stop at the bathroom. When she came back out she continued down the hall. Robie lost her but picked her back up again about a minute later. She'd taken her blouse off and replaced it with a sweatshirt. Part of him wanted to go over and see her. Then he saw her lift up a long black dress on a hanger with a sheet of plastic over it. It had been draped over a chair. She took the plastic off and held the dress up to her. It was a strapless gown, Robie could see. She lifted up another garment. It was a matching jacket. The last items she picked up were three-inch black heels.

Annie Lambert was going out on the town tonight, it seemed. And why shouldn't she? thought Robie. Part of him felt jealous, though. It was an odd emotion for him. It didn't sit well.

He sat down, put his feet up on a leather ottoman, and gazed at the ceiling. He was so tired, couldn't remember the last time he'd truly slept. He drifted off and awoke with a start some time later. From the foggy recesses of his mind he remembered something and drew out his phone. He brought up the photos he'd taken of the guest register at the hospice.

He scrolled from screen to screen, not expecting to find much of interest. And he didn't. The only name he recognized was Gabriel Siegel from about a month ago. That made sense because Siegel had admitted he'd last visited Van Beuren at that time.

He scrolled to another page. There was nothing.

He hit another page. Nothing again.

But then something caught his eye.

It wasn't a name.

It was a date.

There was an entire day missing in the guestbook. He enlarged the screen as big as he could. He looked at it closely. Down in the far left corner of the frame he spied it.

A triangle of paper. It would have gone unnoticed by anyone looking at the guestbook itself. It was too small. But with the pixels swollen to an unnatural size on his phone, Robie knew what it was. The remains of the page that had been ripped out of the book. Probably while the front desk had been unoccupied.

Why would someone have taken a page from a hospice guestbook?

There could only be one answer. They wanted to cover up whoever's name had been written in there. They wanted to wipe away the record of someone who had visited Elizabeth Van Beuren.

Was it Broome? Getty? Wind? Two of them? All three?

Siegel had told him that he hadn't seen Broome for ten years and hadn't seen Wind or Getty since Gulf One. Cassidy had said he hadn't seen any of them since the war except for Getty.

But what if Broome or Getty or Wind had found out that Van Beuren was here and had come to visit her while she was still lucid? Siegel had said she was in and out of it. And had she let something slip? Something that had led to all three of them having to be silenced? It seemed a bizarre notion, but it was no more strange than any of the other theories that had floated through Robie's mind lately.

Robie looked at the date before and after the missing page. Eight days ago. That would fit with the timeline. Siegel hadn't been targeted since he'd stopped coming a month ago. Rick Wind had been the first to die. Counting back, it seemed that Wind might have been killed shortly after he had possibly visited Van Beuren. And if Curtis Getty hadn't come to the hospice, that would explain the heated discussion that the waitress at the diner, Cheryl Kosmann, had witnessed. Broome had told Getty. He then might've told Wind. Or it could have been the other way around. Robie couldn't know for sure without seeing which of them had visited the woman. Getty didn't have a car, so it was doubtful he'd driven all the way out to Manassas.

No chance could be taken. Husbands, wives, and an ex-wife, who was also a potentially dangerous government lawyer, had to be killed.

The Broomes had managed to escape. For a time. But with Robie's involuntary help they had managed to get them too.

Robie's mind next drew to the timing of the insertion of the ventilator.

It kept a terminally ill woman alive.

But it also did something else.

It prevented her from saying anything during her lucid moments.

From saying anything else!

They had put the tube in her to shut the poor woman up.

But whatever she had told one or more of her former squad members had been the reason they had been killed.

Robie raced out of his apartment and took the elevator down.

He had a hospice visit to make.

90

Visiting hours were over. But Robie's repeated raps on the glass front door brought an attendant. He flashed his badge and was allowed in.

"I need to see Elizabeth Van Beuren," he said. "And I need to see her now."

"That's not possible," said the attendant, a woman in her thirties with short blonde hair.

"She hasn't been transferred out of hospice, has she?" asked Robie.

"No."

"What, then?"

The attendant was about to say something when the nurse Robie had spoken to before came forward.

"So you're back?" she asked. She was clearly not pleased.

"Where is Elizabeth Van Beuren? I need to see her."

"She can't see you."

"That's what she said. But why?" asked Robie, his gaze digging into the nurse's features.

"Because Ms. Van Beuren passed about three hours ago."

"What happened?"

"The ventilator tube was removed. She passed peacefully an hour later."

"Who ordered the tube removed?"

"Her doctor."

"But why? Wouldn't he have to get permission from her family?"

"I really can't speak to that."

"Well, who *can* speak to it?"

"Her doctor, I suppose."

"I'll need his name and number, right now."

Robie called and spoke with the doctor. The physician was reluctant to discuss the matter with Robie until Robie said, "I'm a federal agent. Something is going on here we're trying to figure out. The only common denominator is Elizabeth Van Beuren. Can you tell me anything? It's vital or else I wouldn't be asking."

The doctor said, "I would not have removed the tube without the family requesting it."

"Who requested it?"

The doctor paused, then said, "Mr. Van Beuren had the medical power of attorney."

"So he told you to remove it. Why the change of heart?"

"I have no idea. I just did what he asked us to do."

"Was it by phone or did he come here in person?"

"By phone."

"Pretty strange that he didn't want to be here when his wife died," said Robie.

"Quite frankly, Agent Robie, I thought the same thing. Maybe he had something more important to do, although for the life of me I can't imagine what that might be."

"Do you know where he works?"

"No, I don't."

"Ever seen him in person?"

"Yes, numerous times. He seemed like a perfectly normal person. He was deeply devoted to his wife. He was intimately involved in her care. I liked him."

"But not devoted enough to be with her at the end?"

"Again, I can't explain that."

Robie clicked off and looked at the nurse. "Is the body still here?"

"No, the people from the funeral home already picked it up."

"And her husband never came in? Does her daughter know?"

"I have no idea. I would assume Mr. Van Beuren has contacted her. He didn't ask us to do so, and thus we couldn't make that sort of communication."

Robie called Vance but still got voice mail. He next called Blue Man, but the man didn't answer either.

Robie raced down the hall to Van Beuren's room. He pushed open the door and saw the empty bed. He drew nearer, picked up the photo, and looked at George Van Beuren. Short hair, muscular physique. Robie wondered if he was maybe military or former military.

The nurse had followed him down the hall and was standing in the hallway.

"Is this really necessary?" she asked.

"Yeah, it really is." He whirled around. "George Van Beuren. You said you've seen him. Was he ever wearing a uniform?"

"A uniform?"

"Yeah, like military or something?"

"No, not that I ever saw. He was just dressed normally." She took a step forward. "We need to collect Mrs. Van Beuren's personal effects and send them along home."

"I'll need that home address."

"We can't give out that sort of information."

Robie took a long stride until he was within a couple inches of her.

"I don't like playing the asshole, but in this case I'm going to. This is a case of national security. And if you have information that might be able to stop an attack against this country and you don't provide it to a federal officer who has requested it, you're going to prison, for a very long time."

The woman gasped, then said, "Follow me."

A minute later Robie was flying down the road in his car.

91

The Van Beurens lived about twenty minutes from the hospice center.

Robie made it there in fifteen.

The homes were solidly middle-class. Basketball hoops. Vans and American-made cars in short asphalt driveways. Do-it-yourself landscaping. Not a butler or Rolls-Royce in sight.

Robie zeroed in on the Van Beurens' house. It was set at the end of the street. The home was dark, but one vehicle was parked in the driveway.

Robie stopped his car at the curb, pulled out his pistol, and crept toward the house. He didn't knock at the front door. He peered in one of the windows. He couldn't see anything.

He hurried around to the back. Putting his elbow through the glass in the back door, he reached through and turned the lock. He pulled a flashlight and made his way through the house. It didn't take him long. He ended up in the front room after clearing the others.

He shined his light around. It hit on various objects

on walls and shelves. He passed one item and then came back to it. He rushed over and snatched it up.

It was a photo of the Van Beurens.

Mother, daughter, and father.

Mom was in her combat fatigues.

Robie's gaze focused on Dad.

George Van Beuren was also in uniform, a very distinctive one. White shirt, dark pants. Dark cap.

It was the uniform of the United States Secret Service Uniformed Division.

George Van Beuren helped to guard the president of the United States.

And then in a flash of synapses Robie finally made the connection.

He was watching Annie Lambert walking down the hall. He had lost her for about thirty seconds. But then regained her. She had changed clothes in those few seconds.

And then Robie forgot all about Annie Lambert and took his mind back to that airplane hangar in Morocco. Through his scope he had watched Khalid bin Talal climb the steps to his jet. After that he had lost sight of the prince for a brief period. And then he had regained him as the Saudi walked down the aisle of the plane and took his seat across from the Russian and Palestinian.

That's when Robie had noticed the straps around the prince's middle. He had assumed it was the straps holding on his body armor. But the prince had not been wearing body armor before he got on the plane. Robie had been watching him closely. He would have seen the outline of the armored vest under the robes. And it took longer than a few moments to put on, especially if one was wearing a long robe and was very heavy in the belly.

What had happened was now clear.

Talal had been warned about a possible hit. He'd had someone, perhaps a double he routinely employed, take his place at the meeting. Maybe he thought the Russian and Palestinian would try to kill him. Maybe he suspected a traitor in his inner circle, or a sniper like Robie waiting to take his shot. He had outsmarted them all. He had had his double die in his place.

Robie thought back to the conversation he had overheard that night. It now took on a critical importance.

Something that everyone assumed was pointless to try.

The weakest link.

Willing to die.

That could only be one possible target.

The president of the United States.

Now the theft of the Secret Service SUV made sense. They had someone on the inside. They had George Van Beuren.

And the fact that they had let Elizabeth Van Beuren die told Robie that the time to make the attempt was right now.

And Talal's billions had bought him people in this country to do his bidding.

Then he remembered something Annie Lambert had told him. When the president got back to D.C., there was going to be a big event at the White House.

He pulled out his phone, did a quick Internet search.

He got the results and raced out of the house.

Tonight the president would be entertaining the crown prince of Saudi Arabia.

Talal was multitasking tonight.

The son of a bitch was going for both men.

92

Robie was halfway to D.C. when he finally reached Blue Man. In terse sentences he told him about his latest deductions.

Blue Man's response was equally terse. He would meet Robie at the White House with backup. And he would alert the appropriate parties.

Twenty minutes later Robie slid his car to a stop at the curb, jumped out, and ran.

He was on Pennsylvania Avenue heading to the front gates of the White House. He looked at his watch. Nearly eleven. He imagined the party would be winding down by now. And if the attempt hadn't occurred yet, it would have to shortly.

He spied Blue Man and a group of men huddled outside the White House front gates. Robie could see that it was a mixture of FBI, Secret Service, and DHS. He saw no uniformed Secret Service around. He assumed it had been determined that they couldn't know how far the conspiracy had gone, so it was best to leave the uniforms out of this.

Robie ran up to them. "Do they know where Van Beuren is?" he asked.

Blue Man said, "He's on duty. We've spoken to the Secret Service agents inside. They're hunting for him now. The problem is, we don't want to show that we're suspicious of anything. Van Beuren may not be the only asset they have in there."

One man in a suit stared over at Robie. He was about six-three with graying hair and a face that seemed to have a worry line for every national crisis he had endured. Robie recognized him as the director of the Secret Service. Robie recalled that the man's father had been a veteran agent with Reagan when he had been shot. It was said that the current director had become an agent at the urging of his old man. And he had sworn that no president would ever die on his watch.

The director said, "You're the one who called this in?"

"I am," said Robie.

"I sure as hell hope you're right. Because if you're not . . ."

"If I'm wrong, nothing bad happens. If I'm right . . ."

The director looked at Blue Man.

"We'll move in through the visitors' entrance. We'll attract less notice that way. Hopefully, they'll snag Van Beuren before we even get in the place."

"And the president?" asked Robie.

"Ordinarily with any threat like this we would have

already moved him either to his personal quarters or to the bunker underneath the White House. But if Van Beuren is involved he'll know that's our protocol and may have set an ambush somehow. So we decided to sequester the president in an atypical place, the Family Dining Room, along with the crown prince, some of the president's staff, and some select VIPs who we know are not threats. No uniforms are part of the security detail. All suits. Van Beuren can't get near him. We did it subtly. Now we just have to find Van Beuren." He said again, "But I sure as hell hope you're wrong about this."

"The fact that you haven't been able to locate Van Beuren yet tells me that I'm right," replied Robie.

They raced to the visitors' entrance and moved quickly through the security checkpoint there. All uniformed Secret Service had been pulled off interior guard duty and massed in a hallway. They had not been told why. Each of them had been questioned. None of them knew where Van Beuren was. He had been assigned to a security perimeter on the lower level, near the library.

He wasn't there.

All rooms on the lower level had been checked.

Robie and the others ran down the hall and up the stairs to the main level of the White House. As they were fast-walking down the Cross Hall toward the State Dining Room, which adjoined the Family Dining

Room, one of the agents with them received a message through his earwig.

"They found Van Beuren," he said.

"Where?" the Secret Service director asked immediately.

"A storage room in the West Wing."

They changed direction and quickly reached the West Wing. There they were directed to the room where Van Beuren had been found.

The door was thrown open by the lead agent. Inside they saw Van Beuren. He was on the floor, unconscious and trussed up. A patch of shiny blood was mixed in with his hair.

One of the agents knelt down next to him and felt for a pulse. "He's alive, but somebody hit him hard."

Blue Man said, "I don't understand this. Why knock out and tie up your assassin?"

Robie was the first to spot it. "His gun is missing."

All eyes went to the man's holster. The nine-millimeter that should have been there wasn't.

Robie said, "He wasn't the assassin. They just needed his weapon. That way they didn't have to try and sneak one past security. He just walked in with it. Part of the plan."

And then Robie remembered the last part of the overheard conversation from the plane hangar in Morocco.

Access to weapons.

Not a westerner.

Decades in the making.

Willing to die.

He said, “The shooter has his gun. They have to be in with the president and the crown prince.”

The director paled. “You mean part of his staff? Or one of the guests?”

Robie didn’t answer. He was already sprinting down the hall.

93

The Family Dining Room was one of the most intimately scaled rooms on the main level of the White House. It was bracketed on one side by the chief usher's office and could also be accessed through the much larger and adjacent State Dining Room. The president and vice president would often have one-on-one lunches there. It was not as elaborately decorated as the far larger East Room or the ornately furnished Green, Blue, and Red Rooms.

Yet if Robie and company failed tonight, it would be the room known forever as where a U.S. president had lost his life.

The group marshaled outside the door to the State Dining Room.

The director said, "We're going to alert agents inside the room that the shooter is probably in there. They've already formed a hard wall around the president and are awaiting my order to get him out of the room."

Blue Man said, "If they do that or start searching people the assassin will fire. In such close quarters and despite the wall around the president, the bullet might hit its target."

"We can't just wait and see if the person acts or not," countered the director. "Protocol says to move and to move fast. I should have already given the order."

Robie said, "How many people in that room total?"

"About fifty," said one of the agents.

"This could turn into a bloodbath," said Blue Man.

The director said curtly, "No one wants that. But my focus is only on the president. We plan to take him out through the chief usher's office and from there to the Entrance Hall."

Another agent said, "And the longer we wait, the less chance we have of getting him out of there safely."

Blue Man said, "What if there's more than one shooter? You could be leading him directly into an ambush."

Robie said, "The shooter must be someone who works here."

"That's impossible," said the director.

"The person was involved in a conspiracy with someone we know worked here. That's indisputable. That could not be an outsider. And many of the people in that room with the president and the crown prince are staffers, correct?"

The director gave a start. "It could be one of the prince's staffers. It was a major mistake to put them in the same room together. Shit!"

Robie shook his head. "Van Beuren was found in the West Wing. Did one of the prince's staffers have access to the West Wing tonight? Because Van Beuren's head injury was recent."

The director looked at one of his men. "Do you have the answer to that?"

"None of the prince's staffers were anywhere near the West Wing this evening."

"Son of a bitch!" exclaimed the director.

Robie said, "People have been paid off up and down the line on this one, sir. The person behind this has lots of money. No one is off-limits. For all we know he might have bought off a Secret Service agent in there."

"I can't believe that," said the director. "No agent has ever been a traitor."

"The same could be said for the uniformed division," said Blue Man. "But it obviously happened. One of the men forming the wall around the president right now could be the backup shooter, with the primary one using Van Beuren's gun."

"But if there is a Secret Service agent on the payroll, why bother getting Van Beuren's gun?"

"Something like this, you have a fallback plan, sir," said Robie. "The stakes are too high. I'm not saying there are two shooters in there. But I am saying that we can't responsibly discount that possibility."

"So what do we do?" asked the director.

Robie said, "Let me go in there. A staffer will know the interior security agents but they won't know me.

Let me go in dressed as a waiter. I can go in under the pretense of bringing in something, maybe coffee."

"And then what?" demanded the director.

"I identify the shooter or shooters and take them out."

"How will you identify the assassin from all of the people in that room?" snapped the director.

Blue Man spoke up. "Agent Robie is very adept at spotting assassins, Director." He drew closer and whispered into the man's ear. "He happens to be one for this country. In fact, he's our best one. If you need a man who can make the kill shots under pressure in a room full of people, he's it."

The director gazed sternly at Robie. "This goes against every protocol and procedure the Service has."

"Yes, sir, it does," agreed Robie.

"If you fail the president dies."

"Yes, sir. But I am prepared to die making sure he doesn't."

"If I can't alert the agents in there about our plan and you pull your gun, they will shoot you."

"It's always in the timing, sir."

The director and Robie locked gazes for a long moment. Then the director said, "Get him a waiter's uniform and a cart of damn coffee."

94

Robie pulled his jacket more tightly around him. The waiter's uniform they had gotten him was for a bigger man. Robie had insisted on this. He couldn't allow a gun bump that someone could spot. He had two pistols, one in his holster, one hidden under the cloth covering the coffee cart. He was also wearing body armor, although at least some of the agents would fire into his head if they thought he was a threat to the president.

The agents inside had been told that the danger was over but to still maintain the wall around the president. The crown prince and his staff were standing in a corner diagonally across from the president, surrounded by other agents. The thirty-odd White House staffers and other guests were in the middle of the room between the prince and the president.

The door opened and Robie wheeled the cart into the room. He had no earwig. Had no means of communication with anyone. The force right outside the door was standing by to rush in after him. The director had his walkie-talkie ready to order his agents not to fire at Robie if he pulled his gun. Yet he knew that would be an impossible order to follow. As far as the director was concerned, Robie was a dead man from the moment he walked into the room.

The door was shut behind Robie and he continued to push the cart along. He gridded the room without seeming to do so.

The Family Dining Room had been established by James Madison and was where many first families ate until Jackie Kennedy created a dining room upstairs in the family quarters. The room was about twenty-eight feet by twenty feet in size. A blue-and-white oriental rug covered much of the floor. There was a blue-and-white marble fireplace surrounded with wall candelabras on either side of the mantel. Above that was a portrait of a woman in nineteenth-century garb. The long dining table that was usually in the center of the room had been shifted to one side, the accompanying chairs lined in front of it. A cabinet blocked off one door. A mirror hung over a Chippendale-style chest. A crystal chandelier anchored the middle of the ceiling. The walls were painted yellow.

Although the VIPs and staffers had not been told of any threat, it seemed, from their anxious features, that some of them realized that the move to this room was out of the ordinary.

Robie's thoughts went back to the overheard conversation at the plane hangar.

Not a westerner.

Decades in the making.

That obviously couldn't be George Van Beuren. He should have realized there had to be a second person.

Robie saw the crown prince hovering nervously in one corner. There was a wall of security around him and his staff. Robie quickly sized up each of the staff members. Some, like the prince, were wearing traditional robes. Others were in suits. The crown prince looked like his black-sheep cousin, Talal. Both fat and both too rich. A lot of damage one could do with all that money, thought Robie. The world would be safer if people didn't have so much damn wealth.

His gaze next swept to the other side of the room.

He could see the president in the middle of the wall of agents. He had possessed dark hair when winning the White House. Now, after three years in office, a good deal of it had turned white. Maybe that was the real reason why the place was called the White House, thought Robie. It quickly aged all the occupants.

There were six agents forming the hard wall around the president. But even with that there were clean shooting lines right to the man if one was close enough. Each agent was looking outward, at possible threats. Robie looked for any agent who was not doing this, who was looking at the president or at other agents. Even if they believed the threat to be over, their vigilance should never relax, for in truth, the danger was never over.

All of the agents' gazes were directed outward.

Maybe there was only one shooter. Robie could use a bit of luck right now, and having only one person to deal with would be lucky indeed.

He rolled the cart farther into the room. He checked the crown prince's corner one more time. If the threat came from there it would be a difficult shot to hit the president.

He turned his attention to the last group.

The staffers and other members of the group sequestered here stood in the middle of the room. They were all formally dressed. Robie saw lots of black. Many of the women wore shawls, jackets, and wraps to cover bare shoulders. Some carried tiny purses, all too small for Van Beuren's sidearm.

The men huddled together. Tuxes were the rule. Suits with pockets and maybe a stolen nine-millimeter from an unconscious guard in one of them.

Most were Caucasian. The majority of them appeared to be westerners, but of that Robie couldn't be certain. But there were about a dozen who looked to be from distant places.

Robie fixed his sights even more on this middle group. Equidistant between the two national leaders, this positioning made the most sense if the plan was to kill both men. It would take miraculous shooting, but it was not impossible for someone who knew what he was doing. The distances involved were short.

I could do it, thought Robie.

The first shot would create a panic. If it hit its target

the focus would momentarily be on the victim of that shooting. As the person fell to the floor, those around him would scream, run, duck.

But it was difficult to fire a gun in close quarters and go unnoticed. Someone would identify the shooter. Agents would rush forward. People would grab at the person. But the shooter might get off another shot. It was certainly feasible.

And with that thought Robie came to understand the order of targets.

President first.

Prince second.

You didn't get this far and kill the second banana first. The president would be the priority target. If the shooter could get off another round, it would be aimed at the prince.

As people came forward to get their coffees, Robie made another sweeping gaze of the room to check for possible position advantages for the shooter.

A group of guests and staffers hung back, clustered around the table. Some had turned chairs around and were leaning on the backs of them.

Mostly women, Robie noted.

Three-inch-heel syndrome. Their feet were probably killing them after the long evening event.

Robie took in the people here one by one until he arrived at the woman.

And then he stopped looking.

Annie Lambert was looking back at him.

She was dressed in black. She had a jacket over her strapless dress.

She held no purse.

Her hands were folded across her chest and rested inside her jacket.

Her hair was done up with a few strands trickling around her long neck.

She looked beautiful.

So this was the reason for the black dress and high heels Robie had seen through his scope. She had told Robie she would be working this event, but he had somehow failed to make the connection.

He promised himself that whatever happened he would save her from harm. She would not die tonight.

Her lips were set in a firm line. She obviously recognized Robie. But she did not smile. She was probably scared, he thought. For a terrible second he wondered if she would raise the alarm about him. To her Robie was an investment banker. Why would he be here dressed as a waiter? Maybe she would think he was here to kill the president. He wondered how to signal to her, but he could think of no way to do so. He just had to hope she would not panic from seeing him.

Yet there was a calmness about her that Robie found enviable under the circumstances. His respect for her grew even more. Her eyes were wide and seemed to take in every bit of him in one glance.

Then he saw that her pupils were also dilated. And then she smiled at him in a way she never had before.

And in that moment Robie saw a side of Annie Lambert he had never suspected even existed.

There was a split second where Robie's mind shut down, as though he'd been struck by lightning. Then his brain immediately fired back up.

He shouted, "Shooter!" He drew his gun.

But with astonishing speed Annie Lambert pulled the gun from where it had been hidden in a compartment in her jacket, aimed, and fired, seemingly all in one smooth motion.

The president was only a few feet away. Her shot hit him in the arm instead of the chest. An agent had grabbed him when Robie had shouted. If the president hadn't moved his heart would have been pierced by the round instead of his limb.

She started to point her gun at the prince. She never made it.

Robie's shot hit Lambert directly in the head and blew out the back, the slug embedding in the wall behind her along with some of the woman's brain and skull. The yellow paint turned red.

She fell backward, hit the table, and slid to the floor.

The Secret Service removed the president from the room so fast his blood barely had time to touch the floor.

Robie heard screams, sensed people rushing in and out. But he simply stood there, his gun pointed down.

All he could do was stare silently at Annie Lambert's body.

95

Robie was in a room at the White House. He didn't know which room and he didn't care. He had been led to it by others and told to wait there.

He sat in a chair and stared at the floor. The light overhead was dim. He heard noises from outside somewhere. People were talking in the halls. Occasionally the sound of a siren reached him.

None of it made an impression on him.

He only saw Annie Lambert's face. Her eyes, really. The pupils big and pulpy, seemingly too large to be contained in such limited space.

He saw the round from his Glock hit her head, explode her brain, and end her life.

He saw this a hundred times. He could not make his mind turn the image off. It kept playing like a video reel. Part of him wanted to place his gun against his temple and make it stop for good.

But they had taken his gun from him and so this was not an option.

Right now that was probably a good thing, he

thought. Right now Robie was not sure he wanted to live. He could no longer make sense of anything.

The door opened and Robie looked up.

"Agent Robie?"

He saw the director of the Secret Service. Behind him was Blue Man.

"Yeah?" said Robie.

"The president would like to personally thank you."

"How is he?"

"Fine. Hospital released him. Thank God the bullet went clean through his arm. More blood than damage. He'll be fine in no time."

"That's good," said Robie. "But there's no need to thank me. Just doing my job. You can tell him that for me." He looked down at the floor once more.

"Robie," said Blue Man, stepping forward. "It's the president. He's in the Oval Office. He's expecting you."

Robie glanced up at the man. Always neat as a pin. Twelve in the afternoon or twelve at night, didn't matter.

Blue Man had a confused look on his face. While he had known that Annie Lambert lived in Robie's apartment building, Robie also knew that Blue Man was not aware of their relationship. And he did not feel like enlightening him.

Robie said, "Okay. Let's go."

The trip to the Oval Office took a few minutes and involved their walking outside and past the Rose

Garden. Before Teddy Roosevelt had had the West Wing created, a series of glass conservatories had occupied the spot. As they trudged along, Robie recalled that Roosevelt had been shot while campaigning for president. The only thing that had saved his life was the thickness of the speech that had been folded up in his pocket. The bullet had hit this mass of paper and it had robbed enough of the round's kinetic energy that Roosevelt had been able to give his speech, albeit while bleeding heavily from the wound in his chest. He had only consented to be taken to the hospital after his speech was done.

They didn't make presidents like that anymore, thought Robie.

And so Roosevelt had lived. And so had the current president.

He had lived because of a bit of skill on Robie's part.

And a lot of luck.

Just like the rolled-up speech.

The president sat behind his desk, his left arm sat stiffly in a sling. He rose when he saw Robie. He had changed clothes. Gone was the tux, replaced by a white dress shirt and black slacks. He looked shaken still, but there was firm resolve in his grip as he shook hands with Robie.

"You saved my life tonight, Agent Robie. I wanted to thank you personally for that."

"I'm just glad you're okay, Mr. President."

"I can't believe that one of my staff was involved. Ms. Lambert, I believe. They tell me there was nothing in her background that would have hinted at this."

"I'm sure it was a surprise to everyone," replied Robie dumbly.

Especially me.

"How did you recognize so quickly that it was her?"

"She had taken a drug, to calm her nerves. Suicide bombers often do this before they detonate. Her pupils were dilated from the drug's action in her body."

"She was drugged, but could still shoot straight?"

"There are chemicals that relax the nerves, sir, without dulling the other senses. And it actually makes you a better shot. Nerves kill the aim faster than anything. And I would assume that even the most gifted assassin would have been nervous tonight."

"Because they would know there was no way out. That they would die," said the president.

"Yes, sir. And she was close to you, only a few feet away. Her accuracy, of course, was important, but not as critical as her speed."

In fact, she was faster than me, thought Robie. Her gun had appeared in a blaze of motion. Aimed, fired, and started to move to the secondary target before he could even get off one shot. It was only his shout that had made the agent nearest the president act swiftly enough to move him so that a mortal wound became something far less.

As though he had been reading Robie's thoughts,

the president said, "They tell me that if I hadn't been moved I would be dead. And I wouldn't have been moved except for your warning."

"I wish I could have stopped her before she fired."

The president smiled and held up his wounded arm. "I'll take this any day over being dead, Agent Robie."

"Yes, sir."

Robie wanted to leave now. He wanted to be alone. He wanted to get into his car and just drive until he ran out of fuel.

"We will honor you suitably another time. But again, I wanted to make sure that I conveyed my personal thanks as soon as possible."

"And again, not necessary, sir. But I appreciate it."

"The First Lady would like to thank you as well."

As if on cue the president's wife walked in looking pale, the night's terror still clearly in her eyes. Unlike her husband, she had not bothered to change. She swept over to Robie and took his hand in hers.

"Thank you, Agent Robie. Neither of us will ever be able to repay the debt we owe you."

"You don't owe me anything, ma'am. I wish you both the best."

A minute later Robie was walking fast down the hall. It was as though he couldn't breathe in here, like he was submerged in water.

He had reached the front entrance lobby before Blue Man caught up with him, showing a speed Robie would not have expected.

"Where are you going?" he asked.

"Somewhere other than here," replied Robie.

"Well, at least it's over," said Blue Man.

"You think it is?"

"Don't you?"

"It's not over," said Robie. "In fact, in some ways it's just beginning."

"What are you talking about?"

"It'll be in my next report."

"The crown prince would also like to thank you."

"Send him my regrets."

"But he's waiting expressly to talk to you."

"I'm sure. Tell him to email me."

"Robie!"

Robie walked out the front door of the White House and kept going.

It isn't over yet.

96

It was still early in the morning.

Robie was in the other apartment. He stared through the telescope to where Annie Lambert had lived. The place would be swarming soon with federal personnel. They would go through every inch of her life. They would find out why she had tried to kill the president. They would discover why she was doing the bidding of a fanatic from the desert world who possessed limitless petrodollars.

Robie thought about what she had told him of her past.

She was adopted. An only child. Parents lived in England. But were they English? What had her upbringing been like?

Again the words of the Palestinian came back to him: *We own that person. Decades in the making.*

Did they own you, Annie Lambert?

Were you decades in the making?

And now you're dead. On a metal slab a few miles from here. Dead from my round fired into your head.

And I slept with her right across the street. I had drinks with her. I liked her. I felt sorry for her. I could have maybe come to love her.

Robie knew that Annie Lambert living in the same building as he did was not a coincidence.

This is still about me. She came to live there because of me.

Prince Talal wants his revenge. He wanted to mess with my mind, screw my life every way he could. And he'll want it even more since I destroyed his plan.

The phone rang.

He looked at the screen.

It was Nicole Vance's cell phone.

He hit the answer button.

He knew what was coming.

"Hello?"

"The package will be delivered to your door in thirty seconds."

"Okay," said Robie evenly.

"You will do what it says to do."

"I hear you."

"You will follow the instructions completely."

"Uh-huh."

The connection went dead.

He put the phone away.

Blue Man had already told him, although Robie had figured it out previously.

Vance and Julie had never made it to the WFO.

They had been taken. This was Talal's fail-safe. All the really good ones had such a plan.

He counted off the seconds in his head. At thirty the manila envelope was slid under his door. He did not rush to it. He would not attempt to capture the messenger. That person would be able to tell him nothing.

He walked slowly to the door, bent down, and picked up the envelope.

He fingered open the clasp and took out the pages.

The first ten were glossy photos.

Him having drinks with Annie Lambert.

Him being kissed by Annie Lambert outside the White House.

Finally, him having sex with Annie Lambert in her bed. He wondered briefly where the camera had been placed for that shot.

Robie dropped the photos on the coffee table and looked at the other pages.

He sifted through them. There was nothing surprising here. He had anticipated most if not all of it.

It is still very much about me.

And Talal wants me. He wants me back where it all started.

The offer was crystal clear.

Him for Julie and Vance.

He considered it a fair trade. If Talal could be trusted. Which he could not, of course.

Yet Robie would still have to accept it. There was one advantage. This would render unnecessary the need for him to search the world hunting for Talal. The prince was summoning him right to where he would be.

Robie had already killed the double. He doubted that Talal had another one in reserve. And as much as Talal wanted to end his life, Robie wanted to end Talal's life even more.

Using Annie Lambert as a vicious tool, Talal had taken something from Robie, something precious, perhaps even inviolate.

He's taken away my ability to ever really trust myself again.

He took the photos over to where the light was better and looked at them again, one by one. Annie Lambert looked like what she might have been under vastly different circumstances: a beautiful woman with a bright future ahead of her. A nice person, wanting to do some good in the world.

She had not been born a killer. She had been raised to become one. An extraordinary one because he had never once suspected, until he had seen those swollen pupils.

I was not born to be a killer either, thought Robie. *But I am one now.*

He pulled out a Zippo from a drawer, carried the photos into the kitchen, and burned them to blackness in the kitchen sink. He ran water over them, let the smoke rise up and wash over his face. He watched as Annie Lambert disintegrated into the bowels of his sink. Then he rinsed the residue down the drain.

Annie Lambert vanished.

Like she had never even existed.

And the Annie Lambert he thought he knew never had.

Robie left the kitchen and started to pack.

The instructions had been explicit. He intended to follow them. At least most of them. For certain key elements he intended to create his own rules.

He assumed that Talal would expect this.

He had beaten Robie in Morocco.

Robie had bested him in Washington.

The next two days would determine who would be the winner of the third and final round.

97

The Costa del Sol was not as warm as the last time Robie had been here. The wind was chilly. The sky was gray. And there was rain in the forecast.

The ride over in the high-speed ferry was rough, the big boat pitching and swaying until it got fully up to speed. Yet even then the twin hulls of the catamaran were beaten by the heavy waves.

Robie wore a leather jacket, dungarees, and combat boots. If he was going into combat he needed the appropriate footwear, he figured. He had no weapons on him. As always, he had to trust that what he needed would be waiting for him. He sat in a seat next to one of the windows and watched the seagulls fighting the swirls of wind over the choppy water. The gray Med lashed up at the hull of the ferry and spray battered the windows. Robie did not flinch when this happened, as did other passengers around him.

He didn't react to things that could not hurt him.

Because of the rough water the crossing took longer than normal. When they pulled into Tangier the sky was growing dark. Robie clambered down the walkway of the ferry and joined the crowd making their way to transportation into town.

Unlike last time, Robie boarded one of the tour buses along with a group of other passengers. When the bus was three-quarters full the doors hissed closed and the driver swung the bus onto the road leading away from the port. Robie looked back once at the ferry and wondered if he would be alive to take it back across the strait.

Right now, he wouldn't bet on it.

The bus ride took about twenty minutes, and by the time it stopped and the doors hissed open again, the rain had begun to fall. While the tour guide took charge of the group, Robie walked off in the opposite direction. His destination had been planned well in advance. There was supposed to be someone waiting for him.

There was.

The man was young, but his features carried the weariness of someone much older. He wore a white robe and a turban and had a jagged scar down the right side of his neck.

It was from a knife, Robie knew. He had a scar too, but on his arm. Knife wounds never healed properly. Serrated blades ravaged the skin too much, tearing up the edges of the flesh so badly that even a gifted plastic surgeon couldn't fix it completely.

"Robie?" the young man said.

Robie nodded.

"You come here to die," said the man matter-of-factly.

"Or something," replied Robie.

"This way," he said.

Robie went that way. They entered an alley where there was a van.

There were five men in the van. They were all larger men than Robie and looked just as fit and strong as he was. Two wore robes, three didn't. They were armed.

Two men searched Robie in every possible way that one could search another.

"You came without weapons," said the young man in an incredulous tone.

"What would have been the point?" replied Robie.

"I thought you would go down fighting," said the young man.

Robie didn't answer him.

He was hustled into the van and driven back out of the city.

The rain was falling harder. Robie did not mind the rain. What he did mind was wind, but that had fallen away. The drops fell straight down. But they fell fast. The storm was moving quickly, he thought.

The van kept going,

About thirty minutes later it stopped and passed through a security checkpoint.

It was not the same private airport. That would have been too easy.

The doors to the hangar opened and the van drove straight in.

A different jet was parked here. It was smaller than Talal's 767. To Robie it looked like an Airbus A320. The man owned two planes that were used by commercial airlines to fly hundreds of people at a time.

Robie was pushed roughly out of the van. The farther away they had gotten from prying eyes, the harsher the treatment had become. He was now completely in their power, so the kick in his back that knocked him to the cement was not wholly unexpected.

The young man said something in Farsi to the man who'd kicked Robie.

Robie picked himself back up and said, "Tell him he hits about as hard as my sister. And if he wants his ass kicked tell him to try that again, only with me facing him."

The young man said, "I will not tell Abdullah that. Otherwise he will kill you."

"No he won't. Because if he robs Talal of his fun, he'll be dead too."

"Is that what you think this is, fun?"

"For him, maybe. Not so much for me."

"You have ruined a great plan."

"I stopped a maniac from screwing up the world."

"I can debate you point by point."

"I don't care what you think you can do. Where are Special Agent Vance and Julie Getty?"

"They could be dead."

"They could be. But they're not."

"How can you be so sure?"

"Again, the fun factor. I know Talal really needs to feel it right now."

"Yes, I do."

Robie turned to see Prince Khalid bin Talal walk down the stairs from his jet.

98

Talal faced Robie. The interior lights had automatically come on, because it had grown dark outside. Robie could hear the rain pinging off the metal roof of the hangar. The large windows on the upper levels of its side walls revealed moisture-laden clouds.

Talal came to a stop about ten feet from Robie. He wore not robes but a stylish three-piece suit that somehow managed to make his portly form look sleeker.

"You look slimmer than your body double, Talal," said Robie. "Not quite as fat, at least."

"You will refer to me as Prince Talal."

"Where are Vance and Julie, *Prince Talal*?"

Talal nodded and the two women were led out of a far corner of the hangar. Vance's face was purple and black. She walked stiffly, as though every step was killing her. Julie had two swollen eyes, she carried her right arm at an awkward angle, and her left leg dragged a little. Their condition made Robie's anger rise, but he willed himself to remain calm. He would need it for what was coming.

When they drew near to Talal he casually snapped

his fingers and the men accompanying the two women pulled them to a stop.

"I'm sorry for all this," said Robie, looking first at Vance and then at Julie.

They stared back at him without speaking.

Robie turned to Talal. "But at least the only one who died was your person. The president is safe."

"The only one to die just yet," said Talal. He smiled. "But you knew her, didn't you? You knew her quite intimately if the photos are any indication."

Vance said sharply, "What photos?"

"I know it was a game to you, Talal," said Robie. "But it's never been a game to me."

Talal wagged a finger at Robie. "I could possibly excuse you for trying to kill me. I could perhaps excuse you for thwarting my plans to assassinate men who would lead the world to disaster. But I cannot excuse you for disrespecting me. My name is *Prince* Talal."

The blow hit Robie from behind, knocking him to the floor. He rose slowly, his ribs aching. He looked at the man who had struck him. Abdullah was the biggest one of them all, and the look on his face was the fiercest.

"My friend here, Abdullah, also does not like your disrespect."

Abdullah bowed slightly in Talal's direction and then spat at Robie.

"Yeah," said Robie. "I can tell." He looked at Vance and Julie. "But now you have me and you can let them go."

"As soon as you came here, as soon as your foot touched dirt in Tangier, you knew that was not possible."

"It's why I came. I expect you to honor our agreement. Me for them."

"Then you are an idiot."

"You don't keep your word?" Robie looked at the others. "So how can they trust you, Talal? You tell them one thing and do another. Leader doesn't keep his word, then what's he worth? Nothing. He's worth nothing."

Talal was unfazed by this. And his men did not seem to even understand what Robie was saying.

"You might try explaining that to them in Farsi, Dari, Pashto, and the old reliable Arabic, but I doubt their opinion of me would change. They do what they do because I pay them far more than they would earn elsewhere."

Robie said, "I'm going to offer you a chance to surrender. I'm only going to offer it once. After that it will be withdrawn and it won't be offered again."

Talal smiled. "You want all of us to surrender to you?"

"Not just to me."

"Who, then? You were not followed here. We know that for a fact."

"You're right. *I* wasn't followed here."

Talal blinked and then looked around. "You speak

gibberish. I expected better from you. You are obviously paralyzed with fear."

"Trust me, it would take a lot more than your fat ass to make me afraid." Before Talal could respond, Robie added, "I'm just making the offer. It's up to you to take it or not. Do you refuse?"

"What I think I will do is watch all three of you die, right now."

"I'll take that as a no," said Robie.

"Abdullah, kill him," said Talal.

Abdullah drew two guns. It only took a moment, but he flipped one pistol to Robie, who used it to shoot three of the men closest to him, including the young man who had first met him. The bullet wound joined the knife wound on his neck as his life ended.

Abdullah fired twice, killing two other guards.

When the other men drew their weapons, Robie emptied his mag at them, grabbed Vance and Julie, and pulled them behind the front landing gear of the jet.

"Cover your ears," said Robie to them.

"What?" said Vance.

"Just do it. Now."

"Abdullah!" he shouted and the big man threw himself to the side and slid behind the van.

An instant later the right-side window of the hangar blew open, shattered by massive rounds from a thirty-millimeter chain gun. Next, rifle rounds fired through this opening slammed into the remaining guards. The shots were fired so fast and with such spot-on accuracy that the men had no chance even to fire back. One by one they dropped until the only one left standing was Talal. When two more men appeared at the door of the jet, they were immediately shot. Their bodies fell to the floor, making dull thunks on the cement.

Outside the window the chopper hovered, its thirty-mil chain gun mounted between the front landing gears now silent. It was a stealth aircraft. And the rain had covered any sounds it had made. Until the chain gun had opened up, that is. There were few things on earth that could cover the noise a thirty-mil made.

Shane Connors slid his self-loading sniper rifle off the metal support and kissed the hot barrel, his longtime ritual. He gave Robie a salute from the chopper and then signaled to the pilot. The chopper slowly moved off.

Robie came out from behind the landing gear and approached Talal. Abdullah rose from behind the van and joined him.

Talal gazed at Abdullah in disbelief. "You betrayed me?"

"How do you think we got on to you in the first place, Talal?" said Robie. "And if you can buy off our people, we can buy off yours."

Robie lifted his gun. Talal stared at him. "So you kill me now?"

"No. It's out of my hands. I'm sorry."

"You're apologizing for not killing me?" Talal said slowly.

The hangar door opened and a gold SUV pulled in. Inside were five men, all in robes. All armed. They got out of the car, lifted Talal up, and carried him to the vehicle. He screamed and tried to break free, but he was a man of little muscle and he soon gave up.

"You're going back to Saudi Arabia, Talal," said Robie. "The Americans have officially turned you over to your countrymen. I think you would have preferred the bullet."

The SUV drove off and Robie beckoned to Vance and Julie.

"There's a chopper outside that will take us to our ride home," he said quietly. "And there's a medical crew on board."

Vance and Julie crept out from behind the landing gear.

Vance hugged him and said, "I don't know how you managed all this, Robie. But I'm sure as hell glad you did."

Julie looked at the departing truck and said, "What will they do to him?"

"There's no reason for you to waste a second of your life thinking about it."

"Why did he kill my mom and dad?"

"I promise you that once we make sure you and Agent Vance are okay, and we put a few miles between us and this place and get some food in both your stomachs, I will answer all your questions, okay?"

"Okay, Will," said Julie.

Robie put one supporting arm around Vance and held his other out to Julie, who took it. They walked over to the waiting helicopter, which had set down in front of the hangar. Within the hour they would be winging their way home.

After that, Robie didn't know. He just didn't care to look that far ahead anymore.

99

Blue Man and Shane Connors were sitting at the small table in the conference room when Robie walked in.

Connors and Robie made eye contact, exchanged a brief nod, and then Robie sat next to him.

Blue Man said, "I've just congratulated Agent Connors on a job well done."

"Got me out from behind a desk," said Connors. "That was reward enough."

Robie eyed Blue Man. "What did Van Beuren tell us?"

"Pretty much everything."

"Why did he turn on his country?"

"Basically money and morals."

"The money I get. Explain the morals."

"Well, the money was not exactly what you would have imagined. It was going to pay for medical bills, with plenty left over for Van Beuren to retire on. Even though they had insurance through the government, it didn't cover some of the experimental treatments that they used to try and save Elizabeth Van Beuren. Without this money, they were going to have to declare bankruptcy. And without the money she wouldn't have gotten the treatments. Unfortunately, they didn't work."

"And the morals?"

"George Van Beuren blamed the U.S. government for his wife's cancer. He said it was exposure to the toxins in the battlefield that led to her illness and death. He wanted his revenge. And the president and one of the leaders of Saudi Arabia were excellent targets for his rage."

"He must've talked to Gabriel Siegel," said Robie. "He thinks the same thing."

"It doesn't excuse treason," commented Connors.

"No, it doesn't," agreed Blue Man.

"And Van Beuren's daughter?"

"Knew nothing about any of it, her father said. And we believe him. Nothing will happen to her."

"But she's lost both her parents now," said Robie.

"Yes, she has."

"Why was Van Beuren knocked out?"

"The original plan had been to leave him completely blameless. You discovering what you did made this impossible, of course, but they didn't know that. So Lambert knocks him out and steals his gun. Van Beuren was going to hang around for a while longer in his job, then retire, and go live somewhere else."

"And all the deaths leading up to that?" said Robie. "George Van Beuren screwed up. He told his wife what he was planning. Maybe he actually didn't even think she was listening or lucid. Maybe he just wanted to get it off his chest. But she had heard him and, being the patriot she was, the lady was pissed. When she was visited by Broome or Wind or Getty, she told them. Van Beuren found out and action had to be taken. Scorched earth. Killed them all."

"You've pretty much nailed what happened," said Blue Man. "It was actually Leo Broome who had visited her. Broome later confronted Van Beuren about what his wife had said. Van Beuren tried to claim that his wife was simply hallucinating. But Talal's people had Broome put under surveillance. Broome told both Rick Wind and the Gettys. That signed their death certificates. They dialed you up to kill Jane Wind because they were terrified her ex had told her something. And it was also the catalyst to set you in motion along the course Talal had planned for you."

"And they put the tube down his wife's throat so she couldn't talk again," noted Robie.

"They actually wanted to kill her, but Van Beuren said he wouldn't go through with it if they did. When the plan was set and about to go off, he took her off the ventilator and she died naturally."

"What about Gabriel Siegel?" asked Robie.

"They wanted us to think he was involved. They called him at work, told him his wife would be killed if he didn't meet with them. I'm not sure we'll ever find his remains. They had no reason to keep him alive."

"The attack at Donnelly's?"

"The Saudis interrogated Talal. He wanted you to suffer. Wanted you to blame yourself for what happened. He was certain you would figure out that you were the real target in all of this. They used a Secret Service van Van Beuren got for them. Stupid on Talal's part because it would naturally swing suspicion that way. But I guess he thought no one was smarter than he was."

"Broome's money?"

"We did some more digging. It apparently was stolen Kuwaiti antiquities. He and Rick Wind were involved. Broome invested well. Wind did not; Curtis Getty was clean."

Blue Man paused and studied Robie. "But even though the president and the crown prince were the actual targets, you were at the center of this, Robie."

"I didn't kill Talal and he decides to find out who I was and then to come after me. When Elizabeth Van Beuren talked Talal saw a way to involve me in all of it. My handler orders the hit on Jane Wind and I'm off and running from one orchestrated event to another."

Connors said, "It was a win-win for them. If you killed Wind and her son and later found out she was innocent they probably figured that would screw you up. And if you didn't pull the trigger on a mother and son, that's why they had the backup shooter. They'd learned of your exit plan on the bus. And they made sure Julie would be there too."

Robie said, "And they probably figured whether I pulled the trigger or not I'd most likely get on the bus with Julie after I figured out who Jane Wind really was."

Blue Man added, "But when they learned Julie came up with the idea of questioning other squad members, the game suddenly became too risky. That could lead to Van Beuren. They would kill Julie, and you too if necessary. Nothing could jeopardize the assassination attempt."

"Guess it all makes sense," said Robie slowly.

Blue Man said, "And Annie Lambert was an even earlier plant. After Talal escaped the attempt in Tangier and found out you were the shooter, he had her move into your building. This was before any of Elizabeth Van Beuren's old squad members found out what her husband was up to. Talal evidently had certain plans for the two of you," he added quietly.

Robie looked down at his hands. He had not brought himself to think about Lambert since the night he had killed her. "She was better than me," he said at last. "Faster, steadier. Never seen anyone that calm in a situation like that."

"She was also drugged," Blue Man pointed out. "Have you ever drugged yourself to carry out a mission?"

"No, but I've never gone into a mission where I absolutely knew I was going to die either," Robie countered.

More uneasy silence followed until Connors asked, "How does an Ivy League-educated young woman from Connecticut end up being a traitor willing to die?"

Blue Man said, "We've done a lot of digging on that and the Saudis were able to get some information from Talal. Her adoptive father was English, the mother Iranian. They had emigrated to Iran while the shah was still in power. Apparently they were brutalized by members of the shah's regime and even lost family members during the course of it. They appealed to their home government and to our government for help but apparentely were turned down. Back then the shah could do no wrong. As you know, we helped keep him in power. After the revolution in the late seventies, the shah was deposed and we lost all of our influence in that country. The Lamberts hated the West, obviously, and apparently America in particular. They returned to England, adopted Annie, moved to America, and raised her as their daughter."

"But they were brainwashing her, programming her the whole time?" said Connors. "For something like this?"

"Apparently for all of her life. There was no guarantee, of course, that she would get a position at the White House. But one can attempt to kill the president in other places as well. Her parents were wealthy and politically active. She was a brilliant student and she was clearly a superb actress. We haven't interviewed one person who had any inkling she was a ticking time bomb. Not one. She led the perfect life. Was able to interact socially, perform outstandingly at work. There was no flaw, no warning sign. It was as though she was two different people residing in the same body."

She was, thought Robie. *She had to be.*

Blue Man paused and looked over at Robie. "She fooled the best we had," he continued. "She was the most remarkable cell plant in my experience. Sort of a true-life Manchurian candidate, only better."

Robie asked, "And where are her parents now?"

"Talal didn't know. Perhaps back in Iran. If so, we can't touch them."

"There's no place we can't touch," said Robie sharply. "And there's a Russian and a Palestinian out there who need to be addressed as well. They were the ones who brought this thing to Talal."

"I know. We're working on that."

The three men fell silent as Robie brooded, Blue Man looked equally pensive, and Connors merely seemed curious.

"There are many ways to hurt people, Robie," said Blue Man finally. "I know you know that."

"Yeah," Robie said brusquely.

"She was trained for this her whole life. And we're all terrified because she didn't fit any profile we have. What if there are more Annie Lamberts out there?"

Connors said, "We have to find them and stop them."

Robie smacked the table with the palm of his hand. "She was the puppet, her life taken from her by her parents. She's dead and they get to live. Tell me what's wrong with that picture?"

"She was a cold-blooded killer," said Blue Man.

"Bullshit! She was what they made her! She never had a chance."

"You're not the best person to make that determination."

"Then who is, some analyst who never even met her? You got an algorithm for that?"

Blue Man said nothing for a few moments. "If it makes you feel better, Khalid bin Talal is no longer among the living."

Robie said nothing, because this meant nothing to him.

"Then there is the matter of Julie," said Blue Man.

"I've got that covered," said Robie abruptly. He rose.

"How?"

"I just do." He looked at Connors. "I owe you, Shane. More than I'll ever have in the bank."

"We're square. Like I said, got me out from behind the desk."

Robie looked at Blue Man. "There are maybe five men I know who could have made the shots Shane did that night. And two of them are in this room. You might want to keep that in mind."

"Rules are rules," said Blue Man.

“No, rules, as we’ve seen, are made to be broken.”

He turned to walk out the door.

“Robie?”

He turned to look at Blue Man, who held up a manila folder. “This was delivered to us by messenger. I believe you received a set too. I think you should take this and do what you want with it. It’s of no use or concern to us.”

Robie took the package, opened it, and glanced at the photos inside. The first one was of him and Lambert on the rooftop bar. The next was of her kissing him in front of the White House. He didn’t look at the rest. He closed the package back up.

“Thanks.”

He walked out the door.

100

Robie drove.

This time Julie was shotgun.

Vance was in the backseat.

They had mostly recovered from their injuries, though Julie still limped a bit and Vance's face was still puffy.

"Where are we going?" asked Julie.

"Somewhere you've already been," he replied.

He had explained what he could to her about her parents' deaths. He had watched her sob, given her tissues. He'd talked with her quietly as her anger grew, peaked, and then faded to more tears. The fourteen-year-old street-hardened kid had finally and fully unraveled in the face of overwhelming misery and grief. But at least she had some closure.

He parked the car and the three got out and walked into the bar.

Jerome Cassidy was waiting for them.

His face was scrubbed pink and he was dressed in what looked to be a new suit with shiny black shoes. His hair had been cut short and lay neatly on his head.

From the whiff Robie got, the man had used hairspray to keep some errant strands in place.

"What are we doing here, Will?" asked Julie, as Cassidy came forward to greet them.

Robie and Cassidy had worked out the story beforehand.

Cassidy said, "He brought you here so I could tell you the truth."

"Truth, what truth?" asked a bewildered-looking Julie.

"I wasn't just friends with your parents." He paused, eyed Robie, who gave a bare nod.

"I was your mom's half brother. That means I'm sort of your uncle. Well, technically I guess I *am* your uncle."

"We're related?" said Julie.

"Yes, we are. And I seem to be the only relations you have left. Now, I know you don't know me or anything, but I have a little proposition."

Julie folded her arms across her chest and looked at him suspiciously. "Like what?"

"Like we take some time getting to know each other. See, the reason I was trying to track you all down was because your dad and my sister really helped me out when I was down. I owed them big. Never got a chance to repay that debt."

"I see where this is going," said Julie. "You don't owe me anything."

"No, Julie, it's a real debt. They loaned me money.

I signed a note. That note was transferable into stock in a company I started with the loan. That company now owns all of my businesses, including this bar. If the note wasn't repaid by a certain date the loan amount plus accrued interest was transferred into stock. The loan never was repaid and the stock was issued. You're a forty percent owner in my business, Julie. I've got the documents to back it up, if you want to see. I should have told you when I first met you, but I was so surprised to see you, I just didn't. But I'm a man of my word. And what your parents did for me changed my life. They earned the right to share in the rewards. Well, since they can't, you should. Because whatever they had now belongs to you. I'm a man of my word and that's just the way it is."

He stopped talking and looked at her uncomfortably.

Julie's suspicious look faded. She glanced at Robie. "Is this really on the up-and-up?"

"We checked out his story. It's all true. You'll be able to go to any college you want. You'll be able to do anything you want."

She looked back over at Cassidy. "So what does that mean for you and me?"

"Well, it means you can live with me. I can even legally adopt you. Or if you prefer, you have the financial means now to have a guardian appointed until you reach the age of eighteen, and live in your own place. It's totally up to you."

"Live with you?"

"Well, it would be flexible. I keep pretty busy, but I've got a housekeeper who's been with me a long time. She's got a daughter about your age. I think it would work out. But again, it's up to you."

"I'll need to think about it," said Julie.

"Absolutely. Take all the time you need," said Cassidy quickly.

Robie said, "Why don't you start trying to get to know each other right now? I don't think Mr. Cassidy here dressed up just to talk to you for a few minutes. Would that be okay, Julie? I can come back and pick you up later."

"I guess that would be okay."

Robie looked at Cassidy and smiled. "Have a good time."

"Thank you, Agent Robie. From the bottom of my heart."

Robie and Vance turned and walked out.

Julie caught up with them before they even reached the car.

"Okay," she began. "That story was total bullshit. What's really going on here?"

Robie said, "I was telling you the truth. You *are* related to him. He cared for your parents deeply. He will care for you deeply. He's rich. Life will not suck."

A smile crept across Julie's face. "Pick me up in two hours."

"I will."

She held up something. It was a small canister. "It's

the paralytic spray you gave me. Just in case he turns out to be a creep."

She walked back to the bar.

Vance said, "I feel sorry for whoever ticks her off."

"I don't. They'll have deserved whatever they get."

Vance looked at him as they got into the car. "You ever going to tell me the real story about Cassidy?"

"No."

"Okay."

Robie put the car in drive and pulled away from the curb.

She touched him on the shoulder. "You doing all right?"

"I'm fine."

"I hate to bring this up, but what did bin Talal mean when he said . . ."

Robie slowed the car and looked at her.

She glanced away and said, "Never mind. So we have two hours. You want to grab some lunch?"

"Yeah, I do."

They ate, talked about things they might do together, but part of Robie wasn't even listening. They said their goodbyes.

As she was climbing out of the car Vance said, "If you keep saving my life I'm really going to start developing an inferiority complex."

"There's nothing inferior about you, Nikki. You're top-notch in my book."

"I don't understand you completely, Robie, but I want to understand you. Does that make sense?"

He looked at her, a smile edging across his lips. "I think you'll have the opportunity."

"I'll hold you to that."

He picked up Julie at the appointed time and drove her back to an apartment the Feds had temporarily gotten for her. It came complete with a housekeeper who packed a gun and could kick the crap out of most intruders.

Before Julie got out of the car she turned back to Robie.

"Is this goodbye like forever?"

"Do you want it to be?"

"Do *you* want it to be?"

"No, not really."

"But you're not sure."

"I don't want you to ever be hurt again because of me."

"Life is what it is, Will. You take it as it comes."

"That's always been my philosophy."

"Where do you think I learned it from?" She playfully punched him in the arm. "Thanks. I mean it. For everything."

"I think I owe you more than you owe me."

"How about we split it down the middle?"

She reached over and hugged him. He was tentative at first, but finally Robie hugged her back.

She got out of the car and slowly walked up to her apartment. She turned back, waved at him, and then, despite her still-gimpy leg, Julie skipped up the last few steps.

Like a kid.

Robie smiled and watched until he could no longer see her.

Her injuries would fully heal. At least her physical ones. And her emotional ones might too, given her age.

Robie could not say the same for himself.

The image of Annie Lambert came bursting into his mind like it had been fired there with a rocket launcher. Every moment they had spent together. Everything they had said to each other. Every possibility he might have given thought to about what could have been between them.

And she had been a killer.

Just like he was a killer.

His had been by choice.

She had had no real choice in the matter.

So who was the guiltier one?

It was like Julie had said. You had to take life as it came. It gave no quarter, spared no feelings. Limited no pain. Put no ceiling on happiness.

This was his world.

He was who he was.

He could not change that.

He was not an innocent.

And the people he hunted certainly weren't innocent.

Maybe the best Robie could do was protect those who actually were.

ACKNOWLEDGMENTS

To Michelle, your extraordinary enthusiasm for this book really meant a lot.

To David Young, Jamie Raab, Emi Battaglia, Jennifer Romanello, Tom Maciag, Martha Otis, Chris Barba, Karen Torres, Anthony Goff, Lindsey Rose, Bob Castillo, Michele McGonigle, and all at Grand Central Publishing, who support me every day.

To Aaron and Arleen Priest, Lucy Childs Baker, Lisa Erbach Vance, Nicole James, Frances Jalet-Miller, and John Richmond, for being the best team a writer could ever have.

To Maja Thomas, who continues to lead the way on ebooks.

To Anthony Forbes Watson, Jeremy Trevathan, Maria Rejt, Trisha Jackson, Katie James, Aimee Roche, Becky Ikin, Lee Dibble, Sophie Portas, Stuart Dwyer, Anna Bond, and Matthew Hayes at Pan Macmillan, for catapulting me to the top in the UK.

To Ron McLarty and Orlagh Cassidy, for terrific audio performances.

To Steven Maat at Bruna, for taking me to the top in Holland.

To Bob Schule, for your friendship, enthusiasm, and editorial skills.

To the charity auction winners: Jane Wind, Gabriel Siegel, Elizabeth and Brooke Van Beuren, Diana Jordison, Cheryl Kosmann, and Michele Cohen. I hope you enjoyed your characters.

To David and Catherine Broome, for the use of your last name, although you're much cooler than the "Broome" characters in the novel.

To Kristen, Natasha, and Erin, because I'd be lost without you.

And last but far from least, to Roland Ottewell for another great copyediting job.

Will Robie may have met his match when he's ordered to kill rogue agent Jessica Reel. With the trap set he quickly finds that there is more to her betrayal than meets the eye.

The second **Will Robie** thriller.

A deadly assassin from North Korea is ordered to destroy the enemy at all costs. With the stakes so high, Will Robie and Jessica Reel face their most lethal mission yet.

The third **Will Robie** thriller.

Returning home after twenty years brings back painful memories for government assassin Will Robie. His father has been arrested for murder, but could he really be guilty?

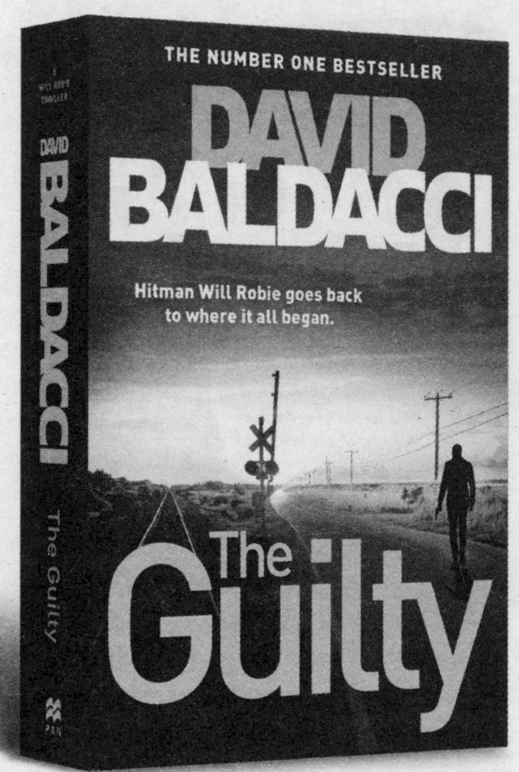

The fourth **Will Robie** thriller.